CRIME

HUNT FOR A SERIAL KILLER

THE BUCK TAYLOR NOVELS

CRIME DELAYED

BOOK 2

CRIME DENIED

BOOK 5

BY

CHUCK MORGAN

COPYRIGHT© 2020 BY CHUCK MORGAN

Printed in the United States of America

First printing 2020

ISBN 978-0-9988730-9-1(eBook)

ISBN 978-1-7348424-0-1(Paperback)

LIBRARY OF CONGRESS CONTROL NUMBER

2020906109

CHUCK MORGAN

CRIME
DELAYED

A BUCK TAYLOR NOVEL

CRIME
DELAYED

A BUCK TAYLOR NOVEL

BOOK 2

BY

CHUCK MORGAN

CHAPTER ONE

How could they be so dumb? All they had to do was stash the carcass and come back for it later. Why did that lady Ranger and her dog have to show up? Up to that point, everything was perfect. The bull elk was huge with a monster rack. He was the biggest elk they had seen in the last month, at least.

Sure, they were a little out of season, and they didn't have a permit for a bull elk, but they weren't hurting anyone. The elk was just standing there, waiting to be shot. What did it hurt? God must have intended for them to shoot it, or he wouldn't have put it there, right?

They were going to stash the elk in their hunting camp. Well, not much of a hunting camp. It was a lean-to made of sticks and pine boughs, but it was a great place to hide out when they weren't hunting. They had all the comforts of home. They had a gas lantern for light; they had a small cooler for drinks, and they had a couple of sleeping bags for when they stayed out at night. They didn't need the sleeping bags because the nights were still warm even at this altitude.

Tonight, they would have come back and butchered the elk. The sled they use to haul out the meat was hidden in the ravine next to the lean-to. All they had to do was load it up and drag it back to the cabin. It was only a couple miles, and they had done it a lot lately. They always took a different track back so that the undergrowth wouldn't get worn down and show the way back to the cabin.

They were the hunters, and everyone depended on them for food. They were the best shots in the group, and they knew how to skin and gut what they shot. The elk would have lasted them a week or two. But now this. The Teacher is not going to be pleased.

The lady Ranger came out of nowhere. One minute they were dragging the elk back to camp, and the next minute there she was, standing on the little ridge with her stupid dog. All she had to do was walk away. Her and that stupid dog. But she didn't.

They had hidden in the bushes. She should have walked right by them and not seen them, but no. The dog had to sniff them out. He had to start barking. She could have kept walking, but she must have sensed them because she pulled the gun out of her holster. They couldn't let her find them or the cabin.

The first rifle shot hit her in the thigh. There was no ballistic armor around her thigh. She went down hard and rolled down the ridge into the ravine. The dog tried to go after her, but the second bullet hit the dog right in the chest. The dog went down hard too. There was a lot of blood. They broke cover and rushed over to the edge of the ravine. The lady Ranger was trying to reach her pistol with one hand, and she was trying to key the mic on her shoulder with the other.

When she saw them, she just froze. Blood was pumping out of her leg. A crimson fountain exploding with each heartbeat. She looked at them and began to plead with them to help her. She had tears in her eyes. They just stood there and looked at her. The lady Ranger started to shake. Her breathing got shallow. She seemed so helpless, just lying there in the ravine. The Teacher had taught them not to let anything they hunted suffer. They understood the kill shot. He raised his rifle and, without any hesitation or doubt, shot her in the forehead.

Where was the dog? They had seen the crimson stain explode from the dog's chest. He went over the ridge, so he must just be on the other side, but he wasn't. Where could he have gone? They wanted to make sure he didn't suffer like the lady Ranger, but he wasn't on the other side of the ridge. They looked around, trying to spot the blood trail, but there was none.

Maybe he was some kind of mystical forest creature. Just like in the stories the Teacher used to tell them around the campfire. It would be a grand prize to take back to the Teacher. He might award them with a knife or a hatchet. But where is he? He couldn't have gone far, but after an hour searching, there was no sign.

They went back to the lean-to and found a camp shovel and headed back to the lady Ranger. The Teacher had told them that all life was sacred, so they knew that he would not be happy if they didn't give the lady Ranger a proper burial, and that's just what they did. The covered her body with dirt and rocks, cut some pine boughs, and further covered the grave in the ravine. Then they said the Lord's Prayer just like the Teacher had taught them. Finished, they headed back to the elk carcass.

Instead of waiting till tonight to butcher it, they decided to do it now. Someone might have heard the extra shots, and they also figured that sooner or later, someone would come looking for the lady Ranger and her dog. They finished dragging the carcass to the lean-to hunting camp. They spent the next two hours butchering the huge elk, loaded up the sled and hauled it back through the woods to their cabin. They would have a big feast tonight.

They would tell the Teacher about the lady Ranger. He would be happy that they had protected the others. They were not sure if they should tell him about the missing dog. The Teacher might not be pleased that they had missed the shot and not killed the dog. He might give one of the others the rifle and let them go on the next hunt. The more they thought about it, the more they convinced themselves that they would not mention the dog.

CHAPTER TWO

Buck Taylor, Colorado Bureau of Investigation Agent and his son David had volunteered to work the burger and hot dog tent at the annual Gunnison Labor Day community picnic and were doing a brisk business. Buck tried to make the burgers the same way his friend Jimmy Palumbo did at the Le Bon Café in Durango. Jimmy's burgers were huge and legendary, and the only food item besides french fries that Jimmy sold in his café/bar, but Buck just couldn't get them to taste the same. Someday he would find out Jimmy's secret.

Gunnison, Colorado, population of roughly 6,200 people, sits at an elevation of 7,700 feet and is the largest city in Gunnison County. Situated along the Gunnison River, the city was incorporated in 1880. The area is a mecca for hunters, fishermen and anyone who enjoys the outdoors. It is home to Western State Colorado University, which was founded as The Colorado State Normal School for Children in 1901.

One interesting historical fact is that during two months at the end of 1918, the residents of Gunnison isolated themselves from the rest of the area to prevent the introduction of Spanish Influenza. All roads were blocked at the county borders, and people traveling through the area by train were not allowed to leave the train. Because of the isolation, no one in Gunnison died of the flu.

North of Gunnison lies Crested Butte, a ski resort community that helps contribute to the winter tourist trade since you must pass through Gunnison to get to the Crested Butte ski area. Gunnison is a picturesque little community in the heart of the Rocky Mountains and appears to be a perfect place to raise a family.

Buck Taylor stands six-foot-tall and weighs in at 185 lbs. Very little of it flab for a 58-year-old man. Buck's hair is salt and pepper with what seemed like a lot more salt than pepper, and he wore it slightly longer than was typically the fashion of the day. Buck lived in Gunnison all his life. He spent seventeen years with the Gunnison County Sheriff's Department before accepting a position with the Colorado Bureau of Investigation. He met and married his high school sweetheart Lucinda Torres, and they raised three children, David, Cassie and Jason. Life was good until Lucy was diagnosed with breast cancer, and for five years, she and Buck fought the battle of her life. A little over a year ago, Lucy lost the battle.

They were just finishing up the latest rush of people when his son's cell phone signaled an incoming call. David looked at the call and answered.

"Taylor," he said. He listened intently to the call, then hung up. David was a police officer with the Gunnison Police Department. He looked a lot like his dad when his dad was his age. Slightly taller and slightly heavier, but the resemblance was striking. Unlike his father, David still moved with the ease of a young man.

David had recently been promoted to sergeant and was now the night-shift supervisor. He liked working the night-shift and had been a patrolman on that shift for many years. He enjoyed the calmness and quiet of the small mountain town in the early morning hours. He also enjoyed those rare occasions when he was able to spend time with Buck. They had a lot in common, and he enjoyed hearing about Buck's latest investigations.

The pair didn't have a lot of time to talk today. The picnic was in full swing, and the park was packed with locals and tourists alike. This weekend was the unofficial end of the summer tourist season, and most of the tourists should have already gone home, but the weather was perfect, and the town was still living the good life.

Tourism was essential for the survival of the town. In the fall, the hunters would descend on the town to get themselves outfitted for the annual trek into the mountains in search of elk and deer and an occasional moose. As soon as the hunters were gone, the skiers would start showing up.

Fishermen would show up all year round, and it was not unusual to see a fly fisherman standing in the middle of the Gunnison River stalking a beautiful Brown or Rainbow trout while the snow came down around him. If there was open water on the river, there would be a fisherman standing in it no matter the weather. Buck Taylor was typically one of those fishermen. Buck's passion for fly fishing was only exceeded by his love of his job as a criminal investigator.

Fly fishing was also his escape from having to deal with the death of his wife of 35 years. Lucy Taylor had spent five years battling metastatic breast cancer. She lost the battle when the cancer metastasized into her brain. She held out as long as she could, but the chemotherapy and the radiation were no longer effective. She died peacefully in her sleep, wrapped in Buck's arms. Buck was devastated by the loss, and now more than a year later, he still missed her. She was his rock and his soul mate.

Buck and the family had gathered one Sunday morning to scattered Lucy's ashes in the Gunnison River, not far from where Buck and his son were now cooking burgers. It was supposed to be a private family affair, but somehow word had spread around town, and a huge group of people showed up. The private affair turned into a huge picnic and celebration of Lucy's life. Lucy would have loved it.

Buck looked at his son as he hung up the phone.

"Something up?" Buck asked.

"Yeah. I need to go to the office. We got a call from the Pitkin County Sheriff's office. They are searching for a missing Division of Parks and Wildlife Ranger, and they have asked for us to start on our side of the mountain and work towards them. She's been missing almost twenty-four hours. The Sheriff has activated the Gunnison Search and Rescue team, and we have been asked to assist."

"Do you need some help?" Buck asked.

"Who's gonna cook the burgers and dogs for this crowd if you leave. I will let you know later if we are looking for volunteers. Can you make sure Judy gets her tent closed up and gets the kids home?"

David's wife, Judy, was in charge of the dessert tent. She also ran the little deli/ice cream shop that Lucy owned and ran for a significant part of her life. When Lucy passed away, Buck had been thinking about selling the little place, but Judy offered to take it over and eventually buy the shop from him. Buck was pleased that Lucy's legacy would continue, and besides, the people in town loved her little place.

But today Judy's assistant was working the shop while Judy and her and David's three kids, Amy, age 16, David Jr also nicknamed Buck, age 14 and Rosalie, age 10, named after Lucy's mom, ran the tent in the park. Buck told David he would take care of everything and not to worry. He also told him to be safe.

David shed his apron and headed towards the dessert tent to let Judy know where he was heading and dashed for his car. Buck threw some more burgers on the open grill and prepared for the next group of hungry tourists. The Mayor of Gunnison, Pamela Sanders, saw Buck working alone and jumped in to help. Buck's mother-in-law Rosalie, who had been sitting in the shade, also walked over and put on an apron.

Rosalie Torres was one of the elders of the community. Pushing seventy-five and five feet two, she was a force to be reckoned with. What she lacked in stature, this still active Latina more than made up for with drive. She was still on the organizing committee for the Labor Day picnic, and she served on almost every volunteer committee that functioned within the county. Nothing went on in Gunnison that Rosalie was not a part of.

Fernando Torres, Rosalie's husband, and Lucy's father ran a small horse ranch just outside the city border. He had also been an outfitter and hunting guide. His love of the outdoors was something he was proud to have passed on to his two daughters, Lucinda, and Rachel, and his son Michael. Life was not always easy for Fernando and Rosalie, but they did the best they could and made sure that their children never wanted for anything.

It was a sad day five years ago when Fernando suffered a heart attack while guiding a couple of hunters up near Monarch Pass. Although the hunters had made a valiant effort to revive him and had succeeded several times, by the time search and rescue reached them, Fernando was gone. The family still missed Fernando every day, but it was okay. His daughter Lucy was with him.

By the end of the day, every one of the fifty or so volunteers were dog tired, but they all had a wonderful time. Buck had also volunteered to be on the teardown team, so after clearing out the burger tent and making sure Judy and the kids had taken down the dessert tent, he spent the next couple hours helping clear the rest of the tents and clean the park. Just before he left the park, he walked over to the little handicapped fishing dock where the family had scattered Lucy's ashes and spent a minute in quiet reflection. He said goodnight to Lucy and headed for home.

Buck was due in the office in Grand Junction the following afternoon for the monthly staff meeting, and he had a bunch of paperwork that needed to get turned in for the cases he had recently closed.

CHAPTER THREE

Buck is assigned to the Grand Junction office of the Colorado Bureau of Investigation, but he typically works from home and handles cases in the central and southwestern parts of the state. He is highly regarded as an investigator by those who know him, and he is often called upon by Governor Richard Kennedy to handle special cases of a sensitive nature.

The phone call he received just as he was getting ready to leave the house for Grand Junction was regarding one of those sensitive cases that required special handling.

Buck recognized the number on his phone as one of the main numbers for the CBI office in Grand Junction. He wasn't sure who was calling, but he hit the answer button.

"Buck Taylor."

"Hey, Buck, this is Paul Webber. Did I catch you at a good time?"

Paul Webber had just recently joined the Colorado Bureau of Investigation as a field agent and had been assigned to the Grand Junction Office. He came to CBI from the Dallas, Texas Police Department and was very highly regarded as an investigator. Paul was a big guy. He stood six feet four and weighed in at two hundred forty-five pounds. A former college football standout at the University of Texas, Paul had spent four years in the Marines before joining the Dallas, Texas Police Department, where he spent six years and was most recently assigned as a homicide detective.

Paul Webber had been assigned to work with Buck on a corruption case out of the city of Montrose, Colorado. The Governor had been approached by the Montrose Chief of Police and asked to have CBI start an investigation of the five city council members. A complaint had been filed by a local real estate broker indicating that something shady had gone on during the annexation negotiations for a new subdivision. The Chief of Police was concerned that handling the investigation out of his department might ruffle some feathers. Montrose was a small western slope town, and everyone knew everyone. He wanted the investigation to be impartial.

Buck liked Paul Webber from the first time he met him. Paul was smart, and he had a tremendous amount of drive. Like Buck, he was also very passionate about investigating crimes.

Buck and Paul had been investigating the entire annexation process for the past couple weeks and had gotten a warrant to look at the finances of each person involved. They were expecting a call from the forensic accountant any time now.

"Hey, Paul. I was just getting ready to leave the house and head to the office. What's up?"

"The forensic accountant just called. We were right. Councilman Meyers definitely tried to hide fifty thousand dollars. The accountant was also able to backtrack the money to the developer's daughter's personal bank account. He is emailing us the findings. We should have enough to make an arrest."

"Great news, Paul. Go ahead and type up the arrest warrant for the developer, his daughter and the councilman. Fax that to the city attorney in Montrose and have her call the judge to get the warrants. I am leaving the house now and will meet you at police headquarters in about an hour. See if you can pull Richards and Baxter away from their desks. We could use them to arrest the developer."

"Will do, Buck. See you in a bit."

Paul hung up, and Buck smiled. He hated when elected officials disregarded their oaths and violated the trust of their constituents. Besides, Councilman Meyers was an arrogant prick. He pushed the speed dial button on his phone and heard the Director's phone ringing.

Colorado Bureau of Investigation Director Kevin Jackson answered the call.

"Hey, Buck. What's going on?"

Kevin Jackson was the youngest person ever appointed to run the Colorado Bureau of Investigation. He spent years working his way up the administrative side of the Colorado Springs Police Department and had made significant changes to the department along the way, but he wasn't just an administrator; he was also a cop and a damn good one. Buck had become very familiar with the Director, and sometimes it seemed as though he worked for the Director instead of for the agent in charge of the Grand Junction field office.

Buck filled the Director in on the events getting ready to unfold in Montrose. He explained what the forensic accountant had discovered and that he had Paul Webber preparing the arrest warrant. He also asked him if it was okay to borrow Agents Richards and Baxter to help with the arrests? He would use the Montrose police as back up. The Director told him that he would call the governor and fill him in. He had no issues with anything Buck told him and told Buck to let him know when the arrests were finished. He told Buck to stay safe. Buck hung up

Richards was Agent James Richards, a ten-year veteran with the Colorado Bureau of Investigation. Richards had spent several years with the Ann Arbor, Michigan Police Department, before deciding to relocate his family to Colorado. He had a slight build and a very bookish look about him. Buck thought he was an accountant the first time he met him.

Baxter was Agent Ashley Baxter. Ashley was five feet four with long blond hair that she usually wore in a ponytail. She joined CBI five years before, right out of the University of Wisconsin. A Denver native, she had no issues moving to Grand Junction and had thrived in her new environment. She typically worked with Richards, and their focus lately was mostly on property crimes like burglary. They had just wrapped up a successful investigation into a series of home invasions and were waiting for their next assignment.

CHAPTER FOUR

J immy Corey was concerned when he woke up Labor Day morning, and his mom still wasn't home. She had promised to be home the night before. They planned to spend Labor Day together, and then they had an important meeting at his school on Tuesday.

Susan Corey had worked as a Ranger for the Division of Parks and Wildlife since graduating from Colorado State University in Fort Collins, Colorado, seven years earlier. She earned a bachelor's degree in animal biology and jumped at the chance to work for the CPW. At five feet seven and one hundred forty pounds, she was in excellent condition to hike the backwoods of the Colorado mountains to enforce hunting and fishing laws and protect the animals in her charge. It was not unusual for her to spend several days in the field searching for poachers or anyone else breaking the law. She didn't mind working alone since she always traveled with Duke, her five-year-old golden retriever.

Jimmy took out his cell phone and pressed the number one key. His mom always told him that if anything ever happened to her that he should call the first preprogrammed number in his phone.

Miguel Vargas answered on the second ring. "Vargas."

"Hi, Mr. Vargas, this is Jimmy Corey, have you heard from my mom?"

Miguel Vargas was the Chief Ranger at the Colorado Parks and Wildlife office in Glenwood Springs. Vargas was fifty years old, five feet ten, and weighed one hundred seventy pounds. He was in excellent health from spending almost thirty years as a CPW Ranger. A job he loved.

"Hi, Jimmy. Last I heard she was due back home yesterday. Did she not get home?"

"No, sir," responded Jimmy. "I have been trying her cell phone since last night, and it just goes to voicemail."

Vargas was now concerned. It wasn't like Susan Corey to stay out of touch.

"Jimmy, let me see if I can find her. Keep trying her phone, and if she comes home, have her call me. I will be back in touch as soon as I hear anything."

Vargas hung up and dialed the CPW dispatcher. Because of the holiday and the perfect weather, most of the eleven Rangers that worked out of Glenwood Springs were on duty. There were still a lot of campers in the woods, and encounters with wild animals were always a concern. He asked the dispatcher to call the troops and have them start looking for Susan Corey's car.

Vargas knew Susan Corey was working a poaching case somewhere south of Aspen, but he didn't have an exact location which was going to make this tough. He was going to need some help. Susan Corey could be anywhere.

Vargas's next call was to the Pitkin County Sheriff. He and Sheriff Earl Winters had been friends for years. The Sheriff recognized the number on the screen and answered his cell phone.

"Hey, Miguel. What's up?"

"Mornin Earl. Hate to bother you on the holiday, but I have a missing Ranger and could use your help."

Vargas went on to explain the situation and that she could be anywhere in the area. Vargas knew Susan Corey was heading into the mountains south of Aspen looking for elk poachers, but she could have been heading home and encountered another issue. The last time the dispatcher talked to her was three days earlier, and she told them she would be hiking into the area around Hunter Peak. The problem is, Hunter Peak is not easy to get to, and there are several old Forest Service roads that you can use to get into the area. After that, it is still a good couple hours to hike in.

The Sheriff listened intently, asked a couple of questions, and told Vargas that he would have his deputies start looking for her truck. He would also activate the Pitkin County Search and Rescue team and call Gunnison County to see if they could start looking from their side of the mountain. There were several old access roads she could have used from Gunnison County as well. The more folks they could get out on the roads looking for her, the faster they could find her truck and narrow down the search area. The Sheriff hung up.

The Sheriff was good to his word, and his first call was to Gunnison County Sheriff James McCauley, who listened and then promised to have his deputies start looking along the back roads and to have his search and rescue team start covering what the deputies couldn't.

His next call was to his dispatcher to call in all his deputies and his search and rescue team and have them meet at the Sheriff's office. His plan was to spread as many cars around the county as possible to try to find Corey's truck.

Meanwhile, Miguel Vargas was doing the same thing with his Rangers, and after assigning search areas, he jumped in his truck and headed for Aspen. As more time passed, the more his concern grew. He knew Susan Corey could take care of herself, but anything could have happened. She could have fallen or somehow gotten injured, she could be lost, although that was unlikely, or, god forbid, she could have encountered the elk poachers, and things could have turned ugly fast. He hoped it wasn't the last scenario.

Vargas called Jimmy Corey back on his cell phone. When Jimmy answered, he explained what was going on and that a lot of people were going to be looking for his mom. He also asked him to look around her small office and see if she left any notes about where she planned to go when she left the house. Jimmy promised he would.

As he was getting ready to head to Aspen, he asked his wife to head over to Susan Corey's house and sit with Jimmy. His wife could read the concern in his eyes and told him not to worry. She would take care of Jimmy, and she would also call his grandparents in Pueblo and let them know what was going on.

CHAPTER FIVE

The Sheriff arrived at his office and waited for his search teams to assemble. While he waited, he pulled up Susan Corey's truck registration through the Division of Motor Vehicles website. The Ranger drove a state-issued 2014 Chevy Tahoe, white, with the Division of Parks and Wildlife logo on the front doors. Just to be on the safe side, he asked dispatch to put out a BOLO, Be On The Lookout, for her truck, just in case she was stranded some place. He also put in a request through her cell phone provider for the last location her cell phone had been used. This might help narrow down the search area.

Once his search teams and deputies arrived at the office, he provided them with Susan Corey's picture, her vehicle registration and assigned each searcher with an area to search. The search teams headed out. The day did not go well, and by nine PM that night, the Sheriff called the searchers in and asked them to meet again the next morning to start searching again. Susan Corey had fallen off the face of the earth, and the Sheriff hated to call off the search, but with darkness setting in, it would make looking down old access roads even harder. Best to wait for morning.

Tuesday morning dawned clear, bright, and warm. Strangely warm for a September morning in the mountains. The searchers started to arrive at seven AM and were just getting their assignments when the Chief Deputy walked into the room and asked everyone to just sit tight for a little bit. The Sheriff was out on a call, which might prove helpful to the search.

The Sheriff and another deputy were on their way to talk with a couple of hikers who found a dog that appeared to have been shot and was lying under a Colorado Parks and Wildlife Chevy Tahoe.

Pitkin County Sheriff Earl Winters was the epitome of a western Sheriff. Tall and broad at the shoulders, Earl wore jeans, a button-down shirt, and a broad-rimmed Stetson. He had a bit of a gut hanging over his belt but was still an impressive man. The large handlebar mustache only added to the old western look. Earl had been Sheriff for over twenty years and had no intention of retiring anytime soon. He loved his job, and he loved his county.

The Sheriff was first to arrive at the location of the call. County Route 13 led south from the Aspen Highlands ski resort, and the road ran out at the Maroon-Snowmass trailhead. This was a very popular trail that led to Maroon peaks, and the parking lot was still crowded even though it was late in the season. The Sheriff didn't have to look hard to find the hikers who had called in the report. There was a crowd of hikers standing around the white Tahoe that was parked down a small side road that led to the parking lot restroom.

The group separated as the Sheriff walked up. The reporting party, Henry, and Lidia Franklin were kneeling next to a full-size golden retriever. On the other side of the dog, another hiker was cleaning the wound and whispering to the dog while working out of a first aid kit. The dog was shaking. The Franklins introduced themselves to the Sheriff.

They had started on a day hike just after dawn and had not noticed the dog at first. As they were walking to the restrooms, they heard what sounded like someone whimpering. That, someone turned out to be the golden retriever. He was lying under the truck crying, and when Lidia crouched down to see if he was okay, she noticed the blood on his chest. She was able to pull him out from under the truck, and that's when she had her husband call 911.

The other hiker who was working on the dog identified himself as Steven Blair. Blair was a registered nurse who had started for the trailhead a few minutes after the Franklins and had pulled out his first aid kit and started working on the wound. He reported that the blood around the wound had congealed, but he couldn't be sure if there was any internal bleeding. He felt the wound might be a day or two old. The dog was too weak to stand and did not look good, but he still managed to lick Blair's hand while he spoke to the Sheriff.

The Sheriff knelt next to the dog and stroked his fur. He slid the dog's collar around and found a name tag. "Duke." The name on the back of the tag was Susan Corey with a phone number.

While the Sheriff was checking the name tag, the deputy arrived and knelt next to him. The Sheriff showed him the name tag, and the deputy nodded. The Sheriff told the deputy to get an emergency blanket out of the back of his patrol car, a Ford Explorer, and he then asked Blair to help him carry the dog to the back of the car. They gently placed the dog in the back of the Explorer, and the Sheriff told the deputy to head for the Pitkin County Emergency Vet clinic.

The Sheriff called dispatch and told the dispatcher to call the emergency clinic and let them know that the deputy was on his way and that the dog looked critical. He thanked the Franklins and Steven Blair and took down their contact info in case he needs to contact them later on.

The Sheriff went back to his truck and pulled a Slim Jim out of his toolbox and made quick work of getting into the Ranger's truck. Once inside, he found the registration and confirmed that it was indeed Susan Corey's truck. Other than some papers sitting on the passenger seat, he couldn't find anything that might indicate where she had gone. The Sheriff was very concerned, and it was now time to call in the cavalry. He locked up the Ranger's Tahoe and headed back to his truck.

"Dispatch, come in."

"Go ahead, Sheriff."

"Dispatch, activate search and rescue, and have them report to me at the Maroon Snowmass trailhead. Call in all off-duty deputies and reserve deputies and have them assemble here as well. Contact Gunnison County and ask if they could activate their search and rescue and coordinate with me when they are ready. I will try to give them a search perimeter as soon as I can. Then put out a statewide broadcast that we have a missing and presumed injured, law enforcement officer, and we are requesting assistance to search a massive area. Foul play is assumed at this point. Got it?"

"Yes, sir. Do you want a call for volunteers for the search?"

"Not until we know what we are dealing with."

The Sheriff then called Miguel Vargas and filled him in on what they had just discovered. Since all of Vargas's Rangers were also armed law enforcement officers, he would mobilize the entire team and have them head to Aspen to assist with the search. The Sheriff asked all the hikers who were still in the area to remove their cars from the parking lot and evacuate the area. This was about to become a crime scene. He used a couple of old buckets and crime scene tape to close off access to the parking lot. It was going to be tight trying to get a lot of vehicles in here, but they would figure it out. Now he just needed to wait for the troops

The Sheriff stood at the trailhead and looked deep into the woods.

"Where are you, Susan Corey?"

It was time to get organized.

CHAPTER SIX

Buck Taylor turned left off Main Street onto S Park Avenue, turned right onto S 1st Street and pulled into the Montrose Police Department parking lot. He parked his state-issued Jeep Cherokee in one of the visitor's spaces and headed for the building. Once inside, he identified himself to the duty officer at the desk and was buzzed into the back and headed for the Police Chief's office.

Police Chief, Paul Sawyer, was seated at a small conference table across the hall from his office. Also in the room was the City Attorney, Beverly Jensen, Paul Webber, James Richards, and Ashley Baxter from the Colorado Bureau of Investigation. Two Montrose police officers, Nunez, and Harding, were also in attendance. Buck was pleased. He had worked with Nunez and Harding before and knew they were top-notch cops. Buck shook hands all around.

"Okay," he said. "Do we have the warrants?"

Beverly Jensen nodded. Beverly was a twenty-eight-year-old, medium height black woman who had landed in Montrose after completing her law degree at THE Ohio State. She was looking for a place to start over after a failed marriage and had fallen in love with the area during a trip early in her college years. From the few encounters Buck had with her in the past, he knew she was smart and dedicated.

"You bet. We have arrest warrants for City Councilman Benjamin Meyers, Reginald Carstairs, and his daughter Regina Carstairs. We are good to go."

"Great," said Buck. "I will take Meyers with Officer Nunez. Paul, you and Harding will take Regina Carstairs, and Richards and Baxter will take Reginald Carstairs. You all have the addresses. This should be simple, but keep on your toes. You never know how people are going to react. Chief, you will be our back up if the shit hits the fan. We all good?"

Everyone nodded, and they headed out the door to their cars. The Chief stopped Buck before he left the building.

"Hey, Buck, I appreciate the work you guys did. This was going to get hairy if we had to deal with one of the city fathers, and you are saving our bacon. Thanks."

"No problem, Paul. As far as we are concerned, the information we received came from a source outside the city, and the first you guys found out about the investigation was when we showed up just now with arrest warrants. That should give you plenty of cover."

Paul Sawyer smiled, and they headed to their cars. Buck, followed by Officer Nunez in his patrol car, pulled out of the lot and headed back down South 1st Street, turned right onto South Park Avenue and turned left onto Main Street. Benjamin Meyers and Associates Real Estate office was just four blocks down on Main street, so just before they got to Junction Avenue, the two cars pulled over to the side and double-parked. Buck put his red and blue flashers on, grabbed the warrant, and exited the car.

Walking briskly, he pushed open the front door to the real estate office and walked right past the receptionist who started to say something, but Buck wasn't listening. He turned the handle of the door marked Benjamin Meyers, and pushed open the door. Meyers was seated behind his desk talking to two clients, one male and one female, and he looked startled when the door burst open and in walked Buck, followed by Officer Nunez.

"Benjamin Meyers. We have a warrant for your arrest on

public corruption charges. Please stand up, step around the desk, and keep your hands where I can see them."

Meyers looked at his two clients who started to get up and were told to remain seated by Officer Nunez. Nunez then looked at Buck.

"Agent Taylor, this is Reginald Carstairs and his daughter Regina."

"Well, well," said Buck. "You two are under arrest as well. Please do not move. Nunez, call it in."

Regina Carstairs started to give Buck a lot of lip and reached into her purse, which was in her lap. Nunez, who had the better angle, saw the handle of the gun before Buck did, drew his service weapon, and placed it at the back of Regina's head. Buck grabbed Meyers, who had just started to stand up and pushed him flat down on his desk and drew his own weapon, and pointed it at Reginald Carstairs.

Carstairs looked bewildered until Nunez pulled the gun out of his daughter's purse, and then he looked scared. Regina just looked hostile and continued to yell profanities at Buck. She ran out of steam and sat back in her chair. Nunez called dispatch and told them to send everyone to the real estate office and proceeded to search each person, one at a time, and put flexicuffs on their wrists while Buck held Meyers down and held his gun on the Carstairs.

The Police Chief was the first to arrive, followed by the rest of the crew from his office. The suspects were read their Miranda rights and then walked through the real estate office and out past the crowd that had gathered on the street. Each suspect was placed in a different patrol car and driven back to police headquarters to be booked, fingerprinted and formally charged.

Paul Webber watched the booking process and said to Buck.

"What are the odds that they would all be together at just the right time?"

"You got me Paul, but boy that Regina sure wanted to go down swinging. I can't believe she went for a gun. What an idiot."

"You got that right," Paul replied. "I will stick around and make sure all the paperwork is covered if you want to head to the office."

Buck nodded, told Richards and Baxter that they could clear out as well and stopped and shook hands with the Chief and officers Nunez and Harding and asked Beverly Jensen if she needed anything else from him.

Beverly told him she was good, and she would call him if anything came up. Buck wished everyone well and headed for his car. Once in the parking lot, he called the Director and filled him in on the arrests.

The Director said, "She actually went for a gun in her purse. What the hell did she think she was going to do? Shoot her way out of the office."

"You got me, Director. I was as surprised as anyone. This could have gone from simple to messy in a heartbeat. I'm heading to the office. Call if you need me."

Buck disconnected the call, slid into his car, turned onto Highway 550 and headed for Grand Junction. He had just gotten to Delta, Colorado, when he pulled over to the side of the highway and turned up the police radio. He hardly ever used the police radio in the car. It was there just for emergencies. He preferred to do most of his calling on his cell phone. It was a little more private.

Buck listened to the statewide officer assistance call. This must be the same Ranger his son David had mentioned. It sounded to Buck like the situation had gone from a missing Ranger to something else entirely, especially when the bulletin mentioned that her dog had been shot. Buck never ignored an officer assistance call. He always figured that someday it could be him on the other end, and he would want everyone to respond. He pulled out his phone and called the duty officer at the Colorado Bureau of Investigation office in Grand Junction. He told the woman who answered that he was responding to the officer assistance call from Pitkin County and would be in touch.

There was no easy way to get to Aspen from where he was in Delta, so he turned onto Route 92. At Hotchkiss, he turned onto Route 133, which would take him to Carbondale, where he would turn south on Route 82 and head for Aspen. All told the drive would take him almost three hours, and he would arrive late in the afternoon. He had no choice. A law enforcement officer was in trouble. Buck flipped on the emergency flashers in his engine grill and hit the gas. He needed to shave some time off the three-hour drive.

CHAPTER SEVEN

The Sheriff was standing next to the Pitkin County Search and Rescue mobile command center when Buck walked up. He had to park almost a mile down the road leading to the trailhead. Between tourist cars and all the emergency vehicles, there was barely room for all the people.

"Sheriff," said Buck. "Heard you could use a hand."

The Sheriff turned and shook Buck's hand. "Buck Taylor. How the hell are you? Been a while."

It had been a few years since Buck had worked with Sheriff Winters, and he was amazed to see that the Sheriff looked the same as the last time he saw him.

"Doin good. Want to fill me in on what you got goin?"

"You betcha," said the Sheriff. "Hey, by the way, was sorry to hear about your wife passin. Always liked that lady. And hey, nice job in Durango last month. Knocked the shit out of the cartel boys." Bucked nodded.

The Sheriff filled Buck in on the search so far. Since Susan Corey hadn't left any information in her car, the Sheriff had no choice but to use it as a starting point for the search and send his teams out in several directions. Because the dog had been shot, the Sheriff had assigned a deputy or an armed Ranger to work with each two-person search team. He wanted someone armed with each group just in case. He was happy to report that the dog was out of surgery, and the emergency room vet felt good about his chances.

The Sheriff walked Buck through the search grids on the topographic map he had laid out on a table inside the command center. Right now, he had fifteen search teams working from several directions and all heading generally toward Hunter Peak. The Gunnison County search and rescue teams were working their way toward Hunter Peak from the south. From this point on, it was just a matter of waiting. And it would be getting dark soon, and he wanted everyone back before dark.

Buck looked at the grids. "Lot of area to cover. Any tracks from the dog?"

"No," responded the Sheriff. "None that anyone could find."

"You got PIS out there? Anyone could find tracks it would be him."

"Can't find him. Truth is, I think he is pissed at me."

Buck waited for an explanation. The Sheriff went on to explain that one of his newer deputies had gotten curious about PIS and had pulled his prints off a soda can and ran them through AFIS, the Automated Fingerprint Identification System. As in the past, the prints came back as flagged, and as in the past, PIS found out that they had run them, and he stormed off to god knows where.

Buck let out a low whistle. "You guys violated his trust again. No wonder you can't find him. Geez. We promised we wouldn't do that anymore. Try to find out his identity."

"I know. Jumped all over the deputy, but nothing I can do now."

"Okay," said Buck. "Since your search teams will be heading back in a little bit, I am going to check into the hotel, and I will try to find PIS and see if I can get him to help."

Buck shook the Sheriff's hand and started the long walk back to his car. Good thing he was in good shape. Buck reached his car, managed to turn around on the narrow road, and headed for Aspen.

Aspen, Colorado, playground of the rich and famous, is the county seat of Pitkin County, Colorado. Aspen has a population of around 7,000 people and sits at an elevation just shy of 8,000 feet. It was originally built as a mining town in the 1880s and was almost abandoned after the collapse of the silver mines in the early 1900s. In the 1930s, skiing started to take the place of mining, and Aspen started looking towards the future, but all that got put on hold during World War II. In 1946, skiing took off for real, and Aspen hasn't looked back since. Once the county seat of the counterculture movement in the United States, Aspen is now home to movie stars and corporate CEOs and boasts the most expensive real estate in the country. A lot had changed over the years, and Buck was never sure if it was a good thing or a bad thing. Mostly it just was, and Buck accepted that.

One thing Buck loved most about Aspen was that it still had its share of quirky characters, and despite efforts to "clean up the city," the city still had a good size homeless and counterculture population. Buck was on a mission to find one of those quirky characters as he pulled his car into a parking space along South Monarch Street next to Wagner Park.

Buck had first encountered PIS about ten years back. PIS, as he was affectionately known, had arrived in Aspen about twenty years ago and had stood out right from the start. At that time, the counterculture movement was in full swing, and drugs were everywhere. Everyone in Aspen either heard of or knew PIS, except that no one really knew much about him. PIS was tall, about six feet two and gangly as folks used to say. He probably weighed one hundred fifty pounds soaking wet. He had long gray hair pulled back in a ponytail and a three-day growth of stubble on his face. The odd thing is that no matter what day or time of day you encounter PIS, his stubble was always the same. It never seemed to grow out or look untidy.

Unlike most of the homeless characters at the time, PIS never smelled like a homeless person. He wore the same clothes every day but never looked dirty or unkempt. His outfit hadn't changed since Buck first met him. He wore calf height, brown leather lace-up moccasin style boots, light gray tuxedo pants with a dark gray stripe down the legs, and a worn white dress shirt now frayed and yellow with age. Around his waist, he wore a bright red cummerbund, and around his neck, he wore a bright red ascot.

No matter what time of year or what the temperature was, PIS always wore the same tattered brown linen coat and a black beret. He looked rather elegant for a homeless person. His only other possession was a well-worn leather backpack that looked like it had traveled the world. The initials, P-I-S, were engraved on the flap, and since no one knew his name, everyone just called him PIS, which he never seemed to mind. His demeanor was always jovial and friendly, and no one ever complained about feeling threatened by his presence. Most striking was his British accent. Not the harsh Cockney accent you associate with street people but a silky-smooth accent that just exuded sophistication.

No one ever saw him panhandling for money, yet he always seemed to have enough to visit one of the local pubs for his nightly glass of cognac. As it turned out, PIS also had an incredible talent, which helped him generate some income on a fairly regular basis. PIS was an amazing tracker. There wasn't anything he couldn't find, whether it be an animal, or a missing child and his abilities had come to the attention of many of the local hunting guides who paid him a daily fee to help them find game for their out-of-town clients. PIS's tracking skills had also come to the attention of the local police and Sheriff, and over the years, he had been involved in finding many lost hikers or missing persons in the rugged mountains surrounding Aspen.

Early on, when he first arrived in Aspen, many people tried to engage him in conversation to try to determine his real name or his background. It was rumored that several times, people had tried to follow him as he left the downtown area and headed for the forest at the end of the day. No one was ever successful. Within minutes of entering the forest, PIS would disappear, leaving his followers bewildered. No one had any idea where he went at night or where he slept, but every morning he was right back downtown walking the alleys between East Hopkins Avenue and East Hyman Avenue rummaging through trash dumpsters. If you asked people to guess PIS's age, you would get answers from forty to eighty. He truly was a mystery.

The Sheriff had run his fingerprints once when an over-zealous deputy tried to arrest PIS for vagrancy, and his prints came back as flagged, meaning some agency had restricted access to his information. PIS had become furious at the intrusion into his privacy, and ever since, there was a truce between local law enforcement and PIS. He would provide his tracking services for free to any agency that needed such services; in exchange, local law enforcement would no longer try to determine his true identity. That truce had lasted almost twenty years, till now.

Buck had first met PIS during a missing person's case Buck had been working in the Aspen area. The case involved a missing heiress, a thirteen-year-old girl who had disappeared from her home in the Woody Creek area. It was never clear if she had walked away from her home or if she had been taken. Security had been tight around the family home, and there were no signs of a break-in. No ransom had ever been demanded, and the body was never discovered, even though Buck and PIS, with the help of the Sheriff's department, worked tirelessly for two weeks and had scoured every inch of the forests around Aspen. It was Buck's only case that remained unsolved, and the case file sat in a prominent place on Buck's desk as a reminder of the one he couldn't solve.

Buck had gotten to know PIS pretty well during those two weeks. More so than anyone else had ever been able to, and he developed a fondness for this unusual character. During those two weeks of hiking around in the woods, Buck learned two things about PIS that he had kept a secret to this day. He found out that PIS's real name was Pheasant Iverson-Smythe. PIS had refused to say anything more about why his first name was Pheasant, and Buck let it go. The other thing he learned, while they sat around a small campfire one afternoon, was even more of a mystery. PIS had pulled an old tin cookie box out of his backpack. Inside the cookie tin wrapped in fine silk was a beautiful china cup and saucer, a silver spoon, a small tea ball for brewing tea and a tiny silver teapot. PIS had also removed a smaller tin containing loose leaf Earl Grey tea, which he proceeded to brew up for himself. The whole image seemed out of place. Buck spotted a worn black and white picture of a beautiful young woman sitting in the bottom of the cookie tin, but when he asked PIS about the picture, PIS almost reverently closed the tin and explained that some things were best left unsaid. Buck could have sworn he saw a tear develop in PIS's eye.

Those two weeks had created a strange bond between these two men. Buck couldn't explain it, and he never tried. He worked with PIS several more times over the years, and it became more apparent to Buck, that as he got older, PIS never seemed to age. PIS also seemed to understand how much it troubled Buck that the case of the missing heiress remained unsolved.

CHAPTER EIGHT

Buck spent the next couple hours, until well after dark walking the streets and alleys of downtown Aspen searching for PIS. His inquiries with local shop-keepers, hoteliers, bartenders, and the homeless he encoun-tered netted the same response. No one had seen PIS for a couple of days. Most couldn't remember the last time they saw him, but they would be happy to let Buck know if he showed up.

Buck checked into his hotel and crashed for the night. To-morrow was going to be a very long day. Before he nodded off to sleep, he asked the spirits of the woods to keep an eye on PIS and Ranger Susan Corey and keep them safe. Buck wasn't religious in the typical sense of religion. He had been raised Catholic, and he and Lucy had tried to raise their chil-dren Catholic but only Jason, their youngest son, had kept organized religion in his life. Buck was more spiritual than religious. He had very little use for organized religion, but he always believed that there were spirits out there keeping an eye on things. He always thanked the spirits for allowing him to catch fish or for allowing him to witness a beautiful sunrise or sunset. Lucy never questioned his beliefs, and she never minded when he discussed his attitudes with his kids or grandkids.

Buck's internal alarm clock went off at five AM, and he showered and dressed, clipped his badge and holster to his belt, and headed out to get something for breakfast before heading down to the trailhead. Stopping at a small gas station and convenience store just before the turnoff for Route 13, Buck grabbed a couple bottles of Coke and water and a few snacks to take with him. He was sitting in his car, eating a microwaved burrito and drinking his Coke when there was a knock on the passenger side window. Buck glanced over and there, standing beside the car was PIS. He hit the button to unlock the door, and PIS climbed into the passenger seat.

"Good morning, Agent Taylor. How very nice to see you again. What a pleasant day it is going to be."

Buck loved listening to PIS's accent, and for a second, he just stared. He had no idea how PIS found him, this far from downtown. He swallowed the piece of burrito he was chewing on and smiled.

"Where have you been?" Buck asked. "People haven't seen you in a couple of days."

"I've been around. I heard you were looking for me. Will we be embarking on another grand adventure?"

Buck nodded. "We have a missing person we need to find. I am heading to the trailhead now and could use your help."

PIS looked serious for a moment. "I told the Sheriff that I would not be available to work with him for a while. Did he send you to find me?"

"No. The Sheriff was very clear that you were pissed. I told him I would find you. This one is important PIS. A female Ranger is missing, and her dog was found shot. We need your help."

PIS stared at Buck for a minute without saying anything. His trust had been violated once again, and Buck understood how important that was to him, but he also had no doubt that PIS would do the right thing.

"I didn't realize it was a Ranger who was missing. Had I known, I would have found the Sheriff and offered my assistance."

Buck simply nodded, started the car, and pulled out of the convenience store parking lot. The sun was just starting to come over the mountains, and Buck knew from experience that the earlier PIS got on the trail, the better and morning light was the best for finding obscure footprints or trail signs.

Buck was able to pull into the Maroon-Snowmass trailhead parking lot and parked next to the rescue command center. The Sheriff, coffee in hand, was standing over the table looking at the search map with the head of the Pitkin County Search and Rescue team. They both looked up at Buck, and PIS approached.

"Buck, PIS. Nice to see you," said the Sheriff.

Buck nodded, but PIS reached out his hand, first shaking the hand of the head of the rescue team and then shaking the Sheriff's hand.

"I must apologize, Sheriff. My behavior of late has been in poor taste, and if you will allow me, I would like to offer my services in the search for the Ranger."

Buck had never seen PIS seem this contrite. He had filled PIS in on the events thus far, and PIS seemed to be extremely concerned about the fate of the Ranger's dog. Buck wondered if the wounded dog had somehow struck a nerve with PIS. Something from his past that triggered a serious response.

The Sheriff accepted his offer of help and Buck, and PIS joined the Sheriff around the map. The Sheriff explained that the rest of the teams would be arriving soon, and then he reviewed where they had searched yesterday and what the game plan was for today. PIS studied the map very carefully as if he was memorizing every trail and landmark, although Buck believed deep inside, that PIS knew these forests like Buck knew his own house.

PIS looked up from the map. "Is it possible to see where

the dog was found?"

The Sheriff explained that the Ranger's truck was still at the scene, and he led Buck and PIS over to where it was parked. PIS got down on his knees and looked under the car. He spotted a small splash of blood on the rocks under the truck, and he reached in and touched it with his hand. He then crawled under the truck as far as he could go and started scanning the area around the truck. He had a dog's eye view of the forest around the truck.

The sun was just starting to cast long shadows across the parking lot as PIS slid out from under the car. PIS was focused on something in the distance, and both Buck and the Sheriff knew better than to interrupt PIS when he was this focused.

CHAPTER NINE

The Teacher was not pleased. Not pleased at all. They had never seen the Teacher this mad. They brought home all that elk meat and had the others cook up some for dinner. Some of the others had found some canned vegetables at one of the houses they raided and also some soup. It was a good meal.

The Teacher then asked them to tell the others how they had shot the elk, and that is when the trouble began. Being the oldest, the hunter told the story the way the Teacher had taught him too. He used words and visualization to bring the others along on the trail as they stalked the huge animal. The others sat and listened, enthralled with the story. Even the youngest sat still during the telling.

They described seeing the animal in the distance, how they crawled and crouch stepped to within a couple hundred yards and how they had drawn a bead on the elk, sighted in on his massive chest, took a deep breath, just like they had been taught, held the next breath and fired. The shot was perfect, and the elk had only been able to run a couple yards before it collapsed in some grass. They chased after it, and when they found it, it was still breathing, so they slit its throat to stop the pain. Just like the Teacher had told them to do. The Teacher looked pleased.

They told the group about dragging the elk back to the hunting camp in the woods and how they were going to hide it and come back to butcher it later, but that the lady Ranger and her dog spotted the camp. The Teacher froze. He asked them to repeat the part about the lady Ranger, which they did. A little more nervously this time.

They described how the dog had sniffed out their hiding spot and how they had no choice but to shoot the lady Ranger in the thigh since she was wearing a ballistic vest. They described how they found her lying in the ravine, how the blood was pumping out of her leg, and she had pleaded with them to stop the pain, and they told everyone that they shot her in the head, so she would no longer suffer, just like the Teacher had taught them.

The Teacher's face grew red with anger. He demanded to know what had happened to the dog. They were now too afraid not to tell the whole truth, so they told everyone that they had shot the dog and had seen it fall, but that after searching for a long time, they were unable to find the dog. They explained that they had gone back to where the lady Ranger was lying in the ravine and had covered her body with dirt and sticks so no one would be able to find her.

The Teacher could no longer contain his anger. He yelled at them for taking a human life, something he always told them never to do. He understood that they were trying to protect the others, but taking a human life was forbidden. He told them they would be punished for taking the human life, and he told them he was very unhappy that they could not find the dog. If the dog made it back to where it had come from, there would be hell to pay, and they had put the others in peril.

The Teacher was certain that the outsiders would come looking for the lady Ranger and her dog, and he now feared that after all this time, they would have to move their camp. He told them that it was all their fault for being so stupid and to get caught by the lady Ranger. He called them dumb and stupid, and a bunch of other words they did not understand, and they knew the Teacher was mad, very mad. He said that if the outsiders found the cabin, they would take the others away to a bad place where they would no longer be able to see each other and that the hunter and the younger one would have to go to jail because of killing the lady Ranger. They had no idea what jail was, but the Teacher made it sound like a terrible place, and the younger one started crying, which just made the Teacher madder. He took the rifle that was in the corner and put it under his bed. He told them not to touch it again until he had come up with a suitable punishment.

The Teacher told the girls to clear the table from dinner and to start moving everything out of the cabin and deep into the mine. They needed to be prepared for when the outsiders came. He told the hunter and the younger one to go out into the woods and make sure the traps were all set. He did not want to be surprised by the outsiders.

The others had never lived anywhere else but the cabin. They were scared and nervous about having to leave. All their stuff, the Teacher's books, and the awards he had given them for doing good things were here in the cabin. Momma was buried not far away, and they were worried that they would never be near her again. Some of the others started to cry.

The Teacher, sensing their worry and concern, started to calm down. He told them all to come back to the table for a minute. He had them all hold hands, and then he read his favorite passage from the bible. "Yea, though I walk through the valley of the shadow of death..." The others listened carefully to the words. They always felt better upon hearing the words.

The Teacher finished reading and told them that he loved them all, even the hunter and the younger one and that he was sorry he had gotten so mad. He told them that human life was precious and that it was wrong to take a life, but that they might now have to take more lives to protect their home. This would make him sad. He hoped that they could get deep enough into the mine so no one would find them and that someday they might be able to come back to the cabin.

The Teacher asked them all to gather up their things as quickly and quietly as possible and start moving things into the mine. They all followed his orders, and the hunter and the younger one left to check on the traps.

CHAPTER TEN

While the Sheriff headed back to the rescue command center to help organize the searchers and give them their assignments, Buck stood next to Susan Corey's truck and watched PIS work. PIS was methodical in his approach to tracking, and it would take all his skills for this one. The dog left almost no trail to follow, so PIS started to expand his circle around the truck. Moving out five yards each time he completed a circle around the vehicle. Several times he had gotten down on his knees or his belly to get a better view of the area.

Buck waited patiently. The rest of the search was going to be organized but not too precise since they had no idea in which direction Susan Corey had traveled. They knew from the Chief Ranger that she was supposed to be searching for the illegal elk camp in the area near Hunter Peak and that several of the search teams had been in that area but found nothing. Once she arrived in the parking lot, something could have changed her mind, and she could have gone off in any direction. This was needle in the haystack time.

Buck's thoughts were interrupted by a call from PIS.

"Agent Taylor. Over here, please."

Buck tried for years to get PIS to call him Buck but to no avail. Even if no one was around, he still called him Agent Taylor. He walked over to where PIS was kneeling on the ground, looking at something in the dirt. Buck knelt next to him and looked at the spot PIS was pointing at. Buck got closer and pulled his reading glasses out of his back pocket. He looked at the ground next to PIS's finger and could make out a single, very light pad impression and contained in that impression was a tiny spot of something reddish-brown. Blood.

Knowing where the first trail mark was, gave them a direction of travel from the Ranger's truck, and with that, PIS started moving in that direction. Buck could hardly see the trail, but there was enough indentation in the undergrowth to give PIS something to follow. Buck ran back to the rescue command center to let the Sheriff know that PIS had a trail and to pick up one of the search team radios. The Sheriff was still going to send out his search teams per the plan they had come up with earlier, just in case the trail PIS was following didn't pan out.

Buck headed back to his Jeep, put on his ballistic vest, grabbed his backpack, a topographic map, handheld GPS unit, and his back up semi-automatic pistol and headed back to the Ranger's truck. PIS was already fifty yards up the trail looking for the next sign, which he found just as Buck was walking up behind him. A spot of blood on a leaf eighteen inches off the ground. Buck couldn't see it, but he trusted PIS, so off they went.

The trail they followed was hardly more than a slight impression in the undergrowth, but it made sense to Buck. If you were a guide running an illegal elk camp, you wouldn't want to have it anywhere near one of the established trails. This trail looked like an old game trail that hadn't been used in years. It was perfect. The last thing you would want is for a tourist to stumble on your camp, and this area was filled with tourists hiking on the many established trails.

PIS was like an old hound dog on a scent. Periodically he would stop and kneel to look at something, or he would stop, scratch his beard and then move ten or fifteen paces into the woods around the trail and circle back toward the trail. Buck soon realized that this was how PIS maintained the sign. If he lost the trail, he would move left or right until he could reestablish the trail. For the most part, the dog seemed to have traveled a fairly straight line. Several times over the next couple hours, PIS would stop and point out where the dog had laid down to rest. Buck couldn't even begin to imagine how much the dog must have been hurting as it made its way back to the Ranger's truck.

Buck was in pretty good shape for a fifty-eight-year-old man, but after four hours of hiking over uneven ground, he needed to take a break. PIS, on the other hand, looked like he hadn't walked anywhere at all. He still wore his linen coat and his beret, and he wasn't even sweating. Buck was mystified. It was early September, but it was still warm for this time of year, and Buck was sweating profusely. PIS did agree to hold up so that Buck could take a breather, and he didn't refuse the bottle of water and the trail mix bar that Buck offered him.

Buck unfolded the topographic map and pulled out his handheld GPS unit. He had been marking waypoints on the map as they had been traveling. PIS came over to look at the map with him. They had traveled in pretty much a straight line from the Ranger's truck, but what they both noticed was that they were not headed to Hunter Peak, at least not directly. If this trail continued, they would travel to the west of the peak. Away from where most of the rescue units were searching.

"What do you think?" Buck asked.

PIS pondered the question and looked once more at the map. "If I had to venture a guess, I would say that something distracted the Ranger, or she had some new information that we were not aware of. There are several trails that lead to Hunter Peak that she could have followed more easily than this trail, yet she chose to bushwhack through the trees. Very odd, indeed."

Buck had to agree. He folded up the map, put it back in his pocket and they headed out again. Twice over the next hour, PIS lost the trail in some rocky terrain, and it took a little bit of time to reestablish the trail. Buck spent that time listening to the other search teams reporting in. No one had anything good to report.

Buck and PIS traveled for about another hour when PIS stopped short and put his hand out so Buck couldn't move past him. At almost that same instance, the radio crackled.

"Search team four to command. We have a serious problem over."

"Go ahead, search team four, this is command."

"Command, we have a man down. One of the Rangers stepped on what appears to be some kind of booby trap. He was impaled in the leg with a sharp stick that just popped out of the ground. He is bleeding badly, and we need a paramedic."

"Search team four. Please begin first aid and try to stop the bleeding. We are sending in the paramedics. Please provide coordinates."

The search team leader gave them the coordinates, and Buck pulled his map out of his pocket. The search team was in the grid next to the one he and PIS were working, a little over a mile from their present location. Buck put the map back in his pocket and started to move in the direction of search team four, but PIS stopped him again. Buck looked annoyed until he saw where PIS was pointing. Just above the surface of the trail, Buck spotted the monofilament fishing line. It was tied to a bush off to their left and was pulled tight across the trail.

"Booby trap?" Buck asked.

PIS nodded. "Yes. Be very careful. Let me see where this goes. Please stand back a couple of paces."

PIS got down on his knees and followed the line without touching it. Five feet off the trail and in dense underbrush, he stopped. The string was attached to a very rudimentary crossbow that had been anchored between two shrubs. The bolt was nothing more than a sharpened stick, but with the tension on the line, it could have delivered a nasty surprise to whoever tripped it. PIS pulled a knife from his pocket, snapped it open with one hand and proceeded to cut the tripwire, and disengage the bolt. He crawled back out of the underbrush.

"Could have been a bit of a nasty surprise for whoever tripped this," he said while handing the bolt to Buck. "It was low enough to the ground to cause some damage, but I don't think it was intended to kill. Just wound."

Buck examined the bolt. "Crude but effective. How the hell did you spot the tripwire? I was looking at where you were pointing, and I didn't see it until you touched it."

"Experience, Agent Taylor. Someone does not want us to find this elk camp."

Buck pulled out his radio. "Command, this is Buck Taylor. Please put the Sheriff on."

"Go ahead, Buck. This is Earl," replied the Sheriff.

"Earl, have all the search teams stop where they are. We just disarmed a booby trap along the trail we are following. There could be more out there."

"All search teams. You heard the man. Hold your positions until we figure this out. Buck, how do you think we should handle this?"

"We are certain we are on the dog's trail. Let us continue forward and clear a path and see where the trail takes us. In the meantime, I would suggest you pull everyone back to the parking lot. Right now, our trail is taking us to the west of Hunter Peak. We will call in as soon as we reach the end of the trail."

"Okay, Buck. Stay in touch. All search teams, backtrack the way you went in and return to the parking lot."

Buck looked at PIS. "Let's keep moving. Slowly."

PIS nodded and started back down the trail.

CHAPTER ELEVEN

S he had to park along the road leading to the Maroon-Snowmass trailhead parking lot. There were a lot of emergency vehicles ahead, and it appeared that the entrance to the parking lot was closed. She had no idea what was going on. She overheard a conversation at the restaurant that there was some kind of police search going on at the trailhead, and she decided to see for herself.

She left her car on the side of the road and walked down to the crowd to see if she could find out what was going on. She pulled the long brown wig down a little snugger on her head, pulled it back in a ponytail, and put on her Denver Broncos ball cap. She climbed out of her car, grabbed her backpack out of the trunk, and slung it over her shoulders. She looked just like all the other hikers that were walking down the road to the trailhead.

As she walked towards the barricade that was set up at the entrance to the parking lot, several disgruntled hikers came walking back from the barricade. Several people told her that the trail was closed until further notice. She thanked them as they passed, figuring that was what most friendly hikers would do.

She stepped up to a crowd of hikers and day users who had gathered at the barricade and listened as the Park Ranger told the crowd that the authorities were in the process of looking for a lost hiker and the park would be closed until the search was concluded.

Most of the hikers took the information as gospel and turned to head for their cars. Some chose to stay and either grumble about the inconvenience or ask questions to try to get more information from the Ranger. She stood to the side of the group and listened. She had learned long ago that you got a lot more information from people if you stopped and listened and watched their body language.

As the other hikers conversed with the Ranger, she heard his words, but more importantly, she noticed his eyes. It was obvious to her that he was not being completely truthful. He was trying to be polite with the crowd, but there was an underlying tension in his face and voice. Answering the same questions, a dozen or more times gets old pretty fast, but the Ranger answered each query with a polite smile.

Satisfied that she was not going to hear anything new, as more hikers and curiosity seekers came and went, she turned and headed back to her car. Being the polite, friendly hiker, she was, she let those just heading for the barricade know that the trail was closed indefinitely. The other hikers politely thanked her before continuing to the barricade to hear it for themselves.

She reached her car, put her backpack back in the trunk, and stood for a minute looking down the road at the barricade. She knew the Ranger was only being partially truthful. It was obvious the trail was closed. So that was the truth. The missing hiker was another story. From the trailhead, she could see the Pitkin County Search and Rescue mobile command center, so obviously, there was some kind of search going on. Typically, in small communities, when a hiker is lost or missing, the Sheriff's office calls for volunteers, but that was not the case here. Most of the volunteers she could see were uniformed searchers, and she also noted a lot of law enforcement types. A lot more than you would see at a simple search, and from the cars she observed, the law enforcement folks had come from many different jurisdictions. She would need to think about this some more.

She climbed into her car and just sat for a minute. Was it possible they had found it? Is that why all the cops were on the scene? In all the time it was there no one had ever stumbled onto it. Was it possible that someone spotted the newer lock? She had purposely taken an old looking padlock from her grandfather's garage so it would not be obvious to anyone looking that the lock was recently changed.

She started to feel a little nauseous and took a sip of water from the bottle between the seats. It couldn't be. She was just getting started. She had tried to be careful, just like she had been taught. She made certain she wasn't followed, and she covered her tracks well. No, it was not possible. No one had discovered it in forty or fifty years. Why now? She started to shake, and she wrapped her arms around her chest and squeezed. The shaking stopped.

She decided that she was just being paranoid and that the cops would not be waiting at her house when she got home. After all, how would they even know about her? She started her car, pulled off the side of the road, and headed home. Even though she felt more confident that this didn't concern her, and it was just a co-incidence that something was going on in the same area, she had this little nagging bug in the back of her head. She would need to be very careful until she worked this all out.

CHAPTER TWELVE

The trail was becoming more obvious as they moved forward. They were finding more and more dried bloodstains on the undisturbed undergrowth, and PIS told Buck that with the amount of blood he was finding, they must be getting close to the end of the trail. He also had to stop once more and expose another booby trap. This time it was a shallow pit about a foot deep covered with a thin layer of sticks and leaves. Almost impossible to see, but it could have been quite effective. Buried in the small pit were a dozen sharpened sticks pointing up, so anyone who happened to step into the pit would have had their foot impaled on any one of the spikes.

PIS spent a few minutes removing the spikes, which were buried a foot or so deep in the soil to keep them upright. At one point, he commented about the fact that what they had encountered so far were very similar to the types of booby traps the Viet Cong used to set during the Vietnam war. Crude, but effective.

Buck started to ask him about the comment, but PIS just ignored him and stood up and said they should keep moving. Buck let it slide, but wondered if he had just been privy to another little tidbit about PIS's life.

PIS moved down the trail with a little more urgency, or so it seemed to Buck. He seemed to be much more focused, and they covered a lot more ground until they arrived at a small rise, and PIS stopped, knelt, and touched something on the ground. Buck climbed up the little rise behind him, stopped to catch his breath, and looked at where PIS had his hand. This blood spot was so obvious that even Buck could see it.

Without saying anything, PIS stood and moved a couple of feet to his left and repeated the process. Buck looked and noticed the second large blood spot. PIS still hadn't said anything. He stood up and moved down the backside of the ravine, where he found more dried blood. He stood and looked around the area. Then he looked at Buck. There was a seriousness in his eyes that Buck had never seen before.

"The dog was shot there." He pointed to the spot where Buck was now standing. Buck stayed silent. "It would appear he fell off the ridge in this direction and landed here." He pointed to another big bloodstain. "There is a good blood trail leading back to the trail we came in on. I am amazed that with the amount of blood that is here, that the dog was able to walk back four point four miles and get back to the Ranger's car. He must have been in terrible pain."

Buck pulled out his handheld GPS and looked at the data. They had traveled four point five miles. He hadn't told PIS how far they had gone, but he hit the number almost exactly. Buck didn't know how PIS had known, but he decided to keep that knowledge to himself. PIS was certainly an anomaly. PIS climbed back up the small ridge and looked around.

"What do you think happened to the Ranger? Any chance she might be still alive?" Buck asked.

PIS stood for a moment, and Buck thought he saw PIS's eyes get a little misty.

"I don't think so." He pointed to the other large spot of blood on the ground a few feet to the right. "This is arterial spray. Notice the many small droplets. I believe the Ranger was shot here." He stood and pointed to a pile of leaves and sticks at the bottom of the ravine.

"I believe we will find the Ranger under that pile of leaves."

Buck pulled his cell phone out of his pocket, clicked on the camera, and took a couple of pictures of the various blood stains as PIS pointed to them. He then put his camera away and looked at PIS. He nodded, and they made their way down into the ravine, making sure to disturb as little as possible.

At the bottom of the ravine, Buck took over, and PIS stood back to let Buck do his job. With great care, Buck began to remove the leaves and sticks from the pile. Below the leaves and sticks, Buck found a layer of loose dry dirt. His heart sank. It was obvious, even to him, that the dirt was recently disturbed, and he moved even more carefully.

Using his hand to brush away the dirt, the face of Susan Corey gradually revealed itself. Her eyes were still open, and Buck could almost sense the horror she must have felt knowing her life was slipping away. The dark hole in her forehead and the lack of blood on her face told Buck that the kill shot had come too late. Buck figured Susan Corey must have been at the end of her life when someone put her out of her misery. He stopped and stared at her face.

Buck had seen a lot of death in his long career in law enforcement, but he had never gotten jaded by it. He was still impacted deeply and seeing Susan Corey's lifeless face made him sit back for a moment and reflect on his own life. It also made him angry that this young woman's life had been cut short, and he vowed to do everything he could to find and punish the person or persons who had done this.

PIS joined him, and together they removed the dirt and debris from the rest of her body. PIS pointed to the bullet hole and the massive amount of blood that stained her green pant leg. Buck nodded and pulled out his camera again. He took pictures of the wounds, of her body as it lay and pictures of the debris that had been piled on her. He looked at PIS.

PIS said, "Whoever shot her knew what they were doing. Shot her below her ballistic vest. She rolled down the slope ended up here, and then the shooter shot her in the forehead. Such a terrible waste. I am truly sorry, Agent Taylor."

Buck nodded. "Without your help, we might never have found her. Thanks for helping to bring her family closure. Now we need to call in the troops. This is now a crime scene."

Buck climbed back up to the top of the ridge and found that he had 2 bars of cell service. He decided not to broadcast the find over the radio, so he used his phone and dialed the Sheriff.

The Sheriff answered on the second ring. "Buck, does this mean what I think it means?"

"Yeah. Didn't want to broadcast it on an open frequency. We found Susan Corey. We are gonna need the Forensic Pathologist and the crime scene guys."

Buck told the Sheriff about what they had discovered. He pulled out his handheld GPS and gave the Sheriff the coordinates for the body and told him how to follow the trail from her truck. He would send PIS back up the trail to meet them halfway, and he would lead them in the rest of the way. He asked him to send in a couple search and rescue guys to carry out the body when forensics was finished, and he requested as many deputies as the Sheriff could spare. This was going to be one tough crime scene to process. He asked him to keep all the other law enforcement folks and Rangers away from the scene.

The Sheriff mentioned that there were several Gunnison County deputies not that far from his location, and he would request assistance from the Gunnison County Sheriff and have his deputies meet up with Buck to help work the scene. This deep in the mountains, jurisdiction lines sometimes get blurred, and Buck told the Sheriff he would be grateful for all the help. The Sheriff would also be calling his homicide team.

Buck hung up and headed back to PIS and the body. He asked PIS if he would head back up the trail and meet the teams coming down. PIS slapped Buck on the back and headed up the ridge. Buck was now alone with the body, and he said a silent prayer and asked the spirits of the forest to watch over her family.

CHAPTER THIRTEEN

B uck pulled a silver and orange survival blanket out of his backpack and used it to cover Susan Corey's body. He had also checked to make sure she still had her weapon, her radio, and her cell phone. It was obvious that robbery was not a motive, so he dismissed that idea and moved on to the next idea. Ambush. Was Susan Corey ambushed, and if so, by whom? Buck was all too familiar with ambushes having survived one while investigating a drug distribution network in Durango, Colorado, a month, or so back. If it hadn't been for luck and his friend Jessica Gonzales, the DEA Agent in Charge of the Grand Junction office, he would not be here today.

The Slattery brothers were prime suspects in a triple homicide Buck had been investigating in Teller County, when he was reassigned to the cartel investigation in Durango. Somehow the brothers had followed Buck to Durango and tried to ambush him in his hotel parking lot. Jess Gonzales was walking through the hotel parking lot on her way to meet Buck just as the shooting started. Buck and Jess killed both brothers, but Buck would never forget how close he came to getting killed that evening. He knew his late wife Lucy would not have been pleased.

He stopped and cleared that memory out of his head. Susan Corey needed and deserved Buck's full attention, and he would not let her down. Buck stood up and looked around the area. The trees were not as dense in this part of the forest. The shot could have come from almost anywhere, so he needed to narrow that down a bit. He walked back up to the top of the ridge to the first bloodstain. He looked down at the bloodstain and noticed the spatter that PIS had first pointed out to him. Most of the spatter appeared to be on one side of the larger stain, so he decided to concentrate his initial search in that direction.

Buck walked back down into the ravine and headed in the direction he thought the shots might have come from. The first thing he noticed was that whoever buried Susan Corey's body left almost no footprints. Whoever this person or persons were, they had skills. Buck moved away from the body. He was still worried about additional booby traps, so he was careful where he placed his feet. Remembering how PIS used a circular pattern each time he lost the trail, Buck followed a similar pattern. Every five feet or so, he would stop and then move right and then left in a semi-circle around the body location.

Buck was just completing his fourth semi-circle when he heard some leaves and sticks crackling in the distance. Buck unsnapped the thumb break on his holster and removed his semi-automatic pistol. He knelt next to an Aspen tree.

"Gunnison County Sheriffs!" a voice called out. "Coming in from the south."

Buck replied, "all clear. Come ahead." He rose and holstered his gun, but kept his hand on the backstrap, just in case.

Buck spotted the two Gunnison County Sheriff's deputies coming through the trees, followed by two Gunnison County Search and Rescue members. He snapped the thumb break on his holster shut. Buck recognized Walt Jenkins. Walt was a corporal and had been with Gunnison County for about six years. The other deputy he didn't recognize.

Walt stepped up and extended his hand. "Buck Taylor, how the hell are you?"

Buck shook Walt's hand, and Walt introduced him to deputy Jimmy Sanchez. Buck shook Jimmy's hand and then shook hands with the two rescue team members, Mike Brill and Connie Hancock, both of whom he knew quite well.

Walt walked over to the body and pulled back the corner. He stood there for a minute, said a silent prayer, and crossed himself. Walt was a devout Christian. He put the blanket over Susan Corey's face and looked around the area.

"Heck of a crime scene, Buck. What do you want us to do?"

Buck explained about his semi-circle search pattern and that they were looking for the shooter's nest. He also reminded them of the possible booby traps. Walt told Buck that they had encountered a booby trap on the way up the hill.

"If Jimmy hadn't tripped over his own feet, he would have gotten an arrow right in his backside," said Walt. "Luckily, the arrow passed right over him and embedded itself in a tree. Who would have ever thought about booby traps in Colorado?"

Buck agreed, and the four Gunnison searchers headed off to continue Buck's search pattern. Buck took the opportunity to take a breather and pulled a bottle of Coke and a trail mix bar out of his backpack. They had been going nonstop since this morning, and Buck was beginning to feel his age. Finishing the Coke and the trail mix bar, Buck headed in the direction of his initial search to help the Gunnison County team. He was just coming up on the first searcher when he heard Jimmy Sanchez call his name.

Jimmy was about forty yards from the body and was looking at something on the ground as Buck walked up. He was soon joined by Walt Jenkins, and they looked at what Jimmy was looking at. The spent shell casing was lying on the ground in plain sight. It didn't appear that anyone had tried to hide it unless someone had missed it.

Buck pulled out his phone and snapped a picture of it. Walt pulled a clear evidence bag out of his backpack and handed it to Buck, who had already gloved up, and he picked up the shell casing between his two fingers and placed it in the bag and sealed it. Buck signed his name to the bag, and Walt placed it in Buck's backpack.

The group also noticed a large puddle of blood near the shell casing. From the way Buck read the scene, it appeared that whoever shot Ranger Corey was probably hiding behind this downed log and pretty much hidden from view. From this vantage point, Buck could see the top of the ridge where Susan Corey was shot. But what was the blood?

Jimmy had moved off from the group and was following the blood trail that led to the little hideout. He called to Buck.

"I think I know what the blood is from."

Buck and Walt walked over to where Jimmy was standing. Jimmy was standing next to a pile of bloody guts.

Jimmy said, "I think someone gutted an elk here. It's not a fresh pile, so I would say a couple of days."

Buck and Walt agreed with his assessment. A picture started to form in Buck's mind. He explained his theory to Jimmy and Walt.

"My guess, at this point, is that someone was hunting out of season, possibly the illegal hunters that the Ranger had been following. The hunters heard her coming and pulled the carcass over behind the downed tree and hid. Something the Ranger or her dog did must have spooked them, and someone shot her in the thigh. Shot the dog too, but the dog managed to crawl away. Susan Corey wasn't as lucky. She fell into the ravine bleeding badly. Someone then shot her in the head, either to shut her up or to put her out of her misery."

Walt looked at Buck. "Man, Buck, if that's the way it went

down, that is pretty cold. Using a kill shot on an animal is one thing, but to kill a person up close, that's something else entirely."

Buck just nodded. He tried to visualize what Susan Corey had been feeling at the time. Lying in a ravine feeling her life pumping out of her thigh and then watching as her killer stood in front of her and calmly points his gun at her and pulls the trigger. Whoever did this was going to pay. Buck made himself that promise.

CHAPTER FOURTEEN

She sits alone in the dark in her room—one small lavender candle burning in a small mason jar on her dresser. The night air is still unseasonably warm, so she has the window open, and she can hear the hubbub of mountain life as it passes by her home. Her parents had gone out to dinner as soon as she got home. They looked frazzled, even more so than usual. It has been hard on them, especially the last three years, since she was away at college. They knew she would be leaving again very soon, and she wondered if they hated her for her decision.

She had lived in Aspen all her life, and for the most part, it had been a good life. Her parents were not rich, and they didn't get involved in the Aspen social scene. They lived in the same little Victorian house on West Hallam Street that her grandfather bought in the nineteen fifties. She was the third generation living under the same roof, and sometimes things got a little crazy.

Her father's father, her grandfather, had come to Aspen a few years after the end of World War II. He had been a soldier in the 10th Mountain Division as the war neared its end and had learned how to ski. Some of his fellow warriors were settling in small communities throughout the Colorado mountains and were working to build up the fledgling ski industry. He thought it might be fun to be a part of the movement.

His best friend, Gus Murphy, found a job with the recently formed Aspen Skiing Corporation and had offered her grandfather a job working as a mechanic on the ski lifts. Having been mechanically inclined all his life, her grandfather took to the job like a fish to water. As the years progressed, his life became more and more fulfilling, and he felt he was living the American dream. He met and fell in love with her grandmother, bought the small Victorian house on West Hallam Street, and raised a son there. It was a perfect life except that the demons were still working hard in the back of his mind.

The demons had always been there as long as he could remember, and his time in the army had only deepened the lust they brought out. He had practiced his craft, as he called it, with great abandon as a young man. Many of the townsfolk around Lynchburg, Virginia thought he was odd, and some feared him. He had grown up on a very rural farm outside Lynchburg. The family's water came from a pump, and an outhouse served their more personal needs. To say they were dirt poor would have been an understatement. His father was a sharecropper and didn't even own the dirt under their little house.

Life had not been easy growing up. He was constantly picked on when he was able to get to school, which was not often, and as things got worse, his father would take to drinking, and he was a terrible drunk. No one was safe from his rage, especially his mother and younger sisters. Numerous times he had watched as his father left his middle sister's room, and he heard her crying inside. As his younger sister got older, the same thing would happen to her. His mother would often come out of her room with a black eye or a bruised lip. He wasn't saved from his father's rage because he was a boy. His father would belittle him all the time about not being good at anything or not being a man. He would work him from dawn til dusk, and then if the mood was right, would beat him senseless for even the most minor infraction.

His escape often took him into unknown territory. He took to following in his father's footsteps and started abusing the animals on the farm. But it didn't stop there. Many of the neighbors complained to the local Sheriff about their pets disappearing. The Sheriff had visited the farm numerous times but never found any evidence that anyone on the farm was involved, but the neighbors knew the truth. What they had no way of knowing was how deep the depravity went.

One afternoon one of the neighbors had confronted him about a missing goat. He had seen the goatskin hanging in a tree along the creek behind the farm. The neighbor confronted him and his father with the evidence, and a fight broke out. By the time the Sheriff arrived, the neighbor was dead. His father, who was covered in blood, tried to put all the blame on himself, but the Sheriff didn't buy it. They were both arrested. His father was convicted and died in prison a few years later. He was convicted and given a choice, jail or the army. He chose the army.

The army was a great place for him. They taught him how to kill. A skill he honed with great enthusiasm. He was so good at it that he was often the first soldier called upon when a Nazi guard needed to be dispatched silently. His knife became his friend, and he used it most effectively when an enemy officer needed to be encouraged to talk. He was a skilled craftsman, and his actions often turned the stomachs of even the most hardened soldiers.

He had been able to keep the demons under control for the first couple years after he moved to Aspen, but they had become too strong for him to ignore. He needed to feed the demons, but Aspen was a small mountain town. Missing people would be noticed. At first, he tried to feed the demons with animal sacrifices. He stayed away from family pets, too close to home, so he focused on wild animals, which were in abundance in the forests around Aspen.

Killing forest creatures with his bare hands was a lot of fun, but it didn't satisfy the demons for long. He needed the sensation and the arousal that came from killing another human being. The incredible satisfaction it would bring as he felt life slip away from someone who had been a living breathing person. He also missed the thrill of the hunt. Finding the right person and stalking them until just the right moment. He loved the challenge.

Her thoughts were interrupted by the commotion down the

hall, so she stood, blew out the lavender candle, and walked down the hall to her grandfather's room. Her grandmother was trying to get the very agitated man to calm down. Her grandmother looked up as she entered the room, and her eyes pleaded for her granddaughter's help. Her grandfather had been getting more and more agitated lately. The past few decades had not been easy for the family.

Since the accident that had left her grandfather a quadriplegic, he had been confined to his bed, but for the past five years, the Alzheimer's Disease had taken a terrible toll on his mind. He struggled to keep his sanity, but his memories were all but gone, and she feared that the demons were winning the final battle for what was left. She knew what to do, so she sat down on the edge of the bed and started to hum a lullaby. It didn't matter what lullaby she hummed; it seemed it was the sound that would calm him down. Her grandmother took the opportunity to increase his morphine drip, and he fell asleep. Her grandmother looked relieved. She sat for a few more minutes, and then left his room, grabbed her jacket, and headed out into the night.

CHAPTER FIFTEEN

Buck and the others stopped searching as they heard the first sounds of the parade of law enforcement personnel approaching the small ridge. Buck wanted to try to keep the crime scene as untouched as possible, so he headed back to the body just as PIS and the Sheriff came over the ridge. The Sheriff looked as solemn as Buck had ever seen him. Buck took a minute to review with the Sheriff what they had discovered, and they planned out the perimeter of the crime scene. They would tape off the area from the top of the ridge, down into the ravine and over to where they had found the probable shooting location. The area was huge.

Since Buck was on scene as a courtesy more than anything else, he let the Sheriff take charge of the crime scene. He would step back and let the locals handle the investigation and would offer his services as needed. The Sheriff called his two homicide investigators over to where he and Buck were standing.

Moe Steiner was a twenty-year veteran of the Sheriff's Department. He was about five-ten and maybe one hundred seventy pounds. He had thinning hair and a large brown mustache. He was dressed in jeans, a T-shirt, and a light jacket. His partner was Jane Fitzpatrick. Fitz, as she was affectionately known around Aspen, was a sixteen-year veteran and had been working homicide for almost ten years. The mother of three and grandmother of two she was five-six and maybe a little overweight. She also had on jeans, a light flannel shirt, and her dark blue nylon police jacket.

Buck shook hands all around. He had first met both investigators when he was investigating the missing heiress ten years ago. His only unsolved case. He knew them both to be exceptional investigators and extremely detail-oriented. He had a feeling that this investigation, because of the location and the size, would be a challenge for both of them.

They had just begun discussing the overall crime scene when the Sheriff's two forensic techs, Claudia Gomez, and Holly Flynn, crested the ridge followed closely by Dr. Emily Parker, the Forensic Pathologist for Pitkin County.

Colorado is one of about a dozen states that still use the Coroner system instead of the Medical Examiner system. The coroner for each jurisdiction is an elected official, and that person did not have to have any experience at being a coroner or even be a medical professional. Anyone could run for coroner. The system was evolving so that the coroner needed to complete a formal training program in death investigations, but it was a slow process. Since unlike in the Medical Examiner system, the coroner did not have to be a doctor, each coroner would contract with a licensed Forensic Pathologist to handle any investigations that required an autopsy. These Forensic Pathologists were usually highly trained doctors, who, in a lot of cases, split their time between several jurisdictions to keep costs down.

Dr. Emily Parker had been the licensed Forensic Pathologist for Pitkin County for five years. She had been a medical examiner in Los Angeles before growing tired of the rat race and decided to relocate her family to the Colorado mountains. A graduate of Harvard University and John Hopkins Medical School, she was very highly regarded and the ultimate professional. Instead of working as a pathologist for several counties, Emily Parker opened a family medical practice in Aspen, where you could still find her most days. At the time, she wasn't sure if she wanted to go back into the medical examiner profession. That changed five years ago with the sudden death of her predecessor, Dr. Ross Malone, who died in a freak skiing accident on Aspen Mountain. Since Dr. Parker was already licensed as a pathologist, she took the job on, temporarily, until they could find a permanent replacement for Dr. Malone. The county was still looking.

She walked up to Buck and the Sheriff and extended her hand. Buck shook her hand.

"Nice to see you again, Agent Taylor. I wish the circumstances were better."

Buck nodded. "Good to see you too, Doc. Sorry for the long trek."

"No worries," she replied. She looked down at the body in the ravine. "Why don't you give me the tour since you found her. Okay with you, Sheriff?"

The Sheriff told her it was fine with him, but he wanted one of his homicide folks down there with them. Fitz stepped forward, and the small group started down the side of the ravine. Buck had worked with Dr. Parker several times before and knew that she would prefer to view the body first before asking for his report. She never wanted her first impressions tainted by the opinions of others. There would be time for that later. Buck and Fitz stood off to the side as Dr. Parker gloved up and knelt next to the body.

While Buck, Fitz and Dr. Parker worked around the body, the Sheriff had a couple deputies tape off the area, and he asked his forensic team to start working towards the body from the shooter's nest, for lack of a better term. Gomez and Flynn grabbed their gear and headed over to where the two Gunnison County deputies stood watch over the possible nest. Once there, they shook hands all around, gloved up, and started working the scene. Walt Jenkins had grabbed the evidence bag with the shell casing in it from Buck's backpack and handed it to Holly and showed her where they found it. He told her that Buck had the pictures of the bullet in situ, as it lay on his phone.

Walt and Jimmy Sanchez proceeded to walk the two forensic techs through what they had discovered during their initial search. They showed them the gut pile from the elk and indicated the direction the carcass had been dragged and hidden behind the downed tree where they found the shell casing. Gomez and Flynn worked the area as thoroughly as possible, considering all the leaves and undergrowth and then started working towards the body. They needed to work fast as the light was starting to fade.

CHAPTER SIXTEEN

Dr. Parker examined both bullet holes, took a liver temperature, and with the help of Buck, rolled the body over to look for exit wounds or other wounds that might indicate a struggle. The bullet that had penetrated Ranger Corey's forehead had exited out the back of her head and was buried in the debris under the body. It had made quite a mess coming out. Dr. Parker called over Claudia Gomez and asked her to collect the skull fragments and brain matter and then see if she could locate the spent bullet.

The bullet that penetrated Ranger Corey's thigh had not exited and was likely buried in the bone. Dr. Parker would dig that out during the autopsy. Buck picked up Ranger Corey's pistol from the ground next to the body and dropped it into the evidence bag that Fitz was holding. He did the same thing with her radio and cell phone.

"Sheriff," Dr. Parker called. The Sheriff looked down from the top of the ravine. "You can go ahead and have the rescue team bring down the body bag. Ranger Corey is ready to leave the scene."

She stepped out of the way as the rescue team came down into the ravine and placed the black PVC body bag next to the body. One of the rescue team members was an Episcopal minister, and he knelt next to the body. As the rest of those in the area bowed their heads, he said a prayer for Susan Corey. He then made the sign of the cross and nodded to the rest of the team. The team gently lifted Ranger Corey and placed her in the body bag. Several deputies climbed down into the ravine, and everyone pitched in to get the body to the top of the ravine. The trail was too narrow for vehicles, so the team would need to carry the body back to the parking lot. With permission from the Sheriff, they headed out. The light was fading fast.

Dr. Parker stowed her gear and removed her gloves. "Agent Taylor, since you were the first on the scene, I would like to hear your impressions." She pulled out her cell phone and clicked on the voice recording app.

Buck waited for Fitz to pull out her phone as well, and then he began.

"PIS and I followed a very poor blood trail from the dog until we arrived at the top of the ridge above us." Dr. Parker looked at PIS, who had been standing off to the side and out of the way, and smiled. PIS nodded back.

"Once we arrived on the ridge, we found two larger blood spots, one from the dog and one from Ranger Corey. The dog's blood trail went off the ridge to the opposite side, and we were able to follow it back to the trail we came in on. The other spot, according to PIS, appeared to indicate arterial spray appeared to point in this direction. We followed the direction of the spray, and at the bottom of the ravine, we found a large pile of debris. I took photos of everything we did and found, from this point on, including the bloodstains on the ridge. After removing the loose leaves and sticks, we found a layer of disturbed soil, which we carefully removed and exposed Ranger Corey's face. The bullet hole in her forehead was obvious. We knew that the forehead wound was not the cause of the blood pool on the ridge, so we exposed the rest of the body and discovered the wound in her thigh. After exposing and photographing the body, and with the help of the deputies and rescue team members from Gunnison County, we continued to search the area. About forty yards out, we found what appears to be the shooter's nest, and we also found a gut pile a couple dozen yards beyond that."

Buck stopped to catch his breath and see if they had any questions.

"And your opinion, Agent Taylor?" asked Dr. Parker

"My opinion is that Ranger Corey happened upon someone or more than one person who had illegally killed an elk. It appears they had been dragging the elk back in this direction when they heard Ranger Corey and her dog and hid the carcass and themselves behind the tree at the end of the crime scene tape. Either Ranger Corey or her dog did something that spooked the hunters, and they shot her through the thigh. Missing her ballistic vest. Ranger Corey then rolled down into the ravine and was subsequently shot in the forehead and buried."

Dr. Parker and Fitz turned off their voice recorders.

"Thank you, Agent Taylor. Your assessment of the crime scene jives with my initial findings. The rest we will confirm during the autopsy."

Buck helped Dr. Parker and then Fitz back up to the top of the ridge, and they headed towards the Sheriff. He was talking with his forensic techs as well as two of his deputies. The available light was fading, and with the fear of additional booby traps, the Sheriff asked all his people to clear the crime scene before it got too dark. He would leave two deputies to guard the crime scene, and they would be relieved in four hours. He would continue this pattern until everyone returned to the scene first thing in the morning to continue looking for evidence.

The Gunnison team headed back south, with the deepest thanks from Buck and the Sheriff, and Buck and PIS followed the rest of the group out of the woods.

"I would like to come back with you in the morning, Agent Taylor, if that is acceptable? I feel I can be of use in tracking these evildoers."

"No problem, PIS. We can meet where we met this morning. Let's say five AM. I'd like to get here before the crowd shows up."

"Very good, sir."

The Sheriff's group, including Buck, the Doctor, PIS and the homicide detectives, caught up with the rescue team carrying the body bag. The rescue team had stopped just shy of the entrance to the trail, and one member of the team was in the process of unfolding an American flag, which he then placed over the body bag. He looked at the Sheriff who nodded, and the somber procession headed into the parking lot.

The path from the trailhead to the waiting ambulance was lined with several dozen Rangers, law enforcement officers, and rescue team members who all now stood at attention and saluted as the body bag was carried past them. It seemed to Buck that even the forest creatures had stopped to show their respect. You could have heard a pin drop it was so quiet. The body bag was gently placed in the waiting ambulance, and those assembled began to head back to their various vehicles.

Miguel Vargas walked up to Buck and PIS, who had moved off to the side of the trail. "I wanted to thank you personally for finding Susan Corey's body." He shook hands with both Buck and PIS. "I don't know how I'm gonna tell her son. They were extremely close, and he is gonna be devastated. We're all devastated. It's been years since we've had a Ranger killed in the line of duty. Susan Corey was one of the best."

Tears formed in his eyes, and he turned and walked towards the ambulance. He would ride to the Aspen Valley

Hospital in the ambulance with the body. He didn't want Susan Corey to have to travel alone. The ambulance pulled out of the parking lot, followed by the contingent of officers, Rangers and rescuers, all with the emergency lights flashing. It was another incredible show of respect.

Dr. Parker stepped up and thanked Buck and PIS for their help. She told them she would perform the autopsy first thing in the morning, and the Sheriff asked Detective Moe Steiner if he could attend the autopsy. Fitz would be back at the crime scene, coordinating the search for evidence. Moe simply nodded.

The Sheriff said, "Okay, folks. It's been a long, sad day. Let's all meet up tomorrow morning and see if we can find the bastards who did this." They all headed for their cars and pulled out of the parking lot, checking out with the deputy who was manning the barricade.

Buck asked PIS if he could buy him dinner, but as he expected, PIS graciously declined, so Buck dropped him off in Wagner Park. He then headed to a local deli, grabbed a sandwich, and a couple bottles of Coke and headed for his hotel.

CHAPTER SEVENTEEN

The younger one sat high up in the tree and watched the people below him. He had been watching when the older man and the crazy-looking man with the funny hat and the ponytail, found the lady Ranger. The Teacher was not going to be happy. Once they found the lady Ranger the older man with the ponytail left, and the other man stayed and started looking around. He was soon joined by four other searchers, and together they found the hiding spot behind the downed tree.

Now he sat watching as more people arrived led by the older man with the ponytail. Some of them gathered around the lady Ranger, and others searched the area inside the yellow string. He would have to wait until dark before he would be able to climb down from the tree and run back to the cabin to let the Teacher know what he saw.

He was fascinated by the little boxes some of the people had. They would hold them out in front of themselves, and then a light would flash. The first time he thought they were shooting the lady Ranger again and this confused him, but they also did the same thing behind the downed tree. He didn't understand. Maybe the Teacher would know what this odd behavior was all about.

As darkness started to settle into the ravine, he watched some of the people put the lady Ranger's body into a black sack, and then they took her away. The others soon followed. Maybe they didn't like being out in the woods at night. He always liked night in the woods. It was peaceful. The others made a lot of noise, and sometimes he just needed to get away, and he would find refuge in the woods.

He waited until almost full dark before he climbed down from the tree. He knew he shouldn't, but he couldn't resist walking back to see where the lady Ranger had been buried. Just before he got to the ravine, he was startled by the two men in dark clothes who were hiding up on the ridge. He froze. He knew how to walk in the woods like the Indians the Teacher used to tell them about when they would have story time. He knew they would never hear him, so he moved a little closer.

These people were dressed in black clothes, and they carried funny looking rifles. They didn't look anything like the rifle he and the hunter used on the lady Ranger. He wondered why they were there. Could it be a trap? The Teacher told them about the war and how the bad people would hide in the forests and then attack without warning. Were there others around? He hadn't spotted anyone else.

He sat for a minute and listened, but they were very quiet. Maybe he should take out the big knife the Teacher had given him for being smart in his lessons and sneak up on them and put them down. He was so close to the one man leaning against the tree that he could stick him before he even knew he was there. Maybe the Teacher would reward him for protecting the others. He might get to use the rifle and become the new hunter. Then he remembered that the Teacher had been upset that they had killed the lady Ranger. He told them that life was sacred and that killing people was wrong.

He was undecided as he watched the two men. He reached out and touched the handle of the small metal object that was wrapped in leather and hooked around the man's leg. The man jumped and looked around. The other man laughed and asked him if he was afraid of ghosts. The man continued to look around, but he never saw the younger one who had scampered back a couple of feet into the undergrowth.

It could be fun scaring the men in the black clothes, but he knew he needed to get back to the mine and tell the Teacher. He backed away from the ridge and circled the far side of the yellow string. He decided to take the long way back to the mine. He did not want to leave any kind of trail for the people to follow. He needed to protect the others.

An hour later, he arrived back at the mine. Even though there was no light coming from the tiny hole in the mountainside, he was able to find it without difficulty. The others were all asleep, but the Teacher was sitting at the old wooden table drinking that foul-tasting liquid from the old bottle. He called it hooch, and he wouldn't let any of them touch it. The younger one had tasted the last little bit that was in the Teacher's old mug after he went to sleep one night, and it burned his throat and belly as it went down. He never touched the foul liquid again.

The Teacher looked up from his cup. He had sad droopy eyes. He told the Teacher all about the people and about them finding the lady Ranger. He also told him about the two men in the black clothes with the funny looking rifles. He waited for the Teacher to tell him he had done a good job of protecting the others, but the Teacher just looked sadder and turned back to his cup.

The younger one knew better than to push the Teacher when he was drinking the foul-tasting liquid, so he walked away and climbed into his bed. He was soon asleep. The Teacher finished his drink and lowered his head to the table. His last thought was that he hoped he could protect the others.

CHAPTER EIGHTEEN

B uck and PIS arrived at the parking lot before dawn and checked in with the bored-looking deputy who was sitting in his patrol car next to the barricade. He reported to Buck that all was quiet and that the third twosome of deputies had checked in about two hours before. He was expecting the second twosome to be walking into the parking lot any time now.

The morning was much cooler than the day before had been, and Buck snugged his insulated Carhart jacket up against the breeze that came rushing down from the higher peaks. Fall was definitely in the air this morning, but it didn't seem to bother PIS. He was dressed in the same clothes he had on yesterday, and his linen coat was unbuttoned. Buck had never seen PIS sweat no matter how hot the weather got, and he had never seen him look uncomfortable in the cold. His three-day stubble looked neatly trimmed, just like always.

They headed down the trail leading back to the ravine. Buck wanted to get there before the crowds showed up. He wanted to see if they couldn't pick up the killer's trail. He was always amazed to watch PIS in the woods. He looked so comfortable. The sun was just starting to lighten the sky, and Buck needed a flashlight to see his way down the trail, but PIS just forged ahead like he had walked this trail a thousand times. The conversation was kept to a minimum as they walked.

About a half-hour into the trail, they heard the second shift deputies approaching, and Buck called out a greeting so they would not be surprised. Buck never liked the idea of surprising people with guns in the dark. The deputies stopped for a minute and exchanged pleasantries. Talked about how cold it had gotten overnight and told Buck about the earlier deputy who thought he felt someone touch his thigh holster. Scared the crap out of him, and everyone had a good laugh.

Buck and PIS told them to have a good day and moved on. Buck stopped for a minute just after they left the deputies. He looked at PIS.

"Any chance what the deputy felt wasn't just his imagination?"

PIS thought about it for a minute. "What is it you Yanks often talk about, the killer coming back to the scene of the crime? That would be pretty ballsy, I must say."

PIS and Buck continued down the trail until they arrived at the ridge. The sun was just starting to come up over the mountains, but the chill remained in the air. Buck called out to the two deputies on duty and announced themselves. He introduced himself to the two deputies. They were familiar with PIS. While Buck talked with the two deputies, PIS took a walk around the perimeter of the ridge. Curiosity about the deputy being touched got the better of PIS, and he started examining the area for tracks or a disturbance of some kind. He found what he was looking for behind the big tree.

"Agent Taylor, a minute if you please."

Buck and the two deputies walked over to where PIS was standing. PIS knelt next to the tree and pointed to a small depression in the leaves.

"Someone was out here last night. I don't think the deputy

imagined anything."

Buck and the deputies got closer and could make out a small boot print in the ground, where PIS had scraped aside the leaves. Buck pulled out his cell phone and snapped a picture of the print.

"How can we be sure it wasn't from one of us yesterday?" Buck asked.

"From my recollection, none of us were near this tree. Besides, this print is way too small. Looks almost the size of a child's print or a small female."

Buck noticed the two deputies move their fingers a little closer to the trigger guard on their rifles and start to look around. Concern was imprinted on their faces. Buck found his hand sitting on the backstrap of his pistol. He looked around the area.

PIS stepped back away the tree and headed down the opposite side of the ridge, clearly looking for a trail. He disappeared from view. The others stood their ground. In the distance, they could hear the rest of the investigators and searchers coming down the path.

As the Sheriff approached, he noted the concern and the tension of the small group on the ridge.

"Buck, what's going on?" he asked.

Buck recounted the conversation they had been having just before the Sheriff arrived. At this point, Fitz joined the group as did the two forensic techs. Fitz was the first one to speak up.

"You seriously think that the killer came back here last night and tried to sneak up on our deputies? For what purpose?"

Buck started to respond when PIS returned to the top of the ridge.

"The deputies definitely had a visitor last night and whoever it was, knew this forest very well and was extremely skilled. The trail disappeared back behind the tree and circled the crime scene. This individual was out far enough that we would not have even looked for a sign that far out. If I hadn't been following the trail from the tree, I would never have seen it. Very clever."

The group looked at each other, not sure what to say, so PIS continued. "I also think this person might have been sitting up in a tree yesterday afternoon watching what we were doing. Found a deep impression under that big aspen just past the downed tree. It looks like someone dropped down off the lower branch."

"How can you be certain?" asked the Sheriff.

"I checked that area under the tree right after we found the shooter's nest. Those impressions were not there yesterday afternoon. I lost the trail about a quarter mile from here, heading northeast."

CHAPTER NINETEEN

The Sheriff was not happy. His first thought was that he had left two of his deputies out in the woods by themselves, and they could have been killed. His second thought was, "who the hell are we dealing with?" The perpetrator was in the woods within the past twelve hours. That was a big head start, and they had a lot of ground to cover. He was going to need some reinforcements, and everyone was going to have to be armed. This was not a job for the search and rescue team.

He called the group together and explained his plan. The forensic team and Fitz would continue to work the scene under the watchful eye of two deputies. He would contact the Sheriff's in Eagle, Garfield and Gunnison counties and ask them to call out their SWAT teams and any deputies they could spare for a manhunt. He asked Buck to call his Director, see if he could remain on the investigation, and then he and PIS would start scouting the area and see if they could narrow down the search area a little. He was still concerned about the booby traps they had found so far, and that would hinder the search.

Buck took a minute to step away from the group and pulled out his phone. He was amazed that he had cell service this far back in the woods. He dialed the Director.

Kevin Jackson answered on the second ring. "Hey, Buck. You still in Aspen?"

"Yes, sir. Things just got a little more complicated."

He went on to explain the most recent events to the Director and told him that the Sheriff would like him to remain on scene and help with the manhunt. He explained about the tracks they found this morning and about the booby traps.

"So you think that the killer returned to the scene, and snuck up on the two deputies last night? To what end?"

"Can't say for sure, sir. But it sure changes the dynamics of the investigation."

"Okay, Buck. You stay. What do you need from me?"

"We could use a little help from the Grand Junction office, whoever you can spare. Might also be wise to get some Troopers down here. This manhunt is going to leave the county stretched pretty thin."

"Okay, Buck. I'll do what I can. In the meantime, you watch your ass. I came close to losing you once; I don't want to go there again." The Director hung up.

Buck put his phone away and went back to talk to the Sheriff. He told the Sheriff it was okay with Director Jackson that he stay and help. He also told him he had requested some help from Grand Junction and had also asked the Director to get in touch with the Colorado State Patrol and have some Troopers fill in for his deputies around the county. The Sheriff thanked him for the idea about the Troopers. He hadn't gotten that far in his thought process.

Buck pulled out the topographic map from his backpack and laid it on the ground. The Sheriff and PIS knelt next to Buck, and Buck asked PIS to point out where he lost the trail. PIS took a minute to orient himself and pointed to a location about a quarter mile from where they sat.

"I think we should start at the shooter's nest and work out. We know where PIS lost the trail from last night, but what bugs me is that we haven't found the trail to their elk camp. We know they killed the elk and dragged it as far as the nest. What we haven't found is where they went after that. I doubt they butchered it here. We would have found evidence of that. They had to continue dragging it out of here, but to where?" Buck said.

PIS agreed. Buck looked to the Sheriff, who nodded in agreement. He agreed that Buck and PIS should try to find that trail to the elk camp. The Sheriff then pointed to three locations on the map. He was going to have his SWAT team follow Buck and PIS from the crime scene. He would have a couple of his deputies or reserve deputies meet up with the SWAT teams from the other counties and come in from three other areas. He would request that Gunnison SWAT approach from the Crested Butte Ski area and head north. One of the other SWAT teams would meet up at the Conundrum Creek trailhead off Route 15 and head southwest. The other team would start from Ashcroft off Route 15 and head northwest. They would all converge on wherever Buck and PIS ended up.

Buck agreed with the plan, and the Sheriff asked his two SWAT deputies who had been the last team on the site this morning to accompany Buck and PIS. The Sheriff would have another deputy meet up with them later and bring them some sleeping bags and some supplies. He would start the SWAT teams out first thing in the morning. This should give Buck a chance to narrow down the trail. The Sheriff stood, shook hands with Buck and his team and told them to stay safe. He then headed back to the parking lot. He had a lot of calls to make and a lot of people to get organized.

Buck looked at PIS. "You good with this. I can't make you stay."

"No problem, Agent Taylor. Happy to serve."

Buck grabbed his backpack and headed down the ridge to the shooter's nest. They needed to follow the elk, but first, they had to find it. That might be easier said than done. Either way, they had a lot of people who were going to be depending on them to get the job done.

PIS started working in a semi-circle around the shooter's nest. He surmised that since they had dragged the elk from the gut pile to the downed tree that they must have been heading in that direction when they encountered the Ranger and her dog. He was both amazed and perplexed that whoever they were following was good enough to outsmart him. That didn't happen often.

PIS was out about a quarter mile from the shooter's nest, and he was getting more and more aggravated with himself for not being able to spot the trail. Elk carcasses are not light, and this one was being dragged across the ground. There had to be a sign. No one is that good. He stopped and looked back through the trees to the shooter's nest. He was on a straight line directly from the gut pile and though the nest. It had to be here. He scanned the area, and then he spotted it.

At first, he wasn't sure he was looking at it. It blended in almost perfectly with the surrounding area. He walked forward, scanning the area for booby traps as he went. The closer he got, the more obvious it became. The undergrowth was denser than in the rest of the area. The sign wasn't much, but to a trained eye, it was just enough. He stepped around the growth and noticed for the first time the cut ends of the branches. He stepped to the front of the mass and spotted the blood on the ground. He marveled at the cleverness of the camouflage. No wonder the Ranger hadn't found this camp. It was practically perfect in its disguise.

PIS gave a short shrill whistle and waved to Buck and the two deputies who had been following farther back. He waved them over.

"Agent Taylor," he said as Buck and the deputies approached. "I believe we have found the hunting camp." Buck looked at the makeshift lean-to and the bloodstain on the dirt floor. He was impressed with its simplicity. He looked around the area, and even to his older tired eyes, he could see the double track that went off to the Northeast. It was a trail made by some kind of sled. A very heavy sled.

CHAPTER TWENTY

She had discovered her grandfather's trophy box a couple of months back and wondered about the significance of the baubles. She knew it was her grandfather's because no one in the family remembered the old cigar box that was hidden in a hole in the wall behind her grandfather's big Craftsman toolbox. She had mentioned it one night at dinner, and no one reacted. Well, that's not exactly true. She thought she saw some kind of recognition in her grandmother's eyes, but that disappeared as fast as it arrived.

She waited until the family was asleep and entered her grandfather's room. He was sleeping soundly, and she hoped that he might wake up in one of his, getting rarer, lucid moments. She hated to disturb him, so she started to leave his room when a low frail voice stopped her in her tracks.

She approached the bed and stood there with the trophy box held out in front of her. Her grandfather stared at the box in her hands and smiled. She hadn't seen him smile much since she had gotten home from college, and it surprised her. He asked her to open the box so he could look inside.

She opened the box and held it so he could see inside. His heart monitor reacted almost immediately, and she was afraid the change of tone from the monitor might wake someone else in the small house. She closed the box and pulled it away from him, but his expression indicated that he wasn't done. She glanced towards his bedroom door to see if anyone might have heard them and then she reopened the box and he looked deep inside. She asked him what all these pieces meant. He smiled and asked her to remove the gold-edged cameo necklace. She held it up for him to see, and he told her that this was the first one.

She was a pretty runaway from somewhere up near Chicago. Her family life had been brutal, so she headed west to find her way in the world. The Korean War was over, and a lot of people were leaving their familiar homes to look for financial opportunities out west. The fledgling ski industry and lax laws were drawing people from far and wide, and Aspen was no exception. The young woman had found work in a small diner just off the highway, and she had found a room with several other young women. Her grandfather had befriended the young woman, and they started seeing each other at night. Her grandmother never knew.

After a few weeks, she told him that she was tired of the cold and had decided to head to California. Her grandfather sensed an opportunity about to disappear, so he told her he would drive her to the train in Glenwood Springs. He knew she hadn't told any of her friends about him, so he wasn't worried about getting caught. That night, as she slipped out of her rooming house, he met her up the highway and loaded her one suitcase in the trunk of his car. She was dressed in a long skirt, pretty white blouse and around her neck was the cameo neckless—a gift from her mother.

Instead of heading north up highway 82, he turned south and headed out of town. He turned down Route 15, which at the time was just a narrow dirt road and found the old fire road that led to Conundrum Creek. She asked him where they were heading, and he told her that he wanted to show her a beautiful sight before she left. He reached the end of the road, parked the car and reached his arm around her shoulders. The syringe bit deep into her shoulder, and she started to yell, but he put his hand over her mouth and held it there until the sedative had time to work.

The snow was not that deep on the old trail through the wood as he carried her over his shoulder. The old mining cabin was dilapidated, but it wasn't the cabin he was interested in. Years before, when he first arrived in Aspen, he spent a lot of time exploring his new home and discovered the old cabin a mile or so down Conundrum Creek. It sat back about a quarter mile from the trail along the creek and was hidden from view. What interested him most about the cabin was the shaft the old miners had dug under the wooden floor of the cabin. The shaft went down about thirty feet and then opened into a large long tunnel. He found old, broken, and decayed wooden shelves and a lot of old mining equipment.

When he first found the cabin, he thought it would be perfect for his needs. He spent several weeks tracking down the owner of the property and discovered that the mining claim that the cabin sat on was owned by a man in Pittsburg who had almost forgotten about the old claim. Through a series of letters and telegrams, her grandfather was able to get permission to work the old claim and use the cabin.

He spent the next couple months cleaning out the space and installing the things he knew he would need. Along the walls, he bolted in chains and shackles for hands and feet. He purchased several kerosene hurricane lamps and built a bed with a straw mattress. The biggest improvement he was able to make in the machine shop at the ski resort maintenance shed. He fashioned a large metal hatch door that he installed over the old rotten wooden shaft door and put heavy-duty hinges and a hasp on it.

The old miners had left an old kerosene stove in the tunnel that they had vented up through the ground a few feet behind the cabin. It would help to keep the chill out of the air and make it a more comfortable space to work in. He also placed his pride and joys in the tunnel. Over the years working at the ski resort, he had managed to use the metal shop and had fashioned several beautiful knives and scalpels. Since he made them all himself, there was no record of him buying them. His space was complete, and his body had tingled at the thought of what would soon be taking *place in his secluded little world.*

Her grandfather's voice seemed to grow stronger as he told her the rest of the story. He had carried the young woman to the cabin and had unlocked the trap door. He lowered her down the old wooden ladder and placed her on the bed while he fired up the kerosene lanterns and the old kerosene stove. Once the space got warmer, he stripped off all the young woman's clothes and tied her to the bed frame. She had a beautiful body, young and subtle. Her breasts were small but perky, and she moaned through the gag as he repeatedly penetrated her. Twice he had to inject her with more sedative to keep her quiet. This was the first time he had ever had sex with someone other than his wife, and he was surprised at how much he enjoyed it, but the night was fading fast, and he needed to get home before his wife woke up.

Now that he was spent, he untied her from the bed and carried her over to the first set of shackles that he had bolted to the wall. Still naked, he hooked the shackles to her hands and feet. She had started to wake up, and the fear in her eyes made him get excited all over again, but he didn't have the time to penetrate her again. He was running out of time. He opened an old cabinet that was hanging on the wall and removed a leather bundle. He placed it on the wooden table under the cabinet and unrolled it revealing his assortment of custom-made knives.

He chose a thin four-inch-long scalpel from the bundle and admired it in the light from the kerosene lantern. He loved how the scalpel glowed under the yellow light of the lantern. He walked over to the young woman and held the scalpel so she could see it. She squirmed hard against the shackles and started to bleed where the metal shackles cut into her hands and feet.

Slowly and almost delicately, he slid the sharp edge of the scalpel along her exposed abdomen. He had used this same technique on several high-ranking German Officers during the war. They were a stubborn lot, but eventually, they all talked. He didn't care if the young woman talked or not. This was not an interrogation.

This was pleasure.

He could hear her screaming through the gag. He spent the next hour slowly slicing the young woman's torso, legs and arms until she passed out. She just didn't seem to have the stamina of the German Officers. It was almost disappointing. He walked over to the leather bundle on the bed and using an old rag, cleaned the blood off the scalpel and his hands. He got dressed and then walked back and turned off the kerosene stove and put his bundle back in the cabinet. If she was still alive when he returned, he would finish the job, but for now, the demons were satisfied. He turned off the kerosene lanterns and climbed out of his workspace. He closed the hatch, made sure the padlock was shut and covered the hatch with the decaying floorboards.

The night had gotten colder, and it had started to snow. He stood for a minute and just gazed at the beauty of the scene. He felt at peace for the first time in a long time. He walked back to his old car and headed home.

CHAPTER TWENTY-ONE

She could feel the heat rising as her grandfather told her the story of his first civilian kill. She hadn't realized how sexually aroused she felt as he described the details of the kill. She felt embarrassed that she was feeling this way and didn't understand what was happening. Her grandfather knew exactly what was happening. He could sense that she had the same feelings he did when it came to taking another's life. He finished his story and looked at the vibrant pink color in her cheeks and the little beads of sweat that had formed on her forehead and cheeks.

He told her that he knew she was the one who would follow him. He could feel it deep in his soul. He told her that he would help her find her way along the path that had been taken from him so long ago. She stared in disbelief at what he was saying. She could never take a human life. She had never killed anything, nor had the desire to do so. Or did she? His description of the kill had stirred something deep inside her—something scary but also something wonderful.

Her grandfather started to speak in dribble and incomplete sentences, and then he closed his eyes and went to sleep. The lucid moment had passed, but she had learned a lot. She looked at the rest of the pieces of jewelry in the little box. Her grandfather just admitted to being a serial killer. One of the first in modern history, yet there had never been any hint that this was the case. She wondered how many more pieces of jewelry would have found their way into his little treasure box if he had not been injured so many years ago. She also wondered how he had kept the demons from destroying him since he was no longer able to feed their needs.

She also wondered if her grandmother knew about his proclivities. She had noticed the change in her grandmother's eyes when she mentioned the old cigar box she had found in the garage. Yet her grandmother never said anything about it.

She looked again at the trophies her grandfather had collected. She wondered about the people they had belonged too. Most of the jewelry appeared to be pieces that would have been worn by young women of the time. She wondered if she would ever be able to get their story from her grandfather. She would need to hurry. She was due back at school in early September. If she was going to act on the feelings that had been stirred up by her grandfather's story, she would need to do it soon.

She closed the lid of the old box, leaned in and kissed her grandfather on the forehead and left his room. The house was quiet as a church cemetery, and she was grateful. She headed back to her room and once inside closed the door and hid the trophy box in the back of her closet. She needed to understand the feelings that her grandfather's story had generated. Was it possible she was a serial killer too?

She had taken psychology classes at school, and she understood that serial killers were psychopaths. She always believed they were evil incarnate and that they would stand out in society like freaks at a carnival. Even though she had never had the opportunity to see her grandfather in his early years, she never considered him to be odd. He had never spoken before of his craft. But now. His story had aroused something deep inside of her. Something she now both feared and found interesting and exciting.

Could it be true that he could sense in her the things that made him do the evil deeds he had told her about? It made her sick to her stomach, and she ran into her tiny bathroom and vomited in the toilet. No, there was no way she could ever be the evil thing her grandfather had become in her eyes. But she was also envious of *him. If the way she felt while he was telling his story was real, the sensation was incredible. She felt more satisfied, sexually, at this moment than she had with any of the college boys she had slept with over the years.*

She knew she needed to pursue the feelings to see if they were real. She was afraid of what she might find and of what she might become, but she needed to find out. She laid down on her bed, her head full of strange thoughts and feelings. She decided the first thing she needed to do was to try to find her grandfather's old cabin and see if the shaft was still locked up tight. She would check that out first and then decide on the next step.

CHAPTER TWENTY-TWO

Buck took pictures of the makeshift hunting camp with this cell phone camera and noting that he still had one bar, sent the pictures along with the GPS coordinates he took from his handheld GPS unit to the Sheriff and Fitz. Fitz would have to bring the forensic techs to the camp as soon as they were finished processing the crime scene at the ravine. Buck pulled a roll of crime scene tape from his backpack and with the help of one of the deputies, ran the tape around the makeshift hunting camp.

Satisfied with the day's progress so far and with the light beginning to fade, the small team decided to wait at the elk camp for the deputy bringing the supplies and hole up there for the night. With the possibility of booby traps still out in the woods, Buck didn't want anyone getting hurt. At first light, they would follow the sled tracks and see where they led. Buck also asked the Sheriff to have the deputy bring one more assault rifle with him. The idea that someone snuck up on the two SWAT deputies at the ravine had everyone a little jumpy.

While one of the deputies cleared the fire ring that someone had worked very hard to try and hide, Buck looked around the elk camp. There wasn't much to see. The bloodstains on the ground that had been covered up with leaves gave Buck the impression that the camp had been used for a long time. There were visible signs that someone had been butchering animals, but no evidence of tools. Whoever had cleared out of this camp had done so with a great deal of skill. There was not going to be much physical evidence for the forensic techs to find.

In the distance, Buck could hear the sound of a small, high-pitched motor. He assumed the deputy bringing in their supplies was on a dirt bike or a small ATV, all-terrain vehicle. Just then, the driver came through the trees and stopped at the yellow crime scene tape. He had been able to maneuver his small ATV along the trail they had left. That was quite an accomplishment considering there was not much of a trail to follow.

The deputy shook hands all around and then offloaded two backpacks and a couple sleeping bags from the small cargo cage on the back of the ATV. He had a Remington AR15 slung over his shoulder, which he handed to Buck.

"Sheriff said you asked for this," the deputy said. "He also sent along some deli sandwiches for dinner, some water bottles, and danishes for breakfast."

Buck was also glad to see that the Sheriff sent along a couple bottles of Coke. He would make sure he thanked the Sheriff.

"Sheriff wanted me to tell you that he has several deputies watching all the known trailheads on both Route 13 and 15 and that the SWAT teams will head out at first light according to the plan you guys came up with earlier."

Buck thanked the deputy for the supplies, and the information and the deputy climbed aboard the ATV and headed back up the trail. He wanted to get out of the woods before total dark. PIS had taken the food bag and was in the process of handing out sandwiches and water bottles. They each found a little piece of the forest and set their tired bodies down for a breather and nourishment.

The two deputies smiled at each other as they watched PIS open his backpack, remove his little tin, and start to brew himself a small pot of tea. Everyone had heard the stories of PIS and his china tea set, but few had ever seen it for real. Buck watched them but said nothing. Buck understood that for PIS, this was a very private moment, and he didn't want to interfere.

PIS looked up at the deputies as he took his first sip of tea from the china cup. "Even in the wilderness, gentlemen, we must remain civilized, and there is nothing more civilized than a good cup of tea."

Everyone chuckled and dug into their meals. The sandwiches were excellent, and as the sun set and the forest became darker, everyone settled in for the night. It would be chilly tonight, but the sleeping bags the Sheriff had sent them would be most welcome.

Buck rolled his sleeping bag out on a bunch of leaves and pine boughs he had cut and made himself an insulated platform to sleep on. He crawled into the sleeping bag and rested his head on his backpack. He had found a spot near the fire pit that gave him a small opening through which to look at the milky way above. This far into the forest, the view of the Milky Way was incredible.

Buck looked up at the sky and thought back to the camping trips his family had taken when the kids were younger. After the kids had gone to sleep, he and Lucy would lie next to each other and stare at the stars. With no city lights to lessen the view, they were able to see billions of stars and even the swirling celestial cloud that flowed through the milky way. It was always magical; only this time, it brought a tear to his eyes, knowing that he would never be able to share another moment like that with Lucy. Buck closed his eyes and drifted off to sleep.

Buck had asked one of the two deputies to take the first watch. Everyone was concerned about having a repeat of the night before and did not want to face the possibility of someone sneaking up on the group.

Buck opened his eyes and scanned the area. He wasn't sure what had woken him, but he sensed something was not quite right. He snapped open the thumb break on his holster and put his hand on the gun. He looked to his left and noticed PIS lying flat on his back with his eyes wide open. PIS turned his head toward Buck.

"We are not alone," PIS said in a whisper. Buck tensed and looked towards the two deputies. They both appeared to be sound asleep.

"Where?" asked Buck.

"Not sure. Could be maybe twenty yards out behind the lean-to. There might be two of them. Can't tell for sure."

"How do you want to handle this?" asked Buck

The fire had settled down into just a pile of hot embers, and the forest was almost as dark as being inside a cave. PIS slid out of his sleeping bag and lying flat on the ground, crawled deeper into the woods behind them. Buck pulled his pistol out of his holster, and with little movement, un-zipped the sleeping bag. He would be ready to move if PIS needed help.

The deputy on the other side of Buck must have sensed something going on, but Buck signaled for him to stay put. The deputy lowered himself back down on his backpack, but Buck saw him pull out his service weapon and place it on top of his sleeping bag. Buck wasn't sure how long PIS was gone, but his internal alarm clock told him it was about twenty minutes. Twenty very tense minutes.

CHAPTER TWENTY-THREE

PIS called out from somewhere behind the lean-to. "PIS coming in." He emerged from the right side of the lean-to. Buck and the first deputy crawled out of the sleeping bags, guns in hand. The other deputy woke up and wondered out loud what was going on. Buck grabbed a log off the pile they had collected earlier and dropped in on the fire. The embers caught the dry wood, and the flames exploded, adding much-appreciated light to the dark forest.

PIS stood next to the fire. "I could account for two of them. I think that was it. The first one was about thirty yards out behind a group of shrubs to the north. He had a clear view of our little camp. The second one was up a tree to the south. No more than fifteen yards. They must have heard me moving through the undergrowth because they moved off before I could get to them. I will check for tracks in the morning."

The one deputy swore under his breath. Buck looked around. "Sounds like the same MO, modus operandi, from the other night at the ravine. You certain they are gone?"

PIS nodded, and Buck and the two deputies holstered their pistols. No one was going back to sleep anytime soon. Buck was amazed at how easily PIS had been able to move around in the dark forest. The guy had some mad skills, and even though Buck never asked, he wondered where PIS had received his training. It didn't come from being a homeless guy in Aspen.

The one deputy asked the question that everyone had on their minds. "What the fuck are we dealing with? What kind of criminal stays in the area of the crime and follows the police around?"

"Good question," responded Buck. "Not any kind of criminal I've ever encountered. Good thing is, we know they are still in the area, and we know there are at least two of them."

Everyone agreed with Buck's statement, but Buck felt uneasy. He wondered why the killers hadn't tried to run? What was keeping them in the area? He didn't have enough evidence to be able to answer that question, so he pushed it to the back of his mind. He would figure out the answer before this was over.

Buck sat back on his sleeping bag and watched the fire. PIS walked over and sat down next to him, and Buck noticed the perplexed look on PIS's face.

"What's got you bugged?" he asked.

PIS thought for a minute. "Either my skills are getting rusty, or we are up against people who have skills that far exceed mine."

PIS was quiet for a minute, and Buck could see he was replaying the whole thing in his head. He said, "I was as quiet as a church mouse when I moved through the woods, yet they had me before I even got close to them, and they were able to scamper off without me having any idea they were moving."

Buck sensed his frustration. PIS had skills in the woods that Buck could only marvel at. If PIS was concerned, then the people they were after were incredibly dangerous. They had already shown themselves to be cold-blooded enough to shoot a human being in the head at close range, and they had proven they were not afraid to sneak up and observe armed law enforcement personnel.

Buck assured PIS that it wasn't his skills that were lacking.

It was obvious that the people they were chasing knew the woods better than they did, and they would just need to be a little more diligent. Buck sensed that they were getting close. They all needed to stay focused.

As dawn started to break over the mountains, and the sky turned a pale shade of pink, everyone in the camp felt a little relieved. They were now able to see around them and some of the concerns from the night before lifted. Each man packed up his sleeping bag, and they each ate a danish for breakfast. PIS had disappeared into the woods as soon as it was light enough to see, and he came walking back into camp.

"Agent Taylor, there were two culprits last night as I had suspected. They both headed off in different directions, but they met up again about a quarter mile from here. I also found the rest of the trail we spotted yesterday. They did a bang-up job trying to hide it, but the grooves from the sled were too deep to hide."

"Excellent, then we have a trail to follow." He looked at each man individually. "We need to stay alert. We know they are good at building booby traps, and they are also not afraid to get close to us. Let's douse the fire and get moving. The SWAT teams will be starting soon. We need a target."

With that, the one deputy emptied a water bottle on the fire embers and stirred them around with a stick. The last thing they needed out here was a forest fire. PIS slung his backpack over his shoulders and started for the sled trail. The others followed a couple of yards behind.

CHAPTER TWENTY-FOUR

They had been following the men for almost an hour when the men settled in for the night. They had lit a small fire, and then all slipped into their sleeping bags. The hunter had a good observation spot just beyond the lean-to, and he watched them all settle in. The younger one was on the other side of the camp up in a big aspen tree.

Once he was confident that the men were asleep, the younger one had climbed down from the tree and snuck up to just outside their camp. He could hear the men breathing; he was so close. At one point, he was going to see if he could reach one of the rifles, but the old man with the ponytail started to move around, so he thought it best to back off. He wasn't sure what he would do if he did get one of the rifles.

The men had rifles that didn't look anything like the old rifle the hunter used. Theirs were all black and had lots of things that seemed to be attached. The rifle the Teacher had given the hunter was just a wooden stock and a barrel. Nothing fancy, but it did a good job on the animals they hunted.

The Teacher had told them all stories about a big war in the jungle and that he had used a black rifle that had things attached to it. It sounded just like the rifle the men were carrying. The younger one thought it would make a great prize to bring one of these back for the Teacher and the Teacher might reward him and let him use the black rifle to hunt with. Since the Teacher's hands shook sometimes, he didn't think the Teacher would be able to use the rifle anyway.

The men had remained quiet for quite some time, so the younger one moved back towards the tree he had been hiding in. The almost unperceivable clicking sound alerted him that something was wrong. The hunter had seen something, so he froze where he was. He glanced back through the trees just in time to see the old man with the ponytail slide out of his sleeping bag and crawl into the woods. The old man with the ponytail made almost no noise as he scooted along the ground.

The younger one watched him for a minute. The old man with the ponytail had skills just like he and the hunter had. He had found their trails and traps. And he wondered if the old man had been taught by the Teacher. The Teacher told them that he taught a lot of men during the jungle war how to survive in the woods. Maybe the old man with the ponytail was one of the Teacher's students. They would need to be careful if that was the case. He might know how to set traps like he and the hunter knew how to do, and that could be dangerous.

The younger one knew he should head back to the safe place, but he wanted to test the old man with the ponytail, so he started to move away from the men's camp. He would work his way back to the trail by making a big circle around the camp. He wanted to see if the old man with the ponytail would be able to track him, so he decided to lead him towards one of the old animal trails that would take the men away from the safe place.

He made small noises as he went, crackling a leaf or snapping a small stick. He was having fun, but then the old man with the ponytail stopped and looked at something on the ground, and while still kneeling looked around. He then set off in a different direction. The younger one wasn't sure what the old man with the ponytail had found, but he was now heading back towards the hunter.

The younger one gave a soft, low-pitched whistle that he knew most people would never be able to hear, but he knew the hunter would hear it. The low-pitched whistle was something momma had taught them all, and it meant danger and for everyone to head back to the safe place. He continued down the old animal trail and then circled back around through the trees and headed home.

The younger one caught up with the hunter just down the trail from the safe place and then hid in the undergrowth and watched the trail for a while to make sure they had gotten away. Feeling confident that they had not been followed by the old man with the ponytail, they reset the booby trap on the trail and headed for the mine.

When they got back inside the mine, the Teacher was just starting breakfast for the others. They told him about the old man with the ponytail and that maybe he was one of the men the Teacher had taught how to survive in the woods. The younger one told him about playing with the old man with the ponytail and that he was as good as they were in the woods.

The Teacher listened to their story and looked concerned. His hands were shaking badly today, and he was having trouble using the knife to put the jelly on the bread. The older girl took the knife and started making the sandwiches. They were running out of bread and some other things, and they would need to plan a raid on one of the big houses.

The Teacher reassured them that everything would be okay and that once the men left the woods, they would sneak into the big empty house up by the ski lift and raid their food stores again.

The teacher sat down on the old chair and rested his face in his hands. The others went about their business cleaning the living area in the mine, but the hunter sat next to the Teacher and rested his hand on the Teacher's arm. The Teacher looked at him, and the younger one and they saw the concern on his face. The Teacher told them to go back down by the cabin and make sure the traps were set just like he had shown them.

The hunter grabbed his rifle, and the younger one went to the old box and took out some metal spikes and a hammer and a spool of old fishing line. The teacher led the younger one to the old green box, and using the key from his pocket, he unlocked the box and opened the lid. The younger one had never seen what was inside the old green box. The Teacher had told them never to touch the box, and they never did.

The Teacher pulled out several old cardboard tubes with strings hanging out of one end. The tubes looked very old, and they were covered in some kind of white powder. He also took out some metal tubes with wires attached to them along with a metal box with a T handle stuck in it. He put it all in an old backpack. He told the others to stay in the cave and that he, the hunter and the younger one would be back in a while. The Teacher slung the backpack over his shoulder, and the three of them headed for the mine entrance.

CHAPTER TWENTY-FIVE

O nce outside the mine, the hunter and the younger one watched the Teacher as he slid one of the metal tubes into each of the cardboard tubes. He then took a big spool of wire that he had taken from the cabinet in the kitchen area and handed it to the hunter and the younger one. He told them to run the wire from the mine entrance back to the cabin. He needed six wire runs to different spots around the cabin, and he pointed out where to run them. They took the spool and headed back towards the mine entrance.

The Teacher was worried. Many times, over the years, people had gotten close to the cabin or the mine entrance, but this felt different. Each time they had been able to either run them off with animal noises or simply hide in the woods or the mine until they passed. These men were on a mission. He had seen determination like that during the war. These men were dangerous, and he was convinced that they were only a scouting party. He was sure that sooner or later, the woods would be crawling with people looking for his little family. The hunter had killed one of theirs, and they were out for blood.

The Teacher had promised momma that he would do everything he could to protect the family, and he had been successful for a long time. Now, however, he was worried that he might not have enough left to do the job. He was getting on in years, and each day, his hands seem to shake a lot more. He was also having trouble talking and doing even the slightest of chores. He was worried about what would happen to the family if he didn't wake up one morning. His thoughts went back to that day so many years ago.

He joined the army right out of high school and had found the family he never had before. His mom worked nights as a waitress at a local greasy spoon, and his dad worked at the car plant in town. His dad was also a drinker, and he had no problem beating on his wife and son when he tied one on, which seemed to be almost every night. The day after graduation, he had headed for the army recruiting station and enlisted. The war in Vietnam was in full swing, and he was able to leave for boot camp within two days of enlisting. He left that little west Texas town and never looked back.

Years of getting beat up by his father had given him an inner strength, and he was able to handle everything the army threw at him. His test scores and his skills during boot camp got him noticed, and he was offered a chance to become an Army Ranger. He thrived in this new environment and was soon proficient with every weapon the Army had to offer, and his escape and evasion skills put him at the top of his class.

He was in the middle of his third tour of duty in Vietnam when something inside snapped. Maybe it was too many close calls while on patrol, or maybe it was that he could no longer stand seeing the kind of destruction and death that war caused or perhaps he just got a conscience, but anyway, he had finally had it with war and killing.

His unit had come upon a small village in the Vietnam highlands that they believed was being used by the Viet Cong. They interrogated the local elder who denied it, but his unit wasn't satisfied. To force the elder to talk, they started shooting the civilians one by one. There were screaming and tears, and then all of a sudden, he lost control of the situation and his unit. He tried to stop the frenzy, but by the time his men were finished, there was nothing they could do except set the village on fire and move down the road. He was grief-stricken, and after brooding about it for a couple of days, he swore to his men that he would see to it that they all paid for the terrible massacre.

A week later, his unit was involved in a horrible battle for a valley that he cared nothing about, and after three days of intense fighting, he'd had enough. Sometime during the third night of the battle, he slipped away from his foxhole and disappeared into the forest surrounding the valley. For several weeks he used his escape and evasion skills to hide from enemy patrols until he crossed into Laos and made his way to Bangkok in Thailand.

No longer in uniform and with long hair and a heavy beard, he looked like some kind of homeless beggar. During his days in Bangkok, he looked for ways to get out of the country, and at night, he would rummage through trash to find anything edible. Eventually, he found work on a tramp steamer with an Indonesian captain who didn't care about papers. He only cared about hard work.

For six months, he sailed around the Indian Ocean before leaving the ship in Abu Dhabi in the United Arab Emirates. With money in his pocket, he was able to fly to Spain and then on to Central America, eventually making his way across the US/ Mexico Border in New Mexico. Airport security at the time was pretty much nonexistent, and no one ever questioned his driver's license. He assumed the army figured he had died in the battle for the valley and had never even looked for him.

He hitchhiked his way north through New Mexico and soon found himself in Aspen, Colorado. He fit right in. The counterculture scene was in full swing, and there were drugs and women everywhere. With his long hair and dirty clothes, he looked like everyone else, but he found that he just couldn't deal with all the people. One day he headed back into the forest, and after a few weeks of just being alone with his thoughts, he stumbled on an old miner's cabin.

The cabin hadn't been lived in for years, but it had good bones, and he was able to use the scraps from the original cabin to fix it up, so it was livable. The miner, whoever he was, had tapped into a small spring, so the cabin had running water, and he also found the old mine a few hundred feet back behind the cabin. He spent the next several years fixing everything up, so he had a rugged but comfortable home, and more importantly, he found the privacy he so badly wanted.

Before leaving Aspen, he bought an old M1 carbine from a pawn shop along with a box of 30 caliber ammo. He was a crack shot and had no problem making sure he had plenty of food to eat. All in all, he had a good life.

CHAPTER TWENTY-SIX

His thoughts turned to the morning he found them. The snowstorm had been furious and lasted three days. When it was over, there were close to three feet of fresh snow on the ground. The temperature had dropped way below freezing, but the little miner's cabin was warm and cozy. He hated the idea of having to go out in the cold, but his fresh meat supply was running low, and he had decided before the storm set in that he needed to do some hunting to replenish his stock. The fact that the storm lasted three days only made his situation worse, so he put on his long underwear, every sweater he owned, which was only two, and his coat, hat, and gloves and head out into the snow.

The day had dawned beautifully. The sky through the trees was a bright robin's egg blue, and there wasn't a cloud to be seen. The fresh mat of snow on the ground was untracked and sparkled in the morning sunlight. He just stood in the doorway of his little cabin and admired the beauty that surrounded him. He closed the cabin door and headed out.

He found the old Ford station wagon on an old Forest Service fire road that hardly anyone ever used. The car was almost buried to its roof. The front wheels were sitting in a ravine off the side of the road. He thought it might be abandoned until he heard a faint cry coming from inside the car. Fearing the worst, he dropped the bundle of snowshoe hares he had shot, and with his hands, he started digging for the driver's door.

It was hard work, and he was soaked to the bone and cold as hell when he cleared enough snow to open the driver's door. He would never forget the sight he found inside the car. The woman sitting in the driver's seat was barely conscious. She was wrapped in a coat and had wrapped herself up in a blanket, but it hadn't helped. Her skin was cold to the touch, and he feared she was dead until she slowly opened her eyes. She stared at him and was able to mutter a short sentence. "Help my babies."

He looked behind her and couldn't believe his eyes. There, filling the back seat and the rear back-facing seat where eight kids all wrapped in blankets with just their little faces visible. He was shocked. Most of them weren't moving, and he knew he needed to do something before they froze to death. He had no idea how long they had been in the car, but their situation was desperate. He told the woman he would go and get help, but with a soft, almost dying voice, the woman pleaded with him not to bring the authorities.

He spent the next hour clearing the doors so he could get the kids out of the car one at a time. The whole gang of them were stiff and barely able to move, but night was falling, and he needed to get this little troop to his cabin before the temperature dropped even more. They would not survive another night in the woods.

Still wrapped in their blankets, the kids helped each other as they struggled through the deep snow, trying to follow the man's tracks. The woman, barely able to walk, managed to carry one of the youngest children, and he had two of them in his arms along with the snowshoe hares. It took several torturous hours of trudging through the deep snow, but his little troop finally reached the small cabin. He opened the door and ushered them all inside. It was going to be a tight fit, but the closeness of their bodies would help them thaw out. Once inside, they all crashed on whatever piece of real estate they could find, and within a matter of minutes, the warmth of the cabin had everyone asleep.

He awoke to the smell of rabbits cooking in the big cast-iron pot. Shaking the cobwebs out of his head, he remembered finding the woman and kids in the car in the woods and hiking back to the cabin. He raised his head from the table he had fallen asleep on, and there, standing in front of his little wood stove, was an angel with a wooden spoon. The woman was taller than he thought she was the night before, and she had the most beautiful long blond hair hanging down her back almost to her waist. For a minute, he just sat there and looked at her.

She turned and was startled to see him looking at her. Her face glowed in the early morning light coming through the old lead glass window. She turned back to the stove and continued to stir the rabbit stew she had prepared. Gradually the children awoke, and soon, the little cabin was filled with more noise than he was used to. It was almost scary. He had lived alone for such a long time that having people around, made him uneasy.

The whole gang gobbled down the rabbit stew like they hadn't eaten in weeks, which might have been the case, and then everyone settled down, and sleep overtook them once again. While everyone was asleep, he hiked back to the car and made several trips carrying what little luggage they had. He had hoped to find something in the car that would explain who she was and how she came to be stuck in the middle of the mountains in a snowstorm with eight kids.

Back at the cabin with their meager belongings, he was able to get some of the answers he was seeking. She told him that she had been driving through the mountains heading for a new start in California. She had family out there who were going to help her with her kids. She had taken a wrong turn after leaving Aspen, and then the storm hit, and she was hopelessly lost. When the front tires went into the ravine, she knew they were in trouble, so she wrapped everyone up in what she could and prayed for a miracle. God had sent him as an answer to her prayers.

She told him she was from Florida and that two of the children were hers from a failed marriage, and the rest were either adopted or in foster care. She said she had permission from Florida to take the kids to California to a new life. He doubted the story right from the first minute she opened her mouth. He had interrogated enough prisoners while he was in Vietnam, and he knew when people were lying to him. This woman was nothing but one big lie.

She never did give him a story he could believe, but over the years, he had stopped asking, and they settled into a quiet life. The kids were growing, and he found a new purpose in teaching them things, important things, like reading and writing but also necessary things like how to pick locks, set up traps, and survive. The kids became very good at breaking into the mansions that had begun to spring up around Aspen over the years. Many of these were second homes for wealthy celebrities and businesspeople, and they were empty a good portion of the year.

They expanded the cabin to accommodate the entire gang and had also set up a second home back in the old mine. This was their safe place in case someone got too close to the cabin. They had used it several times recently as it seemed there were a lot more people hiking in the woods

Things went along fine until one morning two years ago when the woman woke up feverish and exhausted. She had tried to stand at the stove to cook breakfast but had passed out. Luckily, he was standing behind her, and he was able to get her into the bed they shared. Over the next several days, she woke up delirious and had no idea who anyone was. The Teacher, as the kids had been calling him, was beside himself with worry, but he knew she would never let him go for help.

On the third day, she didn't recognize him or the children. On the fourth morning, she didn't wake up at all, and her breathing was shallow and labored. She stopped breathing later that day.

In all the years they had lived in the cabin, the Teacher never got the whole story from her. He was able to glean that she had started in West Virginia and that somewhere along the road, she had decided to start kidnapping small children who were too young to know any better. She never told him how she chose the kids to kidnap or what she intended to do with them, and she never explained why their parents didn't come looking for them, but over the years, they had all become one big family, and he stopped asking.

The children had chosen a beautiful spot above the mine for her grave. From there, she would have a view of the entire area, and they were pleased with their choice. They had dressed her in a dress she had made, that she always intended to wear for a special occasion, but never had. She looked beautiful. The Teacher wrapped her in a blanket, carried her up the mountain to the gravesite, and laid her in the shallow grave the oldest boys had dug. Each child had been told to find something special in the woods that they thought momma might like, and they each placed their special treasure in the grave with her. The Teacher then shoveled the dirt back into the grave, and then they all said the Lord's Prayer.

The Teacher knew that any chance of ever finding out her true story was now gone forever, and he decided that the most important thing at this point was to keep his little family together. He had grown very fond of the children over the years and took great pride in teaching them the things they would need to know as their lives progressed. He also wondered what would happen if they, one day, decided to leave the cabin. They were approaching that age where they would want more out of life than what was available in their little family group.

And now here they were setting up defenses and traps to protect their little family from the outside world. He had no doubt his children would be able to survive in the real world. He often would sneak into Aspen at night to steal food and other things they needed, and he always tried to bring back a current newspaper or a new book to help them with their education. He was amazed at how smart the children were and how quickly they learned new skills. He was also surprised at how quickly they learned to break into houses or stores without leaving any signs of having been there. Their survival skills, thanks to him, were top-notch.

He had known for a while now that his days were numbered. He had read up on Parkinson's Disease in a medical book the children had stolen from a doctor's house, and he believed that this was the ailment that was causing the hand tremors. He didn't think he had long to live, but as long as he had a breath to take, he would do all he could to protect his family.

CHAPTER TWENTY-SEVEN

PIS was very quiet as he scanned the ground around him. Once they found the first booby trap, in a spot that PIS had checked during his nighttime chase of their two followers, it was decided that Buck and the two deputies would stay several yards behind PIS. He had been able to disarm the trap, but they didn't want to take any chances. Whoever they were chasing had been able to set up the trap in the dark, while being pursued by PIS.

Buck had spoken with the Sheriff by radio right after they had gotten on the trail. He had a decent signal, and he was able to give the Sheriff their coordinates from his handheld GPS unit. The Sheriff reported back that the SWAT teams were just starting to enter the woods, and based on Buck's coordinates, they should meet up in a couple of hours.

"Sheriff, please be sure to remind everyone about the booby traps. We have uncovered several more since we left yesterday." Buck said.

"You got it, Buck. Everyone has been told to be careful. By the way, the guys from Gunnison are coming up on horseback so they may get there before the rest of the teams. You guys stay safe."

Buck wrapped up his radio call, and they started back down the trail. PIS had moved ahead, and Buck and the two deputies had lost sight of him. Buck wasn't sure where the feeling came from, but his head told him to stop, and he held up his fist. The two deputies knelt and raised their assault rifles in a defensive position.

Buck had his assault rifle slung over his shoulder, and he pulled it around and took the same position as the deputies. They stopped and listened. All Buck could hear was the breeze rustling through the trees. Then the deputy, Manning, pointed to his ear and pointed off to the left. Buck strained to listen. Then he heard it. There was movement off to the left. Buck couldn't tell how far off, but it was just within his hearing range.

Buck looked ahead for PIS, but he still couldn't see him. Deputy Manning moved to his left while staying in a crouch, while Deputy Sanchez shifted to the right and covered the trail they had just come down with his rifle. They waited.

Buck had learned a little bit about the two deputies while they were eating their sandwiches the night before. Deputy Rick Manning had been with the Pitkin County Sheriff's department for about three years. He had been born and raised in the county, and his Dad owned a gas station and convenience store in Carbondale. He was single and had served two tours in Afghanistan as a Marine before joining the department.

Deputy Michael Sanchez had been with the department about six years. He had been a standout bull rider in high school in Waco, Texas, and had hoped to move into the PBR, Pro Bull Riders Association, after graduation, but a bad trip on the back of a fiery bull ended with a career stopping knee injury. Unable to fulfill his lifelong dream to be a pro bull rider, Michael spent a couple of years just bumming around the western US before he settled in Dillon, Colorado. When he heard about an opening in the Pitkin County Sheriff's office, he applied and was surprised to be one of three people chosen for the three jobs available. Two years ago, he married a local girl, and they had a beautiful baby girl. His promotion to the county SWAT team had been a highlight of his life to this point.

Buck wasn't sure what to do at this point. He didn't want to move deeper into the woods because, with booby traps still a real possibility, this could be a trap to draw them in. He was just about to decide on a plan when he spotted a bright red spot coming through the trees. Everyone tensed until they spotted PIS.

Buck and the deputies stood as he approached, and he stepped onto the trail and stopped to catch his breath. Buck looked at him with a questioning expression.

"Sorry, Agent Taylor. Didn't mean to cause a stir." He caught his breath. "We were being followed again. Only one this time, but close enough that I spotted him through the trees. I didn't want to lose him, so I broke off the trail and tried to circle around him."

"It looks like you didn't catch him. What happened?" asked Buck.

"Didn't need to. I think we are getting close," said PIS

"Well, what are we waiting for? Let's go get him!" said Deputy Sanchez.

"Hang on there young fella. This one is very crafty, and it could be a trap."

PIS looked at Buck. "There is an old miner's cabin up ahead about half a mile. I didn't get too close, but it looks abandoned. The person I was following disappeared into the woods behind the cabin." PIS went on to tell them that he had encountered two more traps while following the person of interest.

With booby traps still lurking in the woods, they would need to approach the cabin with caution. Since PIS was unarmed, Buck suggested he remain back on the trail once they got close to the cabin. PIS just laughed and headed down the trail. Buck looked at the two deputies who both just shrugged their shoulders. Buck nodded in agreement, and they headed off after PIS. This time they kept a little more distance between each other, and Sanchez covered their rear.

The trail they were following had almost disappeared when they caught up with PIS, who was now kneeling behind a downed tree. He pointed over the tree and Buck, and Manning knelt next to him. Sanchez had taken a position behind another tree and was acting as lookout.

Buck spotted the little cabin about fifty yards off through the trees. It sat in a little clearing in the trees. He scanned the area. As far as he could tell, the cabin appeared to be abandoned, but where had the person gone that PIS had followed? There were no visible trails leading away from the cabin.

Deputy Manning handed Buck a small pair of binoculars, and Buck studied the area around the cabin. It looked abandoned, just like PIS had told them, but he had an uneasy feeling. They needed to clear the little cabin so they could continue trying to follow their person of interest. Buck had the two deputies move off the trail to the right and left. PIS reminded them to watch where they placed their feet, and they both acknowledged that they understood. The two deputies would approach the little cabin from the sides while he and PIS approached the cabin head-on. Once again, Buck suggested that PIS stay back while he approached the cabin, but PIS just smiled.

Buck started moving down what was left of the almost invisible trail, and PIS followed a couple of yards behind him. That was the agreement they had reached since PIS was unarmed. Both deputies had moved off the trail and were working their way toward the cabin keeping Buck and PIS in sight. Buck, with his rifle up to his shoulder, moved at a slight crouch. Whenever he could, he would step off the trail and hide behind an available tree. He continually scanned the area with his rifle as they approached the cabin.

The explosions caught them totally off guard. The first explosion went off just to the right of Deputy Manning and knocked him to the ground. The second explosion went off a few seconds later between the cabin and Deputy Sanchez, who dove for cover behind a large aspen tree. Buck and PIS had just reached the cabin when the first two explosions occurred. Right after the second explosion, PIS reacted and threw himself against Buck driving him away from the cabin. They both hit the ground just as the front of the cabin exploded. The air was filled with flying pieces of wood and glass. Buck and PIS covered their heads with their arms and tried to bury themselves deeper into the leaves and the undergrowth. The sound was deafening.

CHAPTER TWENTY-EIGHT

She had spent a good part of her summer vacation, trying to locate her grandfather's torture chamber. She knew it was somewhere along Conundrum Creek, but she was having a great deal of difficulty locating it. She didn't have much time to spend with her grandfather since she was working in a local restaurant, so she missed out on a lot of lucid moments. Those few times, she was able to sit and talk with him; he didn't make a lot of sense.

The last time she found her grandfather in a mood to talk, he spent most of the time talking about his second kill. He had asked to see his treasure box again, and she went and pulled it from the hiding space behind the big toolbox in the garage. He spent a lot of time looking at the small treasures, but he kept coming back to a thin silver bracelet. He would stare at it for a few seconds, look at something else, and then repeat the process as if drawn to it.

She knew better than to interrupt his train of thought, so she waited until he was ready to tell his story. She took the bracelet from the treasure box for him; he stared at it and sat back against his pillow.

The young woman who owned the bracelet was from Maine. He couldn't remember the city, but he sure remembered her. She was petite and pretty. He couldn't remember how old she was, but she was old enough to drink, and that was where he found her. She was on her way to Oregon to meet up with some friends from high school.

Her family didn't know she was in Aspen. She told them she was going to Florida for spring break, but she changed her mind at the bus station and decided to go to Oregon, where her high school boyfriend was going to school. He found out that the boyfriend had no idea that she was on her way. She would be perfect. He discovered that the girl from Maine had no place to stay in Aspen and almost no money for food, so he found her a place to sleep in an old shed behind the maintenance shop.

Even though he was older than she was, he liked the way she flirted with him. Her attention got him very excited. When he would visit her after work, she always seemed pleased to see him, and she seemed to enjoy teasing him. He figured that the bright red lipstick was just for him. He told her about a hot spring located south of Aspen and that they could go there. Clothing was optional, which didn't seem to bother her.

Telling his wife he had to work a night-shift, he met the girl at the shed, and they headed for the old forest service road that led to the hot spring. Before they had even gotten to the spring, she had started to take off her clothes in the car. She reached over at one point and ran her hand along the zipper in his pants. He almost smashed into a tree along the narrow dirt road.

He pulled the car off the road and into the forest in a spot he had picked for its privacy. Once he stopped the car, she started to unbuckle his pants. He was more than ready as she straddled him in the front seat. He was so preoccupied that he almost forgot the syringe he had placed in the door pocket. She was so preoccupied that she never even flinched when he pushed the needle into her shoulder. They both exploded together, and then she passed out in his arms. He pushed her off and got out of the car. Pulling up his pants, he finished dressing and went to the passenger side door and pulled her out onto the ground.

The area was as dark as a cave, but he had memorized the trail back to his little house of horrors, and a half-hour later, he was unlocking the hatch under the floor of his miner's cabin and lowering her down into the shaft. Once he got her down to the bottom of the shaft, he tied her to the bed just as he had done the first time and raped her for several hours until he was exhausted.

He then dragged her over to the shackles attached to the wall and bolted her in. He admired her naked body for quite a while before he got started. She was almost perfect. Once again, he opened the cabinet and removed his knife collection, and after careful examination, he chose a ten-inch-long filet knife.

He stripped off his clothes and approached the unconscious young girl. He had read an article about an old Chinese torture technique called lingchi or death by a thousand cuts. The Chinese had used this technique to torture people prior to its abolishment around 1905. It involved using non-lethal cuts and slices to ensure that the victim survived for a long time. He was excited to see how many cuts he could make on this young girl before she died. He wanted to wait for her to regain consciousness, but he was getting excited, so he decided to begin.

At some point early on, the young girl woke up, and the fear in her eyes only made his excitement greater. He realized that although he was enjoying the experience that he needed more practice in controlling his cuts. He felt that some were way too deep, and after only an hour, the young girl was bleeding profusely. He knew he should slow down and take his time, but he kept getting more and more excited.

He was disappointed when the young girl passed out for good. He had been keeping count and had only gotten to two hundred slices. He would need more practice. He sat for a minute on the end of the bed and admired his handy work. He liked what he saw.

He cleaned up his tools, got dressed, and turned off the kerosene lantern. He was exhausted but excited by the prospect of practicing this technique some more.

She tried to ask her grandfather for better directions to the shaft, but he just leaned his head back into his pillow and fell asleep. She found herself getting more and more excited as he described the technique. She wondered if she would have the strength to perfect what her grandfather had started. She put the bracelet back in the box and headed back to the garage to hide the box.

She felt very pleased with herself that she was giving her grandfather the chance to relive his life from so long ago. She hoped when he rested for the last time that he would feel good about his life. She was glad she could help him relive those memories.

She would need to continue her quest to find the hidden shaft and the old cabin on her own. She felt like she was getting close. She felt she was ready to follow in her grandfather's footsteps and maybe even develop a technique of her own. She wanted nothing more than to make her grandfather proud of her.

CHAPTER TWENTY-NINE

The Teacher's hands were shaking so badly that he had to show the younger one how to insert the blasting cap into the dynamite instead of doing it himself. He stressed the need for total concentration. The dynamite had been in the mine for years and was very unstable. He told the younger one that one wrong move and he would blow them all up, but the younger one was a fast learner, and he was able to finish the prep work without incident.

The Teacher now led them out the front door of the cabin and showed them the locations he wanted them to place the dynamite sticks. Each one was buried in the ground and covered with leaves, sticks and rocks. The hunter completed running the wires from the cave entrance to each location.

The Teacher showed them how to connect the wires to the blasting caps, and then they headed back to the mine entrance. Once there, the Teacher went back inside the mine and returned carrying a metal box with a metal T-shaped handle sticking out of it. He explained that when the time came to protect the family, they needed to connect one wire from each set to the two little posts at the top of the box. Before connecting the wires, they would need to pull up on the T-shaped handle, so it was ready to work.

The hunter laid out each wire run, in order of placement, on the ground just outside the mine entrance, so they were ready. The Teacher then took the first set of wires and connected one wire to each post, tightening the two wing nuts down on the wire. He told them that when the time came, they would need to push down on the T-shaped handle. That would set off the dynamite.

The Teacher wanted them to follow a specific order if they had to set off the explosives. Right outside first, followed by left outside, and then the one that was set inside the cabin door. If that wasn't enough, they had a second set of explosives between the cabin and the mine, and they were to follow the same procedure. He explained that this was a similar procedure to one that the US Marine mortar crews used in Vietnam during the jungle war. They would drop a mortar round into each of the four corners of a grid and then drop the fifth round into the middle. The idea was to cause the enemy to move from outside the grid into the middle and then drop a round right on their heads. He told them it was a very effective strategy. They both told him that they understood.

The Teacher also had them add a few more booby traps between the cabin and the mine entrance. He cut down a few small aspen trees and had the hunter, and the younger one stack them at the mine entrance to hide the door. He looked around the area between the cabin and the mine entrance. He had done everything he could to protect the family.

He told the younger one to head off into the woods and keep an eye on the men, and he had the hunter hide in the large aspen tree that was about twenty yards away from the door and keep his rifle handy. He was hoping the men would get to the cabin, find it abandoned, and keep going, but he needed to be ready.

While the Teacher headed back into the mine to check on the others, the younger one headed off into the woods, being careful not to trip over the wires they had run along the ground. He was very proud that the Teacher had chosen him for this task. He was the best tracker in the family, and someday he would be able to take the rifle and become another hunter.

The younger one caught up with the men about a half mile from the cabin. He stayed off the trail about fifty yards and hid amongst the trees and the undergrowth. He watched them for a while, and then he realized that the old man with the ponytail was no longer with the group of men on the trail. Panic set in as he looked around the area but couldn't find him. He decided to move to a different location.

As he slipped through the woods, he almost ran into the old man with the ponytail. If he hadn't pulled back at the last moment and crawled under a downed tree, the old man with the ponytail would have seen him for sure. He waited for the old man to pass and then snuck around the tree on the opposite side and headed back toward the cabin. The old man with the ponytail was good, and the younger one spotted him through the trees at the same time the old man spotted him.

The old man was moving straight towards him, so he ducked down into a small ravine and headed back in the opposite direction from which he was traveling. His path would take him away from the cabin, but he needed to shake the old man. He stayed in the ravine for about half a mile, then climbed out, circled around the trail the men had come in on, and headed back towards the cabin on the opposite side of the trail.

He looked around but could not see the men. He felt good that he had been able to get away from the old man. He had gone a long way out of his way to escape the old man, and he was worried that he might not get back to the cabin before the men got there. He made it to the mine entrance just as the men split up and started to approach the cabin. Two of the men moved off to the right and left sides, and the other man and the old man with the ponytail headed towards the cabin. They were all pointing their rifles in the direction of the cabin except for the old man with the ponytail. He didn't seem to have a gun. Maybe their group was set up just like the family. The men with the guns were the hunters, and the old man with the ponytail was like him, the tracker.

The younger one took up his position behind the aspen trees they had cut and stacked at the mine entrance and pulled the metal box with the T-shaped handle closer to the door. The Teacher had closed and bolted the mine entrance door to protect the others. It would be up to the hunter and the younger one to hold off the men. The younger one couldn't see the hunter in the aspen tree, but he knew he was there. Now they just had to sit and wait. Unfortunately, they didn't have to wait long.

CHAPTER THIRTY

The first explosion almost bounced the Teacher out of bed. He had laid down on the bed to try to get rid of the headaches that seemed to plague his days lately. The others were doing their studies and were, for the most part, quiet. The explosion caused dust and bits of rock to fall from the ceiling of the mine, and as he tried to stand up, the others screamed, scattered, and hid under anything they could find.

The Teacher was disoriented for a moment, and when he tried to stand up, his legs gave out from under him, and he crashed to the floor. He covered his head with his arms as bits of rock and dust rained down on his head. He looked around the mine to make sure no one had been injured and then was able to get his legs back under him, and he headed for the mine entrance.

The second explosion caused him to stagger and bang into the mine wall. More dust and debris came down from the ceiling, and he told the others to cover up. Some of them had crawled under the table, and a few crawled under the bed. They all looked confused and frightened.

He reached the mine entrance and was about to unlatch the door when the third explosion knocked him off his feet, and his head slammed into the dirt floor of the mine tunnel. He reached up to his head, and his hand came away covered in blood. His disorientation was back with a vengeance, and he was having trouble figuring out where he was. His first thought was that he was still in Vietnam and that the base was under attack. He looked around for his weapons, but he had none. He knew that wasn't right, so he must not be in Nam. His mind started to clear as two of the others ran up to him and tried to help him move so he could prop against the wall.

He was having trouble focusing and having trouble trying to figure out why there were kids sitting in the dark with him. His mind cleared, and he started to remember. He could hear the others choking on the dust that had now filled the dark mine. He didn't understand what had happened. Could it have been a cave in farther back in the mine? He just couldn't get it worked out in his head.

All of a sudden, his brain cleared enough, and he remembered that he had been working with the hunter and the younger one and that they had set explosive charges around the cabin in case anyone got too close to the mine. It still wasn't making sense in his already fragile and now concussed mind. He knew he needed to help the others, but he was having trouble getting his legs to work. He needed to get them out of the mine before they all choked to death.

It's amazing how sometimes one thing or event can bring about clarity. For the Teacher, that event was a series of gunshots coming from the other side of the mine entry door. He heard the first shots and realized that the hunter and the younger one were outside the mine, and they were in trouble. He had left them to protect the others, and he had gone to sleep. He needed to get to them to help them. It was his job to protect the others, not theirs. He had made a promise to momma. He had to do something.

He managed to get up on his feet with the help of two of the others, and then he told them to run back and hide with the others. He found the latching bolt on the door and was just in the process of swinging the door open when he heard semi-automatic gunfire and lots of it. The men who were searching for them must have found them. The younger one had blown the first three charges, and then the hunter had opened fire from his concealment spot in the big aspen tree. Now the men had opened fire on them both. He felt helpless and knew he needed to do something to help them.

Staying low, he looked out of the mine entrance and spotted the younger one right next to the door. The plunger sat on the ground next to him, and he was leaning back against the wall of the mine with his knees up against his chest and his hands covering his head. The Teacher had never seen him looked so frightened.

The Teacher crawled out the door on his belly and slid under the stacked aspen trees and wrapped his arms around the younger one. He held him as the bullets flew. While he held the younger one, he could still hear the unmistakable sound of the M1 carbine going off to his right. The hunter was making a valiant effort to defend their home, but the semi-automatic fire he heard was withering. The hunter didn't stand a chance.

Staying low to the ground, the Teacher half crawled, and half ran towards the big aspen tree. He no longer heard the M1 carbine. All he heard was the semi-automatic weapons fire. As he neared the tree, he realized his worst fear. The hunter's body hung limply from the branch about eight feet off the ground with a lot of blood flowing from the bullet holes in his chest. The M1 carbine lay on the ground under his body.

With a lull in the rifle fire, the Teacher was able to reach up and pull the hunter's body down from the tree. He reached into the hunter's pocket and pulled out two more clips for the rifle. He ejected the spent clip and slapped in a new clip.

His mind was back in Vietnam, and he needed to protect the men he had abandoned during the firefight. Feeling twenty-four again, the Teacher jumped up, raised the rifle to his shoulder, and charged towards the cabin. He had been able to get off two rounds before the first bullet hit him in the shoulder, but he didn't stop. He pulled the trigger twice more as he ran toward them. The next couple rounds hit him square in the chest, and he flopped back onto the ground.

He looked to his left and saw the younger one hooking up the next set of wires to the plunger. He had to stop him before he got killed, too. The Teacher tried to turn on his side, but the pain was intense. He held up his hand and tried to get the younger one's attention. He was too late. The explosion went off two feet from where he had hit the ground, and he felt his body being flung into the air. The last thing he saw as he hit the ground was the bullets slamming into the younger one as he tried valiantly to get the next set of wires connected to the plunger. Then the lights went out, and the Teacher was finally at peace.

CHAPTER THIRTY-ONE

Buck was lying on the ground, trying to catch his breath. PIS was lying partially on top of him. His first thought was, "this must be how all those quarterbacks felt when I pummeled them into the ground as a defensive back for the Gunnison High School Cowboys, all those years ago."

Buck had been a standout high school football player and could have gone to almost any college he chose with a full scholarship, but he chose to join the army instead. With his teammate Hardy Braxton covering the left side of the line, they had broken just about every state high school record for defensive play. During senior year they had been called the "Wrecking Crew," and many of those records still stood today.

Buck had his arms over his head as debris rained down on top of them. He tried to shake the cobwebs out of his head but was having trouble focusing. He could feel blood dripping down his neck, and his ears were ringing. He tried to move, but he was pinned to the ground. The debris falling from the sky slowed, and PIS slid off Buck. Buck looked over at PIS and noticed the pain in his eyes.

"You okay?" he asked.

"I think I caught a piece of shrapnel in my shoulder," replied PIS.

Buck picked his head up off the ground and reached over PIS. Buck was amazed at what he saw. Sticking out of

PIS's shoulder was a five-inch-long piece of wood. Buck slid closer. He didn't see a lot of blood, but he knew this wasn't good. He told PIS not to move.

He was trying to get his radio off his belt when the first shots hit the wood that had fallen around him and PIS. He dragged PIS closer to the woodpile and then picked up his rifle off the ground. He needed to locate the sniper. He raised his head over the fallen logs, but couldn't pinpoint where the shots were coming from. The remains of the cabin partially blocked his view downrange. He rested his rifle on the top of a log and started to sight in through the scope when he heard rapid gunfire coming from both sides of him.

Deputies Manning and Sanchez were both behind trees and had engaged the sniper with withering fire. Buck looked through his scope in the direction they were firing and saw the bullets as they tore big chunks of wood out of an aspen tree about forty yards to their left.

Both deputies stopped firing, and for the moment, silence returned to the forest. Buck scanned the area with his scope. The movement from the right side was low to the ground. He had to look twice, not certain he had seen any movement at all. As he watched the big tree, he spotted another person stand up and pull something out of the tree. Deputy Manning must have seen the same thing, as he once again opened fire at the tree.

With his clip empty, Manning dropped the clip and was ramming a new clip home when a figure jumped up from the ground under the aspen tree and charged towards them. Several bullets hit the tree that Manning was hiding behind as the figure ran forward, firing as he came. Buck and Sanchez returned fire, and Buck saw the man falter, and a red stain appeared on his right shoulder. Remarkably, the man kept coming and was firing again—this time towards Manning, who had regained his position behind the tree.

Buck sighted in on the man the best he could, and both he and Sanchez opened fire at the same time. Buck could see the bullets as they struck the man square in the chest, and he flew backward and hit the ground. Everyone froze for a minute.

Manning had come out from behind his tree and, with his rifle raised had started to move towards Buck. Buck climbed to his feet and kept scanning the area for any other danger. The explosion caught them both off guard and the dove for cover. Buck looked up just in time to see the body in the woods fly thought he air and land hard on the ground. He wasn't sure what had just happened, but there was someone else out there with them and that someone still had explosives.

Sanchez looked up, and something led his eye to a stand of aspen trees. The stand didn't look natural as the trees were too close together, and from his location, the trees looked more like they were leaning against something. He spotted movement behind the trees and fearing the worst he opened fire on the trees.

Buck, Manning and Sanchez held their positions and scanned the area. PIS was now lying comfortably against a fallen log from the cabin, and Buck was amazed at how calm he appeared. Like getting stabbed in the back with a chunk of wood was an everyday occurrence. He put his hand on PIS's good shoulder and signaled for him to stay where he was.

Manning and Sanchez converged on Buck's position.

"Fuck, Buck. What the hell just happened?" asked Sanchez.

Buck shook his head. "Got me. I feel like we've been in a war zone." He shook his head to try to clear the ringing in his ears.

The forest had been quiet for a few minutes, and Buck

suggested they head toward the big tree and see what they could find. The three men spread out, and with rifles raised, they moved towards the tree. Buck was the first to reach the guy who had charged them. Kneeling next to the body, he touched his two fingers to the side of the guy's neck and checked for a pulse. There was none, which he pretty much figured, after watching the guy get shot repeatedly and then blown up.

He picked up the rifle that was lying next to the body—an old M1 carbine. Buck hadn't seen one of those in years. It was a good rifle in its day and was still used by the military. He slung the rifle strap over his shoulder after checking the body to make sure there were no other weapons. He looked up as Sanchez waved him over to the big aspen tree.

He was almost to the tree when he heard a voice coming from his radio. He pulled the radio from his belt and keyed the mic. "Go ahead, Sheriff," he replied.

"Are you guys, okay? We heard explosions and gunfire. What's your status?"

Buck was just about to answer when he heard rustling in the trees coming from the trees to the left of where they had entered the little clearing. Buck, Sanchez and Manning found cover and scanned the area.

"Buck Taylor. Gunnison County Sheriff's Office." Came a shout from the woods.

Buck stepped out from behind his cover and still with rifle raised called out.

"Come ahead. Slowly!"

The four Gunnison County deputies, all wearing camouflage, stepped out of the woods into the clearing and looked around. Buck lowered his rifle.

Walt Jenkins, with the Gunnison County Sheriff's Office, had been with Buck when they found Ranger Susan Corey's body. He walked up to Buck, and they shook hands.

"Jesus Buck. What the hell happened? You guys, okay?"

"Yeah, mostly," replied Buck. "Got one man injured."

Jenkins looked towards PIS. "Masters, take a look. Masters has paramedic training." Deputy Masters headed towards PIS, pulling out his first aid kit as he went.

Buck held up his hand to Jenkins and lifted the radio to his mouth.

"Sheriff, we are good. PIS has been injured, and we are going to need transport. We are also going to need the Forensic Pathologist and Forensics. Gunnison County just arrived. Over." Buck gave the Sheriff the coordinates from his handheld GPS and clipped the radio back on his belt

Deputy Sanchez yelled for Buck and ducked back behind the tree. Buck and Walt Jenkins headed for Sanchez while the other two Gunnison County deputies headed for the stand of aspen trees with Manning. As Buck approached, he saw Sanchez kneeling next to a body on the ground.

Sanchez looked up as Buck approached. "He's just a kid for Christ's sake. We killed a kid." Sanchez had tears in his eyes.

Buck and Jenkins knelt next to him and looked at the body on the ground. Sanchez was right. Buck figured the kid couldn't be more than fifteen of sixteen. He had blond hair and blue eyes that were now clouded over in death. He had been shot multiple times. Buck put his hand on Sanchez's shoulder. Nothing he could say right now was going to change the way Sanchez was feeling.

Buck looked at Jenkins, who just nodded. They headed over to where Manning and the other two deputies were standing, and the scene was even worse. Lying behind the stand of aspen trees was the body of another young boy. This one looked to be no more than twelve or thirteen. Next to him on the ground was an old plunger for setting off explosives. The plunger looked to be a hundred years old, and Buck was amazed that it still worked. Manning did not have tears in his eyes, but Buck could sense that he was going through the same emotions that Sanchez was feeling.

Walt Jenkins tapped Buck on the arm and pointed to two sets of wires lying on the ground next to the body. "Looks like the kid wasn't finished."

"Yeah," replied Buck. "We better see where those go."

Buck headed off, following one set of wires, while Jenkins followed the other. They each found what they expected about forty yards from the body. The dynamite was very old and coated with white residue. Although he knew the dynamite was not connected to a timer, Buck also knew that this dynamite was very unstable. He found a stick and stuck it in the ground. He then pulled a piece of yellow crime scene tape from his backpack and tied it around the top of the stick. He walked over to where Jenkins was standing and repeated the process.

CHAPTER THIRTY-TWO

The Sheriff was following closely behind his SWAT team as they traveled along an old fire break that they had picked up on the west side of Conundrum Creek. Based on the radio report he received from Buck earlier in the morning, they should be within a mile of Buck's current location. The two other SWAT teams were coming in from Gunnison County to the south and from the Maroon Snowmass trailhead to the west.

The first explosion stopped everyone in their tracks as it reverberated through the valley. The high peaks helped to amplify the sound, but it also made it difficult to determine the direction from which the sound came. The second and third explosions did nothing to change that, but that didn't lessen the concern the Sheriff felt. His SWAT team had already disarmed two booby traps, so there was concern with moving through the woods any faster.

The rifle fire that followed did nothing to alleviate the Sheriff's concerns, and the semi-automatic return fire just increased his anxiety level. "What the hell is going on?" he thought to himself. It sounded like a full-scale invasion was happening in his county. He grabbed the radio off his belt and called Buck. The lack of a response was not unexpected. Buck and his team were deep in the woods, and he might be having getting out a signal.

He called the other two teams to see if they might have a better feel for which direction the sound was coming from.

The Gunnison County SWAT team reported that they were about ten minutes from the location Buck had last reported, and they were certain the shooting was coming from there. They told the Sheriff they would forego a little bit of safety and pick up their pace. The team coming from the trailhead was still too far away from Buck's last position, but they would pick up the pace since they were following Buck's trail and assumed that all the booby traps along the trail had been exposed.

The shooting stopped, and the Sheriff was able to reach Buck. "Go ahead, Sheriff," said Buck.

"Are you guys, okay? We heard explosions and gunfire. What's your status?"

There was a lengthy delay, and the Sheriff started to get impatient. He was about to key the mic again when Buck responded. "Sheriff, we are good. PIS has been injured, and we are going to need transport. We are also going to need the Forensic Pathologist and Forensics. Gunnison County just arrived. Over."

The Sheriff was not happy to hear the request for the Pathologist. That meant that somebody was dead. He keyed the mic and called his dispatcher. He asked the dispatcher to call the county Forensic Pathologist and his two forensic techs and to call the paramedics and activate the Pitkin County Search and Rescue team. Finally, he asked the dispatcher to call Olaf Gunderson and have him bring a couple of his ATVs and a couple of his guides to the Conundrum Creek trailhead. Olaf had been a fixture in Aspen for longer than anyone could remember, and he owned an adventure company. The trail the Sheriff and his team were on was somewhat decent for the most part, and Olaf's experienced mountain guides should be able to maneuver their ATVs along most of it.

Finished talking to the dispatcher, the Sheriff put away his radio and directed his SWAT team to start moving towards Buck's last GPS fix. He had no way of knowing how many people were dead, but he was glad the shooting had stopped, and that Buck sounded like everyone except PIS was okay. Despite their most recent disagreement, he liked that old curmudgeon and he hoped he wasn't hurt too bad.

It took the Sheriff and his SWAT team another forty-five minutes to reach Buck's location. He stood at the edge of the clearing and looked around. In the middle of the field stood a smoldering pile of what he imaged was once a miner's cabin. The field was covered with debris. He spotted the two sticks in the ground with the yellow caution tape hanging from them, and he directed his deputy who was trained as a bomb tech to have a look and see what needed to be done.

He spotted PIS propped against a log. One of the Gunnison County deputies was wrapping tape around the chunk of wood so it wouldn't move. They would not attempt to remove the piece of wood until PIS was safely at the hospital. The Sheriff walked over and knelt next to PIS.

"You doing okay?" asked the Sheriff.

"Don't worry after me, Sheriff. Been hurt a lot worse than this," replied PIS.

The Sheriff looked at the Gunnison deputy and noticed him frown. He separated the back of PIS's shirt that he had cut open to access the wound, and the Sheriff could see scars all over PIS's back. It looked like someone had whipped him unmercifully at some point in his life. The Sheriff was stunned. There was so much they didn't know about this Brit. Maybe someday they would get the whole story.

He patted PIS on the shoulder and stood up. The deputy told him that PIS should be fine. He didn't think the piece of wood was embedded too deeply, and PIS didn't seem to be in too much pain. He even refused the painkillers the deputy had offered him. The tape job should hold the wood in place as long as they didn't jostle him too much. The Sheriff thanked the deputy and asked where Buck and the others had gone.

The deputy pointed toward a large aspen tree, and the Sheriff and his SWAT guys headed in that direction. Some noise to his right attracted his attention, and he stopped. The rest of the SWAT team came through the trees along the trail that Buck had cleared. The Sheriff asked them to secure the area and start hanging crime scene tape around the entire clearing. The rest of the team was directed to grab some evidence flags and cones and start walking the clearing, marking anything they found that didn't look natural.

He headed off in the direction of the voices he could hear through the trees and stopped short as he reached a point where he was able to see the mine entrance. He could not believe his eyes.

CHAPTER THIRTY-THREE

Buck asked the remaining Gunnison County deputies to search the area between the cabin and the mine entrance to make sure there were no other threats. He checked the younger one for a pulse but found none, which didn't surprise him. Sanchez was holding up okay. He kind of set in his head that maybe the bullets that had killed the two boys hadn't come from his gun. It gave him some solace even though he knew that he was one of the top shooters in the department, but with all three of them shooting, anything was possible.

Buck and Manning were standing to the side of the mine entrance discussing the safest course of action to enter the mine when they heard what sounded like coughing coming from deep inside the mine. They both raised their rifles and looked into the deep recesses of the pitch-black mine.

Buck gave a short shrill whistle to get the attention of the Gunnison deputies and waved them over to the mine. Deputy Sanchez had composed himself and joined the group by the entrance. The Gunnison deputies each had night vision goggles in their backpack, so Buck asked them to lead the way. The dust was so thick in the air that the night vision goggles proved useless, so the deputies raised them off their eyes. With rifles raised and minimal light from Buck's flashlight and the flashlights on the rifles, they entered the mine entrance.

Buck noticed that the door they entered was a substantial

piece of construction, definitely designed to keep people out of the mine. He wondered if the guy lying dead in the clearing built the reinforced door, and also wondered what he was trying to hide behind it. Once inside, even the flashlights had trouble cutting through the inky black darkness and dust that surrounded them.

Buck kept his flashlight pointed forward and followed behind the three Gunnison SWAT deputies who had separated and now walked down both sides of the tunnel, hugging the walls as best they could. Manning followed Buck, and Sanchez remained by the mine entrance door to cover their backs.

After what seemed like an eternity to Buck, but was only a few minutes, they entered what appeared to be a large room, and they crouched lower and moved to opposite sides of the space. Buck and Manning held their position in the tunnel and waited.

"POLICE. NO ONE MOVE!" came a shout from Walt Jenkins. "We are armed, and we will shoot!"

Buck could hear quiet movement along with sniffles and tiny coughs. The air was heavy with dust, and even Buck coughed as they stood listening. Walt Jenkins moved back down the tunnel and moved next to Buck.

"We can see a couple of people, and they look like more kids. They are hiding under a table. Can't tell how many. What do you want to do?" asked Jenkins.

"Let's get as much light in the space as we can and see what we are dealing with. Be ready for anything," replied Buck.

"You got it," Walt responded. He keyed his mic. "Okay, guys. Let's get all the flashlights turned on. Stay cool."

All at once, three more flashlights lit up the space. The seven flashlights combined made a dent in the darkness, and it was enough for Buck and the others to see four faces looking up at them from under a table. The faces appeared to be covered with soot. They looked scared.

While the deputies held their guns at the ready, Buck moved into the room and knelt next to the table. He told the kids to crawl out from under the table one at a time. At first, there was hesitancy, then one of the girls crawled out. She was soon followed by two more girls and a boy. Buck heard movement on the other side of the room, and all guns turned that way. Two more girls crawled out from under a small bed that was pushed against the wall. To say the deputies and Buck were stunned would be an understatement.

Buck looked at the first girl who had crawled out from under the table. "Are there any more children in here?" he asked.

The girl who looked about ten or eleven years old looked around the space and then looked at Buck and shook her head no. Some of the kids were still coughing, and Buck and the deputies were finding it hard to breathe themselves, so they pointed the kids towards the door and started walking.

Buck was the first one to exit the mine and was glad to see that Sanchez had pulled an emergency blanket out of his backpack and covered the young boy lying next to the mine entrance. He was followed by six children, all of whom appeared to be around ten or eleven. Once outside, Buck, and the deputies pulled some water bottles out of their packs and gave the kids a chance to get the dust out of their throats.

Buck noticed that each kid looked at the rescue blanket as they came out of the mine, but no one said a word, they just looked sad and confused. Manning looked at Buck and Jenkins and signaled for them to follow him away from the kids. When they were far enough away for the kids not to hear, he said,

"What the hell did we just uncover?"

Buck looked back at the kids who were now sitting on the ground in a small group.

"Be damned if I know. One old guy and eight kids. I can't even imagine. I better radio the Sheriff and let him know what we found."

Jenkins nodded in agreement as did Manning, and Buck pulled out his radio. He was just getting ready to push the mic when they heard movement at the front of the cabin and spotted the Sheriff and the SWAT team entering the clearing.

CHAPTER THIRTY-FOUR

The Sheriff approached the group of kids sitting on the ground and just stared. He turned and headed over to where Buck and the others were standing.

"What the hell, Buck?" he asked.

Buck shrugged his shoulders. "You got us. We were just wondering the same thing."

The Sheriff looked back at the kids and then back at Buck. Buck went on to explain about the explosions and the shootout. He excused himself from Manning and Jenkins, and he and the Sheriff walked over to look at the dead kid by the mine entry. The Sheriff pulled the cover back just enough so the other kids couldn't see and then replaced the blanket. They next walked over to the aspen tree, and Buck showed the Sheriff the body of the older boy. The Sheriff didn't say a word.

Their last stop was the body of the old man. The explosion had done a little damage to the body, but it was the bullet holes in his chest that had killed him. The Sheriff stood for a long minute and then looked at Buck.

"I checked on PIS as we came in. He doesn't seem to be the least bit concerned that he has a chunk of wood embedded in his shoulder. I've got transport coming so we can get him out of here." He stood for a second as if deep in thought. "Honest opinion, Buck. What do you think we have here? Is this some kind of cult or some weird sex thing or what?"

"I have no idea, Sheriff. This is a new one on me. I've seen a lot of abused kids in my day, but these kids don't look abused to my eyes. The way they held hands coming out of the mine, I almost get the feeling they are some kind of family."

The Sheriff looked at Buck. "Seriously? And who's this old guy, the father of these kids?"

Buck said. "I don't think so. These kids all appear to be about the same age. The kid under the tree looks to be the oldest we have seen so far, and the one by the mine entrance looks to be a little bit older than the rest. I doubt they are siblings in the usual sense."

"Fuck, Buck. This is going to be a mess. I better let social services know. This is going to make their day." The Sheriff walked off, pulling his radio off his belt as he went.

Buck took the opportunity and walked over to check on PIS. The Gunnison deputy who had been working on him explained that all things considered, PIS seemed to be doing remarkably well. Buck sat on the ground next to PIS and looked at him.

"I hate to be a bother, Agent Taylor. Much ado about nothing," said PIS.

Buck looked at PIS. "You have a five-inch-long chunk of wood stuck in your shoulder. I don't think that's much ado about nothing."

PIS didn't say anything further, so Buck continued. "You pretty much saved my life back there. Thank you for that. How did you know the cabin was gonna go up?"

PIS smiled. "You are quite welcome, even if all I did was push you out of the way. As far as the cabin. The pattern suggested an old tactic your US Marines used in Vietnam. The Marine mortar crews would drop their mortar rounds in a square pattern starting with the four corners. The enemy would move away from the corners into the center of the square, and then the Marines would hammer the center with successive rounds, essentially obliterating the enemy. It was highly effective."

Buck thought about it for a minute. "You think the guy we killed could be former military and might have spent time in Nam?"

PIS said he thought it was a good possibility. He hadn't seen the man before he was killed, but based on the techniques, it was possible. Buck wanted to talk to the Sheriff about PIS's thought, so he stood up, patted PIS on his good shoulder, and headed off to find the Sheriff. It was just about the same time as the final SWAT team group showed up.

Buck found the Sheriff, and they both stood watching the Sheriff's bomb tech, remove the blasting caps from the two sticks of dynamite that Buck had marked earlier. The bomb tech walked over and told the Sheriff that the dynamite was very old, and even removing the blasting caps wasn't going to make the dynamite safe. He suggested leaving them where they lay and just keeping everyone away from them. The Sheriff agreed.

Buck told the Sheriff about his conversation with PIS. He also suggested they might run his prints through the military and see if there was anything to PIS's idea. The Sheriff agreed. He told Buck that the transport would be on-site in a few minutes along with the Pathologist and Forensics. He was planning to send the kids back first, along with a couple of deputies. PIS would go out with the kids so they could get him to the hospital. The Sheriff told Buck about the scars on PIS's back. Buck had no idea.

They heard the ATVs before they saw them. Olaf Gunderson had delivered in spades as ten ATVs drove into the clearing. Olaf waved to the Sheriff, who waved back. Dr. Emily Parker walked up to Buck and the Sheriff, followed by the two forensic techs, Gomez, and Flynn. The Sheriff walked off with the two techs and left Buck standing with the doctor.

"Looks like we meet again, Agent Taylor," she said. "Do you always make a habit of being where the bodies are?" She smiled, and Buck laughed.

"Seems so, Doc. It's my curse, I guess," he replied.

Buck asked her to follow him, and he would show her the bodies. It would be getting dark in a couple of hours, and the Sheriff wanted to get everyone out of the forest by nightfall. They stopped at the older male's body first, and the doctor knelt and looked at the wounds. She noted the pieces of wood and debris that were buried in his back and side, and Buck explained that besides being shot, he had also been blown up. She looked at Buck with a confused look.

Buck suggested he show her the other two bodies, and then he would be willing to answer any of her questions. He led the way to the boy under the aspen tree. She knelt and gave the body a quick perusal. She stood up, and her face said it all. Nothing needed to be said, so they headed for the younger boy over by the mine entrance. As they approached, she looked at the kids sitting on the ground.

Buck took her by the elbow and led her to the blanket that covered the third body. She pulled back the blanket and just stared for a minute. The age of the young boy was easy to see. The bullets that had killed him had done a lot of damage, and she counted about a half-dozen wounds. She looked up at Buck and then replaced the emergency blanket over the body.

"This is all so senseless. Was there no other way?" she asked.

"Sorry, Doc. We were under attack from several directions, and we had to defend ourselves. We didn't know two of them were kids until it was all over. Everybody feels bad."

Just then, a small figure appeared behind Buck, and a soft

voice asked. "Excuse me, sir. When will the Teacher be coming back?"

Buck and the doctor looked at each other. Buck knelt next to the young girl.

"What's your name, sweetie?" Buck asked

"I'm Sarah. It's my turn to cook, but I don't know what to make."

She was so calm; it was almost unnerving. Buck thought for a minute. "Is the Teacher what you call the older man?"

"Yes, sir. Will he be back soon?"

Buck thought about his answer. "The Teacher is not going to be coming back. He was hurt badly and..."

"Is he dead?" she interrupted without batting an eye.

Buck looked at the Doctor and then back at Sarah. He decided to be straight with the young girl and see what would happen. The Doctor nodded.

"Yes, Sarah. I am afraid he is dead."

"Can we put him in the ground next to momma?"

Buck asked Sarah where momma was buried, and she pointed to a trail that ran up the hill beyond the mine. He asked her if she would show them, and she started to walk away. With Sanchez keeping an eye on the rest of the kids, Buck waved for the Sheriff to follow them, and he and Dr. Parker followed the little girl up the trail.

About a quarter mile up the trail, the little group, with Sarah in the lead, stopped at a small clearing that overlooked the valley below. The view was incredible. Sarah stopped next to a pile of stones and pointed. There was a wooden cross stuck in the rock pile. "This is where we put momma so she could visit God. Teacher said she would be happy here."

Buck, Dr. Parker, and the Sheriff just stood for a minute and watched the activity in the clearing below. The Sheriff suggested they head back. The ATVs were ready to make their first trip back, and they were burning daylight. Dr. Parker took Sarah's hand, and they all headed down the trail to the ATVs.

CHAPTER THIRTY-FIVE

Her grandfather's lucid moments were fewer and fewer as the summer progressed, and even helping him look through the treasure box didn't bring out any more stories or, more importantly, the location of the mine shaft. She grew more and more frustrated, thinking she was not going to be able to fulfill what she felt was her destiny. Time was running out.

She spent most of her free time when she wasn't working at the restaurant, searching the area along Conundrum Creek. She even enlisted the help of some of her friends but to no avail.

Her luck changed just two weeks before she was scheduled to head back to Florida for school. Two miles from the Conundrum Creek trailhead, she found what looked like an old seldom used game trail that she had promised to come back to, but over the summer, she had forgotten about it. It was a bright Saturday morning, and the main trail was busy with tourists. She remembered the tiny trail and decided that this was the day she would follow it. Her frustration level and this strange sudden need had been building the last couple weeks, and she felt like she was going to explode. If she didn't find the mine shaft soon, she might have to improvise, which was never a good idea.

Over the summer, the little game trail had become even more overgrown, and she walked past it twice that morning before she saw the faint trail as it snaked off deeper into the woods. Bushwhacking through the trees and the undergrowth, she walked for about a quarter mile before she found what looked like the re-

mains of an old cabin. There wasn't much left, just some old logs in a pile. She could make out bits and pieces of what looked like old wooden shingles and also what might be the remains of an old door.

Pulling on a pair of work gloves she brought along, she started to move the logs and debris until she exposed what looked like part of an old wooden floor. Her excitement grew as she struggled to clear more of the floor. She tried to be as quiet as a church mouse so as not to attract the attention of any of the hikers using the main trail. Several back-breaking hours later, she had almost the entire floor exposed, and her heart sunk. There was no visible trap door or loose boards, and she sat for a minute and just held her head. All that work. Could she be in the wrong place? She knew this would be her last chance to explore before leaving for college, and she felt terrible.

She was about to leave when she noticed one board that kind of stuck out above the others. The sun must have just cast the right shadow because she hadn't noticed the board earlier. Grabbing a thinner stick, she wedged the stick against the edge of the floorboard and applied pressure. It took several tries to get the stick to catch, and she almost fell over when the board popped loose from the floor. She dropped her stick and pulled up the board with her hands.

She stood there for a moment and just stared. There, below the floorboard, was a rusted metal hatch. She almost screamed out with joy, but then remembered all the hikers. She began removing the rest of the floorboards until she exposed the entire hatch. It was just like her grandfather told her, except for a lot of years of rust. She removed a small pair of bolt cutters she had taken from her grandfather's garage and set the jaws around the old lock, which it surprisingly cut through with almost no effort.

She stood for a moment and thought about what she was about to do. She had hunted for this place all summer, and now it was hers. She also realized that once she opened the hatch and climbed down inside, her life would change forever. Any smart person would call the authorities and have her grandfather arrested. He was a serial killer, possibly one of the first. He was also someone she had always looked up to. Could she possibly turn him in?

She thought about the two choices she could make. She could put all the floorboards back and walk away, never to return, or she could continue on the path that felt more and more right and follow in her grandfather's footsteps. Did she have it in her to take a human life? Unlike most of the serial killers she had read about this summer, she had a good life. She had never killed an animal. Hell, she never even thought about killing anything until she had discovered her grandfather's treasure box. Now it was all she could think about. The idea was enough to get her aroused.

She cleared all the thoughts out of her head and opened the hatch. Her heart skipped a beat when the old rusty hinges made a loud squeak. She froze and listened for a minute, hoping the noise hadn't attracted some unwanted attention. She made a mental note to bring some oil from her grandfather's garage and oil the hinges.

Looking down into the dark void, she spotted the old metal ladder hanging against the side wall of the shaft. It looked like it had very little rust on it. The smell emanating from the shaft was not at all unpleasant and just smelled dry and old. Pulling her flashlight out of her backpack, she turned it on and scanned the bottom of the shaft, which looked a long way down. She was hoping she wouldn't find the shaft filled with spiders, or rats, or even snakes, but the floor of the shaft just looked dusty.

Gathering up her courage, she set her foot on the first rung of the ladder, and, using the door for support, she started to climb down into the tunnel below. She reached the floor of the shaft without incident and scanned the tunnel before her with the flashlight. The tunnel was roughhewn with an occasional brace supporting the roof, but to her amazement, the tunnel was only about ten feet long before it opened into a chamber that was *exactly as her grandfather had described it.*

There against one wall was an old wooden bed. The mattress was old and was covered with an old horsehair blanket. She had to stop for a minute as she visualized her grandfather having sex with the women he brought here. She couldn't picture her grandfather as a rapist, so her mind made the image more pleasant than it probably had been. She spotted the shackles on the opposite wall, and could still see faint brownish stains on the dirt floor. She assumed it was blood, and she felt unsure of her path. Her stomach twisted into a knot, and she felt like she wanted to vomit, but she forced it back down and continued her search.

The old cabinet was hanging on the wall above an old wooden table, and she opened the cabinet. The leather roll was still neatly tied as she picked it up and placed it on the table. She unrolled the bundle and stepped back. The various knives her grandfather made shined bright in the light of her flashlight. They looked brand new. She picked up one of the thin scalpels and was amazed at how sharp it still was. It was as if time had stood still since the last time her grandfather was here. She put the scalpel back and examined some of the other knives.

A sudden thought occurred to her, and she put down the knife and pulled a pair of blue nitrile gloves out of her backpack, along with a clean white rag. She wiped down the handles of the knives she had touched and rolled them back up in the leather bundle and returned it to the cabinet. She closed the door and wiped the small knob on the cabinet. She would need to be careful from here on out.

She looked around the chamber and spotted another tunnel running deeper into the mountain. Following the tunnel, she came to another chamber a little ways back. This chamber contained several stacked beds with very rickety frames. She assumed this must have been where the miners would have slept, but as she got closer, she noticed the lumps that were lying on each bed. She pulled back an old oilcloth cover, which pretty much fell *apart in her hand, and jumped back startled*

Stacked on the bed were two mummified bodies. They were brown with age and appeared to be women. She recovered and checked the other beds. The bodies were stacked on top of each other, several to a bed. They all appeared to be naked. She counted fifteen bodies, which seemed odd. Her grandfather's treasure box contained sixteen trinkets. She wondered where the sixteenth body was. She spent a few minutes examining the bodies without touching them, and she could make out lots of tiny cut marks in the now withered skin.

She had never asked her grandfather how he had disposed of the bodies after he was finished with them. The sight before her put an end to any speculation. The answer was he didn't, which is most likely the reason he had never been suspected of a crime. No bodies were ever discovered, so no crime was committed. It made sense.

She threw what was left of the oilcloth tarps back over the bodies, and left the chamber. She found the old kerosene stove and the lanterns as she was walking back through the first chamber, but she had no idea how to work them, so she decided she would bring down a couple of lanterns. She could make improvements to the space when she came home from school for her next break. She climbed up the ladder, remembering to wipe the rungs clean of her fingerprints. Once back above ground, she closed the hatch and wiped the old hasp.

She had been carrying with her, the entire summer, an old padlock that she found in her grandfather's garage, and she hooked it through the hasp. She figured an old lock would draw less attention than a new one if someone found the hatch. She replaced the floorboards, and then covered the floor with the debris she had removed earlier. Satisfied and very excited, she headed for the trailhead and her car.

CHAPTER THIRTY-SIX

Once the Sheriff felt confident that there were no other threats in the area, he released the SWAT teams. Each group headed back in the direction they came. The mood was somber, and there was little conversation as they departed the scene. The kids had been taken out, along with PIS, on the first ATV run. The ATVs had returned a little bit ago and were waiting for Dr. Parker to release the bodies so they could transport them back to the trailhead and the awaiting ambulances.

The Sheriff spent a few minutes in conversation with Buck, and then with a hearty handshake, thanked him profusely for his help the past couple days. The forensic techs had taken Buck's rifle, along with the rifles of Manning and Sanchez. They would now be evidence. Manning and Sanchez would be placed on paid leave until the investigation into the shooting was over.

The Sheriff asked Buck to stop by the Sheriff's office as soon as he could and write out a statement. Since Buck was not going to be part of the investigation, the Sheriff released him, and he and the two deputies started the long walk back to their cars, which were up at the original trailhead.

As they approached the first crime scene, they ran into Moe Steiner and Jane Fitzpatrick. They had hiked back to the scene of Susan Corey's death, one last time, and were getting ready to head back to the trailhead when they heard all the explosions and shooting. The SWAT team passed them a while before, and they started to follow in the same direction. The Sheriff had called Fitz a little bit ago and asked them to head his way.

Fitz waved to Buck as they approached. "Crazy day, huh?" she said.

Buck and the deputies filled her in on what had transpired. Moe opened his notebook when the conversation began, and he was taking notes as the conversation progressed. Buck told them about PIS's conjecture that the older victim might have had military training, maybe having spent time in Vietnam, and Moe made a note to contact the military. He also told them about the gravesite that the young girl Sarah had told them belonged to momma. Fitz pulled out her phone and dialed a number.

Gary Cummings, the elected Coroner for Pitkin County, answered his phone on the second ring. He exchanged pleasantries with Fitz, and then Fitz asked him if they were able to exhume a body that was buried in the woods without an exhumation order. Gary explained that since it was part of the investigation, they should have no issue, but that he would issue an exhumation order anyway, just in case. She would be covered. Fitz thanked him and hung up.

Buck wished her and Moe good luck and told them to call if they needed anything, and he and the two deputies continued up the trail. Sanchez still seemed to be having issues with the death of the two boys. It was true that they were killed while trying to kill Buck and the deputies, but he was still having a hard time dealing with it.

When they reached their cars, Buck thanked the two deputies for all their help and told them to call if they needed anything. He held Sanchez back a minute and reached into the glove box of his car. He handed Sanchez a business card for Susan Lewis, Psychologist.

"If you need someone to talk to, give her a call," Buck said.

"She is terrific, and she helped me a lot after the shootout in Durango. Tell her I sent you."

Sanchez looked at the card and was about to say something when he hesitated and put the card in his pocket. "Thanks, Buck. I might give her a call."

They shook hands, and Sanchez headed for his car and a couple of days off. Buck slid into his Jeep after putting his gear in the back and just sat for a minute and enjoyed the quiet. He had mixed feelings about not being involved in the investigation, but he also knew that Steiner and Fitzpatrick were very good at their jobs, and he had no doubt they would get to the bottom of it.

He thought about the kids for a minute, and what a strange situation he had walked into. He would check on them in a couple of days and make sure they were good. He pulled out his phone and called his boss.

Kevin Jackson, the Director of the Colorado Bureau of Investigation, answered.

"Hey, Buck. I was ready to file a missing person's report on you. You okay?"

"Yes, sir. It's been a hard couple days," Buck replied.

The Director, no surprise to Buck, had been kept apprised of the entire chain of events by the Sheriff and told Buck he was proud of him. He was also sad that it was Buck that was the one to find the body of Ranger Susan Corey

Buck filled the Director in on the latest events. He told him about the explosives, and about the shootout, the two dead kids, and about the other kids, they found in the mine. When he was finished, there was a long silence on the other end of the phone.

The Director said, "Two dead kids, that's rough. You going to be okay, or you need to talk to someone? And another shootout. Is there something you're not telling me?"

"No, sir," replied Buck. "My head is on straight. Besides, I still have the number for the Psychologist you had me see after Durango. Things are good."

Buck changed the subject. "I am going to stick around here for a couple of days. I need to fill out a statement for the Sheriff and be available for the shooting investigators. May get in a little fishing while I am here."

"Okay. Call if you need anything." The Director hung up.

Buck was an avid fly fisherman, and he tried to get in a little fishing whenever he could. Besides the statement he needed to give the Sheriff, he also wanted to head over to the hospital to check on PIS. He started the car and pulled out of the lot.

CHAPTER THIRTY-SEVEN

PIS had just come out of surgery when Buck arrived at the hospital. He was in recovery and still a bit groggy when Buck badged his way past the charge nurse and walked into the room. PIS looked up and smiled when he saw Buck.

"Agent Taylor, how good of you to come by."

Buck stood by the side of the bed. "You look pretty good for a guy just had surgery. They taking good care of you?"

"Surgeon says I should be able to get out of here in a day or two. The piece of wood only penetrated about three inches, and it didn't hit anything vital. Going to be sore for a while."

"Good to hear," said Buck. He shook PIS's hand. "You need anything you call me. I owe you."

PIS just nodded his head and then sunk back into the pillow and closed his eyes. Buck left his business card on the table next to the bed and walked out the door. His next stop was the Sheriff's office.

He left the hospital, turned left onto Route 15, and turned right onto Main Street. He reached the Sheriff's office in about five minutes and pulled into the parking lot. He walked into the office, presented his ID to the desk officer, and was buzzed through. He headed down the hall to see if the Sheriff had gotten back from the crime scene yet.

The Sheriff was sitting behind his desk. He was talking to a deputy who was seated in one of his visitor's chairs, but he waved Buck in. The deputy stood up, nodded to Buck, and walked out the door. Buck took a seat.

"Statement could have waited till tomorrow, Buck."

"That's okay. Want to get it down on paper while it's still fresh in my mind," replied Buck.

They spent a few minutes discussing the events that had transpired, and Buck told the Sheriff he had visited PIS at the hospital, and not surprisingly, he looked like he was hardly bothered by the whole thing. They chatted about PIS for a few minutes and speculated on the source of the scars they had seen on his back. He certainly was an interesting fellow.

The Sheriff stepped around his desk and shook Buck's hand. He thanked him for his help and led the way to the conference room down the hall. He found a pad of paper and a pen and told Buck to take his time. The Sheriff walked out and closed the door. Buck started writing, and by the time he was finished, two hours later, he had written a small novel. Buck prided himself on details, and he double and triple checked his statement before he stood up to find the Sheriff.

The Sheriff was on the phone, so Buck set the pad down on his desk and turned to walk out. The Sheriff held the phone against his chest and called after him.

"Funeral procession for Susan Corey is tomorrow afternoon. We are starting from the hospital parking lot at 1 PM. The family is not planning a church service, so the procession will head from here to the cemetery in Glenwood Springs for a graveside service. Thought you might like to be there."

Buck thanked the Sheriff and headed for his hotel. He needed a shower and a bunch of sleep. Buck was surprised that it was so dark when he walked out the front door of the Sheriff's office. He hadn't realized he had spent so much time writing his statement. He swung by a local deli that was still open, grabbed a sandwich and a bottle of Coke and headed for his hotel.

He had just opened the door to his hotel room when his phone rang. He recognized the number and answered the call.

"Hey, dad. Are you okay?" asked his oldest son David.

"Hey, David. Yeah, I'm good. A little tired. It's been a long couple of days."

"I just ran into a couple of the Gunnison County SWAT guys in the bar, and they said you were involved in another shoot-out. For real?"

Buck took a few minutes and gave David the Reader's Digest version of the events of the last couple of days. About the hunt for Susan Corey, and then the hunt for her killers, and finding a family of children living in the woods south of Aspen with an old guy. He also acknowledged that there was, in fact, another shootout.

"Must have been rough finding out you guys shot two kids. Not sure how I would have reacted."

"Yeah," replied Buck. "The one deputy, Sanchez, took it pretty hard. Gonna take a while to put this one behind us."

"Listen, Dad. You need anything you let me know. And you better call Cassie and fill her in. Her team was heading to a fire along the Arizona/New Mexico border, but she might have seen something about the shooting on the news. I haven't seen the news story yet, but the SWAT guys said they mentioned that you found the Ranger's body."

They said their goodbyes, and Buck hung up the phone. He didn't want to listen to Cassie, his middle daughter, tonight, but he knew she would be pissed if he didn't call. Cassie had quit law school a couple of years back and took a wild-land firefighters job with the Helena Hotshots out of Helena, Montana. Much to her mother's dismay, she had thrived in

CHUCK MORGAN

her new job. Right up until her death, Lucy still didn't like the idea of her daughter willingly putting herself in danger. It was bad enough that her husband faced certain danger all the time in his job.

Buck dialed Cassie's number. Cassie answered on the fourth ring.

"Hey, dad. Everything good? We are just getting ready to head into the woods. What's up?"

"Hi, kiddo. I just wanted you to hear it from me first and not the news. There was another shootout today. I'm okay."

Buck gave her the same quick version of the story he had just given his son. When he was finished, there was silence on the other end of the line, and he wondered for a second if he had dropped the call.

"Did you shoot one of the kids?" she asked.

"Won't know for a couple of days. There were three of us shooting, and we were pretty much shooting blind. The people shooting at us were well hidden."

"Okay. I've got to run, but I will call when we come out of the field. Please be careful. I don't know if I could handle losing you too." Cassie hung up, and Buck just sat there for a minute and looked at the phone. Cassie had been very close to her mother, and she had taken her death hard, even though they had all been expecting it for over five years. When it finally happened, though, it still hurt, and Cassie was still grieving, as were they all. Buck's whole world revolved around Lucy. She really was his soul mate.

Buck stripped off his clothes and jumped into the shower. The water felt good, and he could feel a little life drifting back into his sore, tired body. He dried off and was getting ready to crawl under the sheets when his phone rang. He looked at his watch. Any time his phone rang this late, it wasn't good.

Buck answered his phone. "Buck Taylor."

"Buck. It's Earl Winters. Hope I didn't wake you, but I may need your help with something."

CHAPTER THIRTY-EIGHT

Buck listened as the Sheriff explained the reason for calling this late. A young couple was heading back to their car after hiking along Conundrum Creek and had stopped near an old collapsed mining cabin to have dinner. They noticed a terrible smell like rotting flesh, or spoiled meat drifting around the cabin. They took a cursory look around the clearing, but couldn't find anything.

The smell was enough to run them off, and they headed back to the main trail. They ran into a couple of the Sheriff's SWAT guys in the parking lot and told them what they had encountered. The two SWAT deputies followed them back down the trail to the turnoff for the side trail and smelled it almost immediately.

They followed the trail up to the old cabin, and after looking around, they noticed a couple of loose boards. When they pulled up the boards, they found what appeared to be a locked metal hatch. The deputies reported that the smell was nasty near the hatch. Since it was getting pretty dark, they GPS marked the location of the cabin and escorted the young couple back to their car.

The Sheriff told Buck that he was able to catch Judge Franklin before he went to bed, and the Judge was in the process of signing a search warrant for the hatch.

"Buck, my guys are going to be focused on the Susan Corey investigation for a while. I could use your help with this. If it doesn't turn out to be anything, you can bug out, but I would like some experienced eyes on this till we know what we are dealing with."

"No problem, Sheriff. I know where the trailhead is. I can meet your guys there in say fifteen minutes." Buck was about to hang up when he had a thought. "Sheriff, can you get someone from public works to bring a small generator and a couple of work lights to the site? Might help if we are going underground."

The Sheriff thanked Buck and hung up. It looked like Buck wasn't going to get any sleep tonight. He knew he should call Director Jackson and let him know what was going on, but he decided to wait until they knew what they were dealing with before he made the call.

Buck put on clean jeans and a clean T-shirt, clipped his gun and badge to his belt and headed out the door. The Conundrum Creek trailhead was about a ten-minute drive through town, so he jumped on Main Street and headed southeast until he reached Route 15. He turned south on Route 15, and a few minutes later turned right at the turnoff for the Conundrum Creek trailhead. He pulled into the space behind two Pitkin County Sheriff's cars.

Buck climbed out of his car and walked around to the rear and opened the hatch. Just to be on the safe side, he slipped his ballistic vest over his shoulders and zipped it up. He put fresh batteries in his flashlight and added three more clips for his 45-caliber pistol in their respective pouches. He added his nylon CBI windbreaker and his CBI ball cap. He locked the rear hatch and headed to the small group of deputies assembled just at the entrance to the trailhead.

Buck shook hands with the four SWAT deputies. Sergeant Jamie Winters, the Sheriff's daughter, would be the lead officer on this little excursion into the unknown. She apologized for dragging Buck out after what he had been through, but she appreciated his help. Buck nodded and suggested they get moving.

It took about an hour in the dark to get to the almost hidden turnoff for the cabin. Without the GPS, Buck doubted they would have ever found it in the dark. He stopped for a minute and checked the air. There was definitely a foul smell in the air. The SWAT officers led the way, and they all commented on the smell as they got closer to the cabin. Buck had a lot more experience than the young SWAT officers, and he was willing to bet good money that they were going to find a dead body. The smell was unmistakable.

The old cabin was just as the Sheriff had described. The old timbers were laying every which way, and most of what lay on the ground were rotten from years of being in the weather. Even the remaining floorboards had seen better days, and Buck saw where the first deputy on the scene had pulled up one of the floorboards. The metal hatch lay below the floorboards, so Buck and the deputies removed the debris and pulled up the remaining floorboards.

Once they exposed the metal hatch, Buck took a few pictures of it from different angles with his cell phone camera. The hatch was covered in rust and still appeared to be sound, so Buck didn't think the metal had rusted through. The smell was intense. Buck took a picture of the padlock while it was still locked. It was definitely not a new padlock. It reminded him of the padlocks his father used to lock up his toolboxes.

Satisfied with the pictures, he switched over to video and asked the deputy with the bolt cutters to cut the lock and remove it. Buck videoed the entire process. Buck stepped back away from the hatch and snapped open the thumb break on his holster. He rested his hand on his gun. The SWAT deputies raised their weapons to the ready position, and Jamie Winters removed the padlock and lifted the hatch, making sure she stayed out of the line of fire from her team.

The smell was overwhelming, and one of the younger SWAT officers disappeared into the woods and threw up his dinner. Everyone stood back to try to let the air clear. Buck took a small jar of Vick's Vapor Rub out of one of the pockets in his ballistic vest and rubbed some under his nose. He passed the jar around, and the SWAT officers followed suit. It helped, but not as much as he had hoped. He was glad that he hadn't put on a good pair of jeans or t-shirt. These were headed for the trash once they were finished. Buck had learned over the years that you can never get dead guy smell out of your clothes. He also knew it would take five or six showers to get the smell out of his hair and nose.

Jamie looked at Buck and asked. "Should we wait for the lights from public works, or should we go in with flashlights?"

"Let's not wait," replied Buck.

Jamie removed a portable electronic gas monitor from her backpack, attached it to a length of rope she carried, and lowered it into the shaft. It would be a bad thing to walk into a mine full of methane gas. She watched the monitor as it reached the floor and then pulled it back up. Nothing so far. Just to be safe, she had her guys pull out their full-face gas masks, and once snug, she stepped onto the top rung of the ladder and climbed down into the dark. She was followed closely by her team. Buck would remain topside until they had cleared the mine.

CHAPTER THIRTY-NINE

The bar was packed, and she had been nursing the same beer for most of the evening. Two of her girlfriends were heading back to college on Monday, and tonight was girl's night out. The noise from the crowd and the laughter at their table made it hard to concentrate, but she was running out of time, and she needed to find the perfect subject.

She had never been able to discuss with her grandfather how he chose his victims. What little she did know didn't help. She knew he chose women who were traveling alone or women who wouldn't be missed, but how did he know. There were well over two hundred people in the bar tonight, and she was having trouble focusing on one or two who might make the cut.

Getting asked to dance every couple songs didn't help either, and her girlfriends kept getting on her case about not drinking. She still had doubts that she would be able to do this. She was still struggling with the fact that she didn't have any of the signs that came with being a serial killer. She had spent time over the summer in the library reading everything she could find on serial killers, and she didn't seem to fit the profile.

Of course, the more she thought about it, her grandfather didn't fit the pattern either, at least the part she knew about him. She wondered how far he would have gotten and how many women he would have killed if he hadn't gotten into the accident that night. The story the family always told was that he was coming home from visiting a friend in Glenwood Springs.

According to family lore, there was a terrible rainstorm that night, and the roads were slick as glass. In those days, the late fifties early sixties, very few family vehicles were available with four-wheel drive. Her grandfather had been coming around a sharp corner, lost control on the slick road, and the car flew off the road and crashed down into a creek bed before flipping over several times and wrapping around a tree. Her grandfather hadn't been found for several days until a county road crew noticed the damaged guardrail on the side of the road.

By the time they were able to get him out of the car and into the hospital, he was, for all practical purposes, dead, but the doctors believed that the cooler temperatures had slowed his body down enough to keep him from bleeding to death. Her grandmother, her dad and his brother Stewart had raced to the hospital as soon as the Sheriff called.

The county had mounted a search for him, but the weather was so poor that for several days the searchers couldn't stay out more than a couple hours. He was lucky the road crew had noticed the guardrail, or he wouldn't have made it. What her grandmother found at the hospital that night was a broken man. The doctors weren't sure he would survive more than a few days, but he surprised everyone and lived another fifty or so years.

His body was broken almost to the point of not being recognized. He had broken his back in several places, and the doctors were certain he would never walk again. Of course, they weren't sure he would ever wake up, so they weren't concerned about his being able to walk. That time would come if he survived. The story was he was in a coma for several weeks, and when he woke up, he was a quadriplegic. Her grandmother had been devastated.

She never doubted that her grandmother loved her grandfather, but she imagined there must have been times when she would have preferred that he had died in that accident. Her grandmother had spent the rest of her life being his twenty-four-hour a day caregiver. She never saw her grandmother complain.

So here she sat in a crowded bar trying to wrap her head around her grandfather's life, and what his legacy might have been had he survived to continue his craft.

She was just about to give up her quest and order another beer when she spotted a tall, good-looking young man who had just entered the bar with some friends. She could feel the excitement build in her very private areas. She wasn't sure if the urges she felt were to make him her first victim or just to have sex with him.

She wondered how she would be able to do it. If she drugged him, how would she get him to the old cabin? There was no way she could carry him; that was for sure. She hadn't considered that part of her plan. This changed everything.

If she invited him into the woods to see something, go skinny dipping in a hot spring, or just to have sex, she might not be able to overpower him when the time came. If he fought back, she would lose. She had never been very athletic. She needed a new plan. She thought about how hard this serial killer stuff was going to be. So many decisions had to be made and evaluated to make sure one didn't get caught.

She turned back to the conversation going on at the table, and she danced a few more dances. Then, in a moment of clarity, she had a thought. Maybe she was looking in the wrong direction. Female serial killers were not all that common, but if she chose a female victim instead of a male, that would throw the whole thing out of whack. If the authorities did discover her little torture chamber, they would start looking for a man. This could work. She would most likely be able to overpower a woman at least until she got good enough and developed her real technique. With all she needed to learn, she needed to make the first kill as easy as possible. She still didn't even know if she could do it.

The initial problem solved; she still had to think about how to get her victim to the cabin. She decided that this first time, she would try to lead the victim to the cabin before she passed out. The hot spring thing might work. She could find a woman to be-

friend—someone who had a little too much to drink and might need a ride home. No one would notice one woman helping another woman who was a little tipsy. It's what women do to avoid predators.

She had been able to score some ruffies from a guy she had dated for a while. She had no idea why he had them, but it didn't matter. He needed money, and he sold her a small bag without any questions. Ruffies were typically called the date rape drug, but the reality was that only a small percentage of rapes were attributed to being drugged. Most rape victims were either drunk or under the influence of some more common drugs. If she could slip her victim a ruffie away from the bar, or even down by the cabin, she wouldn't have to worry about getting the body there herself.

CHAPTER FORTY

T he SWAT team assembled at the bottom of the ladder and assumed a defensive posture. Sergeant Winters signaled the team to move forward, and with rifles at the ready position and flashlights on, they moved down the tunnel side by side. As they entered the first larger chamber, they broke off to either side of the tunnel and covered the room with their lights.

Two of the SWAT members moved down the right side of the room, and two moved down the left. Sergeant Winters and her teammate had just reached the old broken-down bed when she heard a yell from the other side of the room, followed by.

"Holy shit!" and "what the fuck!"

She turned towards the sound and saw, in the lights, what had caused such a reaction from her teammates. The body appeared to be hanging from some old shackles that had been mounted to the wall. It was blackish purple, bloated, and almost unrecognizable. Sergeant Winters stepped over to her teammates while the fourth SWAT member cleared the rest of the room. She looked the body up and down. Even with their masks on, the smell was almost overpowering. The skin was already starting to slough off the bones, and in another couple days, the body would have ended up in a lump on the floor.

She lowered her rifle and pointed to the cut marks that covered the body. They were coated in dry blood and were starting to spread open as decomposition caused the body to expand. There was a dry pool of blood under the body that had mostly disappeared into the dirt floor.

The room was bathed in light, and the three SWAT members almost jumped out of their skins. The other team member who had cleared the room had discovered a couple of battery-operated lanterns on an old wooden table and turned them on. That was when they noticed the victim's eyes. They could almost feel the fear that this person had experienced. It was utterly ghastly.

Sergeant Winters directed two of her members to continue searching the tunnel that they could now see at the opposite end of the chamber from where they had entered. She and her other teammate began searching the body chamber. She spotted the old cabinet hanging on the wall over the table with the lanterns on it and opened the door revealing a rolled-up leather bundle. She left it where it was. She would let Buck, or the forensics team do the honors. Her job was to secure the space.

A voice came over her radio. "Sarge, you need to come back here and see this."

"What is it Eddie?" she responded

"Not sure I can describe it. You better come take a look."

She closed the cabinet, and she and her partner headed down the tunnel following the lights from their flashlights. They had gone a few yards down the tunnel when they saw another room and the faint glow of her team's lights. She entered the room and stopped in the doorway, unable to believe what she was looking at. Her teammates had removed some old deteriorating covers from some old rickety beds, and there on the beds were a whole shit load of mummified bodies. All appeared to be naked and all appeared to be female.

"What the hell did we just walk into?" she asked no one in particular.

One of her teammates responded. "Looks like one of those old Egyptian tombs they show on the Discovery Channel."

She couldn't agree more.

"Okay. Don't touch anything else. Let's go back the way we came. This is a crime scene, and we need to clear out."

She left the room and headed for the ladder, followed by the rest of her team. Once up the ladder, they all removed their masks and tried to breathe clean air, but the air around them still smell like dead guy. They moved away from the hatch, and Buck followed. He gave them a minute to catch their breaths.

"Okay, Sergeant. What did you find down there?"

"Not sure, Buck. There is a fresh body hanging up that looks like it was tortured unmercifully, and we found a room full of mummified bodies. Looks like all women and looks like they were all tortured as well."

"Alright. Let's tape off the area and prepare for a long night. I called the Sheriff a little bit ago and asked him to have the public works guys bring out an exhaust fan and one hundred feet of flexible air duct besides the lights and generator. See if we can get rid of some of the smell. I need to call the Sheriff back. He is not going to be happy."

The Sheriff was still at his desk. It had been a long couple days, and he still had a bunch of paperwork to get through. His cell phone rang, and he looked at the number.

"Fuck, Buck. I guess I ain't gonna get much paperwork done tonight, am I?"

"Sorry, Earl. This might be as bad as it gets."

Buck went on to describe the scene that Sergeant Winters had described to him. He asked the Sheriff to call Dr. Parker, the Forensic Pathologist, and also have the fire department bring out some Scott Pak breathing tanks. The Sheriff asked Buck about forensics. His forensic techs were still at the other old mine gathering evidence, and so were Fitz and Steiner. He was spread pretty thin.

"You want me to call Denver and see if they can spare me to work this with you guys?"

"Sure would appreciate the help. Thanks, Buck," the Sheriff replied.

Buck hung up from the Sheriff and dialed the Director.

A very sleepy voice answered the phone. "Buck, don't you ever sleep?"

"Sorry to wake you, sir, but it's important."

"It always is when you call. Okay, I'm awake. Let's hear it."

Buck described the scene, just as he did with the Sheriff, along with the Sheriff's request for help. Although Buck had statewide jurisdiction, it was always the policy of the Colorado Bureau of Investigation to work with local law enforcement only when they requested help. Buck had, for the most part, always abided by that time-honored tradition. When he finished, the Director gave a low whistle. "I assume you are thinking serial killer? Should we call in the FBI?"

Buck replied. "I'd like to hold off until we know more. The Sheriff's team is spread pretty thin. I'd like to roll the forensics team from Grand Junction and also bring in Paul Webber to give me a hand. He did good on the Montrose thing."

"Okay, Buck. I will call Stan and have him roll everyone. Anything else?"

Stan Greenheck was the Agent in Charge of the Grand Junction office of the CBI and technically Buck's direct boss. However, over the past couple of years, Buck had been working more for the Director and the governor than he had for

Stan, and it always bothered him, but Stan was always good-natured about it because Buck got results and he was Buck's boss. That was good for him.

"Yes, sir," Buck replied. "Do we have any Forensic Pathologists on standby that we can call? Dr. Parker out here is already up to her hips in dead bodies, and I am sure she would appreciate the help."

"I will start making calls. Looks like we are going to be waking up a lot of people. How do you always get involved in shit like this?"

"Just right place, right time, I guess. Thank you, sir." Buck hung up his phone.

CHAPTER FORTY-ONE

The public works crew and the fire department arrived while Buck had been on the phone with the Director. Sergeant Winters and her team were helping them set up the generator, and two of her guys went back down into the mine to string up some temporary lights. The smell in the area around the shaft had dissipated a little, and it was easier to breathe.

Buck's phone rang, and he answered. "Hey, Paul. Sorry to get you out of bed."

"No worries, Buck. Don't usually get a call from the Director at three o'clock in the morning. He filled me in, but I wanted to check with you before I left Grand Junction to see if there was anything else you needed from here?"

"Thanks, Paul. No, I think we have everything covered. Get here when you can, but don't kill yourself. We aren't going anywhere anytime soon. Oh, and Paul. Wear your oldest clothes. Something you won't have a problem throwing away when we are done."

"That bad, huh?" Paul replied.

"Yeah. That bad. See you soon." Buck hung up. It was time to head down into the mine. Buck was glad he wasn't claustrophobic. This would be a bad week to have that problem. Buck walked over to the two firemen who had brought in the Scott Pak breathing apparatus, and they helped him put on one of the tanks. Buck was familiar with the system and had used one on several occasions.

Buck checked his cell phone battery to make sure he had enough juice for pictures and climbed down into the shaft. His first mental note was to have forensics check the hatch cover side walls and ladder rungs for prints. He stepped foot on the dirt floor and was pleased to see that the lights were working just fine.

Sergeant Winters stepped foot on the floor next to him and told him to follow her. She proceeded down the short tunnel and into the first chamber. With the lights on, it wasn't nearly as foreboding. Buck asked her to hold up as he took out his cell phone and took a couple of overall pictures of the chamber. They then proceeded over to the body.

Buck took multiple pictures of the body in situ. What Sergeant Winters described was even more gruesome under the lights. The body was naked and obviously female. Both hands were shackled to the wall, and her feet were shackled as well. The body was covered with hundreds of slices, some deeper than others. The number of very shallow cuts was amazing and varied in length from a small knick to one across her stomach that must have been a foot long.

"You ever see anything like this before?" asked Sergeant Winters.

"No, but I have read about it. It's an ancient Chinese method of torture. Can't recall the Chinese name for it, but it translates to something like death by a thousand cuts."

"You must read some weird books," she responded.

Buck laughed. It helped to break the mood a little.

"Okay, Sergeant. Let's see the rest."

Sergeant Winters showed him the bed, which he photographed from several angles, and then she opened the cabinet to reveal the leather roll. Buck took pictures of the roll and then removed it from the cabinet and laid it on the old wooden table. While he did that, he also took pictures of the

LED lanterns that were on the table. They appeared to be fairly new.

Buck switched his phone camera to video and asked the Sergeant to open up the roll. She untied the two leather strings and unrolled the bundle. She stepped back as Buck panned his camera along the length of the bundle, and then he put his phone away.

"Oh my god!" exclaimed the Sergeant.

"Yeah," replied Buck. With his gloved hand, he picked up one of the scalpels and brought it closer to his face mask. "Beautiful workmanship," he said.

He placed it back in the bundle and stepped aside as the other two SWAT members pulled the flexible duct past him. He heard the exhaust fan fire up, and almost immediately, the air seemed to get better. Buck lifted off his facemask and took a breath. He could work in here now without the Scott Pak. He lifted it over his shoulders and set it on the ground turning off the airflow. Sergeant Winters did the same thing.

Buck left the bundle laid out on the table and followed the Sergeant down the next tunnel. They stepped into another small chamber, and sure enough, there were four rickety wooden bunk beds, and on each bed were several mummi-fied bodies. Buck pulled out his phone and photographed each bed and then a couple of overall shots of the room it-self. He walked around the room, stopping at each bed and looked at each body.

Even with the mummification, he could see that these women had all been tortured with the same method as the newest victim in the other room.

Sergeant Winters voiced the question he had been form-ing in his mind.

"It looks like these women all died the same way as the woman out front, but these bodies look positively ancient.

Can't be the same killer, can it?"

Buck looked at her. "Excellent question, Sergeant. I would think not, but the methods look very similar." He turned around and headed back to the front chamber. Dr. Parker had just entered the room and was looking at the body hanging off the shackles. She looked at Buck.

"Remind me the next time you come to town to take a vacation, okay?" She smiled, and Buck and the Sergeant laughed. He knew she was partly serious.

They followed the same path as he and the Sergeant had followed earlier and returned to the front chamber. Dr. Parker looked depressed. She had never performed an autopsy on a mummy before, and now she had fifteen of them. She told Buck that CBI Director Jackson had called her on the way over and told her he was flying in several experts on mummies from the Museum of Nature & Science in Denver. He also had two more Forensic Pathologists en route, and they should be here in a couple of hours.

"Alright," said Dr. Parker. "Let's start with the newest body."

She and Buck gloved up, and she approached the body. Dr. Parker was very thorough as she probed the body, examining every cut mark. After about forty minutes, she stepped back and removed her gloves.

CHAPTER FORTY-TWO

She had spotted the girl about an hour before, while she was dancing with that hunky Rusty Grover. The girl was moving past the empty tables and sneakily drinking what was left in the empty glasses. She could see the girl was getting pretty loaded.

The girl was cute, with shoulder-length blond hair pulled back in a ponytail. She had a faded blue streak in her hair on the right side. She was wearing a pair of ripped jeans, an old sweater and sneakers that had seen better days. The girl made it through several empty tables before the bouncer came and spoke a few words to her and escorted her out the front door and into the street.

She excused herself from the group and headed for the restroom but veered off, and after checking to make sure her friends didn't see her leave, she walked out the front door. The night had gotten a lot cooler than it had been a few hours ago, and she shivered as she pulled her jacket tighter around her.

She wasn't sure if she was that cold or if her nerves were kicking in. Was she really about to do this? She still had doubts about her role as a killer. On some level, it felt right, but on other levels, she wondered if she was just doing this because she was fascinated by her grandfather. She always looked up to him, and finding out he had killed several women in his younger years didn't change her opinion of him.

She got into her car and pulled out of the parking lot. She had no idea where the girl had gone, so she started driving up and down the streets and alleys. She had only gone through two alleys when she found her behind one of the hotels looking in the dumpsters and then staggering down the alley.

The girl looked a little startled when she pulled up next to her and rolled down the window. She asked the girl if she would like to get some real food, and as it penetrated through her booze fogged mind, the girl told her that she would like that. The girl climbed into the passenger seat, put her head back into the headrest, and fell asleep.

She stopped at the all-night convenience store and bought the girl a burrito and a bottle of water. She slipped the ruffie into the bottle of water and shook it up to make sure it dissolved. The girl was still sound asleep, so she headed for the trailhead. This might be easier than she imagined.

She pulled into the trailhead and pulled the car as far off the road as she could. Next, she walked around to the passenger side of the car and opened the door. She shook the girl a couple of times until she started to wake up. She told the girl that she had food for her and a place to stay, but she needed to get out of the car and walk with her.

The girl took the burrito, unwrapped it, and started to eat like she hadn't had food in a couple of days. She washed the burrito down with a big swig of water. The girl half stumbled out of the car, and she held her by the arm and started down the trail. She wasn't sure if it was the ruffie or the booze, but the girl just stumbled along with her like a little lost puppy. There was no conversation.

By the time they reached the old cabin, the girl was almost incoherent and proceeded to pass out. She had to drag her limp body the last twenty feet to the shaft. She unlocked the padlock and opened the hatch. She stopped for a minute and listened to the sounds around her. She didn't hear any people, which was just as she expected. She grabbed the coil of climbing rope that she had left at the top of the ladder and ran the rope around the girl's chest. She put on her gloves and lifted the girl over the edge of the hatch.

Even though the girl couldn't have weighed more than a hundred pounds, it surprised her how difficult it was to lower her, and the roped slipped through her hands, and the girl fell the last fifteen feet down the shaft. She hit the ground hard.

She stepped onto the top rung of the ladder and started down, pulling the hatch closed as she went. She reached the bottom and stepped onto the ground. The girl was still unconscious, so she untied the rope and dragged her to the chamber. Once there, she stripped off the girl's clothes and threw them in a corner.

She had trouble holding the limp girl in place and hooking up the shackles, and by the time she was finished, she was sweating. She stood back and looked at the girl hanging against the wall. Her body was thin, and she had small pert breasts. She looked like she hadn't eaten well in quite some time.

She walked over to the old bed and undressed while watching the girl. She laid down on the bed and tried to get herself excited, but it just wasn't happening. Maybe it was the nerves, or maybe, unlike her grandfather, there just wasn't a sexual component to her needs. She decided to just get on with the cutting.

She opened the cabinet and pulled out the old leather bundle. Once untied, she rolled it out on the table and pulled out a thin scalpel. She walked over to the body and stood for a minute. She was trying to figure out how to begin.

Her first slice was very tentative, and the scalpel barely drew any blood. She was almost disappointed. The second slice was across the girl's stomach, and that one drew a lot of blood. The girl twitched. After a few more slices, she figured out just how much pressure to exert, and she began to make progress.

By the time the girl started to wake up, she had lost so much blood that she wasn't able to offer much resistance. She tried to scream through the gag, but nothing came out. The girl's eyes showed the fear she was experiencing, and it made her cut even faster as she watched life leave the girl's eyes. The ground at her feet was covered in blood, and she stepped back and admired her handy work.

She had been keeping track, and she had gotten to almost five hundred slices before the girl died. She was proud of her accomplishment. Not bad for a first-timer. She used a container of water she had brought down earlier to scrub her scalpel and wipe the blood off herself. Surprisingly there wasn't much.

She put the scalpel back in its place in the bundle, rolled up the bundle, and placed it back in the cabinet. She walked back to the old bed and put her clothes back on. She once again looked at the girl. She was pleased, and she felt no remorse. As a matter of fact, she didn't really feel anything. Maybe she did have the killer gene in her like her grandfather. She checked to make sure she hadn't left anything, turned off the lanterns, and climbed back out of the shaft.

Morning was still a few hours away, so she locked up the hatch replaced the floorboards and the debris and headed for her car. She felt exhausted. Killing someone slowly was hard work. She might have to pick up the pace on the next one.

CHAPTER FORTY-THREE

Dr. Parker stepped back from the body and leaned against the table under the cabinet. "Death was from massive blood loss. I counted roughly five hundred slices of varying depth and length. The autopsy will tell more, but I think the cut along her throat might have nicked the artery. But even if it didn't, she wouldn't have lasted much longer than she did. Based on the decomp, I'm gonna guess she has been down here about a week, maybe a week and a half."

"Can you tell anything about the killer from the cuts?" Buck asked.

"Not really. There are a few cuts that look like they might have been tentative. Possibly the first couple slices. What surprises me is that there are no signs of resistance in the cuts. It looks like she didn't fight back or try to twist out of the way. I will bet we find some kind of drug in her system when we get her on the table."

Dr. Parker told Buck it was okay to remove the body. She was going to see if she could do some preliminary work on the mummified bodies in the other room. Buck asked Sergeant Winters to have the paramedics come down and take out the fresh body. She told him that his forensic team had arrived from Grand Junction, and they were carrying in their equipment, and also that Paul Webber was upstairs. Buck thanked her and asked her to send everyone down. He would wait for them here so that Dr. Parker wasn't alone.

The paramedics and the firefighters were the first to climb down the ladder, and some of them openly gasped when they walked into the chamber and saw the body hanging there. The paramedics pulled out a poly body bag and laid it on the ground in front of the body. The firefighter using a cordless side grinder proceeded to cut through the shackles, and they gently lowered the body onto the body bag and zipped it up.

Paul Webber and the CBI forensics team entered the chamber. They were all wearing one-piece white Tyvek overalls with their hoods up, Tyvek booties, surgical masks and nitrile gloves. Buck watched as they each stopped and looked at the body as the firefighters and paramedics lowered her onto the body bag.

"You okay, Paul?" Buck asked. Paul looked a little green.

Paul answered hesitantly. "Yeah. I'm good. Been a while since I saw a body like that. Wow."

Buck walked Paul and the forensic team through the mine just as he had Dr. Parker. He pointed out areas he wanted printed and swabbed for DNA. They ran into Dr. Parker in the second chamber. She had had one of the SWAT officers help her move the bodies very gingerly off the first bed and was kneeling next to the three mummified bodies taking pictures. She looked up as Buck and his team entered the already crowded chamber.

Buck introduced her to Paul Webber and the forensics team. She would be spending a lot more time in this chamber, so they needed to strategize so as not to be tripping over each other. Until the bodies were removed from the mine, Dr. Parker was in charge, and she would direct the forensic team to gather evidence she felt was vital while they also followed their procedures. It was going to be a very long day for everyone.

Buck could see that Paul Webber needed some fresh air, so

he suggested they head topside. Once outside the shaft, Paul took off his mask and unzipped his jumpsuit.

"Oh my god, Buck. What the hell have you gotten us into?"

Buck was just about to answer when his phone rang. Buck looked at the number and answered the call. "Yes, sir, Director?"

"Hey, Buck. I think I have everyone you need heading your way. Can you fill me in?"

CHAPTER FORTY-FOUR

Buck described the scene inside the mine to the Director while Paul stood next to him and listened. Buck told him about the condition of the fresh body and about the mummified remains in the back chamber. He told him about the knife set they had discovered. He thanked him for getting the team assembled as fast as he did, and for the help, he had summoned to give Dr. Parker a hand with the autopsies.

The Director asked Buck to speculate on the scene. Buck never liked speculation. He preferred to have the facts in front of him, but he knew that anything he told the Director would stay within a small circle.

"Well, sir. It looks like we have two different crimes here. We have what appears to be some very old multiple murder serial killings, and then a much more recent kill carried out in what appears to be a similar manner. We have no idea how long the mummified bodies have been here, but we know that the most recent murder occurred within the last week to week and a half. No way at this point to know how the two crimes are related, but from my very cursory observation, I would say they definitely have a relationship."

The Director listened as Buck spoke. He interrupted only once with a question which Buck answered as best he could, and then he told Buck to stay in touch and call if he needed any help. Buck hung up his phone. He was just going to talk to Paul as the Sheriff entered the clearing, followed by several people who looked like grad students and an older gentleman wearing a safari hat.

"Buck, I ran into Professor Frederick Standish in the parking lot. These young folks work with him." Buck introduced himself to the Professor and his team. The Professor shook his hand.

"Pleasure to meet you, Agent Taylor. I am a Professor of Archeology at the University of Colorado Boulder, and these young men and women are some of my top grad students."

The Professor appeared to be in his fifties but seemed to be very fit. He wore green cargo pants and a safari shirt with his sleeves rolled up. He and each member of his team carried a backpack. They all looked like they came ready to work.

The Professor continued. "When Director Jackson called me this morning and described what you found, I was intrigued. He expressed the urgency of the situation, so I gathered up my team and headed right out. We'd like to get to work right away."

Buck asked Sergeant Winters to escort the Professor and his students back to the rear chamber to help Dr. Parker, and they all disappeared down the shaft. The Sheriff followed them down the ladder.

Buck hadn't noticed that the sun had come up, and he looked at his watch. He needed some sleep, but there was a lot to do. "Paul, I need you to head over to the county clerk's office and the tax assessor's office and see if you can figure out who owns this cabin. If it was part of a mining claim, the path might get a little convoluted, but see what you can find out. Second, take some pictures of the lanterns on the wooden table. They look brand new. See if you can find out who in town sells that brand and then see if maybe someone has security footage of the purchase."

Paul zipped up his suit and replaced his hood and mask and headed back down into the mine. Buck found his backpack and pulled a warm bottle of Coke out of the mesh sleeve on the side. He took a long drink and sat down for a minute on the pile of logs that used to be a cabin.

The Sheriff climbed out of the hatch and walked over and sat down next to Buck. The sun had cleared the mountains, and it was shaping up to be a beautiful fall day. The aspen leaves around the cabin were starting to turn yellow, and the contrast to the green of the pine and spruce trees was a magical sight. The summer had been unusually wet, and that meant that along with the yellows, there would also be a large amount of red and orange colors this year.

Buck was thinking about the times that he and his late wife Lucy used to sit on the handicap dock at the park in Gunnison and look out over the Gunnison River at the aspens on the other side. Lucy always loved the fall colors. Buck wiped a tear from his eye. He missed her very much.

"You okay, Buck?" The Sheriff asked.

"Yeah," Buck replied. "Well, what did you think down there?"

"Not sure what to think. I'm worried that we have someone trying to imitate a bunch of killings from a long time ago. Scares me to think we might have a serial killer in our little town. Was also wondering if I should call the FBI and get them involved.?"

Buck looked at the Sheriff. "Let's hold off on the FBI until we know more. I will take care of them. You have enough on your plate right now. How is Fitz coming with identifying the old guy at the other mine?"

The Sheriff filled Buck in on the investigation so far. The Doctor had pulled the two bullets from Susan Corey, and the state crime lab had determined that they came from the old guy's M1 carbine. The woman's remains had been unearthed from the mountaintop grave, but they were waiting on Dr. Parker to perform the autopsy. So, nothing on that front yet. Moe Steiner had taken pictures of all the kids along with DNA swabs and fingerprints, and he was running them through every system available, both state and federal, looking for any matches to missing kids. He mentioned that Fitz had been having trouble getting any kind of response from the military on any possible ties the old guy had to one of the services.

Buck stopped the Sheriff and pulled out his phone, looked up a number and dialed.

"Hey Buck, how are you, brother?" answered Jess Gonzales, the Agent in Charge of the DEA's office in Grand Junction.

"Doing great, Jess. Good to hear your voice," Buck replied.

Jess gave Buck a rundown on where things stood with the Durango investigation, and Buck gave her a quick debrief on the shooting of the Ranger.

"We all heard about the Ranger getting killed. Heard you were involved. You got a drug angle on this one?" Jess asked.

"Sorry, Jess. No drug angle, but I need a favor for Sheriff Winters over in Pitkin County. His homicide folks are looking into a possible military angle on the old guy that was killed, and his investigator is not getting much help from the military. You did such a great job getting us the info on the Green Beret in Durango I was wondering if you might be able to push someone to help the Sheriff?"

"For you, Buck, anything. Let me make a few calls. Can you text me the contact info for the lead investigator?"

Buck said he would, and they chatted for a few more minutes. Buck hung up the phone and pulled up Fitz's contact info and texted it to Jess.

"Thanks, Buck. I appreciate that," said the Sheriff. He

looked at his watch.

"I need to run. The procession for Susan Corey starts in less than two hours. See if you can make it." The Sheriff stood up, shook Buck's hand, and headed down the trail. Buck had almost forgotten about the procession for Corey. He would need to make some time to be there.

Paul Webber came out of the hatch and took off his mask. He had pictures of the lanterns, and he also had digital fingerprints from the girl in the front chamber. He had gotten them from the forensic tech and told Buck he was going to swing by the Sheriff's office and run them through AFIS.

Buck stood up, grabbed his backpack, and told the deputy who was now manning the crime scene entrance that he would be back in a while. They both signed out with the deputy, and then he and Paul headed down the trail towards their cars. Buck needed to shower before he went to the service for Susan Corey. He stunk of dead guy, and he didn't want to offend anyone. He told Paul where he would be, and they parted company in the parking lot. Buck headed for his hotel.

CHAPTER FORTY-FIVE

The funeral procession for Ranger Susan Corey pulled out of the hospital parking lot and turned onto Main Street. The procession was led by a Pitkin County Sheriff's patrol car with lights flashing. It was followed by a Colorado Parks and Wildlife Department pickup truck full of flowers that had been delivered to the coroner's office over the past couple of days. The pickup was followed by the black hearse bearing the flag-draped coffin carrying the body of Susan Corey. Behind the hearse was the Sheriff, and then a contingent of over one hundred cars and emergency vehicles from Pitkin County as well as several of the towns and counties surrounding Aspen.

Buck pulled out of the parking lot as the last emergency vehicle passed in front of him. He had gotten back to the hotel and taken three showers to try to get rid of the smell. He wore his cleanest pair of jeans and a clean T-shirt. He hadn't expected to be here this long, so he hadn't packed anything more than the three days supply of clothes in his GO bag.

The procession traveled along Main Street and then turned onto Highway 82. Buck was amazed at the outpouring of love and support as they traveled through town. All along the sides of the road, people were standing and waving American flags. Even after the highway had begun, there were crowds of people on the road. Susan Corey was getting a hero's send-off. Something she very much deserved.

As the procession crossed the line between Pitkin and Garfield Counties, several Garfield County Sheriff's patrol cars and emergency vehicles joined the procession. The procession turned off Highway 82 and proceeded up Grand Avenue to the Rosebud Cemetery. The procession stopped behind a black limousine, and everyone exited their vehicles and lined up along both sides of the pathway leading to Susan Corey's grave.

Buck felt a little underdressed with all the spit and polished class "A" uniforms that were lined up on the walkway, so he walked behind the honor guard and stood off to one side. Miguel Vargas, the Chief Ranger for the Glenwood Springs office of the Colorado Parks and Wildlife Department, stepped up onto the path. He was dressed in his class "A" uniform, forest green pants and short jacket, tan shirt with a green tie, and his green "Smokey the Bear" hat. He was escorting an older woman and man whom Buck figured must be her parents. Behind him, a female Ranger, also in Class "As" escorted a young man in a dark suit. This must be her son.

The flag-draped casket was carried by six CPW Rangers and followed the family. Everyone along the path stood at attention and saluted as the casket went by. Buck placed his hand over his heart. He was surprised as a shadow crossed his side, and he turned to find PIS standing next to him. His right arm was in a sling, and he was dressed as always, except today instead of a bright red cummerbund and ascot, PIS was wearing a forest green cummerbund and ascot. He stood alongside Buck and placed his hand over his heart.

To say Buck was surprised to see the Brit was an understatement. He just had surgery yesterday, and here he was looking like his old self, except for the sling. Buck also noticed that the hole made by the piece of wood that had pierced his linen coat was sporting a brand-new black patch.

The casket reached the gravesite, and everyone along the

path filled in around the family who were sitting in the front row. Miguel Vargas gave a moving eulogy, and several Rangers from her office also spoke about Susan Corey. A local chaplain continued with the service. Buck gathered from the service that Susan Corey was not a religious person. It was a beautiful service under a clear blue Colorado sky, but it didn't have much of a religious tone to it.

The chaplain finished the service, and the six Rangers who had been part of the honor guard folded the American flag and presented it to Susan Corey's mother. In the distance, a bugler played taps. The family stood and headed back to the limo, and Vargas announced that there would be food and drinks available at the CPW office. Buck and PIS followed the crowd, and Buck offered PIS a ride to the CPW office, which he accepted.

Once in the car, Buck looked at PIS. "Surprised to see you here today. Did you escape from the hospital?" he asked.

"Doctor said I was a miraculous patient and that I could leave whenever I was ready. Couldn't stand being locked up inside that long. The sheriff was nice enough to give me a ride up here. It was quite a moving procession."

Buck agreed, and they headed over to the CPW office for refreshment. In the parking lot of the CPW building was a huge white tent, so Buck and PIS headed that way. Once inside, they each grabbed a sandwich and a bottle of water and began milling about. Buck was amazed at how many people showed up, and PIS was amazed at how many of those people Buck knew.

Buck and PIS walked over to the table where the family was sitting, and Miguel Vargas stood and introduced Buck and PIS to Susan Corey's parents and her son. He mentioned that they had been instrumental in finding Susan and her parents thanked them profusely. Buck was a little embarrassed, but PIS was his jovial self and launched into a lengthy conversation with the family. Buck stepped away and signaled for Miguel to follow him.

Away from the table, Buck asked Miguel how the son was holding up. Miguel explained that even though his grandparents lived in Pueblo, they had agreed to move up here and stay in Susan's house until Jimmy graduated next year. Buck knew that a fund had been set up for the boy and asked Miguel how they were doing with raising money. Buck donated money that morning before he left his hotel room.

Miguel said, "Craziest thing. A lawyer showed up at the bank in town that was handling the donations and gave the bank a certified check for one hundred thousand dollars. He also had a letter telling the bank that a college fund had been set up in James Corey's name at a bank in the Bahamas and that the bank would cover all of Jimmy's college expenses for a four-year degree to any college Jimmy chose to attend. The bank manager had been stunned, but he checked it out, and both the check and the account in the Bahamas are real."

"That's amazing. No idea where the funds came from?" asked Buck.

"Not a clue. Jimmy has a guardian angel, someplace." Miguel shook Buck's hand. "Thanks for everything you did for Susan. You ever need anything you give us a call. We owe you." He walked back to the family and sat down at the table.

Buck watched as PIS shook hands with Jimmy and his grandfather and gave his grandmother a big hug. He shook hands with Miguel and headed back to where Buck was standing. Buck had an idea running around in his head, but it didn't want to land. He watched PIS interact with Jimmy Corey, and he wondered to himself, if it was possible, that the money and the college fund somehow came from PIS. "Nah. How was that even possible? After all, this is PIS we are talking about. But then again, who was PIS, really?"

Buck and PIS headed back to Buck's car. Once inside, Buck told PIS about his conversation with Miguel and about the money. PIS never reacted. He just said how nice it was that someone was looking out for the young man, then he closed his eyes and went to sleep. Buck woke PIS as they pulled into the parking lot of the hospital, and PIS thanked him for the ride and stepped out of the car. Buck watched him walk through the front door to the hospital. He pulled out his phone and called Paul Webber.

CHAPTER FORTY-SIX

The thrill of the kill had started to fade. She had gone home that night and slept like a baby. The next morning, she still felt wired. The response hadn't been sexual, but the kill had still excited her. She felt better and better about her technique as the night wore on. She got an adrenalin jolt when the girl woke up and realized what was happening to her. If only it had lasted. The cut she had made across her neck must have hit the artery. She thought she was shallow enough, but there was a little spurt of blood that wouldn't stop. She would have to remember that for the next time.

She had been hoping there would be a next time before she had to leave for college, but it was not meant to be. She had been back to the bar every night after work since the first kill, and this would be her last night in town, and she had not been able to find the next victim. She finished her drink and told her friends at the table that the next round was on her. Instead of waiting for the waitress, she walked up to the bar.

The woman behind the bar was the owner. She hadn't met her personally, but this was where she and her friends hung out all summer, so they got to know who was who. The bartender/owner walked up and asked her what she needed. She gave her the order for three beers and laid a twenty-dollar bill on the bar.

The bartender/owner came back with three beers and stared at her for a minute. She was beginning to feel a little self-conscious when the bartender/owner finally spoke.

She had admired the necklace she was wearing and wondered where she had found such a pretty piece? She told the bartender/owner that she had found it in a pawn shop in Florida. The bartender/owner looked at it a little closer and then said something that chilled her to the bone.

The bartender/owner told her she had a necklace very similar to that one, but she lost it when she was involved in a car crash many years before. The necklace belonged to her grandmother, and she had borrowed, well stolen it, when she ran away from home. She was in a crash just outside of Aspen, and the necklace had disappeared. No one at the hospital remembered seeing it.

She asked the bartender/owner if she remembered anything else about the crash, but she said that she must have fallen asleep after she was picked up hitchhiking on the highway, and when she woke up in the hospital several days later, she couldn't remember anything about the crash. The police told her that the man who picked her up was likely going to die and that she was lucky to be alive.

She left the twenty on the bar, picked up the three beer bottles, and walked back to her table. She was too stunned to talk. Luckily her friends were doing enough talking, so they never noticed.

She had taken the jade necklace out of her grandfather's treasure box. She had admired it since she found the box, and she decided that it would be one thing to remember her grandfather with. He had been slipping in and out of consciousness for the past couple of weeks, and the family was not holding out much hope. Since it was her last night in town, and she was certain no one would have any idea where the necklace came from, she decided to wear it out. How in the hell could she have ever guessed that someone would recognize the necklace? What a huge cluster fuck.

She needed some air, so she excused herself and walked out the front door and stood on the sidewalk. The air was fall crisp, and it felt good. Her thoughts turned to the woman at the bar. She didn't remember anyone ever mentioning that there was a passenger in the car with her grandfather the night he crashed. Is it possible this woman was in the car with her him? How could that have gotten missed in the family stories? More importantly, was it her necklace that was in her grandfather's treasure box?

She put her hand up to her open mouth. "Oh, my god." This woman was supposed to be her grandfather's sixteenth victim. That's why there were sixteen mementos in the box but only fifteen bodies in the mine. He was on his way to the mine to kill her when the crash occurred. But why had no one ever mentioned a second person in the car?

The bartender/owner did not appear to know who was driving the car that night. She had no recollection of the accident. Her grandfather must have already drugged her when he crashed the car. She didn't know what he used as a sedative, but whatever it was, it had to be fast-acting and very powerful. Powerful enough to induce amnesia?

She felt a chill run up her spine, and then in a moment of clarity, she struck on an idea. One that would hopefully keep her focused while she was away at school. She would finish what her grandfather had started that fateful night so long ago. She would take care of his sixteenth victim. She would need to devise a plan for this kill. It would take time, and it would need to be perfect. The bartender/owner was no slouch. She ran a bar. She would probably be tough to deal with, and she had a pretty good build, even after so many years. She pictured the woman in her younger days and understood why her grandfather had chosen her. She must have been a real looker in her day because she was gorgeous now.

This was awesome. What better way to honor her grandfather than to finish his journey? She felt her excitement build just like it had the night of her first kill. It was a shame. If she only had more time. But that's okay. She would be back at Christmas. She would start working out the plan in her head, and by Christmas, *it would be perfect. She just knew it. Her grandfather would be so proud of her.*

She stepped back into the bar and shook off the chill from the night air. Her body was warm and tingling. She sat back down at the table where her friends were still talking away and took a sip of her beer. She looked over the top of the bottle and stared at her next victim.

The next morning her father and mother packed up the car and drove her to Denver for her flight back to Jacksonville. She hugged them and stepped into the security line. She wrapped her hand around the jade necklace and said a silent prayer that her grandfather would live long enough to see her complete his final act. She smiled as she went through security and waved goodbye to her parents.

CHAPTER FORTY-SEVEN

B uck left the hospital parking lot, turned right onto Main Street, and pulled into the parking lot for the Sheriff's office. He entered through the front door, showed his ID to the officer at the front desk, and was buzzed into the back. He found an empty desk in the bullpen, sat down, and pulled his laptop out of his backpack.

The first step in any murder investigation is the creation of the murder book. This was pretty much the entire investigation in one place and would include interviews, forensic reports, autopsy reports and crime scene photos. It was also a chronological listing of how the investigation has progressed.

Over the years, Buck caught up with the rest of the world and started to use the murder book template on his laptop. In the old days, everything was done with paper and pencil. The problem was that there was only one book, and anyone who needed access had to go to wherever the physical book was located. This was tough since Buck was very rarely in the same place for long. The laptop made it simple since it was always with him, and it also gave instant access to anyone who needed to either review something or add a report.

Buck started with the title page and entered the name of the community and the date. The file automatically opened a new case number, and that number would be everyone's source of reference for anything related to the case. His next task was to build the chronology of the crime.

Buck was very meticulous about his investigation notes, and between the chronology and the case summary, he spent over two hours sitting. He got up to stretch his legs and walked over to the soda machine in the corner, and bought another Coke. His third of the day, so far. He found a couple of boxes of cold pizza in the refrigerator and grabbed two slices and popped them into the microwave. "Hell of a lunch," he thought, as he walked back to the desk he had been using.

Buck pulled out his cell phone, connected the micro USB cable to his laptop, and downloaded all his crime scene photos. He spent the next two hours reviewing each picture and attaching labels to them before placing them in chronological order. His final task was to enter the emails for everyone involved in the case, send them an alert that the file had been uploaded, and was now available for use. He closed his laptop and went to see if Fitz or Moe Steiner were in the office.

He spotted Moe Steiner walking back from the central printer and followed him back to the office he shared with Fitz. He was just about to ask Moe if they were making any progress on identifying the old man from the cabin when Fitz walked in, followed by a tall, sharply dressed black man with close-cropped hair. He wore civilian clothes, but his military bearing was obvious. He had on a nylon jacket with a patch on the front right, and ARMY CID emblazoned in white letters on the left.

Fitz introduced Buck and Moe to Major Richard Cranston. They shook hands all around. Moe suggested they get out of the cramped office and move to the conference room down the hall. Once seated around the conference room table, the Major opened the computer bag he had slung over his shoulder and pulled out a file. He slid the file over to Fitz and sat down.

"First, I would like to apologize for taking so long to get

back to you. I didn't realize the urgency until I received a call from headquarters in Washington. I was told this was a top priority," said the Major. Buck silently thanked Jess Gonzales.

The Major continued. "The fingerprints you uploaded caught us all off guard." He pointed to the file. "They belong to First Lieutenant James Michael Forester. Lt. Forester has been listed as missing and presumed dead since 1968. He was awarded a bronze star posthumously for bravery during the battle from which he disappeared. Although an extensive search was made after the battle, his body was never found. He has been in our POW/MIA registry since that time, until today."

Fitz read through the file and slid it over to Buck. Buck had seen his fair share of military files just like this one as an Army MP. He scanned the file. Lt. Forester had entered the Army in 1965 as a ninety-day wonder. He went from civilian to army officer with only ninety days of training before he was shipped off to Vietnam. It was said during the Vietnam war that the lifespan of a fresh Lieutenant was about sixteen minutes. Forester had beaten the odds and had been involved in several large-scale operations while in-country.

Buck closed the file, slid it to Moe, and looked at the Major. "Why are you here, Major? I am sure the Army has better things for a Major to do than to drive from Denver to Aspen to deliver a simple file. You could have sent the file by email. What's not in the file?"

Fitz and Moe looked at Buck and then at the Major. They weren't sure what was happening. The Major looked at Buck and pulled another file from his computer bag and slid it over to Buck. Buck opened the file and started to read. He finished and slid the file to Fitz and Moe.

The Major sat back in the chair and said. "Lt. Forester and his unit were being investigated for an attack on a village just south of the DMZ. This was right after the My Lai massacre, and the army was very sensitive to having its units running amuck and killing civilians. Lt. Forester and several of his soldiers were slated to be arrested within a day or two of the battle they were in. No one outside CID had been told of the arrest, so we doubt he ran because of it. The information that was gathered during the investigation was that Forester tried to stop the carnage, and he threatened to have the men responsible brought up on charges. Our sources indicated that he took the massacre to heart, and was extremely depressed that he had not been able to stop it. Our first assumption when we couldn't locate him was that he might have been fragged by his own men. We could never prove it, so we were back to, he was either killed during the battle, taken prisoner, or he finally had enough and just disappeared into the forest. Until your fingerprint inquiry came through, we just weren't sure. Now we are."

The Major stopped to catch his breath. Buck looked at Fitz and then Moe. He said to the Major, "What is the Army's interest in this moving forward.?"

The Major thought for a minute. "We have a conflict. He was cleared of all charges and awarded the bronze star. He is also now a deserter, a kidnapper, possibly a murderer and was involved in a shootout with police. He is an MIA who has been located and should be treated as a hero, but the circumstances make that almost impossible."

Buck closed his eyes and scratched his forehead. "Unless Fitz or Moe disagree, all indications are that he was protecting the children he was with. How he got those children is still under investigation, but you are correct, he is still a deserter, and as a former soldier myself, I cannot see the army giving this man a military burial. My feeling is that the body will remain with us until the Army can notify any existing relatives, and if they choose to take the body, that will be up to them. I would suggest the army remove his name from the

POW/MIA registry and close his file."

Moe and Fitz had nothing to add. Buck had spoken from his heart, and he felt the Major agreed with him. The Major handed his business card to Fitz. "We are already in the process of making the notification. If no one claims his body, please give me a call. No matter what happens, I will see that he gets a decent burial, even if not necessarily a military funeral."

The Major stood, shook hands all around, and Fitz led him down the hall to the main entrance. Moe and Buck discussed the Major's visit and came to the same conclusion. They weren't sure what the Army was looking for, but they didn't find it here. Fitz had returned to the conference room, and they spent a few minutes discussing both cases thus far.

Moe had been bringing back a report from the printer when he had first encountered Buck, and he showed the report to Buck and Fitz. The report came from the State Crime Lab in Pueblo. The bullets that killed Ranger Susan Corey came from the M1 Carbine they found at the old cabin. Now they just needed to figure out who pulled the trigger.

Buck was beat, and he said goodnight and headed for his car. He couldn't remember the last time he'd slept.

CHAPTER FORTY-EIGHT

Paul Webber spent most of the day behind the counter at the Pitkin County Clerk's Office going through book upon dusty book of property ownership records, trying to pinpoint the owner of the old mine and cabin. Not all the mining claims were digitized, so it was pretty much all handwork. He was able to find the general location of the cabin on the county plat map, but after that, his trail hit a lot of roadblocks trying to identify individual mining claims in an area that had several dozen claims.

With the help of several of the nice ladies in the Clerk's Office, he was able to narrow down the claim to just a couple, and then he hit pay dirt, as the old miner's use to say. He found the original claim for the land under the cabin and spent the rest of the day following sale after sale until he got to what he believed was the last purchase.

He felt good about what he found since the last time the mining claim changed hands was in the early 1940s. The claim had not changed hands since. Now he was working his computer trying to locate the person who had last purchased the claim. He was just about to give up for the day when he found a motor vehicle registration for one Marvin Bishop Jr. He had been searching for Marvin Bishop, and this was the closest he had gotten.

The only problem was that Marvin Bishop was fifty years old. He couldn't have purchased a mining claim in the 1940s, but perhaps his father or grandfather had. He was able to run a reverse directory search and found a number for Mr. Bishop. Marvin Bishop lived in Castle Rock, Colorado. Based on his address, he lived in Castle Pines, a very exclusive gated community, just south of Denver and full of huge mansions.

Paul dialed the phone number he found and was pleased when the call went through. The call was answered by a woman with a heavy Spanish accent. "Hello, ma'am," he said. "I am looking for Mr. Marvin Bishop. My name is Paul Webber, and I am an Investigator with the Colorado Bureau of Investigation."

"Dr. Bishop is not home right now. Could I take your number and have him call you back?" she responded. Paul gave her his cell phone number and told her it was urgent that he speak with Dr. Bishop as soon as possible. She promised to pass on his number and hung up.

Paul hoped his next task would be a bit easier, but as he dove back into the internet, he soon realized that it was not going to be. It seems that half the outdoor stores in Aspen carried the lantern they had found in the mine, plus, it was also available online through Amazon.

Paul decided to let that search wait, and he pulled the picture he had taken of the victim's face and decided to hit some of the bars and restaurants in town and see if anyone had seen her. He needed to get something to eat anyway so this would be a great opportunity

Since he had been cooped up all day in the musty archives, he decided to do his search on foot. He left the Clerk and Recorder's Office, crossed Main Street and headed south on Galena Street. His destination was Wagner Park, but he stopped along the way to grab a deli sandwich and a bottle of water. Once sated, he continued on his journey.

Paul worked his way through the homeless people in the park and was getting frustrated. The picture was not the best sample of what someone looked like, and the more squeamish in the park turned their heads away when he showed it to them. He found a small group of young men and women sitting together at a picnic table and approached them with the picture.

As each person looked at the picture, one young girl mouthed, "Oh my god," and covered her mouth with her hand. It was too late. Paul heard her, and he asked her to look at the picture again.

"Do you know this girl?" Paul asked.

The girl looked at the picture again. "It looks like Blue, but she left town a couple of weeks ago."

Paul asked her to look at it again. Then one of the young men in the group asked to see it again, and he agreed with the young girl.

"What do you know about this girl, Blue?" Paul asked.

The group didn't appear to know much. She had shown up in Aspen a couple of weeks back and was only around for a little while before she left. One young man said he thought she came from some a small town in North Carolina, or someplace back east. The group kind of agreed. She wasn't all that talkative, and she stayed to herself. The girl who first identified her said she use to spend a lot of time in the alley behind the Jackpot Bar.

Paul spent a few more minutes talking to the group and then thanked them and headed for the Jackpot Bar and Grill. Halfway there, his phone rang, and he answered. "Paul Webber."

"Uh, hello, Detective Webber. This is Dr. Marvin Bishop. My housekeeper said you left an urgent message. How can I help you?"

"Thanks for calling back, Dr. Bishop."

Paul went on to explain the reason for his call and that

he was trying to reach a Marvin Bishop, who owned a small group of mining claims in the Aspen area. Dr. Bishop thought for a minute and then told Paul that his father might have once owned some worthless mining claims, but he would need to talk to his father and look through his father's papers.

Paul asked him to please do that, and then asked for his address and asked if it would be possible for him to come by tomorrow and meet with Dr. Bishop's father. Bishop explained that his father suffered a stroke about five years back, and he couldn't guarantee if his father would be able to have a conversation, but that the detective was welcome to come by at around noon. His father was best in the mornings.

Paul thanked the Doctor and hung up. He felt good about his progress, so he continued walking to the Jackpot.

CHAPTER FORTY-NINE

The Jackpot Bar and Grill had been an Aspen institution for years. It was dark and smelled like old beer and vomit, and it was one of the most popular places in town for the younger set. They had live music five nights a week during the summer, and the food was marginal at best. Paul walked through the front door and almost gagged, but he squared up his shoulders, stepped up to the bar and asked to speak with the manager.

The bartender looked him up and down. "Maggie Stevens. This is my place. You, a cop?"

Paul pulled out his CBI ID card and held out his hand. "Paul Webber, Colorado Bureau of Investigation." Maggie shook his hand. She had a firm handshake. Paul also noticed that she was an attractive woman. He figured she must be in her fifties, but he would find out he was wrong.

Maggie Stevens was in her seventies. She told Paul she had owned the bar since the early 1970s. She bought it with her ex-husband. Paul asked her how long she had been in Aspen, and she told him that she had been involved in an auto accident in 1964, and spent several months in the hospital in a coma. She went through several months of rehab, and when she was finished, she decided to stay in Aspen. Over the years, she worked in several bars until she and her ex-husband were able to buy the Jackpot.

"What can I do for CBI?" she asked.

Paul explained the reason for his visit and asked her if he

could show her a picture of the person he was looking for. He told her the picture was a little disturbing. He opened up the gallery app on his phone and held the picture up for Maggie to see.

"Girl doesn't look too good," commented Maggie. She looked closer, and then she yelled across the floor for the big guy who was setting up a podium at the front door. Boomer was her head bouncer, and she showed him the picture.

"This look like the girl you threw out of here about a week or so ago?" she asked him. He looked closer at the picture. "She looked much better that night than she does in this picture, but yeah, sure looks like her. Found her wandering around from table to table finishing off anything that was left in the glasses after people left the bar."

"Anyone pay any particular attention to her while she was here?" Paul asked.

Boomer thought for a minute. "Not really. She was pretty much by herself until I sent her packing."

Paul thanked Boomer and Maggie and walked back out into the clean mountain air. He stopped a few more young people as he walked down the sidewalk, but he wasn't able to get any more information on the woman they called Blue. He was a little discouraged, but he had made progress. He headed back to his car, but first, he wanted to stop off at the Sheriff's office to see if anything came back on her prints.

He walked through the front door of the Sheriff's office, presented his ID to the desk officer, and was buzzed through the locked door. He found the young woman who had helped him send the prints through the AFIS system and asked her if anything had come back on his prints. Nothing yet.

He sat down at the empty conference room table and dialed Buck. Buck had climbed out of the shower and was getting ready to put his head down when his phone rang. He checked the number and answered his phone.

"Hey, Paul. What's up?"

Paul filled him in on the conversations with the young people in the park, and the conversation with the owner and the bouncer at the Jackpot. He told him about what he found on the mining claim, and his conversation with Dr. Bishop. He told Buck he was going to drive over to Denver in the morning to interview the doctor and, hopefully, his father. Buck told him he had done a good job, and to let him know how things went in Denver. Buck was going to meet up with Dr. Parker and the archeology team, and see if they were making any progress. He was also going to check with forensics and the crime lab. He reminded Paul that the murder file had been uploaded, and to make sure he recorded the information from his multiple interviews.

Buck disconnected the call. He pressed speed dial one and heard the Director's phone ringing. The Director answered, and Buck filled him in on the progress so far. He told the Director what an excellent job Paul Webber had done with tracking down the mining claims and getting somewhere on the girl's identity.

He also told the Director about the visit from the Army CID agent. He relayed the conversation as best he could remember it, and then voiced the same question to the Director.

"I just can't figure out what the Army was after today. I got the feeling that maybe they wanted us to clear this guy so they could honor him. Seemed a little weird."

The Director agreed and then asked Buck a question he hadn't thought of yet. "What's the possibility that this guy Forester has friends or relations in high places?"

Buck thought for a minute. "Hadn't thought of that possibility. I'm going to suggest to Fitz that they take a little bit deeper look into their suspect. Thanks, Director."

The Director hung up, and Buck dialed Fitz's cellphone. When she answered, he told her about his feelings about the army's visit and suggested she look into Forester's background a little deeper now that they had his military file. They talked for a few more minutes, and then she hung up. Buck crawled into bed and shut off the light.

CHAPTER FIFTY

Paul Webber turned off Highway 287 onto Happy Canyon Road and pulled up to the main gate for Castle Pines. He presented his ID to the guard at the gate and gave him the address he was seeking. The guard walked into the guard shack, made a phone call, and returned to the car. He handed Paul back his ID, gave him directions to the address, and opened the security gate.

Paul missed his turn once and managed to circle back and find the home of Dr. Marvin Bishop Jr. Dr. Bishop lived on a quiet cul-de-sac. The house, although not as large as Paul expected, was set back amongst the trees. He could see a nice view of the mountains from behind the house as he pulled into the driveway.

Grabbing his computer bag, Paul walked up the sidewalk and rang the doorbell. The door was answered by an older Latina wearing a lavender maid's uniform.

"Mr. Webber?" she asked. "Please come in. The doctor is waiting for you."

Paul stepped into a beautifully appointed entry foyer with marble tiles and light wooden millwork. He followed the housekeeper to an open door where she stepped aside and directed him in. Dr. Marvin Bishop Jr. rose from his desk and met Paul with a strong handshake.

"Is it Agent or Detective Webber?" he asked.

"Paul will be just fine, Doctor, and thank you for seeing

me." Paul sat down in one of the leather guest chairs across the desk from Dr. Bishop.

"I only hope you haven't driven all this way for nothing. My father seems to be having a good morning, but I am not sure how much he will be able to answer. He suffered a stroke five years ago, and we brought him back to Colorado from his home in Pittsburg. His memory skills are a little off, and he has very little use of his left side."

Paul told the Doctor that anything that might help would be appreciated. The Doctor handed Paul a stack of legal documents and explained that these were all the documents he could find related to his father's dalliance with buying up mining claims in the Colorado Mountains. It seemed that his father had seen the writing on the wall when it came to World War II, and he thought the country would need plenty of gold and silver if it entered the war. He thought he would get rich.

Marvin Bishop Sr. had, over the years just before World War II, purchased eleven small mining claims in the Colorado high country. All sight unseen, and all pretty much worthless. Dr. Bishop explained that his father had never been to Colorado prior to five years ago after he suffered his stroke. He was just always fascinated with the old west and wanted to be able to say he was a part of it. A law firm in Denver, that specialized in mining claims, handled all the purchases.

He went on to explain that his father joined the army, as every able-bodied man had done after Pearl Harbor and saw action as an Army Engineer. Once the war was over, he returned to Pittsburgh and began a career as a mechanical engineer until he retired in 2000, after the death of his wife.

Paul had listened intently as Dr. Bishop spoke, and made a lot of notes in his little notebook that he always carried. He now looked at the papers that Dr. Bishop handed him. The

Doctor was correct. There was not much new information in the stack. He pulled out the documents for the claim he was interested in and looked through the pages. He had gotten pretty much the same information from the Clerk and Recorders Office in Aspen.

"Would you like to meet my father now, Paul?" asked the Doctor.

Dr. Bishop stood up, as did Paul, and they walked down a hallway to a room off the kitchen. Dr. Bishop knocked and opened the door.

"Dad, you have a visitor," he said as they entered the room. Paul looked around the room, and the first thing he noticed was a larger version of the mountain view he had seen from the driveway. He also noticed that other than a hospital-style bed, there was very little medical equipment in the room. The Doctor was standing next to a leather recliner.

The gentleman sitting in the recliner was quite old. He was wearing a white button-down shirt with a red, white and blue striped bow tie. He looked very dapper.

"Dad," said the Doctor. "This is Paul, and he would like to ask you a few questions about some of your old mining claims. Would that be alright?"

Paul stepped up to the recliner and shook a very frail, almost translucent, hand. There was a noticeable droop on the left side of Marvin Bishop's face, but his eyes were bright and shiny. Paul sensed there was still a lot of Marvin Bishop behind those eyes.

Paul sat down in the chair the doctor had brought over.

"Mr. Bishop. Thank you for seeing me today. I only have a few questions if that's okay?"

Marvin Bishop responded with a garbled answer, and Paul looked at the Doctor who translated that it was okay and to please proceed. Paul showed Marvin Bishop a picture of the old cabin from his phone and asked him if he recognized the building. Marvin Bishop shook his head no. The rest of the conversation didn't go much better. Marvin Bishop confirmed what his son had said that he had never even been to Colorado prior to 2000. Paul was able to make out some of his words, but a lot of what Marvin Bishop said was garbled, and Paul could see the frustration building in Marvin Bishop.

Paul was looking through his notes. He asked Mr. Bishop if he had ever leased his claims to anyone or allowed anyone to work the claims? Bishop said something that he couldn't make out. Dr. Bishop moved next to his dad and asked, "Dad, can you repeat what you just said?"

Marvin Bishop looked frustrated, but he repeated what he had said. Paul looked at the doctor, who shrugged his shoulders. It had sounded like Marvin Bishop had said, "wicked smilley."

"Dad, we don't understand what you are trying to say."

The Doctor looked at Paul. "I think he is getting tired. We should let him rest. I am sorry you came all this way for nothing."

Paul stood up and gathered up his papers. He followed the Doctor back to the door when they both turned, startled by the noise. Marvin Bishop was using his good right hand and was banging furiously on the metal tray table next to his chair. He kept repeating the same thing. "Wicked smilly." Dr. Bishop rushed to his side and tried to calm him down, but he kept banging and trying to communicate.

Paul knelt on the other side of the recliner and, in a soft voice, said. "Mr. Bishop, did you let someone work this claim after you bought it?"

Marvin Bishop stopped banging and smiled at Paul, who dug into his computer bag and pulled out a blank piece of paper and a wide tip black marker. He put it on the tray and slid the tray closer to Mr. Bishop. He took the cap off the marker and placed the marker in Mr. Bishop's good right hand.

Slowly, and with an engineer's precision, Mr. Bishop started to write on the paper. The Doctor looked at Paul, and Paul just smiled. It took a few minutes, and then Mr. Bishop reached out and handed the marker back to Paul. Paul put the cap back on the marker and picked up the paper. "Richard Smiley."

Paul shook Mr. Bishop's frail hand and thanked him for his time. He put the paper in his computer bag and followed Dr. Bishop out the door, gently closing it behind him.

Dr. Bishop looked at Paul. "How did you know what he was trying to say?"

"I didn't," said Paul. "I just had a feeling he was trying to tell us something important. My dad, after his stroke, always tried to write down things he wanted to say. Thought it was worth a try."

"Well, thank you for your patience, and I sure hope this helps your investigation."

Paul thanked him for his hospitality and walked out the front door. He put his computer bag in the trunk of his car and pulled out his phone. He called the CBI office in Grand Junction and asked for Agent Ashley Baxter.

"Hey Bax, it's Paul," he said when she answered the phone.

"Paul. What's up? Thought you were with Buck?"

"Right now, I'm in Denver. Have you got a few minutes to do a computer search for me?" He gave her the information he had gotten from Marvin Bishop and told her he would be back in Aspen in couple hours and if she found anything to call Buck.

He disconnected the call and dialed Buck's number, but

the call went straight to voicemail. He left a message telling Buck what he had found in Denver and that he had Ashley Baxter running it down on the computer. He hung up, started the car, and pulled out of the driveway. Today was a good day.

CHAPTER FIFTY-ONE

Buck stopped by the hospital to check on PIS, only to find out that PIS had checked himself out of the hospital late the night before. He thanked the nurse and walked out of the hospital, got in his car, and headed for the Conundrum Creek trailhead.

He was just pulling into the parking lot when his phone rang. He looked at the number and answered the call.

"Hi, Max. What's up?"

"Hi, Buck. How's my favorite cop?" she said.

Maxine Clinton was the head of the State Crime Lab in Pueblo. A former Biology Professor, Max had been running the lab for the past twenty years. She was about sixty-four years old, slightly overweight, and had been married to her husband for just about all her adult life. Buck had seen Max converse fluently and eloquently with college professors and business leaders, and he had seen her drink just about every cop she ever met under the table. She was a bourbon girl and proud of it. She considered Buck Taylor, one of her closest friends, and Buck felt the same way about her.

"Doing good, Max."

"Are you working with Jane Fitzpatrick on the Aspen shooting?"

Buck explained that although it was not directly his case, he was still helping out when and if he could. Max told him that she used an open order for an overnight DNA test to run the DNA from the female that had been buried. The Director had approved it for the investigation into the drug cartel in Durango, but she hadn't used it because that investigation had moved so quickly. She knew this case in Aspen was a top priority, so she went ahead and authorized the test.

That's what Buck liked about Max. She wasn't afraid to step up and make decisions. "Did you get any results?" Buck asked.

"You bet. I just emailed them to Fitz, but since it was your DNA test, I wanted to let you know I had used it." She gave Buck a quick rundown. "DNA belonged to Corrine Everheart. She's a real piece of work. She has a juvenile record that will need to be unsealed. She has an impressive arrest record for someone who was only thirty-five when she fell off the planet and disappeared. Drugs, gambling, prostitution, assault, and oh yeah, kidnapping. She was only out of lockup for five months when she left West Virginia and was never seen again."

"Nice work, Max. I'll follow up with Fitz later today. Thanks."

Max ended the call the same way she had been doing for years. "You're a good man, Buck Taylor. God will watch over you. Stay safe." She hung up.

Although Buck hadn't been to church since he received his confirmation, he always appreciated Max's little blessing. It wasn't that he didn't believe in God. He wasn't sure what he believed in. He didn't like organized religion, but he never held that against anyone. A lot of people prayed for his wife during the five years she fought metastatic breast cancer, but in the end, Lucy still died. Although he was mad at first, he soon realized that in order to be mad at God, he first had to believe in God, and he just never got there. He always felt there were forces in the world that he couldn't explain, and he always thanked the river spirits whenever he had a chance to do some fly fishing. He just didn't have a place for one God in his life. He never held Max's beliefs against her. He always figured that it couldn't hurt if she believed he was worthy.

Buck stepped out of his car, grabbed his backpack, and started down the trail. The day had dawned a little overcast, and there was a chill in the air. The leaves were changing colors, and almost every day, it seemed, there was more gold in them thar hills. He enjoyed this time of year. Fall was Lucy's favorite time of year, and they enjoyed many fall walks together on the trails around Gunnison before she was no longer able to walk without a cane. The walks stopped when she needed a wheelchair to get around. Then it was just little jaunts on the concrete sidewalks in the park along the river. Even after all this time, he still missed her every day.

Buck reached the old mine cabin just as Professor Standish and his archeology students were taking down their tent and packing up their tools. He had passed a couple of firefighters on the trail who were carrying out the last body bag. Professor Standish stood with his hands on his hips, looking around the site. He spotted Buck as he entered the clearing.

"Morning, Professor. Looks like you guys are wrapping up. How did it go?" Buck asked.

"Oh, good morning, Agent Taylor. We had a fascinating time. It isn't very often we get to use our archeological procedures on a modern site. We learned quite a bit."

Professor Standish went on to explain to Buck the procedures they had followed and some of their preliminary finding. He mentioned that much of what they had uncovered would need to be verified in the lab, but he spoke with a woman at the State Crime Lab, and she was making sure his tests had top priority.

Buck saw how excited the Professor had gotten, and he listened intently, but he needed a few answers, so he interrupted the Professor's debrief.

"Professor, is there any way from your exam to determine if this was the work of one person or several?"

The Professor asked one of his students to bring over his laptop, and he fired it up and opened it to a series of photos. Buck moved in for a closer look. The Professor pointed his pen to the pictures that contained detailed images of some of the cut marks and slices. He pointed out some similarities and also some discrepancies as he called them. Then he stepped back.

"Based on what we were able to see, it is our opinion that all these bodies were killed in the same manner by the same person."

"Any idea how long ago? I'm guessing this cabin has been around since the late 1880s, but obviously, the hatch appears to be newer."

"Quite right, Agent Taylor. We did a little research and determined that the screws in the hatch were most likely purchased sometime during the 1950s. We are having one of the welds tested, but we feel confident that it will show about the same age. The wooden furniture in the mine is from the early 1900s, as is the old kerosene stove."

"How about the bodies, Professor?" Buck asked.

"The lab tests on the skin and the carbon dating should corroborate our findings, but we would estimate that based on several factors, the bodies were killed and left in the mine sometime during the mid-fifties to early sixties."

Buck thanked the Professor and asked him if he could email him a preliminary report of their findings as soon as possible. The Professor said that would not be a problem, and he should have something ready first thing in the morning. He took Buck's business card with his email address on it and headed off to join his students in their packing.

CHAPTER FIFTY-TWO

B uck put on a pair of nitrile gloves, slung his backpack over his shoulder and climbed down the ladder into the mine. He noticed the blue fingerprint dust on the ladder, and he reminded himself to check the murder book and see what evidence the forensic team had sent to the lab.

He stood at the entrance to the first chamber and scanned the area. He had been over the space several times himself, and he knew the forensic team had gone over every square inch with a fine-tooth comb, but Buck had found over the years that no matter how thorough the teams were, sometimes things got missed. It was more important now that there was no one in the space, and all the evidence had been removed.

The space looked different. The bed frame was still there, but the old straw mattress had been removed, as had the little wooden cabinet, and the leather roll of knives. He noted that the team also removed a significant amount of dirt from under the old shackles. He assumed they would be looking for a DNA match, but he figured if they found one, it would have to be a modern connection since DNA hadn't even been discovered in the mid-fifties. He continued to scan the chamber.

Finding nothing else, he moved down the tunnel to the back chamber where the mummified bodies had been found. Here too, the old straw mattresses had been removed. He pulled his flashlight out of his backpack, shined the light under all the bed frames and along the ceiling—nothing much to see here.

Buck was turning to head back to the ladder when he had a thought. He had no idea how far back into the mine the forensic team had gone. He knew the SWAT deputies had done a cursory check just to make sure there were no other bodies around, but he wasn't sure if the tunnel had been thoroughly searched. He turned on his flashlight and headed down the tunnel.

The beam of light from his flashlight was barely holding its own as the darkness of the mine tunnel surrounded him. Buck had never been claustrophobic, but the darkness in the mine was blacker than anything he could remember, and it filled him with dread. Shaking off the closeness of the dark, he continued down the tunnel until he came to the end. He panned his flashlight around the tunnel.

There was nothing to see at the end of the tunnel. Whatever work had happened here happened a long time ago. He had no idea what he was even looking for. Maybe just a clue to who had been the last person to do any kind of work in the tunnel.

He could barely see the light from the back chamber as he turned and started back down the tunnel the way he had come. He was swinging the flashlight beam back and forth and almost missed it on the first pass. He took a step back and moved the flashlight over a small pile of debris that was pushed up against the wall.

A glint from something shiny caught his eye as the flashlight passed over the pile on the third pass. Buck knelt and started to move the debris around. He spotted a flat metal object about the size of a quarter and picked it up. Although it was slightly rusted and dirty, Buck recognized it immediately. It was a partially rounded square with two red swords crossed over a blue background, and the banner across the top said "Mountain." This pin belonged to a member of the 10th Mountain division. He also knew right away that this pin was a lot younger than the mine.

Buck pulled a small plastic evidence bag out of his backpack and noted the date and time. He also set it back on the ground, where he found it and took several pictures with his cellphone. He placed the pin in the evidence bag, sealed it, and signed his name across the flap.

Buck continued his search of the tunnel but found nothing else of interest, and headed for the ladder. Once outside, he closed the hatch and removed the Sheriff's padlock from the hasp.

Buck called the Sheriff, and he answered on the second ring. Buck told him what he found in the tunnel, and they discussed what the pin represented. One issue the Sheriff brought up was the fact that several men who lived in the county, had once been part of the 10th Mountain Division. Many of the men who trained with the 10th, essentially America's first skiing soldiers during World War II, were involved in the startup of America's recreational skiing industry. A lot of former soldiers had settled in Aspen, Vail and Steamboat and were the driving force in opening skiing up to the masses. The Sheriff personally knew of at least ten former members who lived in the county. He would have one of his deputies put together a list for Buck.

The Sheriff asked Buck if he could stop by the office when he had a minute. There were two investigators from the Arapahoe County District Attorney's office who wanted to interview Buck about the shooting involving the two kids. The County Attorney had requested an outside agency handle the shooting investigation since two kids had been killed.

Buck told the Sheriff he was on his way and that he could also have the Public Works guys get the generator, the lights and the fan. He asked the Sheriff to see if they could weld the hatch shut so no one could enter it.

Buck hung up and checked his messages. Paul Webber had called with the name of a person of interest. There was also a call from his youngest son Jason, just checking in to make sure he was alright. He heard about the death of the Ranger, and Buck's involvement. He didn't mention the shooting, which Buck was glad of. Jason was much more sensitive than his brother and sister, and he took everything to heart. He had been very close to Lucy, and he still seemed to be struggling with her death.

Buck called Jason, got his voice mail and left a message telling him that he was fine, and he would call soon. He grabbed his backpack, slung it over his shoulder, and headed for the car. He felt good. The pin in his pocket was their first solid lead.

CHAPTER FIFTY-THREE

B uck pulled his car into the Sheriff's office parking lot and turned off the engine. He sat for a minute, and then pulled out his cellphone and dialed Hank Clancy, Special Agent in Charge of the FBI's Denver office. Hank answered on the second ring.

"Buck Taylor. How the hell are you?"

Hank had been an integral part of the investigation of a Mexican drug cartel trying to set up a distribution network in Durango that Buck had headed. With the help of several local, state and federal agencies, they eventually broke up the cartel's operation and, in the process, made the largest drug bust in history. Hank, despite being a FED, was good people, and he and Buck had a good working relationship.

Buck and Hank chatted a few minutes about the results of the drug bust in Durango, and where things stood with the investigations that continued as a result of their raid. He then took a few minutes to fill Hank in on this new serial killer investigation in Aspen.

"So, the real reason for my call is to see if the FBI has any record of a serial killer operating in Colorado in the late fifties early sixties?"

"Geez, Buck," said Hank. "You don't want much, do you? I will admit that I am intrigued. Fifteen mummified bodies in a mine shaft. How crazy is that?"

"Yeah," replied Buck. "I've never run across anything like

this before. New one on me."

"I'll bet the Sheriff is just thrilled?" said Hank.

Hank went on to explain that multiple murderers were not called serial killers back in the fifties and sixties. That wouldn't happen until the early seventies. He told Buck that it was unlikely their records had been digitized that far back, but he would have one of his clerks start researching, and see if they had anything that might help. He asked Buck to keep him informed, and if he needed the FBI to get involved, to just give him a call. Buck hung up.

Paul Webber was just starting up the stairs to the front entrance to the Sheriff's office when he spotted Buck walking across the parking lot. He waited at the top of the stairs.

"Hey, Buck. Did you get my message?"

"Yeah," replied Buck. "Sounds like making the drive to Denver was worthwhile."

Paul filled him in on the visit with the Doctor and his father as they walked through the doors, showed their ID's and were buzzed through. Buck set his backpack down on the conference room table and grabbed a seat. He removed the 10th Mountain Division pin in the evidence bag from his pocket and laid it on the table.

While Buck opened his laptop to the murder book page, Paul examined the pin.

Buck looked up from his laptop. "Any chance that this Doctor Bishop or someone in his family might have known about the mine?"

"I doubt it," Paul replied. "His kids are teenagers, and he told me that they were all fascinated when they found the mining claim deeds. His father, Marvin Sr., had never mentioned ever owning the claims, and the deeds were locked away in an old safe that had been in Marvin Sr.'s garage in Pittsburg up until five years ago. I don't see any involvement on their part."

Paul went on to tell Buck about the outburst from Marvin Sr. and that it appeared that Marvin Sr. had allowed someone to work the mine. Since Marvin didn't believe there was anything of value in the mine, he gave this person permission with no written contract or anything.

Buck pulled out his cellphone, hooked it up to his laptop and downloaded the pictures of the pin he took in the mine. He then looked over the forensic reports that had been uploaded so far. The forensic team had found some fingerprints. Many were degraded, but they were working through them. They found a bunch of residue on the old mattress and were separating the stains to run DNA. They were not hopeful.

He had an email from Dr. Parker saying that she would be doing the autopsy on the young woman this afternoon, and asked Buck if he could join her. He checked his watch.

His email notification chimed, and he looked to see what had come in. There was a new email from Professor Standish. He opened the email and read the preliminary report. The report covered everything they had discussed earlier in the morning. Buck saved it to the murder book.

"Paul, I am going to drop in on the autopsy of our newest victim. Why don't you follow up on the information you got about her so far?"

Buck stood up and started to close down his laptop when one of the deputies walked in and handed him a piece of paper with eleven names and addresses on it.

"Sheriff asked me to put this together for you. It's everyone we know of who were once in the 10th Mountain Division."

"Thank you, deputy," said Buck. He looked over the list and handed it to Paul.

"Start working through this list. I will call you when I am done at the autopsy, and we can split up what's left of the list."

Paul grabbed his computer bag and headed out the door. Buck walked down the hall to find Fitz when a voice called his name. Buck turned around to find two people walking towards him.

"Agent Taylor. Detectives Young and Lee, Arapahoe County District Attorney's office. Do you have a few minutes for us?"

Buck checked his watch. He had about an hour before the autopsy, so he followed the detectives into an interview room. They asked him to hand his service weapon and any backup weapons he had to a deputy standing outside the door, which he did, and then they closed the door and asked him to take a seat.

Detective Young was about forty years old, Buck figured. He was tall and appeared to be very fit. He had blond hair, which was starting to turn gray and bright blue eyes. His partner Detective Lee was a short Asian woman. She looked to be somewhere in her thirties, and she had dark hair and dark eyes. She smiled at Buck as he sat down.

CHAPTER FIFTY-FOUR

Detective Lee read Buck his Miranda rights, which was a standard part of an interview like this, and Buck declined counsel and signed the paper indicating such. Buck had nothing to hide. They asked Buck if he minded if they recorded the interview, and he told them that was fine. Detective Young asked him to tell them about the events leading to the shooting. Buck knew they had a copy of his statement, and they would use his words now to corroborate what he had put in his written statement.

Buck spent the next twenty minutes describing the events of the search for the Ranger's body, and the subsequent search of the area that led to the old cabin and the mine. He explained about the explosions, about returning fire, and about finding the kids dead, along with the old soldier, who had since been identified.

The detectives listened and took a lot of notes on the pads they had in front of them. Buck finished and sat back in his chair. Detective Young opened up a manila folder that sat on the table in front of him and started looking through the pages.

"Any ill effects from the shootout in Durango? I understand you sought professional help?" asked Young without looking up from the papers. He then looked up and stared at Buck.

Buck was caught a little off guard, but he remained calm. He had used the same technique himself many times. He was curious how they got his medical records. The psychologist he had seen, once, had been at the request of the Director.

Buck calmed his breathing. "No ill effects," Buck said. "I went to the psychologist once, as is routine in CBI for any agent involved in a shooting."

Lee made a note on her pad. Young continued. "From your report, you and the two deputies came under fire and returned fire. Were you able to identify who was shooting at you?"

"Have you ever been involved in a shootout, Detective?" Buck asked.

Detective Young looked a little offended. "My record has nothing to do with your actions, Agent. Please confine your answers to the case at hand."

"As I stated in my report, and also to you just a minute ago. We came under attack as soon as we entered the field. The explosions occurred first, followed by the shooting. When the cabin exploded, I was thrown to the ground by our tracker, who received a serious injury. The deputies identified where the shooting was coming from, and they returned fire. The older man charged out of the woods firing as he ran, and we all shot back. When the next explosion occurred, we spotted movement in the trees and fired. We had no idea that kids were involved until we cleared the scene. My view of the scene at the large tree was partially blocked by the remains of the cabin."

The questions continued along that same vein for a few more minutes, and Buck was getting annoyed. He answered every question truthfully, but he started to sense a bit of hostility on the part of Young. Lee hadn't said much during the interview so far. Buck decided it was time to put an end to the interview. He looked at his watch.

Young kept at it. "Do you have any remorse, Agent, for the

two kids that were killed, or is it just another day for you?"

"Look," said Buck. "No one likes to see kids get hurt or killed. We were in a shootout with an unknown number of individuals. We didn't have time to ask them their ages. We are all saddened by their deaths, but it was them or us. They chose the course of action that resulted in their deaths. Now, if you have no further questions, I have an autopsy to get to."

Buck pushed his chair back and stood up. He turned for the door when Young said. "So, you're a big deal hero cop, and you're too good to answer our questions. You have a trail of dead bodies following you, Agent, and I mean to find out if you're a hero or a killer!"

Buck stopped at the door and turned to face Young, who was now on his feet. He started to step toward the table when Detective Lee grabbed Young's arm.

"Tom, you're out of line. I need you to back off."

Young looked at Lee and then at Buck. Buck had misread the dynamic. He now realized that Detective Lee was the lead investigator, and Young was the pit-bull. It was his job to get under Buck's skin and try to provoke a response, and Buck had almost fallen for it.

Detective Young walked away from the table in the opposite direction from Buck. Detective Lee came over to Buck and held out her hand.

"I apologize, Agent Taylor. You have been truthful with us today, and I allowed the line of questioning to drift away from the reason we are here. You are free to go."

Buck shook her hand, and she signaled the deputy outside the interview room to unlock the door. Buck walked out, retrieved his weapons, and ran into the Sheriff, who indicated for Buck to follow him. Once inside the Sheriff's office, he closed the door and sat down behind his desk.

"Shit, Buck. I am sorry about that interview. I watched

most of it, and if you hadn't stopped it, I was going to. Young was way out of line. The interviews with Manning and Sanchez went just fine. Any idea where the hostility came from towards you?"

"No idea. I've never met either one of them."

Buck and the Sheriff talked for a few minutes about both cases. The Sheriff told him that Professor Standish called and reported that his students were having some luck rehydrating the fingers of some of the mummies, and were working with his fingerprint tech to try to get some clear prints. They had also shipped the samples off for quick DNA analysis.

Buck thanked the Sheriff and went in search of Fitz and Steiner.

CHAPTER FIFTY-FIVE

B uck found Fitz and Steiner in their cubicles. Both were on the phone, but Fitz held up a finger and pointed to her visitor chair. Buck lifted a pile of file folders off the chair, set them on the floor, and sat down. Fitz spoke for a few more minutes and then hung up.

"Hey, Buck. How's the serial killer case coming?" she asked.

"Good. Heading for the autopsy in a few minutes. Did you talk to Max Clinton at the State Crime Lab?"

Fitz told Buck she had spoken with Max and had gotten the information on Corrine Everheart. She told him she had just gotten off the phone with a detective in Charleston, West Virginia, and that he was familiar with her disappearance in that city, and would send her everything they have on her. She was no stranger to the police in West Virginia. He was also going to start running down, missing children around ten years old, and see what turns up. She told him that Moe was in the process of uploading the kid's pictures to the missing and exploited children's database, and was going to send out a national alert to see if they could figure out where she grabbed the kids.

"I heard you had a little run-in with Detective Young. Also heard you kept your cool. Thought you might be interested in knowing that I have the ballistics report. Came in about an hour ago. They only matched one bullet from the rifle you were using, and that was a non-fatal wound in the old man's shoulder."

Buck let that sink in a minute. "I wonder what his deal was then? I felt like he was mad at me, and I have no idea why."

"Shit, Buck. You've been through more on the job in the last two months than most cops deal with in a whole career. My guess is he was just jealous and wanted to see how far he could push you. Good for you that you didn't respond."

"Thanks, Fitz. Hey, do me a favor and ask the Sheriff if you can send a copy of the report to my Director. I'd appreciate that. By the way, does it say who had the kill shot on the two kids?"

She clicked open a page on her laptop and turned the screen so he could see. Buck read the report and then stepped back. His expression said it all.

"Thanks, Fitz."

Buck headed down the hall to the Sheriff's office. He stuck his head in the door. "Earl, you got a minute?"

The Sheriff waved him in, and he shut the door.

"Looks serious, Buck. What's up?"

"Fitz just showed me the ballistic report on the two kids. I just wanted you to know that Sanchez took the death of those two dead kids hard, and was struggling with the possibility that he was the one who killed one or both. I thought you should know his mental state before you show him the report. I also asked her to send a copy of the report over to CBI if it is okay with you."

"Sure thing, Buck and thanks for the heads up on Sanchez. This is gonna hurt him bad if that's the case. He's a good deputy. I would hate to lose him over this."

Buck stood up and walked out of the Sheriff's office. He walked out the front door and headed for the hospital and the autopsy on the girl from the mine.

Dr. Parker was already underway when he entered the autopsy suite and apologized for being late. Buck stood in the corner as Dr. Parker and her assistant went through the autopsy step by step, recording everything she did on both video and audio. Buck stood through many an autopsy in his career, but he never got used to seeing young people on the table. He noted that the girl seemed very thin for her height. She also had other scarring on her body that looked older than the cut marks. Now that the body was washed, the number of cuts and slices was impressive.

Dr. Parker concluded the autopsy while her assistant closed up the Y incision. She removed her gloves and apron and walked over to Buck.

"Afraid there is nothing unusual here, Buck. She died of massive blood loss caused by the cuts. She does have evidence of some superficial bruising, but those appear to be several weeks old. I do not think they are related. She is also very malnourished; twenty maybe twenty-five pounds under average weight for her height. We'll have the results of the tox screen in a week to ten days. I hope they find something because the idea that she suffered through this torture while she was awake is going to keep me up nights."

"Thanks, Doc. By the way. How you doing with the mummies?"

"Last time I spoke to the pathologists next door, they had gone through ten of the bodies and were going to stop for the day and pick it up tomorrow. I will email you a preliminary report tonight, but it will be almost identical to the report on this young lady."

She turned to leave, but Buck stopped her. "Almost identical Doc. What's different?"

She signaled for Buck to follow her, and they headed to the room next door that was being used as an additional autopsy suite. One of the mummies was still on the table, and she pulled back the sheet to expose the body.

"I will tell you, Buck, in all my years of doing this work in LA, I never worked on a mummy before. Professor Standish and his team were incredibly helpful. It was quite the learning experience if you like to learn stuff like this." She pointed to the cuts on the chest of the mummy.

"Professor Standish and Dr. Richland both agreed that the cuts on the mummies appear to be deeper than those on our young lady next door. Their opinion is that the mummies they have looked at so far were mutilated by a man. There was also vaginal tearing evident. In other words, these ladies were raped just prior to their deaths."

She continued. "Our young lady has no sign of being raped or sexually abused in any way. In comparing the cut marks from our victim to the others, they cannot say with one hundred percent certainty that our victim was the work of a man. They feel the cuts were done with a lot less pressure, and some even appeared to be tentative. They were not as smooth and clean as on the mummies, even though the same knives were used. The end result was the same. She still bled out and died just like the mummies, but my guess is it took longer."

CHAPTER FIFTY-SIX

Buck leaned back against the counter and let what Dr. Parker just said sink in. Because all the mummies were women and the latest victim was also a woman, he hadn't thought about the fact that the serial killer could be a woman. He felt a little sexist. Women were just as capable as men at creating evil, but his mind automatically went to a man because of the conditions. The brutality of the torture, the work being done in a mine, the bodies just left to mummify, and the fact that the crimes were committed during the late fifties or early sixties. It all added up to a man being the perpetrator.

Since the latest crime imitated the original crimes in such great detail, his mind just went to the same place for some of the same reasons. The doer was a man. Could he be that wrong? He was going to have to change the way he looked at the crime.

"You okay, Buck? You look perplexed," said Dr. Parker.

"No, not perplexed. Pissed off," replied Buck. "I feel like such an idiot. It never crossed my mind that the killer of our latest victim might be a woman. I made a judgment without having all the facts."

"It's okay, Buck, we all do it. Now you have the facts, so go look at this case from a different angle."

Buck thanked the Doctor for her time and walked out of the hospital to his car. He opened his phone and called Paul Webber. Paul answered, and Buck asked him if he had eaten dinner yet? It was getting late, and Buck realized, too late, that he missed lunch. He asked Paul to meet him at "The Ranch." "The Ranch" was an excellent steakhouse in town, mostly a local joint, and didn't have the same kind of prices some of the other restaurants in town had.

Paul Webber found Buck seated at a booth at the back of the restaurant. Buck had his back to the wall. Force of habit. Paul slid into the booth, and the waitress came by. He ordered a beer and pulled out his notebook.

Buck filled him in on his conversation with Dr. Parker, including the possibility that the latest victim was killed by a woman. Paul looked at Buck with a surprised look in his eyes.

"Wow, Buck. Never even considered that as a possibility. A woman serial killer? There aren't many of them."

He looked pensive for a minute, and Buck said. "Paul. What are you thinking?"

"I was just wondering if our current serial killer could be a female relative or someone like that, who has or had a close relationship to the old serial killer?"

Buck thought about that but held his thoughts as the waitress came by to take their orders. Once the waitress left, Buck took a sip of his soda and looked at Paul.

"Great thought, Paul. Let's put that on the back burner for a minute. Fill me in on your conversations with the 10th Mountain veterans."

Paul opened his notebook. "Of the eleven names on the list, I was able to meet with nine of them today. I'll tell you Buck; it's sad. These guys gave everything for their country, and half of them can't even remember their names. Six of the ones I met today have serious Alzheimer's. Their families let me look through some of the memorabilia they kept, but I couldn't find anything related to a Richard Smiley. Two of the vets still had all their faculties. One guy thought he remembered a Richard Smiley, but he wasn't sure. The other one didn't recall the name, but he had some great stories to tell me. The last poor fella has been bedridden for decades and is in some kind of comatose state. I have two more to see tomorrow."

He read through his notes. "Oh, here it is. One guy suggested I call Sam Brinkman; he operates a small 10th Mountain Division museum in Minturn. He said they used to keep records of the guys who went through training. Might find something on Richard Smiley there."

The waitress delivered their steaks, and the conversation lagged while they ate. Paul mentioned that he had talked to Ashley Baxter at the office, but she hadn't had any luck looking for Richard Smiley either. She was expanding her search to other states, and she was waiting for the army to get back with her. Paul asked if Buck knew how the other case was going, and Buck filled him in on the identity of the man and the woman. He told him that they were publishing the kid's pictures to see if they could attract some leads.

Once finished with dinner, Buck laid out the plan for the next day. He asked Paul to follow up with the last two vets. He took the phone number for Sam Brinkman, said he would follow up with him, and he told Paul to meet him at the Sheriff's office at lunchtime, and they would strategize further. They got up, paid their bill, and headed for the parking lot.

Paul hopped in his car and headed for his hotel. Buck decided to take a walk. The night was cool and fall crisp, and he needed to clear his head. He was mad at himself for almost getting lured in by Detective Young. He was also mad that he had been so focused on the location of the crime and the fact that old mines and rough men go together, that he ignored the possibility that the new killer could be a woman. He wondered if he was losing his touch.

Buck walked a couple of blocks and stood looking out over the Roaring Fork River. This time of year, the river was running low, and it sparkled in the moonlight. He wished he had grabbed his fly rod out of his car. There was nothing like fly fishing to clear one's mind. Once that little fly hit the water, all your focus had to be on the interaction between the fly and the fish. You couldn't think of anything else.

He thought about the times when Lucy use to sit on the bank of a river somewhere and watch him fish. Even though she never took up the sport, he just loved having her there, and she seemed to feel the same way. She would sit on the bank, and later after she got sick, in a lawn chair, and read or crochet. He missed her a lot, and he was also glad she wasn't here right now because she would kick his ass for having doubts about his abilities. She was one tough Latina. Buck stepped away from the river and pulled out the phone number Paul had given him. It was late, but this was important.

"Sam Brinkman."

Buck introduced himself and apologized for the lateness of the call. Sam told him not to worry, that since his wife died a few years back, he usually was at the museum late. Buck explained the reason for his call and the information he was looking for. Sam promised to get back to him as soon as he had anything to share.

CHAPTER FIFTY-SEVEN

Buck had just finished entering the latest information in the murder book on his laptop and was getting ready to look through the latest forensic updates when his phone rang. He looked at his watch and noted the lateness of the hour, but he answered the phone.

"Buck Taylor."

"Agent Taylor. Sam Brinkman here. I hope it's not too late?"

"No, Mr. Brinkman. I was just doing some computer work."

Sam interrupted. "I found some information for you, and I knew you said this was important, so I wanted to get back to you right away."

Buck smiled. "Mr. Brinkman, I didn't expect you to work on this tonight."

"Not to worry, Agent Taylor. I don't have anything to go home to, and I do love a challenge, so I got right on it. Took a bit to find the right timeframe, but I do believe I found the information you were looking for."

Sam Brinkman went on to explain that there was indeed a Richard Smiley in the 10th Mountain Division during World War II. He had been in the training class during the winter of 1943 at Camp Hale in Minturn. Sam went on to explain that when he left the training camp, he was a corporal. He also told Buck that Corporal Richard T Smiley was killed in action in Italy in April 1944.

Buck had started to feel upbeat when Sam called. Now his bubble just burst. "Mr. Brinkman. Any doubt about the information?"

"Unfortunately, not. I have a copy of the telegram from the army to his mom and dad. Sad. He was only 22 years old. War is such a waste of young lives. Sorry, I don't have better information for you."

"That's okay, Mr. Brinkman. You have been a huge help." Buck stopped short as an idea bounced around his brain. "Sir, if I could ask you one more thing? Does your information list where the soldiers are from or where they enlisted?"

"Yes, sir. It lists both if that information was available at the time. You need to remember that this was during the war, so the recordkeeping might be a little messy. A huge number of young men joined the various services during the war. Many were underaged and used fake ID's, and many joined to escape the law or a bad marriage or some other reason. Patriotism was not always the reason for joining the military."

"Can you email me a list of the soldiers who were in the same training class as Corporal Smiley, along with their home cities or where they enlisted?"

"No problem. I will get on it right away."

Buck knew there would be no arguing with Sam Brinkman. Sam was on a quest, and Buck figured he'd have the list on his computer in the next couple hours. He gave Sam his email address and thanked him for his help. He sat back in the desk chair and thought about the information Sam Brinkman had given him. Someone had given false information to Marvin Davis when that person asked for permission to work one of Marvin Bishop's mining claims. Unless Bishop was mistaken and had the name wrong, the person who had used that name didn't just pull it out of thin air. That person had some kind of relationship with Richard Smiley.

Buck started viewing the forensic results when his computer notified him of an incoming email. Buck was wrong. It didn't take a couple of hours for Brinkman to pull together the information Buck had asked for. It took less than an hour. He made a mental note to stop in and visit Sam Brinkman the next time he was in the Vail area.

Buck opened the email and clicked on the attachment. He looked at the list that Brinkman had put together. There were one hundred and fifty names on the list, and he worked his way down the list. He found Richard Smiley about two-thirds of the way down the list. Richard Smiley had listed his hometown as Monroe, Virginia, and he had enlisted in Roanoke, Virginia. He ran his finger down the list. He was able to find six other enlistees with some town in Virginia listed as their home address. He found that seven men enlisted in Roanoke. There were also six more who had nothing listed for the state of their enlistment. He copied down the names on the pad on his desk.

He started to look for the list of the local 10th Mountain vets when he remembered that the list was printed, and he had given it to Paul Webber. He hated to stop when he felt he was just starting to get momentum, but he didn't want to wake Paul. Besides, he needed some sleep himself. He closed his laptop, turned off the lights, and laid down on the bed.

The ringing phone snapped Buck awake out of a deep sleep. He grabbed his phone off the table next to the bed and looked at the number.

"Hey, Hank, what's up?"

"Mornin, Buck. Did I wake you?" Hank Clancy asked.

"No. I had to wake up to answer the phone," Buck said, and he heard Hank laugh on the other end.

"Listen, Buck. Check your email when you are fully awake. One of our clerks worked overtime, but she thinks she might have found something for you. She could not find any kind of active multiple-victim murder investigation from back in the fifties and sixties in Colorado, but she did find old records of six women who went missing around the same time period."

"What makes her think these six women might be connected to our case?"

"According to the reports from local investigators, these six women were traveling across the country for various reasons, and the last place anyone ever saw or heard from them was in Colorado."

"Excellent, Hank. I will pull up the email and take a look at the files. Any chance there might be fingerprint cards on these women?"

"These six have print cards, but remember this was a very transient time in America. After World War II and Korea, a lot of people were on the move. I looked at the files, and most of these women were escaping something. Abusive husbands, bad relationships, and some just had a whim to travel. Not a lot of people were fingerprinted in those days unless they got caught. A couple of them were picked up as vagrants or prostitutes. Not unusual for a single woman on the road. Take a look. My clerk is continuing to follow up, and I will call you if we find anything else."

Buck thanked Hank and climbed out of bed. He opened his laptop, put on his reading glasses, and opened the email and the attachment. Hank was right. Most of these women had lived horrible lives, but the thing that struck him most is that each of these women had tried to disappear. It was just pure luck that someone missed them.

Buck was just about to call Paul Webber when his phone rang. It was Ashley Baxter from the office. "Hey, Buck. I found

Richard Smiley. The Army is sending me his file. Should have it in a few minutes."

"Nice work, Bax," said Buck. "Send it to me as soon as you get it, and thanks."

Buck hung up and called Paul Webber. Paul had just arrived at the home of the tenth name on his list. Buck asked him to take a picture of the list and email it to him. Buck hung up and headed for the morgue. On the way, he called the Sheriff.

"Hi, Earl. Can you have your fingerprint tech meet me at the morgue?"

"Hey, Buck. She is already there. The Professor and the pathologists think they have had good luck rehydrating a couple of fingers on each mummy, and they want to get them into the system."

Buck told the Sheriff about the files that Hank Clancy had sent him and said he would meet the tech there; he was on his way. He hung up his phone, jumped in the shower, and then found his cleanest shirt and pair of jeans. Buck could feel the momentum building.

CHAPTER FIFTY-EIGHT

The fingerprint tech was uploading a print scan into her computer when Buck walked into the morgue. He opened his laptop, pulled up the files from the FBI, and clicked on the fingerprint cards. He slid his laptop over to the fingerprint tech and stepped back to give her room to work. The two pathologists were at the other end of a long row of morgue tables and were working with Professor Standish and two of his students as they ran the digital fingerprint scanner over the hand of the next body.

"Professor. Looks like you've had some success?"

The Professor turned to look at Buck. "Much more than we dared hope for. We used some different techniques that have been used on mummies by other archeologists over the years, and we found two methods that worked better than expected. We are now in the process of checking with the scanner to see if the prints are legible."

Buck was just about to ask about the process when he heard a shout from the fingerprint tech. "GOT ONE!"

Buck and the Professor turned and headed over to the tech. She was almost shaking with excitement. Buck looked at the scan and the old print card side by side, just as she had, and he could see it as clear as day. They had their first hit. He slid his laptop back around and clicked on the file for Martha Collins.

Martha Collins was 22 years old in 1963 when she ran away from an abusive marriage. She was originally from

Appleton, Wisconsin. Her mother reported her missing two weeks after she left her home. No missing person's report was filed by her husband. Buck just shook his head. She had been arrested in Denver in June of that year for vagrancy. She never made her court appearance, and an arrest warrant was issued for her. She was never heard from again. That is until now.

Buck stepped away from the tech and called Hank Clancy. Hank answered, and Buck filled him in. Hank sounded almost as excited as the fingerprint tech was. He told Buck that the clerk found two more possibles, and she was emailing them over to him. Buck hung up and congratulated the tech and the Professor and his team. Nothing they had so far would help them find out who the killer was, but it would go a long way to giving some of these family's closure.

Buck transferred the rest of the fingerprint cards to the tech's laptop and closed his computer. He would let them get on with their work. He headed for the door when he ran into Dr. Parker coming down the hall. She looked excited.

She held up a paper as she approached. "We identified your victim." She handed Buck the paper. It was a copy of an AFIS report. "Her name was Margret Mary Trumaine. According to the report, she was listed as a runaway. She had just turned twenty-one years old, and her prints were on file in New Orleans because she was involved in a bar fight, and had been arrested with her boyfriend. A bench warrant was issued a month ago for failure to appear."

Buck looked over the report and pulled out his phone. He dialed the number on the report.

"Stevenson."

"Hi, Detective Stevenson, my name is Buck Taylor, and I am an agent with the Colorado Bureau of Investigation. I think we found a young woman you have been looking for."

Buck took a few minutes and explained the circumstances surrounding his call. He told the Detective about what they had found in the mine and the hit they just got back from AFIS.

"That's a darn shame, Agent Taylor. That young girl never had a chance. She had an abusive father and an extremely abusive boyfriend. By the time I had contact with her, she was so far under his thumb; I couldn't get her back. She was very meek and mild. Unfortunately, the fact that she is dead doesn't surprise me. I expected her boyfriend would do it, but a connection to a decades-old serial killer case. That's fascinating. You get done with this case you should write a book. Can you send me a copy of the autopsy report for my files?"

"Sure can, Detective. Would you be able to email me a copy of whatever you have on her? I'd like to get to know her a little better."

"You bet, and thanks for the call." Buck and Detective Stevenson exchanged email addresses, and Buck hung up.

Dr. Parker looked at him. "You don't let any grass grow under your feet, do you, Buck?"

"Can't afford to. The dead can't speak for themselves. That's my job. This young girl didn't ask to die this way, and I won't let her death be meaningless."

Dr. Parker could see the intensity in Buck's eyes. She realized that everything she had heard about his dedication and his pit-bull attitude was true. Buck thanked the Doctor and headed for his car. He headed for the Sheriff's Department. There was a bug in the back of his brain, and he couldn't quite get it to development.

Buck pulled into the parking lot, grabbed his backpack out of the back, and headed inside. The desk officer buzzed him in without checking his ID. He walked into the empty conference room and pulled out his laptop and his notepad. He grabbed a bottle of Coke from the small refrigerator in the corner and sat down.

The first thing he pulled up was the forensic reports. He searched through until he found the evidence summary. The techs found several fingerprints, and it always amazed him that they could pull prints that were decades-old, but under the right conditions, there was no telling how long prints could last.

It was obvious from the report that the killer hadn't used gloves, or he had and just got careless. They found partial prints on some of the knives in the leather bundle. They pulled a decent print off a ceramic coffee mug that was also in the cabinet with the leather bundle, and they pulled a couple of usable prints off the kerosene can and the fuel cap on the kerosene stove.

The forensic techs ran the prints through AFIS, and the military, but so far hadn't gotten any hits. This didn't surprise him. Fingerprinting was only used in dealing with criminals, so if the perp had never had any contact with the law, the chances of his prints being in the system were slim to none. He didn't know if the military printed enlistees, but he doubted it. During the war, he imagined they just ran as many men as possible through the enlistment process, with very few questions asked.

CHAPTER FIFTY-NINE

Buck was going through the report looking for the evidence that could relate to the newer killing when Paul Webber entered the conference room. Paul looked exhausted.

"What's going on, Paul?" asked Buck. "You look beat."

Paul explained that he had just spent four hours with two 10th Mountain Division vets in a retirement home just north of town. "These guys love to talk about their time in the 10th. Their stories are incredible. I wish I had the time to write their stories down. Someone should. What incredible men."

"So, besides the stories, were they any help with Richard Smiley?"

Paul opened his notebook. "Both men remember a Richard Smiley, but they couldn't agree if he was killed in Italy. One thought he was, and one thought he wasn't. They had a lot of arguments like that as they were telling me their stories. They did both remember that Smiley was one of the hillbilly boys. They said that several hillbillies from back east somewhere, had all come into the unit together. Said they were thick as thieves, and pretty much stuck together. Said the other guys in the unit used to call them squirrel eaters, and most of the unit stayed away from them."

Buck asked Paul to pull out the list of the vet's names he gave him, and he opened his laptop and clicked on the attachment from Sam Brinkman, the 10th Mountain Division museum curator. Paul slid him the list. Buck opened his notepad to the list he had created from Sam Brinkman's list of the men who enlisted in Roanoke, Virginia. It was a long shot, but then, so far, everything was. He checked the names on Paul's list and then on his list. No matches. Paul could see the frustration on Buck's face.

Buck pulled his laptop closer and started working his way down the list from Sam Brinkman. He had listed only the men who indicated they were from Virginia and had enlisted in Roanoke. He remembered that Sam had told him that some names on the list didn't have that information. Buck had planned to go back to them after he checked out the ones on his list. Now was the time.

Buck found six names on the list that did not contain either their hometown or their place of enlistment. Buck pulled out his phone and dialed Sam Brinkman. Sam answered his phone and listened as Buck told him what he was looking for. Sam Brinkman told him he would get back to him as soon as he had what he needed. Buck hung up.

Buck now took the time to update Paul on the morning's activities in the morgue. Paul was fascinated with the whole idea of fingerprinting the mummies. He was also thrilled that they had identified their victim. The conversation reminded Buck of something he meant to do, and he opened his email, and sure enough, there was the email from Detective Stevenson. The file from New Orleans was attached. The note in the email from the Detective said, "Thanks for the autopsy report and the photo. Definitely, our girl. Heading over to her mom to make the notification. Let me know if you need anything else and good luck."

Buck opened the file. The first thing he noticed was how much the young girl had changed. The girl on the morgue table was much thinner than the girl in the booking photo. Her hair was also shorter now and had a tint of blue color in a streak down one side. Her booking photo showed a girl with bright eyes and blond hair. She looked ten years younger in the photo. She had gone downhill fast.

Buck read the booking information and read through the arrest report. Detective Stevenson was very thorough, and Buck appreciated how well organized the reports were. He stopped reading and turned his computer around so Paul could see it. Paul read the report and commented about a tragic life. Buck couldn't agree more.

Buck had just stood up from his chair when Fitz walked into the room. She looked as tired as Paul did. She filled Buck in on her case. The pictures they had posted on the Missing and Exploited Children's website had been paying off, at least in the quantity of information they were getting, if not the quality. They had a few decent leads on several of the children and had already arranged with the police in Kansas City and Omaha to take DNA swabs of possible extended family members for two of the kids. DNA had already linked the momma, Corrine, with one of the kids. The oldest boy that had been killed was her biological child.

Fitz excused herself so she could get back to answering calls. They brought in several of the volunteer reserve deputies to help out with the calls, many from the news media around the country. Their case had gone viral. Fitz wasn't sure that was necessarily a good thing. She picked her coffee mug up off the table and headed out the door. Buck started to pace when his phone rang.

"Agent Taylor, I have the information you were looking for," said Sam Brinkman.

Buck had no doubt that Sam Brinkman would come through. "Thanks, Mr. Brinkman. Go ahead." Buck grabbed his pen and his notepad.

"Only one of the six names you gave me came from Virginia. Thomas Hawkins listed his hometown as Lynchburg,

Virginia, and he enlisted in Roanoke. Can't tell you why it wasn't in the report. Like I said last night. This was war, and a lot of things slipped through the cracks. I also called one of my contributors in Vail. He wasn't in this unit but was in the unit that completed training just before this group, but he remembers the hillbilly boys. Said they were an odd group, and they stuck to each other like glue. Didn't have any contact with them after he shipped out. I hope that helps?"

"Thanks much, Mr. Brinkman. Helps a lot." Buck hung up his phone and filled Paul in on the conversation. Paul read through his notes. "I spoke with Mr. Hawkins's son yesterday. This is the guy I mentioned who was bedridden and comatose. His son said his father was injured in an accident and had been bedridden ever since. He has been comatose the last two weeks. The doctor doesn't hold out much hope."

Buck sat back in his chair. Something was nagging at him, but he just couldn't put his finger on it. He was just about to say something when his phone rang.

"Buck Taylor."

"Agent Taylor, Frederick Standish here. Do you have a minute?"

Buck said he did, and the Professor filled him in on their progress. They had identified five of the women so far and had just opened up the fingerprint cards for the two most recent reports that Buck had sent the fingerprint tech. The Professor was ecstatic about their success, and Buck was impressed with what they had been able to do so far. The Professor promised to report back and hung up. Buck filled in Paul.

Buck's phone rang again, and this time he recognized the number and answered the call.

"Yes, sir?" he said

"Buck, I just heard from Max that Professor Standish and

his team are having some pretty good luck with getting prints from the old victims. Anything on the newest victim?"

Buck told the Director that, so far, they didn't have anything on the killer. He filled him in on the information they received from Sam Brinkman, and also from the detective in New Orleans on the latest victim. The Director seemed interested in the 10th Mountain connection to the original crime. They talked strategy for a few minutes; then Buck hung up.

Buck pulled up the forensic report on his computer and looked through the evidence collected section. He found what he was looking for on the second page. The techs pulled a relatively fresh DNA sample from the old straw mattress. There was a small stain on the old horsehair blanket that covered the mattress. The note indicated that they had not found a DNA match in the database.

CHAPTER SIXTY

Buck asked Paul if he could run down the street and pick up a couple of deli sandwiches. Paul headed out the door, and Buck spent the time going back through the murder book on his laptop. That little nagging bug was still in the back of his mind, and he couldn't shake it. He knew that solving crimes as complex as this was in the details, so Buck went back to the details.

Buck was still reviewing the photos, and the evidence notes when Paul returned with a couple of Italian subs. They took a break and ate their sandwiches. Buck got up to throw away the sandwich wrapper when his phone rang. It was Max Clinton, the head of the State Crime Lab. Max was excited. She told Buck they had gotten a DNA hit off one of the mummies. It wasn't a solid match, but it was definitely familial. She said it might be a cousin or an aunt or uncle. She forwarded the information to the Galveston, Texas police department since the DNA report had been filed by them. She was waiting to hear back.

Buck and Max talked a while about the progress, and how much success they were having with this case. Nothing related to the killer, but the fact that they could identify these victims was pretty amazing. Buck was just about to say something else when the nagging little bug hit him right in the forehead. He told Max he would call her later and hung up.

Buck sat down and looked at the list from Sam Brinkman

and looked at the notation he had made next to Thomas Hawkins's name. He looked at Paul.

"You said Thomas Hawkins was bedridden and comatose, right?" he asked.

Paul checked his notes. "Yeah. Bedridden for several decades, comatose in the last two weeks. What are you thinking?"

"Was Hawkins injured in the war?" asked Buck.

Paul looked at his notes. "His son just said he was injured in a car crash. Didn't say when, or if he did, I didn't write it down. What are you thinking?"

"What would cause an active serial killer, who had already killed fifteen women, to stop killing?"

Paul thought about it for a minute. "Typically, it would be death or imprisonment." Then Paul's face lit up. "Or an accident that left him a quadriplegic. Shit!"

"Exactly," Buck replied. "Head downstairs to the archives and see if the clerk can find a report on an accident from some time in the sixties that left the victim a quadriplegic."

The Sheriff stuck his head in the door. "You guys are getting pretty loud. You got something?"

While Paul grabbed his notepad and headed out the door, Buck filled the Sheriff in on what they had discovered today. The Sheriff sat back and listened. He was aware of all the activity at the morgue. The thought about the accident he felt was on the right track. He told Buck to let him know if he needed more help, and he headed for his office.

Buck picked up his phone and dialed Virginia Gonzales, the Pitkin County Attorney. Virginia picked up her phone. "Hi, Buck. Figured you'd be calling sooner or later. What do you need?"

Buck spent the next twenty minutes walking her through

the evidence they had developed so far. She, too, was impressed with the work the Professor and his team had been able to do. Science was amazing. Buck asked her about the possibility of getting a warrant for fingerprints and a DNA sample from Thomas Hawkins. Virginia thought for a minute.

"Buck, I agree with your theory. We are a little light on physical evidence linking Thomas Hawkins to the mummies, but I think I can get Judge Donnelly to issue a warrant for the samples. Give me a little bit, and I will call you back."

Buck hung up. The momentum was building. He pulled his laptop closer and started inputting what they had learned in the past couple hours. He also shot a quick email to the Director to let him know what the latest theory was.

Buck hated waiting, but he had no choice. They had a lot of irons in the fire, and Buck just needed to wait to bring it all together. The samples from Thomas Hawkins could seal the deal. He pulled up the evidence report from the murder book and went back to the second page. As he had read before, the techs found what they felt was a fresh stain on the old mattress blanket, but they had not been able to find a match in the national DNA database.

Was it possible that someone related to Thomas Hawkins decided to start down the same road? The mine shaft was not easy to find, and he doubted that someone who just happened upon it, would decide to become a serial killer, or that someone who had the makings of being a serial killer, would go looking for a great place to kill people, and would think the shaft was perfect. Those were just too far in the extreme to be plausible. But someone who knew the original killer and had been able to discuss it. That was more of a reality—especially the methodology of the crimes.

It was not easy to discern from the mummies, how they were killed. As the bodies shrunk, a lot of the slices and cuts had closed up. The only way someone would find out how they died was to discuss it with the killer. Buck thought for a minute. Paul had mentioned that he had spoken with Thomas Hawkins's son. Buck figured that this son would be Buck's age or older. He couldn't recall ever reading about a serial killer who started his career that late in life. Of course, it was possible that the son was a killer for a long time, and had just not been caught, but Buck recalled the conversation with Dr. Parker and about the uncertainty about the killer being a man.

Buck picked up his phone and called Max Clinton at the crime lab. "Hey, Buck. How's my favorite cop?" Typical Max. She always answered his calls the same way.

"Hey, Max. Got a question. The stain the techs found on the old mattress blanket that they have listed as sample 17. Do we know if it came from a man or a woman?"

Buck could hear Max clicking the keys on her computer. "According to the report, the sample came from a woman. What are you looking for, Buck?"

"Just a wild hair. Did the lab do a DNA comparison between the victim and the sample?" More keys clicking

"The lab did do a comparison," said Max. "The sample did not come from the victim. That should be in the notes in your murder book."

Buck looked at the note section of the forensic report. "I don't see that in the report. When was the report you are looking at uploaded?"

Max put Buck on hold for two minutes. She came back on the line apologetic. "Sorry, Buck, the tech just uploaded the latest report twenty minutes ago. If you've had the report open, it probably didn't refresh, so you don't have the latest version."

Buck said, "no worries, Max." He hit the refresh button on

the report, and sure enough, there was the note. He thanked Max and hung up.

Buck called over to the Clerk and Recorders Office and asked the clerk if she could check a few birth records for him. He had no idea how long Thomas Hawkins had lived in the valley, but it was worth a shot. He gave her the information, and she promised to call back as soon as she had something. Buck sat back and closed his eyes.

CHAPTER SIXTY-ONE

The Clerk from the Clerk and Recorder's Office called back and gave Buck the information he had been waiting for. There were four birth records related to Thomas and Judith Hawkins. Thomas and Judith had two sons, Thomas Jr., born in 1950, and Mathew, born in 1952. She also found a death certificate for Mathew in 1953. The cause of death was listed as undetermined. Buck assumed it was probably SIDS related. Back in those days, many children's deaths, if spontaneous, were listed as SIDS. Sudden Infant Death Syndrome. It was a catch-all phrase for "we don't know what caused the death."

She also found two birth certificates under Thomas Hawkins Jr. and Sarah Jane Westover. They had two children. Thomas, the third, born in 1985, and Alicia born in 1995. Buck thought, "a change of life baby." He thanked the Clerk and hung up.

Paul came rushing back into the conference room, carrying an old dusty file folder. "It took some time to go through the boxes, but we think we found it."

He laid the file on the desk and caught his breath. Buck waited.

"Thomas Hawkins was involved in a single-vehicle rollover accident in July of 1964. It happened between Carbondale and Aspen. According to the report, the car slid on the rain-soaked highway, crashed through a barricade and rolled down the embankment. It wasn't discovered for three-days until a highway road crew stopped to check out the damaged guardrail and spotted the car in the ravine. Thomas Hawkins was the lone occupant in the car and had been crushed when the car slammed into a tree at the bottom of the ravine. Hawkins suffered serious internal injuries and a broken neck. The investigating deputy made a note in the accident report that the doctors did not think that Hawkins would survive." Paul stopped to catch his breath, and Buck pulled the report across the table and started going through it himself.

Paul came around the table, and Buck slid the report over to him. There was something else he wanted Buck to see. He flipped a couple of pages and slid the report back to Buck. He pointed to a faded note written by the deputy along the edge of the page. Buck pulled out his reading glasses and looked at the note.

Paul saw that Buck was having trouble reading the note, so he filled him in. "The deputy made a note to check on the condition of the female victim. Identity unknown."

Buck looked at Paul. "You just said that Hawkins was the lone victim. What does this mean?"

Paul smiled. "I think someone doctored the final report. The official accident report makes no mention of a female victim. I think someone missed this note from the deputy when they typed up the final report. Someone hid the fact that Thomas Hawkins was not alone in his car at the time of the accident."

Buck removed his glasses. "Shit, Paul. Do you think this could have been victim number sixteen, and the accident happened before he had a chance to finish the job?"

Paul responded, "it's possible, but why would someone cover it up? Do you think someone in the Sheriff's office, at the time, knew about the killings and was trying to protect Hawkins?"

Buck looked at the signature on the report. Deputy Ernest Rivers. Buck grabbed the report and headed out the door to find the Sheriff. He found him sitting in his office, reading a report. The Sheriff looked up.

"Do you remember Deputy Ernest Rivers?" Buck asked.

The Sheriff thought for a minute. "Ernie was a deputy back in the sixties. Why? What up?"

Buck set the accident reports on his desk and explained the anomaly. The Sheriff looked at the reports, reread the accident report from the deputy and the final accident report, and set the reports back down on his desk.

"Got me, Buck. Old Tom Glover was Sheriff back in those days. He was a tough old bastard, and he ran a tight ship. Nothing happened in this county that Tom Glover didn't know about. I can't believe one of his deputies would fake a report. To what end?"

Buck replied. "Maybe to hide a serial killer?"

The Sheriff sat back and scratched his head. "Fuck, Buck. How confident are you that Hawkins is the guy? Maybe it was just a simple clerical error."

"Is this Ernie still around? Can we talk to him?" asked Buck.

"No, Ernie died about ten years back," responded the Sheriff.

Buck gave the Sheriff the rundown on what they had. When Buck finished, the Sheriff just sat there. "Okay. What's the next step, the DNA, and fingerprint samples?"

"Yeah. Soon as I hear back from Virginia. Do you know the family?"

"No," replied the Sheriff. "Let me know when you are ready to head over, and I will come along."

Buck left the Sheriff's office and headed back to the conference room, where he filled Paul in on the conversation he just had with the Sheriff.

"Do you think a cop would cover up multiple murders?" asked Paul.

"I don't think so. I mean, it's possible Earl is right, and it's just a clerical error. What bothers me is that there is no follow up from the deputy. That I can't explain."

Buck had just sat down at the conference table when Paul grabbed his notebook and started furiously flipping pages. He stopped and read his notes.

"Fuck," Paul said. "Excuse me. I thought so. Maggie Stevens."

"Maggie Stevens, what?" replied Buck.

"Maggie Stevens is the owner of the Jackpot Bar and Grill. I spoke with her early on when we were trying to get a line on our victim. She mentioned that she had lived in Aspen since her accident. She said she was involved in an accident in the sixties and had no memories of the event before waking up in the hospital."

Buck looked at him. "Go talk to her and see if you can jog some of her memories. We might have a living, breathing victim of our serial killer?"

Paul grabbed his notebook and his backpack and headed out the door.

CHAPTER SIXTY-TWO

Buck was starting to get a little antsy, so he decided to take a walk down to the river. He hated waiting for things to happen, and it seemed that that was all he was doing today. They made a great deal of progress in a short amount of time, and he felt they were right there. As he stood at the river's edge and watched the water flow by, he felt that they were close to wrapping this one up.

He was about to head back to the Sheriff's office when his phone rang. He checked the number and answered the call.

"Hey, Virginia. Are we good?"

Virginia Gonzales responded, "got your warrant. What are you waiting for?" She laughed.

"Awesome. Can you fax it over to the Sheriff's office? Oh, I hate to do this, but do you think you can get warrants for the rest of the family as well?"

Buck explained why he needed the rest of the family's DNA. He waited for a response.

"You think someone else in the family is our new killer? Seriously? A family of killers living here in Aspen, and no one knew. You have got to be kidding. Okay, I will try, but see if you can get them to give the samples voluntarily."

Virginia hung up, and Buck walked back the three blocks to the Sheriff's department. As he entered the building, the desk officer handed him the fax copy of the warrant. He buzzed Buck through the door, and Buck headed for the Sheriff's office.

The Sheriff was talking on the phone, so Buck waved the fax and pointed to the conference room. He nodded, and Buck headed for the conference room. He was closing up his laptop when the Sheriff entered the room. He slid the warrant over to him and put his laptop in his backpack.

"Can you have your fingerprint tech meet us there?"

The Sheriff pulled out his phone, called the tech, and gave her the address. He told her to stay in her van until he called her to come in.

Buck called Paul, who said that he was just wrapping up with Maggie Stevens, and he would meet them at Thomas Hawkins's house. Buck and the Sheriff walked out of the building and climbed into the Sheriff's car. He pulled out of the parking lot and headed for the address on West Hallam Street. He pulled to the curb behind the county's forensic van and signaled the tech to wait. He and Buck crossed the street and walked up to the cute little Victorian house.

The Sheriff knocked on the door. The door was opened by a heavyset, middle-aged woman with gray hair and glasses. He introduced himself and Buck and asked if they could come in. Once inside, Buck closed the door.

"How can I help you, gentlemen?" asked Sarah Jane Hawkins.

They had agreed on the way over to let the Sheriff do most of the talking since these were his people. Buck was never offended at being considered an outsider. Many times, it proved valuable to have the locals handle the locals.

"Ma'am, we have a warrant to get a fingerprint scan and a DNA swab from your father-in-law." The Sheriff handed her the warrant.

She looked at the warrant, confused and unsure what to do. She stepped to the door to the living room and called out. "Tom, can you come here a minute? The police are here."

Tom Hawkins came walking in, wiping his hands on a rag. He was medium height, slightly overweight, and he had a short haircut and a neatly trimmed beard.

"What do you mean the police are here? What do they..." He stopped short and looked at the Sheriff and Buck. His wife handed him the warrant. He pulled a pair of reading glasses out of his pocket and read the warrant. He looked up at Buck and the Sheriff.

"What the hell is this all about? You want fingerprints and DNA from a man who is on death's door and has been bedridden since 1964. Are you kidding?"

The Sheriff looked at Buck. Buck responded. "We have reason to believe that your father was involved in several murders during the late fifties early sixties."

Sarah Jane Hawkins put her hand in front of her mouth. Tom Hawkins looked at Buck as his anger seethed. "What the fuck are you talking about? You think my dad is a serial killer? How dare you come into my house and make that kind of accusation! Get the fuck out!"

Buck stepped forward. "Mr. Hawkins, I know this may be a shock, but we wouldn't be here if we didn't have proof. The warrant permits us to be here and to take the samples. You are welcome to call your attorney, but he will tell you the same thing."

Buck watched as Tom Hawkins balled his fists, and he stared daggers at Buck. Buck looked him in the eye. "Mr. Hawkins," Buck said softly. "Please think very carefully about what you are about to do. We understand your anger, but the samples are important, and you do not want to make the situation any worse."

"Thomas, step back." The voice came from a short elderly

woman with a walker who entered the room. Her words to Tom seem to diffuse the situation instantly. He turned and was about to say something when she held up her hand and silenced him. "He may be your father," she said, "but he is still my husband, and I will deal with this."

Tom Hawkins started to protest, but once again, his mother raised her hand for silence. Tom backed off and sat down at the kitchen table.

"Gentlemen, I am Judith Hawkins. If you would follow me, please."

The Sheriff pulled out his phone and called the fingerprint tech to come in. He was just putting it away when Paul Webber arrived at the door. Paul looked around at those assembled and wondered what he had missed. The Sheriff, Buck, the fingerprint tech and Paul followed Mrs. Hawkins through the house to what appeared to be an addition that had been built onto the original house.

CHAPTER SIXTY-THREE

She pushed open the door, and they all entered a cozy, if not large room. The oxygen tank in the corner hissed as Thomas Hawkins breathed. He was lying in a hospital bed with the blanket pulled up to his chest. He had on striped pajamas and was clean-shaven. It was apparent to everyone that Thomas Hawkins was well taken care of.

Mrs. Hawkins sat down on the chair that was next to the bed and held her husband's hand. She nodded to the fingerprint tech who pulled the portable digital fingerprint scanner out of her backpack and ever so gently slid it across his fingers. She then pulled a DNA swab out of her pack, broke the packaging, and gently lifted the old man's lip and swabbed the inside of his mouth. Mrs. Hawkins sat and watched, holding her husband's hand the entire time.

The fingerprint tech opened her laptop and pulled up the prints that had been recovered at the mine. She spent a few minutes comparing the prints from the mine to the scans, and then she looked up at Buck. She nodded her head. Mrs. Hawkins lowered her eyes, and a tear fell on her hand.

Buck turned his head and noticed Tom Jr. and Sarah Jane, standing in the doorway. They both looked stunned. Tom broke the silence. "Mom, did you know about this?"

She looked at her son. "I would like to talk to these gentlemen alone for a minute. Will you please excuse us?"

Tom Jr. looked hurt and like he wanted to fight, but instead, he just turned around and walked out. Sarah Jane followed closely at his heels. Buck asked the fingerprint tech to go back to the kitchen, finish her analysis, and log the report. She nodded and left the room.

Buck, the Sheriff and Paul Webber stood and watched Mrs. Hawkins. She was looking at her husband, and no one wanted to disturb her. She reached over and took a tissue from the box on the table and wiped her eyes. She looked up at Buck and the others. She asked Buck to close the door.

Mrs. Hawkins kissed her husband on the forehead and then began. "My husband was a good man. Up until his accident, he took good care of the boys and me." She wiped her eyes, and Buck could see the sadness in that statement. "He was a loving husband and father, but I always sensed that there was something beneath the surface. He worked a lot of late hours in those days, but his paychecks never revealed any extra money. Up until you walked in, I always believed that he was having an affair or many, for that matter. He would always shower before coming to bed, after a long night, but I could always smell the sex on him. It never occurred to me that he might be a killer. He never seemed the type, but I know he was troubled. I was young and naïve, and despite what I have just told you, I always loved him. I still do. When our little Mathew passed away, he was the rock I depended on."

She sat for a minute and looked down at her husband. She wiped more tears away from her eyes. No one spoke.

"I can only assume that from the young lady's reaction, his fingerprints match fingerprints that were found at a crime scene. What will happen now? He doesn't have many days left, and I assume you can't arrest him. What's next?"

Buck looked down at Mrs. Hawkins. "I am not sure, ma'am. That will be up to the county attorney. May we ask you a couple of questions?" She nodded yes, and asked Buck to please open the door. Buck turned and opened the door and saw a new person in the room. He was the spitting image of Tom Jr. This would be Thomas the third. They all rose from the couch.

Paul pulled out his laptop and turned on the voice recorder app. He nodded to Buck. As the others all listened, Buck walked Mrs. Hawkins through the evidence they had gathered over the last couple of days. She had no idea that her husband had been in contact with the owner of the mining claim. She told them he had worked as a mechanic for the Aspen Skiing Company almost from its inception. They talked about his skills as a metal worker and welder. Periodically there would be a gasp from one of the family members, especially when Buck described the scene in the mine.

Mrs. Hawkins held her husband's hand through all of Buck's questions. For a frail little old lady, she was amazingly strong. He hoped the crash wouldn't come later, but he knew it would. It always did.

Buck asked Mrs. Hawkins if she would allow them to search the house and property. She said she would, and then he asked if the rest of the members of the family would allow them to take DNA and fingerprint samples. They still needed to eliminate them as suspects in the recent murder. They all agreed. Buck asked Tom Jr. if his daughter was around. Tom told Buck that she had left the week before to go back to college in Florida.

Mrs. Hawkins looked up at Buck. "I assume you will want to see his jewelry collection? He thought I didn't know about it, but I did. I just assumed it was to help him relive his conquests. I had no idea they were what you would call trophies."

Buck looked stunned, "yes, ma'am."

"Tommy, would you please show these gentlemen your grandfather's toolbox? The trophy box is in a space in the wall behind the toolbox."

Paul stepped through the door and followed Thomas the third. The Sheriff stepped out of the room and called dispatch to send out his forensics team. He asked that they dispatch a couple of deputies, and to notify the Aspen Police and let them know what was going on.

Buck sat with Mrs. Hawkins. He needed to clear up the anomaly with the accident report. He waited until the Sheriff returned. "Mrs. Hawkins, have you ever read the report about the night your husband was injured in the accident. We found a discrepancy, and unfortunately, there is no one left alive, except you, who might be able to explain it."

Mrs. Hawkins sat there for a minute and looked at her husband. She smiled through the tears and looked at Buck. "I had asked Tom not to change the report, but he wanted to do it for me."

"I'm sorry, ma'am. Who is this Tom that you are talking about?" At this point, Tom Jr. and Sarah Jane stepped into the doorway. Mrs. Hawkins looked at them and then back at Buck.

CHAPTER SIXTY-FOUR

The affair with Pitkin County Sheriff Tom Glover had started innocently enough. Tom was a deacon in her church, and they had met at several of the church's social events. Her own Thomas never wanted to attend church with her. She never understood why until today.

It had started as just coffee, but she was feeling that her husband was growing more distant from her every day. A few months before the accident, it had turned into something more than just coffee. She had been feeling underappreciated, and she needed someone to talk to. She called the Sheriff to see if he would like to stop by for coffee. Her Thomas was at work, and her son was in school.

The coffee visit turned into two hours of intense lovemaking. It was funny. Judith didn't feel any regret after it happened. She still loved her husband, but the time she spent with Tom Glover was something else entirely.

Tom was the one who came by the house that day to tell her they found Thomas's car in the ravine and that he was on his way to the hospital. It was touch and go whether he would live or die. Tom Glover now became her rock.

"Tom told me about the woman they found in the ravine. She had been thrown from the car and was seriously injured. He wanted to protect me from public ridicule, so he told me he would take care of it." Mrs. Hawkins said.

She had begged him not to do anything that would jeopardize his career, and he had laughed at her. He was the Sheriff of the county, and he could do anything he wanted to. "He asked Ernie to remove any mention of the girl from his notes. Tom wrote the accident report up himself, and Ernie signed it without question."

A tear formed in her eye. "Tom helped me get through all the hard days that would follow, as I had to deal with Thomas's injuries, get a job and keep my son fed and clothed. Tom was always there for me."

Buck asked her how long the affair lasted. She looked down at her hand, holding Thomas's hand. She said, "It lasted until the day Tom died, almost ten years ago. That was the saddest day of my life."

Her family just stood in the doorway in shocked silence. Their whole world had been torn apart today. It was horrible to watch. Tom Jr. and Sarah Jean excused themselves and walked out the front door. The forensic team arrived just as they were leaving. The Sheriff stepped away to give the team instructions and asked the fingerprint tech to get the swabs from the rest of the family.

Paul returned with Thomas the third and walked into the room. In his hands was an old cardboard cigar box. He handed it to Buck. Buck opened the box, and just as Mrs. Hawkins had said, the box was filled with jewelry. Buck was no jewelry expert, but nothing in the box looked expensive. Some of it looked like it might have sentimental value.

Mrs. Hawkins held out her hand and asked to see the box. Although it was evidence, Buck wanted to gauge her reaction now that she knew the truth about where the pieces came from. He handed her the box, and she slowly opened it. She sat for a minute and just looked inside the box. She reached in and started moving pieces around. She got a funny look in her eyes. Buck watched her as she seemed to count the pieces one by one. She did this several times. She looked up, and Buck thought he could see fear in her eyes.

"Ma'am, is something wrong?" Buck asked.

Mrs. Hawkins sat for a few minutes, just looking in the box. She closed the box. "There is a piece missing," she said.

"Are you certain?" Buck asked. He took the box from her hand and opened the lid.

"There were sixteen pieces in the box. I checked it now and then to be reminded of how many women he had cheated with. The piece that's missing is a little jade horse on a silver necklace."

The house was now full of forensics people, and Mrs. Hawkins asked Buck if he would close the door. Paul reached behind him and pushed the door shut. Buck was trying to understand what was happening. There were fifteen pieces of jewelry in the box, and they had fifteen bodies in the morgue. The numbers worked unless one of the pieces belonged to the sixteenth victim. The woman who almost died in the accident that night. Paul was thinking the same thing as he looked through his notes.

"Agent Taylor, what I am about to say is very hard for me, and it will destroy my son and his wife." She paused for a minute and let go of her husband's hand.

"My granddaughter, Alicia, found the jewelry box. I saw her with it one day when she thought I was asleep on the couch. She was coming out of this room and headed back to the garage. She spent several days in here talking with her grandfather, over the summer, when he had a lucid moment." She started to cry.

She looked at Buck with pleading eyes. "Please don't say anything to my son."

Buck looked at Paul. "Would you have one of the techs look through Alicia's room and see if they can find anything that might contain DNA? Toothbrush, hairbrush, anything."

Paul left the room, and Buck reached over and rested his

hand on Mrs. Hawkins's hand. "I hope I have done the right thing?" she said.

Buck stood up. He left Mrs. Hawkins sitting there with her husband. The poor woman's entire life had just unraveled. He felt bad for her. He walked through the house and stepped out onto the front porch. The Sheriff walked up beside him. Together they just stood there in silence.

The Sheriff broke the silence. "Hard day, my friend. Wouldn't want to be these folks."

Buck looked at him and shook his head. He told the Sheriff about the conversation they had had about her granddaughter. "What are we going to do?" he asked.

Buck knew what they were going to do. "As soon as the DNA results are back and we confirm what Mrs. Hawkins told me, we are going to issue an arrest warrant for Alicia Hawkins and have the Jacksonville, Florida police arrest her. I will let Hank Clancy at the FBI know. He might want his guys to track her down since she could be considered to have fled the state to avoid prosecution."

The Sheriff pulled out his phone. "I'd better call Virginia Gonzales and see how she wants to handle this. We can't arrest the old guy, but I'm not sure what to do." He stepped away and walked across the lawn.

Paul stepped out on the front porch. "I just spoke with Maggie Stevens at the Jackpot Bar and Grill. She confirmed that she had a little jade horse pendant on a silver chain but that it had disappeared from the hospital after the accident. She never saw it again until a young girl showed up at the bar a week or two back and was wearing a little jade horse pendant. Something in her mind triggered a memory, and she asked the girl where she got the necklace. The girl told her she found it in a pawn shop in Florida. Maggie didn't think anything of it once the bar got busy, but she swore that the girl was watching her the rest of the night."

CHAPTER SIXTY-FIVE

Buck asked Paul to head back to the Sheriff's department and upload his notes to the murder book. Paul headed for his car, and Buck took another pass through the house. Mrs. Hawkins was still sitting next to her husband. As Buck looked in the door, she smiled at him and lowered her head. Buck checked in with the forensic team. He found the Sheriff and told him to call if they needed him. He would be back in the Sheriff's office in the morning to file his reports and put the finishing touches on the murder book.

As he walked towards his car, he pulled out his phone and dialed Max Clinton. He told her what had happened in the last couple of hours, and asked her to rush through the DNA samples she would be receiving for Alicia Hawkins. She promised to get her team on them as soon as they arrived. She ended the call the way she always did.

"You are a good man, Buck Taylor. God will watch over you. Stay safe."

Buck hung up his phone and walked to his car. He sat in his car and pulled out his phone again. He called the Director who answered on the first ring.

"Hey, Buck. What's up?"

Buck filled him in on the day's events. He asked a few questions and then said, "You guys did a great job, Buck. You solved fifteen decades-old serial killings and are about to close out a serial killer who is just getting started. Congratulations."

Buck thanked him, hung up, and sat for a few minutes. He started his car and pulled out. He had intended to go back to his hotel and work on the murder book, but the car seemed to have a mind of its own, and he found himself parked along the river. He stepped out of the car and walked to the edge. The moon was full, and the water sparkled. He stood there just watching the current when he sensed a presence behind him. His hand went instinctively for his gun.

"Sorry to have spooked you, Agent Taylor." Buck relaxed and turned around. PIS stood behind him and smiled.

"I heard it was rather a rough day."

Buck smiled and filled PIS in on the events of the past couple of days. He asked PIS how his shoulder was doing, and PIS told him that he had been hurt worse and not to worry. When Buck was finished, he sat down in the cool grass and looked out over the river. PIS sat down next to him, and that is where they stayed until the sun came over the mountains. Buck stood, shook PIS's hand, and walked to his car. When he turned and looked back at the river, PIS was gone. Buck laughed and started the car.

The next few days were a blur as Buck and Paul continued to pull together forensic reports and log incoming information into the murder book. Virginia Gonzales had decided to indict Thomas Hawkins for the murders in the mine. She did not issue an arrest warrant because she knew he wasn't going to be alive that much longer. Professor Standish and his team continued making progress and identified nine of the fifteen women. He wanted to keep going, but he had serious doubts that they would ever identify all of them. Hank Clancy agreed, and by the end of the week, he pulled his clerk off the case and assigned her other work. Buck found out later that the clerk received a commendation for her excellent work in piecing together the victims.

Fitz and Moe Steiner continued to follow leads on the kids from the other mine. They had solid DNA matches on two of the kids and were waiting for the families to arrange flights to Colorado. The Missing and Exploited Children's Network led to the possible identification of two of the other children, and those leads were being followed up by police departments in St. Louis and Fort Collins, Colorado. The phones were still ringing, but not as often. Corinne Everheart's uncle in West Virginia arranged to have her remains, and the remains of her identified son, shipped to him for burial.

Major Richard Cranston, the Army CID investigator, arranged to have James Michael Forester's remains shipped to an Army base outside of Washington, DC. Buck had no idea how the Army was going to handle his burial, and he decided he didn't care. As far as Buck and the Sheriff were concerned, it was now an Army matter.

Buck stopped by the Hawkins home a few days after that fateful day. To say the family was morose would be an understatement. The family moved around like zombies. All but Mrs. Hawkins. Buck found her sitting, in the cool afternoon air, on a love seat on the front porch. She was wrapped in a blanket and was just staring into space when Buck walked up the sidewalk.

Buck sat next to her, and she put her hand on top of his. She said, "Thomas will be at rest soon. He will face the lord and have to answer for his deeds. My solace is in the fact that you might give closure to those who have lost loved ones. Thank you for all you have done."

Buck started to stand up when she said, "please find my granddaughter."

She pulled her blanket around her a little tighter and looked across the yard.

The DNA from a toothbrush that the forensic team found

in Alicia's room was a solid match for the stain on the old mattress blanket from the mine. Virginia Gonzales issued an arrest warrant for the murder of Margret Mary Trumaine. The FBI also issued a federal arrest warrant for murder and interstate flight to avoid prosecution. The FBI, along with the Jacksonville Police, raided her dormitory, but there was no sign of Alicia. All her belongings were still in her dorm room, but Alicia was nowhere to be found. The FBI reported back that there was no sign of a little jade horse pendant on a silver chain.

Buck and Paul finished compiling the murder book, and Buck emailed a copy to the Sheriff and Virginia Gonzales. They boxed up all the physical evidence that had been returned from the state lab, along with samples from the morgue. The Sheriff had his evidence clerk label and seal the boxes and take them to storage.

Paul headed back to Grand Junction the next morning, and Buck found himself standing knee-deep in the cool waters of the Roaring Fork River. After several hours, he had only landed one fish, but it didn't matter. He could feel his mind clearing more and more as he focused on the fish.

EPILOGUE

Alicia Hawkins was unrecognizable. She had a dark tan, and she had cut her hair short and dyed it purple. The phone call from her older brother came just in time. He didn't want to believe the things they were saying about her, and he wanted her to come home to clear her name. She promised she would, but she had made a promise to her grandfather. She would finish his legacy. One day soon, she would return to Aspen and finish his job.

Alicia hated the fact that she couldn't go home for her grandfather's funeral. She now, more than ever, understood him. She understood the force that drove him to do what he had done. She could feel that force growing stronger in her every day.

She managed to get out of her dorm room, and across the street to the park, just before all the cops showed up. She was surprised to see the men and women with their FBI emblazoned jackets. It made her feel important. She sat in the park and watched for several hours as they carried out her stuff and talked to the other students in the dorm.

She waited until dark and then hitched south until she got to Tampa. She bought some purple dye at a local drug store and rented a cheap hotel room. When she was finished, she looked in the mirror and was pleased with the transformation. Over the following weeks, she made her way farther south until she couldn't go any further.

Alicia walked out of the bar and stepped into the warm

Key West sun. She put on her sunglasses and looked from side to side. She spotted the young girl a block down the street. The girl had arrived on the bus two days ago and looked lost. Alicia had been watching her since she arrived. She looked like a runaway, and she was perfect.

The sun was setting, and all the tourists were heading to the beach to wait for the green flash. People swore that the flash was visible for just a second, just before the sun went down, but Alicia had never seen it. She watched the girl walk along the beach, looking in the trash cans as she passed. Occasionally she would pull something out of the trash look at it, sniff it and eat it.

Alicia watched the young girl walk along the rocks towards the small tropical forest. She reached her hand into the back pocket of her shorts and felt the thin knife. She reached up to her neck and wrapped her hand around the little jade horse pendant on the silver chain. She smiled a wicked smile and headed off after the girl.

CHUCK MORGAN

CRIME DENIED

A BUCK TAYLOR NOVEL

CRIME

DENIED

A BUCK TAYLOR NOVEL
BOOK 5

BY

CHUCK MORGAN

CHAPTER ONE

Alicia Hawkins sat at the end of the long wooden bar and appeared to be focused on the beer in front of her. What no one in the bar realized was that Alicia Hawkins was hunting, and her eyes were slowly and casually moving from seat to seat and table to table in search of her next victim. She had become a predator of the highest level. The top of the food chain, when it came to humans, and the predator needed to be fed. Alicia Hawkins was a serial killer.

She had walked into the bar a couple hours before and found a seat where she could observe the entire room. She was a pretty young woman with purple-streaked blond hair that was tucked up under a straw cowboy hat. She wore tight jeans and a snap-front Western shirt, open just enough to attract the interest of the cowboys and ranch hands who frequented the bar. Being the social person she was, she danced several dances to the local country band and politely thanked the cowboys for their offers to take her home for the night. Tonight, Alicia Hawkins was not interested in casual sex, even though she was attracted to several of the local ranch hands. Tonight, she had a purpose, and had any of the cowboys realized what that purpose was, they would have avoided her like the plague.

Alicia Hawkins had arrived in the middle of nowhere, Oklahoma, a couple days before and had settled into the isolated cabin she'd found on one of those vacation rentals by owner websites. Since all the arrangements were made online, she never actually met the owner, which was just as well, since the fewer people to see her, the safer she felt. The new driver's license and credit cards she'd bought off the dark web worked perfectly, and she was glad she'd spent the extra money to buy the best product available.

She'd left Florida a couple weeks back and was heading, in a roundabout way, towards Colorado to fulfill a promise she'd made to her dying grandfather. In her wake, she'd left several bodies and a task force of federal agents scratching their heads, wondering where her next victim would show up. During the year she had been on the run, she had sliced up seven women in Florida and Colorado, one in Mississippi. Then, to throw off the task force, she'd made a quick trip up to Georgia and left two dead women in that state before heading towards Louisiana and Texas, where two more homeless women died terrible deaths.

She'd lucked out on her second night in Oklahoma when she picked up a young female hitchhiker with no local family. The offer of a place to spend the night and a home-cooked meal was too much to pass up for the young runaway. The sleeping pills Alicia placed in the young woman's wine incapacitated her enough so Alicia could carry her to the basement, strip off her clothes and tie her hands and feet to the wall. Alicia Hawkins then stripped off her own clothes, opened the roll of assorted knives and scalpels she had carefully laid out on the table and spent the next five hours making various-sized incisions all over the woman's body.

She took her time and even stopped now and then to admire the woman's body. She had a thin waist and large, firm breasts, and even though Alicia never reached the kind of sexual pleasure her grandfather had described, she found herself getting aroused as she ran her hands over the woman's body. The drugs started to wear off after the first hour, and Alicia had to gag the woman to silence her screams. Her pleading, tear-filled eyes begged for the pain to stop, which made Alicia increase the speed and depth of the cuts, while using one hand to take care of her own arousal. When the woman's heart stopped beating, Alicia stepped back, admired her handiwork and lay down on the floor and slept. She was exhausted and sexually satisfied. She was also pleased that she was getting closer to her goal of keeping her victim alive until she reached one thousand cuts.

Alicia Hawkins had chosen this cabin because it sat all by itself at the end of a rural lake. The nearest neighbors were almost a half mile away, but she was still fearful that the screams of her victims might attract unwanted attention. For peace of mind, once she settled into the cabin, she took the canoe that was stored in the garage, rowed around the entire lake and noticed one other vacation home that appeared to be occupied. It was late in the season, and she was glad that most of the tourists had gone by the time she got there.

The bar was loud and crowded with cowboys and cowgirls from the local cattle and horse ranches that covered the county. It was Friday night, and they all had money to burn and were looking to let off some steam. Alicia Hawkins was sipping her beer and was about to give up when she spotted her next victim—but she wasn't sure. She'd come into the bar looking for another woman, but across the room, sitting at a table full of well-muscled, tanned cowboys sat a young man who seemed to be the brunt of the jokes that were going around the table. She had already danced with and refused the advances of several of the cowboys at the table, but this young cowboy looked like he might fit the bill. He wasn't well built but was skinny and seemed shy. He didn't seem to be enjoying the razzing he was getting from the others and looked like he wanted to escape.

Alicia Hawkins sized him up. She'd started her career as a serial killer by choosing female victims because they were easier to control and more trusting of going off someplace with another woman. It also made her unique in the serial killer world. She felt she was ready to move up to men, but she needed to make sure it was the right man. She knew she had the skills, and she had experimented with several types of fast-acting sedatives, but she was concerned that she could still be overpowered by a man, especially one of these well-built cowboys. She was not a big woman, but her strength had improved with each victim. Looking at this young man, she believed she could do it. She felt herself getting aroused as she sat there, watching him in the mirror behind the bar.

After several minutes of doubt and internal struggle, she decided that tonight was the night. She watched as the young cowboy picked up some money off the table, stood up and walked towards the bar. He was standing there waiting for his drinks when she walked up and sat on the barstool next to him.

"You don't look like you're having much fun," she said. "Maybe I can fix that for you."

The young man looked around as if he was unsure who she was talking to.

"Are you talking to me, ma'am?" His voice cracked, and he swallowed hard.

"Yes, silly, I'm talking to you. Haven't you ever talked to a woman before?"

She laughed, and the young man turned a bright shade of red. He was embarrassed, and he glanced over his shoulder to the table where his coworkers had gone quiet and were watching in disbelief, since most of them had already struck out with the new girl. The bartender set six beers on the bar, and he looked at her and then his buddies, tipped his hat and walked the drinks back to the table. She could hear loud conversation and a lot of goading, and she sat there and waited. It was his move.

The laughing continued, and the young cowboy stood up, squared his shoulders and walked back towards Alicia. She turned to face him.

"You ready to get out of here?" she said. "I know a quiet place we can go where we won't be disturbed."

The young cowboy swallowed hard and nodded his head. Alicia set a twenty on the bar, turned and tipped her hat to the young man's friends. They could still hear the laughs and the catcalls as they left the bar.

Alicia Hawkins had an easygoing charm, and she soon had the young man telling her his life story. He'd left home at sixteen after his mother died, and his father fell deeper into the bottle. He'd heard that his dad died a couple years later, which made him an orphan—a lot better than when he had a family. He was trying to make it on his own and had always dreamed of working on a big ranch. He loved horses. He'd been in Oklahoma a couple weeks.

She turned the car down a dark lane, almost invisible between the trees, and drove a quarter mile to the house by the lake. She led him inside and lit a fire in the fireplace. The young man stood in the doorway, not sure what to do, so she walked over and took his hand and led him towards the bedroom. She sat him down and offered him a beer, which he accepted, and she told him to take his clothes off while she headed for the kitchen.

Since this was her first time with a man as a victim, she decided to use the same sleeping pills on him that she'd used on the runaway. Once he was out, she would use the sedative cocktail to incapacitate him. The sleeping pills in the beer would take effect pretty quickly, so she would need to move fast.

She walked into the bedroom and found him standing next to the bed, naked. It was obvious that he was ready for her, so she handed him the beer, and he took a big, long drink while she stripped off her clothes. She lay down on the bed, took him in her hands and gently guided him in. The first minute or so was pure pleasure, and she found she was enjoying him until she sensed the pills kick in. She reached under her pillow, pulled out the syringe and pushed it into his shoulder. He never felt the needle go in, and within a couple seconds, he stopped moving.

She pushed him off, slipped out of bed and put on a fluffy white robe that was hanging behind the door. She tried to lift him and was surprised that he weighed a lot more than she expected. She needed a plan B, so she went downstairs to the basement and brought back two pairs of shackles, a chain and her knife kit.

Alicia Hawkins clamped the shackles on his hands and feet and chained him to the bed. She typically didn't work on her victims while they were lying down, but this was a new experience and called for a change in her methods. She would need to think about this aspect of her work before she picked up the next guy. Who knows? Maybe if they were lying down, they might stay alive longer. It was something to find out.

She filled a glass with red wine and stood there admiring the young man. For someone so thin, he was certainly virile, and she wished he had been able to stay awake a little longer. She could feel the arousal beginning again, so she stripped off her robe and pulled a beautiful three-inch scalpel from her kit. It was her favorite tool; it made an incision as thin as a human hair. It was a thing of beauty.

CHAPTER TWO

Alicia Hawkins hadn't become a serial killer in the usual manner. She didn't tear the wings off butterflies when she was a kid, and she never killed a neighbor's cat. She even used to volunteer at the Pitkin County animal shelter, and she loved the family dog. For the most part, her childhood was perfectly normal, with no signs of anything strange in her makeup. She was a perfectly normal college student until that summer a year ago when she made the discovery that would change her life.

She'd discovered her grandfather's trophy box a couple months back and wondered about the significance of the baubles. She knew it was her grandfather's because no one in the family remembered the old cigar box that was hidden in a hole in the wall behind her grandfather's big Craftsman toolbox. She had mentioned it one night at dinner, and no one reacted. Well, that's not exactly true. She thought she saw some kind of recognition in her grandmother's eyes, but that disappeared as quickly as it had arrived.

She waited until the family was asleep and entered her grandfather's room. He was sleeping soundly, and she hoped that he might wake up in one of his—getting rarer—lucid moments. She hated to disturb him, so she'd already started to leave his room when a low frail voice stopped her in her tracks.

She approached the bed and stood there with the trophy box held out in front of her. Her grandfather stared at the box in her hands and smiled. She hadn't seen him smile much since she had gotten home from college, and it surprised her. He asked her to open the box so he could look inside.

She opened the box and held it out to him. His heart monitor reacted almost immediately, and she was afraid the change of tone from the monitor might wake someone else in the small house. She closed the box and pulled it away from him, but his expression indicated that he wasn't done. She glanced towards his bedroom door to see if anyone might have heard them, and then she reopened the box, and he looked deep inside. She asked him what all these pieces meant. He smiled and asked her to remove the gold-edged cameo necklace. She held it up for him to see, and he told her that this had been the first one.

She was a pretty runaway from somewhere up near Chicago. Her family life had been brutal, so she'd headed west to find her own way in the world. The Korean War was over, and many people were leaving their familiar homes to look for financial opportunities out west. The fledgling ski industry and lax laws were drawing people from far and wide, and Aspen was no exception. The young woman found work in a small diner just off the highway, and she found a room with several other young women. Alicia's grandfather befriended the young woman, and they started seeing each other at night. Her grandmother never knew.

After a few weeks, she told him that she was tired of the cold and had decided to head to California. Her grandfather sensed an opportunity about to disappear, so he told her he would drive her to the train in Glenwood Springs. He knew she hadn't told any of her friends about him, so he wasn't worried about getting caught. That night, as she slipped out of her rooming house, he met her up the highway and loaded her one suitcase into the trunk of his car. She was dressed in a long skirt and a pretty white blouse, and she wore the cameo necklace around her neck. A gift from her mother.

Instead of heading north up Highway 82, he turned south and headed out of town. He turned down Route 15, which at the time was a narrow dirt road, and found the old fire road that led to Conundrum Creek. She asked him where they were heading, and he told her that he wanted to show her a beautiful sight before she left. He reached the end of the road, parked the car and reached his arm around her shoulders. The syringe bit deep into her shoulder, and she started to yell, but he put his hand over her mouth and held it there until the sedative had time to work.

The snow was not that deep on the old trail through the woods as he carried her over his shoulder. The old mining cabin had collapsed years before, but it wasn't the cabin he was interested in. When he'd first arrived in Aspen, he spent time exploring his new home and discovered the old cabin a mile or so down Conundrum Creek. It sat back about a quarter mile from the trail along the creek and was completely hidden from view. What interested him most about the cabin was the shaft the old miners had dug under its wooden floor. The shaft went down about thirty feet and then opened into a long tunnel. He found some old, broken-down and decayed wooden shelves and some old mining equipment.

When he'd first found the cabin, he thought it would be perfect for his needs. He spent several weeks tracking down the owner of the property and discovered that the mining claim that the cabin sat on was owned by a man in Pittsburg who had almost forgotten about the old claim. Through a series of letters and telegrams, her grandfather was finally able to get permission to work the claim and use the cabin.

He spent the next couple of months cleaning out the space

and installing the things he knew he would need. Along the walls, he bolted in chains and shackles for hands and feet. He purchased several kerosene hurricane lamps and built a bed with a straw mattress. He was able to make the most significant improvement in the machine shop at the ski resort's maintenance shed. He fashioned a metal hatch door that he installed over the old rotten wooden shaft door and put heavy-duty hinges and a hasp on it.

The old miners had left an old kerosene stove in the tunnel that they had vented up through the ground a few feet behind the cabin. It would help to keep the chill out of the air and make it a more comfortable space to work in. He also placed his pride and joy in the tunnel: over the years working at the ski resort, he had fashioned several beautiful knives and scalpels at the metal shop. Since he'd made them all himself, there was no record of him buying them. His space was complete, and his body tingled at the thought of what would soon be taking place in his secluded little world.

Alicia's grandfather's voice seemed to grow stronger as he told her the rest of the story. He had carried the young woman to the cabin and unlocked the trapdoor. He lowered her down the old wooden ladder and placed her on the bed while he fired up the kerosene lanterns and the old kerosene stove. Once the space got warmer, he stripped off all the young woman's clothes and tied her to the bed frame. She had a beautiful body, young and subtle. Her breasts were small but perky, and she moaned through the gag as he repeatedly penetrated her. Twice he had to inject her with more sedative to keep her quiet. This was the first time he had ever had sex with someone other than his wife, and he was surprised at how much he enjoyed it, but the night was fading fast, and he needed to get home before his wife woke up.

Now that he was totally spent, he untied her from the bed and carried her over to the first set of shackles that he had bolted to the wall. She was still naked, and he hooked the restraints to her hands and feet. She had started to wake up, and the fear in her eyes made him get excited all over again, but he didn't have the time to penetrate her again. He was running out of time. He opened an old cabinet that was hanging on the wall and removed a leather bundle. He carefully placed it on the wooden table under the cabinet and unrolled it, revealing his assortment of custom-made knives.

He chose a thin four-inch-long scalpel from the bundle and admired it in the light from the kerosene lantern. He loved how the blade glowed under the yellow light. He walked over to the young woman and held the scalpel so she could see it. She squirmed hard against the shackles and started to bleed where the metal shackles cut into her hands and feet.

Slowly and almost delicately, he slid the sharp edge of the scalpel along her exposed abdomen. He had used this same technique on several high-ranking German officers during the war. They were a stubborn lot, but eventually, they all talked. He didn't care if the young woman talked or not. This was not an interrogation. This was pleasure.

He could hear her screaming through the gag. He spent the next hour slowly slicing the young woman's torso, legs and arms until she finally passed out. She didn't have the stamina of the German officers, and it was almost disappointing. He walked over to the leather bundle on the bed and, using an old rag, cleaned the blood off the scalpel and his hands. He got dressed and then walked back and turned off the kerosene stove and put his bundle back in the cabinet. If she was still alive when he returned, he would finish the job, but for now, the demons were satisfied. He turned off the kerosene lanterns and climbed out of his workspace. He closed the hatch, made sure the padlock was shut and covered the hatch with the decaying floorboards.

CHAPTER THREE

Alicia could feel the heat rising inside her as her grandfather told her the story of his first civilian kill. She hadn't realized how sexually aroused she'd felt as he described the details of the kill. She felt embarrassed that she was feeling this way and didn't understand what was happening. Her grandfather knew what was happening. He could sense that she had the same feelings he did when it came to taking another's life. He finished his story and looked at the vibrant pink color in her cheeks and the little beads of sweat that had formed on her forehead and her upper lip.

He told her that he knew she was the one who would follow him. He could feel it deep in his soul, and he would help her find her way along the path that had been taken from him so long ago. She stared in disbelief in response to what he was saying. She could never take a human life. She had never killed anything, nor had the desire to do so. Or did she? His description of the kill had certainly stirred something deep inside her. Something scary, but also something wonderful.

Her grandfather started to speak in dribble and incomplete sentences, and then he closed his eyes and went to sleep. The lucid moment had passed, but she had certainly learned a lot. She looked at the other pieces of jewelry in the little box. Her grandfather had just admitted to being a serial killer. One of the first in modern history, yet there had never been any hint that this was the case. She wondered how many more pieces of jewelry would have found their way into his little trophy box if he had not been injured so many years ago. She also wondered how he had kept the demons from destroying him since he was no longer able to feed their needs.

She was curious whether her grandmother knew about his proclivities. She had definitely noticed the change in her grandmother's eyes when she mentioned the old cigar box she had found in the garage. Yet her grandmother had never said anything about it.

She looked again at the trophies her grandfather had collected. She wondered about the people they had belonged to. Most of the jewelry appeared to be pieces that would have been worn by young women of his time. She wondered if she would ever be able to get their stories from her grandfather. She would need to hurry. She was due back at school in early September. If she was going to act on the feelings that had been stirred up by her grandfather's story, she would need to do it quickly.

She closed the lid of the old box, leaned in and kissed her grandfather on the forehead and left his room. The house was quiet as a church cemetery, and she was grateful. She headed back to her room and, once inside, closed the door and hid the trophy box in the back of her closet. She needed to understand the feelings that her grandfather's story had generated. Was it possible she was a serial killer too?

She had taken psychology classes at school, and she understood that serial killers were psychopaths. She'd always believed they were evil incarnate and that they would stand out in society like freaks at a carnival. Even though she hadn't had the opportunity to see her grandfather in his early years, she never considered him to be odd. He had never spoken before of his craft. But now. His story had aroused something profound inside of her. Something she now both feared and found interesting and exciting.

Could it be true that he could sense in her the things that made him do the evil deeds he had told her about? It made her sick to her stomach, and she ran into her tiny bathroom and vomited in the toilet. No, there was no way she could ever be the evil thing her grandfather had suddenly become in her eyes. But she was also envious of him. If the way she'd felt while he was telling his story was real, the sensation was incredible. She felt more satisfied, sexually, at this moment than she had with any of the college boys she had slept with over the years.

She knew she needed to pursue the feelings to see if they were real. She was afraid of what she might find and of what she might become, but she needed to find out. She lay down on her bed, her head full of strange thoughts and feelings. She decided the first thing she needed to do was try to find her grandfather's old cabin and see if the shaft was still locked. She would check that out first and then decide on the next step.

Alicia Hawkins started slowly. She wanted to savor every minute of her new project. The slices on the young cowboy's chest were long and shallow. She wanted this to last, so she was extra careful. After almost an hour, the sedatives started to wear off, so she put the gag in his mouth and tied it around his head. His eyes grew wider with each cut, and he tried in vain to scream. By this point, Alicia was in the deep end of the sexual arousal pool, so she decided to stop and enjoy the opportunity. She started stroking the young man, and when she felt he was ready, she climbed on top of him and guided him inside. He tried to squirm and buck her off, but all that did was increase her arousal. She rode him like she had never ridden anyone before, and when she looked down, she was covered in blood, his blood. She ran her hands over her body and smeared the blood around her breasts. The sensation grew until she couldn't handle it anymore, and she exploded in ecstasy. It was the most incredible thing she had ever felt. She lost complete control of herself and made several slices in his chest, deeper than she wanted.

The young cowboy screamed through the gag, and his entire body convulsed. She slid off the bed and finished her glass of wine. She now understood the sexual arousal that her grandfather had told her about but she had never experienced. She now realized what she had been missing with the women she had killed. Contentment made her sleepy, so she lay on the floor and wrapped a blanket around herself and fell asleep. This young cowboy had a lot left to give, and she planned to take it all.

The sky was still dark when Alicia woke, and she stood up and stared at the young cowboy. Sometime during the night, he had passed out, but he was still breathing, so she wasn't done quite yet. She continued slicing his body while stroking him, her arousal growing to incredible levels, and she climbed on him again. He'd lost a lot of blood, but he was still able to please her in ways she'd never expected, and she screamed as the climax exploded, but she noticed that he no longer fought like he had earlier in the evening.

Twice more over the next couple hours, she pleasured herself while continuing to slice him. The sheets and pillows were soaked with blood, and she had so much blood on her body that she looked like she'd been in a fight. He passed out, for the last time, as the sun rose over the tops of the trees, and Alicia put down her scalpel, walked to the window and watched the mist rising from the lake. The scene was so peaceful. Nothing like the scene in the room behind her.

She turned and walked back to the bed. The young cowboy was no longer breathing, and she covered him with the bloody sheet. She was exhausted, but exhilarated, so she climbed onto the bed and fell asleep next to the body. She dreamt about her grandfather.

CHAPTER FOUR

Alicia's grandfather, Thomas, had come to Aspen a few years after the end of World War II. He had been a soldier in the 10th Mountain Division as the war neared its end and had learned how to ski. Some of his fellow warriors were settling in small communities throughout the Colorado mountains and were working to build up the fledgling ski industry. He thought it might be fun to be a part of the movement.

His best friend, Gus Murphy, found a job with the recently formed Aspen Skiing Corporation and offered Thomas a job working as a mechanic on the ski lifts. Having been mechanically inclined all his life, he took to the job like a fish to water. As the years progressed, his life became more and more fulfilling, and he felt he was living the American dream. He met and fell in love with Alicia's grandmother, bought the small Victorian house on West Hallam Street, and raised a son there. It was a perfect life, except that the demons were still working hard in the back of his mind.

The demons had been there as long as he could remember, and his time in the army had deepened the lust they brought out. He had practiced his craft, as he called it, with great abandon as a young man. Many of the townsfolk around Lynchburg, Virginia, thought he was odd, and many of the neighbors feared him. He had grown up on a very rural farm outside Lynchburg. The family's water came from a pump, and an outhouse served their more personal needs. To say they were dirt poor would have been an understatement.

His father was a sharecropper and didn't even own the dirt under their little house.

Life had not been easy growing up. He was constantly picked on when he was able to get to school, which was not often, and as things got worse, his father would take to drinking, and he was a terrible drunk. No one was safe from his father's rage, especially his mother and younger sisters. Numerous times he had watched as his father left his middle sister's room, and he heard her crying inside. As his younger sister got older, the same thing would happen to her. His mother would often come out of her room with a black eye or a bruised lip. However, he wasn't saved from his father's rage because he was a boy. His father would belittle him all the time about not being good at anything and not being a man. He would work him from dawn till dusk and then, if the mood was right, would beat him senseless for even the most minor infraction.

His escape often took him into unknown territory. He chose to follow in his father's footsteps and started abusing the animals on the farm. But it didn't stop there. Many of the neighbors complained to the local sheriff about their pets disappearing. The sheriff had visited the farm numerous times and never found any evidence that anyone on the farm was involved, but the neighbors knew the truth. What they had no way of knowing was how deep the depravity went.

One afternoon one of the neighbors questioned Thomas about a missing goat. The neighbor had seen the goatskin hanging in a tree along the creek behind the farm and confronted him and his father with the evidence, and a fight broke out. By the time the sheriff arrived, the neighbor was dead. His father, who was covered in blood, tried to put all the blame on himself, but the sheriff didn't buy it, and they were both arrested. His father was convicted and died in prison a few years later. Thomas was convicted and given a choice: jail or the army. He chose the army.

The army was a great place for him. They taught him how to kill, a skill he honed with great enthusiasm. He was so good at it that he was often the first soldier called upon when a Nazi guard needed to be dispatched silently. His knife became his friend, and he used it most effectively when an enemy officer needed to be encouraged to talk. He was a skilled craftsman, and his actions often turned the stomachs of even the most hardened soldiers.

Thomas had been able to keep the demons under control for the first couple of years after he moved to Aspen, but they became too strong for him to ignore. He needed to feed the demons, but Aspen was a small mountain town. Missing people would be noticed. At first, he tried to feed the demons with animal sacrifices. He stayed away from family pets—too close to home—and focused on wild animals, which were in abundance in the forests around Aspen.

Killing forest creatures with his bare hands was fun, but it didn't satisfy the demons for long. He needed the sensation and the arousal that came from killing another human being. The incredible satisfaction it would bring as he felt the life slip away from someone who had been a living, breathing person. He also missed the thrill of the hunt. Finding the right person and stalking them until just the right moment. He loved the challenge.

Alicia Hawkins woke slowly, stretched and lay there for a minute, thinking about the incredible night she had experienced. She felt her grandfather would be proud of her. Her skills had exceeded her wildest dreams, and she was ready to fulfill the promise she'd made to her grandfather before leaving for college. She had wanted so badly for him to still be alive when she felt she was ready to deliver on that promise, but that was not to be. Tears formed in her eyes when she thought about her love for him and her desire to live up to what he saw in her. She looked over at the lump under the bloody sheet.

She now believed she was strong enough to include men in her future endeavors. She had proved that to herself with the young cowboy. In all that ecstasy, she lost track of how many slices she had inflicted on him but knew he lasted longer than almost all the women, and she smiled. The more she thought about the previous night, the more excited she got, and she took a few minutes to pleasure herself again.

She couldn't remember ever feeling this satisfied, and she liked the way she felt. Standing up from the bed, she could feel the dried blood that covered her body crack as she moved. She walked into the bathroom, turned on the shower and stood under the hot water as it washed over her body, taking flakes of dried blood with it. The water that collected at the bottom of the shower was crimson, and it continued to amaze her how much blood the human body contained. She was also amazed at how much effort it took to scrub off the crusted blood, but by the time she was finished and stood in front of the mirror, she could see that her body almost glowed. She wasn't sure if it was the sex or the blood, but she liked the way she looked.

Alicia took a few minutes to clean the dried blood off the knives she'd used the night before and made sure they sparkled before she put them away. She had bought the knives at various flea markets while she was in Florida to replace the knives her grandfather had made by hand in his workshop. She'd left the knives in her grandfather's underground lair in Aspen when she made her first kill, and the authorities were on the tunnel so fast, she couldn't get back and retrieve them. It broke her heart and made her angry how things had turned out.

She made herself a huge breakfast because she was starving, and while she ate, she pulled out her laptop and looked at the news. She was thrilled that she had a government task force named after her, and it was fun keeping track of where they were. She laughed at how far behind her they were with the investigation. She had them running all over the Southeast, and they had no idea she was long gone. This was notoriety her grandfather had never achieved during the years he killed.

She liked to think about the number of kills her grandfather might have accomplished had it not been for the accident that crippled him, but it was okay because she was closing in on his number and had plans to far exceed it. Once she made good on her promise, she planned to head for California. The stories she read made it sound like a good place for serial killers to operate. She stopped and looked up from her coffee. "Oh, my god," she said out loud. "I am also now a rapist, just like my grandfather." She laughed and finished her coffee.

She knew she should get packed and hit the road, but she wasn't concerned. When she'd rented the cabin, she told the owner that she was looking for solitude and didn't want any housekeeping services for the entire week. Since she had gotten so lucky the first two nights she was in town, she still had four days before her rental was up. She also needed to make sure she ended up in Colorado at the right time to deliver on her promise. She couldn't risk getting caught before she delivered.

She washed the dishes by hand and put them back on the shelf. The sheets and towels were shot thanks to all the blood, so she decided to leave them where they were. She knew the evidence techs would do an excellent job of gathering everything up. The person she felt bad for was the housekeeper, who would show up in four days and find a bloodbath. She hoped whoever that person was had a strong stomach.

She wasn't concerned about leaving her DNA. The FBI knew who she was, and she figured that leaving her DNA all over the crime scene would help them know it was her and not a copycat who had committed the crime. It was important to her that they had her kill numbers correct. Mostly because she wanted to surpass her grandfather, but also so they would understand the symbolism of the promise she'd made to him.

CHAPTER FIVE

The promise began quite by accident on a cool summer night in the Jackpot Bar in Aspen. When Alicia had found the trophy box, there were sixteen pieces of jewelry in the box, but there were fifteen mummified bodies in the tunnel. There was a small jade horse pendant on a thin silver chain in the trophy box that she had admired, and she decided to wear it for a night out with her girlfriends before they all headed back to college.

The thrill of her first kill had started to fade. She had gone home that night and slept like a baby. The next morning, she still felt wired. The response hadn't been sexual, but the kill still excited her. She'd felt better and better about her technique as the night wore on. She'd really got an adrenaline jolt when the girl woke up and realized what was happening to her. If only it had lasted. The cut she had made across her neck must have hit the artery. She'd thought she was shallow enough, but there was a little spurt of blood that wouldn't stop. She would have to remember that for the next time.

She had been hoping there would be a next time before she had to leave for college, but it was not meant to be. She had been back to the bar every night after work since the first kill; this would be her last night in town, and she had not been able to find her next victim. She finished her drink and told her friends at the table that the next round was on her. Instead of waiting for the waitress, she walked up to the bar.

The woman behind the bar was the owner. Alicia hadn't really met her, but this was where she and her friends had hung out all summer, so they got to know who was who. The owner walked up and asked her what she needed. She gave her the order for three beers and laid a twenty-dollar bill on the bar.

The owner came back with three beers and stared at her for a minute. She was beginning to feel a little self-conscious when the owner finally spoke.

She had admired the necklace Alicia was wearing and wondered where she had found such a pretty piece? She told the owner that she had found it in a pawn shop in Florida. The owner looked at it a little closer and then said something that chilled her to the bone.

The owner told her she had had a necklace very similar to that one, but she'd lost it when she was in a car crash many years before. The necklace belonged to her grandmother, and she had borrowed it—well, actually stole it—when she ran away from home. She was in a crash a couple miles outside of Aspen, and the necklace had disappeared. No one at the hospital remembered seeing it.

Alicia asked the owner if she remembered anything else about the crash, but she said that she must have fallen asleep after she was picked up hitchhiking on the highway. When she woke up in the hospital several days later, she couldn't remember anything about the crash. The police told her that the man who had picked her up was probably going to die and that she was lucky to be alive.

She left the twenty on the bar, picked up the three beer bottles, and walked back to her table. She was too stunned to even talk. Luckily her friends were doing enough talking, so they never noticed.

She had taken the jade necklace out of her grandfather's treasure box. She had admired it since finding the box, and she decided that it would be one thing to remember her grandfather by. He had been slipping in and out of consciousness for the past couple weeks, and the family was not holding out much hope. Since it was her last night in town, and she was certain no one would have any idea where the necklace came from, she decided to wear it out. How in the hell could she have ever guessed that someone would recognize the necklace? What a huge clusterfuck.

She needed some air, so she excused herself and walked out the front door and stood on the sidewalk. The air was fall crisp, and it felt good. Her thoughts turned to the woman at the bar. She didn't remember anyone ever mentioning that there had been a passenger in the car with her grandfather the night he crashed. Was it possible this woman was in the car with him? How could that have gotten missed in the family stories? More importantly, was it her necklace that was in her grandfather's treasure box?

She put her hand up to her open mouth. "Oh, my god." This woman was supposed to be her grandfather's sixteenth victim. That's why there were sixteen mementos in the box, but only fifteen bodies in the mine. He had been on his way to the mine to kill her when the crash occurred. But why had no one ever mentioned a second person in the car?

The owner did not appear to know who was driving the car that night. She had no recollection of the accident. Alicia's grandfather must have already drugged her by the time he crashed the car. Alicia didn't know what he'd used as a sedative, but whatever it was, it had to have been fast-acting and very powerful. Powerful enough to induce amnesia?

She felt a chill run up her spine, and then in a moment of clarity, she struck on an idea. One that would hopefully keep her focused while she was away at school. She would finish what her grandfather had started that fateful night so long ago. She would take care of his sixteenth victim. She would need to devise a plan for this kill. It would take time, and it would need to be perfect. The owner was no slouch. She ran a bar. She would be tough to deal with, and she had a pretty good build, even after so many years. Alicia pictured the woman in her younger days and understood why her grandfather had chosen her. She was probably a real looker in her day, because she was gorgeous now.

This was awesome. What better way to honor her grandfather than to finish his journey? She felt her excitement build like it had the night of her first kill. It was a shame. If she only had more time. But that was okay. She would be back at Christmas. She would start working out the plan in her head, and by Christmas, it would be perfect. She just knew it. Her grandfather would be so proud of her.

She stepped back into the bar and shook off the chill from the night air. Her body was warm and tingling. She sat back down at the table where her friends were still talking away and took a sip of her beer. She looked over the top of the bottle and stared at her next victim.

The next morning her father and mother packed up the car and drove her to Denver for her flight back to Jacksonville. She hugged them and stepped into the security line. She wrapped her hand around the jade necklace and said a silent prayer that her grandfather would live long enough to see her complete his final act. She smiled as she went through security and waved goodbye to her parents.

Unfortunately, the FBI screwed up her plans for coming home at Christmas, but she decided a better way to honor her grandfather would be to kill his sixteenth victim on the first anniversary of his death. That anniversary was now a couple weeks away, which made her timing so important. She wrapped her hand around the small jade horse pendant, and tears filled her eyes.

She was about to close her laptop when a news article

caught her attention, so she sat back down at the table and pulled up the story. The article was mostly about her first kill in Aspen, the one that had started it all, and how the discovery of the body coincided with the death of a local wildlife ranger, another anniversary that was fast approaching.

There was a picture below the article, and her anger began to grow as she looked at the picture and continued reading the article. The picture was of Colorado Bureau of Investigation agent Buck Taylor, the cop who'd led the investigation that discovered her grandfather's underground tunnel, and that also led to the discovery of her first kill.

Although her grandfather had already been dying at the time, she blamed Buck Taylor for her grandfather's death, which she had convinced herself occurred sooner than it should have because of all the pressure from the investigation. The truth was that her grandfather had been in a coma before Buck Taylor ever entered his life, but her twisted mind didn't see it that way. She also blamed him because she was unable to get back to the tunnel for her grandfather's knives.

She thought about how awesome it would be if she could find a way to get to Buck Taylor while she was in Colorado. If she could end his life like he had ended her grandfather's life, that would be perfect. She knew getting to a cop would be difficult, but maybe, if she had the time, she could find out if he had any family nearby. She could take out members of his family and hurt him like he'd hurt her and her family.

Her mind was working on a plan when she noticed the other person standing next to Buck in the picture. She looked closer and recognized the person. He was a homeless man who had been around Aspen almost her entire life. The article mentioned that the homeless man had helped Buck with several cases over the years, and a new plan started to grow in her mind. If she couldn't get to Buck, maybe she could take out the homeless man, his friend. After all, how hard could it be to kill a homeless person? He looked old and skinny. It should be a piece of cake.

She closed her laptop, packed her suitcase and backpack and looked around the cabin. From the front door, you couldn't see that anything was amiss. She smiled, locked the door and headed for her car.

CHAPTER SIX

The home invasion team had watched the house for the past couple days, and they decided that the time was right. The dossier their stepmom had put together was thorough, and they found no anomalies. The team didn't understand how she'd gotten all the information, and they never asked. They knew she'd spent a significant part of her life working for the government. They each knew their assignments, and all they had to do was execute the plan.

The family they had been watching followed the same schedule every night. Dinner at six, then there was an hour of homework, and then they all moved into the den for two hours of family time. Tonight was movie night; the lights in the rest of the house went off, and the reflection of the bigscreen TV could be seen through the blackout drapes covering the family room windows.

The team figured they would give the family an hour and then make their move. They put on their one-piece spandex suits, placed the hoods over their heads, strapped on their weapons belts and covered the entire outfit with black nylon windbreakers. They looked like ninjas or an elite commando unit, and even though there were only three of them, they were as highly trained as any commando unit.

An hour after sunset, they were ready to make their move. Jessie pulled out her laptop and tapped into the family's digital assistant; she could hear the movie in the background. Typing in the code her stepmom had given her, she asked the digital assistant to turn off all the perimeter alarms and also disconnect the panic buttons. Her final task was to tap into the Sheriff's Office dispatch center and check to make sure she hadn't triggered any silent alarms. Everything was ready.

The team left their nest in the woods and made their way across the field behind the house to the patio door that was on the opposite side of the house from the family room. Slipping out his lockpick set, Earl went to work on the lockset, and within fifteen seconds, the door was unlocked. He slipped the tools back in his jacket pocket and slid open the door.

They waited for a minute to make sure there wasn't a dog they might have missed. Confident that they were good, they walked through the house, pushed open the door to the family room, flipped on the lights and charged into the room with pistols drawn.

The family responded like all the other families had. First, there was confusion, then a sense of fear and finally screams, as Earl and Toby grabbed the father and mother and threw them to the floor.

"What the fuck do you want?" shouted the father as he tried to reach his daughter and son, who were now being held at gunpoint.

"Take what you want, but please don't hurt my children," said the mother. The brothers sat on top of the father, bound his hands behind his back and slipped the gag into his mouth.

Jessie always found it funny that the mother was willing to give up her treasures to save her children, but there was never any mention of saving her husband. She hated these rich fucks, and after she left their houses, she always felt like she needed a shower. She looked over and watched Earl tie the kids to straight-back kitchen chairs they'd carried into the room. Her other brother, Toby, picked up the mother, set her down on the third chair and duct-taped her to it. Jessie could see the fear in the mother's eyes as she repeatedly turned her head to look at the kids. The kids looked petrified.

They positioned all the chairs in a square in the middle of the room and turned down the volume on the movie. Jessie stood watching the movie for a second and then turned to the mother.

"I love this movie," she said. "I hope your kids will still love it after we leave." The two brothers left the room and fanned out through the house. They knew exactly where to find the most expensive jewelry and rare paintings. The family's art collection was impressive. She figured being the CEO of an internet data security company paid well. She also laughed at how easily their stepmom had cracked Mr. Bigshit's home security system.

The brothers walked back into the family room and set down their now-bulging duffel bags. Toby walked out of the room and headed out of the house to get their SUV, which was parked nearby on a side road.

"Did you get the keys?" she asked Earl.

"They were not in the locked drawer in his office. Couldn't find them anywhere," he said.

She walked over to the father and ripped off the duct tape that was holding the gag in his mouth. The gag was soaked, and as she pulled it from his mouth he spit and sputtered.

"Where are the keys?" she asked.

She could see the defiance in his eyes, and he refused to answer. She pulled out her black semiautomatic pistol and rested it on his shoulder.

"Let's try this again. Where are the keys?"

"Fuck you." She was amazed at how calmly he said it. "You don't scare me with this macho bullshit. I will make sure they throw the book at you."

She looked him straight in the eyes and walked over to the mother. She started unbuttoning the mother's blouse, exposing her lacy bra. She could see the fear in the mother's eyes.

"I am going to have my two helpers rape your wife and then your daughter. She's, what? Sixteen? I'll bet she's still a virgin. My boys are going to change that. Now, where are the keys?"

"Fuck you, bitch. I don't have to tell you anything."

She looked at her brother, and he saw something he had never seen before. There was anger in her eyes, and she walked over and hit the father with the butt of her gun, creating a bloody gash across his forehead. She could hear the mother and the children scream into their gags. She looked around the room and spotted what she wanted on a nearby table. She grabbed the metal bowl, dumped out the popcorn and walked over to the father.

"One more chance. Where are the keys?"

He was about to speak when she slammed the side of his head with the metal bowl. Her anger welled up, and she hit him twice more with the bowl. Her brother stood there stunned, as blood flew all over the marble floor.

"Where are the keys?" She hit him again with the bowl. Blood covered the side of his head, and he leered at her.

"Fuck you, bitch. Do you know who I am?"

She hit him once again with the bowl. "Not only do I know who you are, I know what you are. You're a rapist and a sexual abuser."

She hit him twice more and grabbed his shirt. "You think

you're a big man because you hurt your wife. Let's see how you like it." She hit him several more times, and his eyes rolled back in his head. His face was a bloody mess, and his head lolled forward, his chin resting on his chest. The floor around the chair was covered in blood.

After a few minutes, her brother walked over and stopped her before she killed him, pulling the metal bowl out of her hand. The mother was bouncing up and down, still strapped to the chair. She walked over to the mother and ripped out the gag.

With tears in her eyes, the mother said, "Please don't hit him anymore. I will tell you where the keys are, just don't hurt him anymore."

She told them where to find the safe in the garage, and Earl walked out to check to see if she was telling the truth. Jessie shoved the gag back in the mother's mouth and stood there pointing her gun at her head.

Toby walked in, looked at the blood all over his sister and saw the unconscious man lying on the floor in a pool of blood.

"Holy shit. What the hell happened?"

"He got in my face, so I took care of him."

He walked over and checked the father's neck for a pulse. He nodded that he found one when Earl walked in with the keys.

"Got them. Let's get out of here. We are over our time."

The brothers grabbed the duffel bags and headed for the garage. Jessie looked around the room to make sure they hadn't missed anything, and then she walked over to the mother, who pulled back out of fear. She leaned down and looked at the mother.

"Your husband is an ass. Everything we took is covered

by insurance, but he wanted to sound tough. He is also an abuser, and he has raped you several times. You don't have to stay and put up with that shit anymore. Now, I don't know if he is going to survive or not, and I really don't care. He got what he deserved. You know it, and I know it. We are leaving. We have been monitoring your house for a week and will continue to monitor it until we are safely away. If you try to break free, we will come back, and we will kill your entire family. Once we are safe, we will alert the authorities and have them send an ambulance."

She turned and walked out of the room. The duffel bags were sitting in the back of their SUV, which sat in the driveway next to a shiny blue 2019 McLaren Senna. Her brothers slid into the SUV and started down the driveway. She climbed into the McLaren, fired it up and sat there for a minute, listening to the car purr. She could feel the incredible power between her legs. She pulled off her balaclava, let down her long blond hair, put the car in gear and hit the gas.

CHAPTER SEVEN

Buck Taylor stood on the flagstone veranda outside the family room of an incredible mansion. He estimated that the stone patio was twice the size of his entire house. He looked across the field towards the forest on the other side. The property was huge. In the distance, he could see the green tracks that indicated the ski runs of the Telluride Ski Resort. Soon winter would arrive, and those green tracks would be snow-covered. He turned away from the view as he heard footsteps behind him on the flagstones.

San Miguel County Sheriff Matt Anderson stepped through the multi-panel sliding wall and walked up to Buck.

"Crime scene techs will be done in a few minutes, and then we can go in." He took in the view Buck had been looking at. "Hell of a place, huh? Must have cost a fortune."

"Yeah, but what do you do with all that ground? There isn't a horse or cow in sight. Not an outbuilding to be seen. Kind of a waste."

The sheriff laughed. "These kinds of folks don't raise livestock. They control all this acreage because they can. It's all about power and the money it takes to buy it, and you know what all that power gets them?"

"Yeah," said Buck. "They become targets for anyone who wants to take it away from them."

The sheriff nodded.

"Tell me about the family," said Buck.

Colorado Bureau of Investigation agent Buck Taylor wasn't an imposing figure, but when Buck was on the crime scene, there was little doubt to anyone around who was in charge. At six feet tall and one hundred eighty-five pounds, Buck was in the best shape of his life. He still looked like he could play football for the Gunnison High School Cowboys, where he and his brother-in-law, Hardy Braxton, were once called the Wrecking Crew, and where they'd broken pretty much every state high school defensive record there was, some of which still stood today.

He wore his salt-and-pepper hair, which had a lot more salt than pepper in it, longer than the style of the day, and considerably longer than when his wife of thirty-four years, Lucy, was still alive. Today he wore a short Carhartt ranch jacket over a T-shirt and jeans. He had the jacket zipped up two-thirds of the way to hold off the chill from the cool north wind. Fall was in the air this morning, and the snow wouldn't be far behind.

The sheriff pulled out his notebook. Buck always felt better when he saw someone else who used a pen and paper instead of a tablet to take notes. He was known around the CBI office in Grand Junction as a technological dinosaur, and he considered himself lucky that his grandkids could help out when he did something to screw up the TV remote.

"The father is Henry Claremont. The mother is Theresa. Claremont is the founder and CEO of Pegasus Data Security. According to Forbes, he is worth about eight hundred million dollars. They bought the land and built this house ten years ago. He also owns several buildings in Telluride. The kids are Michael, age ten, and Sandra, age sixteen."

Buck didn't ask for the details of the case. He liked to walk through a crime scene for the first time unencumbered by the thoughts and opinions of others. It was a process that had worked well for him throughout his thirty-six years in law enforcement.

The sheriff was about to continue reading his notes when a tall, dark-skinned forensic tech wearing a white Tyvek suit and hood stepped out of the patio door and pulled off his surgical mask.

"You're good to go, Buck. We have everything we need," he said.

"Thanks, Franklin. Any usable prints?"

Franklin Williams was the lead forensic tech for CBI; he'd been assigned to a series of home invasions Buck and his team had been investigating for the past four weeks. So far, the perps hadn't left any fingerprints or DNA at any of the scenes, which was frustrating everyone.

"We ran elimination prints on the family, and we got the dad's prints off a bourbon bottle in his office. The daughter told us he was the only one who touched the bottle. We found two sets of unidentified prints, but there are two housekeepers that work alternate weeks. We'll run them through the system and see if anything pops, but we pretty much got nothing, again."

Buck could sense Franklin's frustration. He was feeling the same way himself. He asked Franklin to have the State Crime Lab put a rush on the samples and told him they could clear out. He nodded to the sheriff, and they stepped through the sliding doors and walked into a bloody mess, literally.

The first thing Buck noticed was the four kitchen chairs sitting in a square in the family room. They still had remnants of duct tape and plastic wire ties hanging off the arms and around the front legs. He stepped carefully around all the blood that had accumulated under one of the chairs. This must have been the chair the father was sitting in. From the amount of blood on the floor, Buck could tell that he was seriously injured.

Buck used his cell phone to take a series of pictures of the chairs, the blood and some close-ups of the tape and wire ties. These would be entered into his crime file once he had a chance to open his laptop. CBI had gone digital a couple years back, so instead of having a blue binder for each case, Buck just had to open a program on his laptop. The new case was automatically assigned a case number, and Buck would list everyone who needed access to the file and send them email invites. All evidence, lab reports, photos, etc. that were part of the case would be uploaded into the file, and anyone who needed access just had to open the file. This was a lot better than the old system where everything was placed in the binder by hand, and Buck would spend half his time trying to track down who had the binder.

For a tech dinosaur like Buck, this made his life so much easier, and he had ready access to anything he needed.

Buck walked through each room of the house and paid close attention to the rooms where items had been stolen. He stepped into the master bedroom and noticed the safe room door sitting open. The door appeared to be part of a bookcase and looked like it was usually closed, but the perps seemed to know where it was and how it opened. Inside he found several shelves with empty slots that at one time held expensive watches. The two jewelry drawers were open and empty as well. Buck made a note on his pad to get a list of everything that was missing from the insurance company. He also wanted to check and see if the cameras he'd noticed throughout the house and the safe room might have captured images of the perps. Whoever these home invaders were, they knew what they were looking for, and they'd taken only the expensive stuff and left the rest behind.

Stepping out of the safe room, Buck noticed the two lighter areas on the walls in the bedroom where pictures should have been. He photographed these and made a note to find out if these had been pictures or paintings.

His final stop was the garage. The safe behind the toolbox was open and empty. There was a hook inside that Buck assumed, at one time, held the key to the missing car. He stood for a minute and looked around the garage. For an amateur car enthusiast, Henry had the space better equipped than the garage and gas station Buck's dad had owned when he was growing up, and his dad had been a professional auto mechanic all his life.

Buck looked out the open garage door and down the driveway.

"How do you get a car like that down the driveway without anyone in the area noticing it? The car had to make a lot of noise," he said to no one in particular.

"You don't," came a disembodied voice from the other side of the garage.

Buck stepped around an MG Spider that was sitting on the lift in the next bay. "Who are you?" he asked the short, dark-haired man in the stained gray jumpsuit, who was removing the front tire from the car.

The man set the tire on the ground, wiped his hands on a dirty rag he pulled from his pocket and stepped up to Buck with his right hand extended.

"Roger Spearman, but everyone calls me Rocket. Pleased to meet you." He shook Buck's hand. "I'm Mr. Claremont's mechanic."

Buck started to say something, then he stopped and stared at the mechanic. "Rocket Spearman, the former NASCAR driver?"

"One and the same," said Rocket.

"I remember your crash in ninety-seven at Daytona. Everyone thought you were dead. How long have you been with Claremont?"

Rocket thought for a minute. "About five years. That's when he bought his first sports car. I keep all his cars running in top-notch condition. It's a shame about the McLaren. Too bad I wasn't here, or I'd have given those thieves what's for."

"Tell me about the car, I'm told it was expensive."

Rocket dug out his phone and pulled up his gallery app. He handed the phone to Buck. "Expensive ain't the half of it. Mr. C paid over a million bucks for that car. It was going to be the centerpiece of his collection. We'll never see that car again."

"Is there a market for a car like that?"

Rocket put his phone away. "Sure as hell is. Cars like that, they only make a couple hundred, if that many. I'm told there are folks in Asia and the Middle East that will pay serious money to get their hands on one. That car is probably already on a boat heading out to sea."

Buck made a couple notes in his notebook. "Do you live on the property?"

"Nah. The Mrs. and I have an apartment in Telluride. Last night we were home. The sheriff called me this morning when they got the call about the break-in, and I came over to check on the family and make sure nothing was stolen. My heart sank when I saw that the McLaren was gone. Damn shame about Mr. C getting beat up. Wish I would have been here to stop the bastards."

Buck thanked Rocket and went in search of the sheriff, who met him at the entrance to the house.

"I see you met Rocket," said the sheriff. "I have the kids sitting in the kitchen, figured you'd want to talk to them next."

"Any word on the father?"

"Flight for Life took him to St. Mary's Medical Center in Grand Junction. It's the closest trauma center. He's in surgery, and his wife is with him. He took a hell of a beating."

"How come they didn't take him to a Level One trauma hospital in Denver? St. Mary's is a Level Three."

"They weren't sure he would survive the trip, and St. Mary's has one of the best neurosurgeons in the country."

Buck nodded, and they walked towards the kitchen to talk to the kids. Ten-year-old Michael had his face in a video game and headphones on. His sister, Sandra, was sitting on the floor with her back against the cabinet, her legs pulled close to her chest.

Buck tapped Michael on the shoulder, and the kid almost jumped out of his seat. Buck asked him to turn off the game for a minute. He set the game on the table next to him.

"Michael, my name is Buck, and I'm going to try to find the people who hurt your dad, but I'm going to need your help. Can you tell me what happened?"

Michael looked like he would rather be any place else than sitting there with Buck. He squirmed and shifted in his seat and poked at his game tablet. When he spoke, his voice was low, and Buck had to listen carefully to hear him. There were also tears and sniffles.

He told Buck about the people in black clothes who came into the house while they were watching the movie, and about watching the girl beat up his dad with a popcorn bowl. Buck asked him if he could describe the people, and he said they had on masks. He did mention that the girl talked like his Uncle Mike, but he couldn't really explain what he meant. By this time, Sandra, still crying, had joined them at the table and had her arm around her little brother.

"The girl had a Southern accent," she said. "Our Uncle Mike lives in Louisiana. Her accent wasn't as heavy as his. More soft and gentle. She seemed to be the one in charge, because she ordered the other guys around, and she was the one who beat my dad." Tears flowed down her face, and Buck handed her a paper towel off the roll on the island.

Buck made notes in his notebook and asked them if there was anything else they could remember about the attack.

"The alarms didn't go off," said Sandra.

"Do you know if the alarms were set?" Buck asked.

"The system is automatic. Once 7 P.M. chimes, the entire house locks down. Dad set it up that way so we wouldn't have to remember to set it. We each have our own access code."

She led Buck over to a console on the wall and punched a couple buttons, bringing up a history page. Buck looked where she was pointing. According to the alarm history, the system armed automatically at 7 P.M. every night, like she said, but at seven forty-five the night before, someone had entered a code and deactivated the alarm.

"That's not one of our code numbers," she said.

Buck wrote the code number down and took a picture of the console. He then pushed a button on his phone and waited for the person on the other end to answer.

"Hey, Buck. What's up?"

"Hey, Bax, I'm sending you a picture of the alarm console. Can you contact the alarm company and see who might have entered the last code at seven forty-five? According to the daughter, the number does not belong to anyone she knows."

"Sure thing, Buck. I'll get right on it."

"Thanks, Bax. I'll call you in a little bit."

Buck hung up. "Good work, Sandra. This could help us out a lot."

"What's a rapist?" They both turned and looked at Michael, and the sheriff stepped away from the door and stood next to him.

"Where did you hear that word?" asked Buck.

Michael looked embarrassed, and he hung his head as if he'd done something wrong. Sandra looked at Buck.

"The woman said it to my mom before they left. She said my dad was a rapist and an abuser." Tears flowed like water. "Why would she say that? Our dad loves us."

The sheriff tapped Buck on the shoulder and nodded for him to follow. Buck left Sandra with her arms wrapped around her brother. Out of earshot, the sheriff pulled out his phone and opened a message.

"This came in on my private email account about ten minutes after we received the nine-one-one call about the break-in." He pushed play, and Buck held the phone up to his ear. A deep furrow formed across Buck's forehead as he listened to the call. He took the phone away from his ear.

"The email message said it was recorded at this location this past weekend, while the kids were staying at a friend's house. That sure sounds like a rape to me, and those voices are definitely the Claremonts'."

Buck played the message one more time. "Do me a favor and forward that to my email. You know these folks. Do you think what we heard is possible?"

The sheriff thought for a minute. "I've been in this business a long time, and I have come to believe that anything is possible. What troubles me is, if this is true, how did someone get a recording of it, and where did they get my private email address?"

"Good questions, for which I have no answer right now," said Buck. "These kids going to be all right here alone?"

"Rocket and his wife are going to take care of the kids until their grandfather can get here."

Buck handed the phone back to the sheriff when his own

phone rang. He looked at the number, frowned and put the phone back in his pocket.

"Look, Buck. I read the reports on two of the other break-ins. The physical violence went way up on this one. You think it's the same group?"

"Everything else fits, Matt, except for the violence. This team has no trouble terrorizing their victims during the attack, but they have never hurt anyone. I hope this isn't an escalation."

Buck thanked the sheriff for his help and headed for his car. His mind was wrapped around the violence he'd heard on the sheriff's phone.

CHAPTER EIGHT

Buck drove away from the house, followed Raspberry Patch Road and turned onto Route 145, heading towards Telluride. He was hoping to get to Grand Junction today so he could interview Theresa Claremont. The voice recording from the sheriff's phone played heavy on his mind. He was hoping he could get her to talk with him about what had happened. He also thought more about how the perps had gotten hold of the voice recording in the first place.

A mile or so north of Telluride, Route 145 took a hard left turn, and Buck headed north. His phone rang, and he frowned as he pulled it from his pocket. Recognizing the number, he answered.

"Hey, Hank. What's up?"

Hank Clancy, the special agent in charge of the Denver office of the FBI, barely let him finish.

"Where are you?"

Buck saw the sign for the Telluride airport. "Just passing the Telluride airport. Why?"

"Good. Pull in and wait at the fixed base operator there. I'm sending a helicopter for you."

Before Buck could answer, Hank hung up. Buck wondered what this was all about, but he knew if Hank was diverting a helicopter to pick him up, it must be important. Hank was a straight shooter and a consummate professional when it came to his duties with the FBI.

Buck pulled onto the road to the airport and climbed the hill to the parking lot. He found a space outside the FBO and pulled in. Telluride Regional Airport sat on the top of a mesa, north of the town of Telluride. In the early days, the local pilots called it the USS Telluride because landing at the airport was like landing on an aircraft carrier. There were steep drop-offs at both ends of the runway, so your approach had to be perfect, and you didn't want to miss it and have to abort your landing because the end of the runway took you straight into a box canyon. Landing at this airport was always an adventure.

Buck pulled out his phone and called Bax. CBI agent Ashley Baxter worked with Buck on a lot of interesting cases, in between working on her own cases. At thirty years old, she was one of the youngest agents in the Grand Junction Field Office, and she valued the time she got to spend with Buck because she learned so much about running an investigation. Bax was also a whiz at doing deep background searches, a talent Buck did not share, so he relied on Bax to help him out. They worked well as a team and had found themselves collaborating more and more as the years rolled by.

Bax answered on the second ring. "What's up, Buck?"

"Hey, Bax. You in the middle of anything right now?"

"No," she said. "I'm waiting for a call back from the alarm company. What can I do for you?"

Buck explained about the short, cryptic call he'd gotten from Hank Clancy. "I was planning on interviewing the wife today, but now, with this, I am not going to be able to get to St. Mary's, and I have no idea when I will be back."

"No worries, Buck. I can cover the interview. What do you think is up with Hank?"

"Not sure, Bax. I'm wondering if it has something to do

with Alicia Hawkins."

"You think they found her, and he wants you in on the bust? Wouldn't that be great?"

"Don't know. Listen, Bax. Something else. I am sending you an audio recording the sheriff received. Listen to the audio and then call me back and let's talk about it."

Buck hung up, pulled up the email and forwarded it to Bax. He grabbed his backpack off the back seat and checked to make sure he had a change of clothes and his laptop. He was closing his bag when Bax called back.

"Oh, my god, Buck. Is that what I think it is?"

"The sheriff and I both think so, which means my going on a trip might be a good thing. I hate to put this on you, but a woman doing the interview might be less embarrassing for her."

"That's not a problem, Buck. How do you want me to handle it?"

"We need to know if the recording is real and if that is her and her husband. If it is, we need to try to figure out how the perps got the recording. We also need her thoughts on what happened last night. You okay with all this?"

"You can count on me, Buck."

Buck smiled at the phone. "Of that, there was no doubt, Bax."

"Buck, you might want to call Jane and see if she can meet me there. Mrs. Claremont might need some moral support."

"Great minds, Bax. She's my next call. I will call you once I know where I am headed with Hank. And Bax. Thanks."

"Travel safe, Buck."

Buck hung up and looked at his watch. He had a few minutes until the helicopter arrived, so he hit another speed dial button and waited.

"Judge Morgan's chambers, Janelle speaking. How may I help you?"

"Hey, Janelle, it's Buck. Is the judge in?"

"Hi, Agent Taylor, please hold on for a second, and I will see." Buck liked talking to Janelle. For someone so young, she was very poised and professional on the phone, and equally so in person. Of course, at Buck's age, everyone seemed young.

"Hiya, Buck," said Judge Morgan. "What can I do for you on this fine day?"

"Well, today, I need to talk to Jane, not the judge."

Judge Jane Morgan, besides being a municipal court judge for Grand Junction, was also the chairwoman of a family trust that helped counsel and find housing and services for women and children that were on the receiving end of sexual violence. With the help of her husband, they had set up a safe house outside Grand Junction and had gathered together a staff of volunteers who were willing to work with these women and children to find the help they needed.

Buck explained the situation with Mrs. Claremont, and the judge listened without interrupting. When Buck stopped to take a breath, she said, "Buck, forward me the audio file. I want to hear it myself."

Buck forwarded the file for the second time and waited while the judge put him on hold. A couple minutes went by, and Buck checked his watch. He heard the helicopter in the distance, and he was about to hang up when the judge came back on the line.

"Buck, if this is real, this woman is going to need our help. I have one more case to hear this afternoon, and I will head over to the hospital to meet Bax as soon as I'm done. Don't worry about a thing. Bax and I can handle this."

The sound of the helicopter was loud as it settled onto the tarmac behind Buck. He covered his one ear and turned away from the craft.

"Jane, I have to run. You're the best. Thanks."

Buck hung up and put his phone back in his pocket, picked his backpack off the ground and headed to the helicopter and his flight into the unknown.

CHAPTER NINE

T he copilot handed Buck a headset as he climbed aboard and pointed to a console on the bulkhead behind the seat, indicating where he could plug in the end.

"Welcome aboard, Agent Taylor. There's water and a couple sandwiches in the cooler next to your feet. Agent Clancy wasn't sure if you had eaten. We will be in the air for about an hour and a half. If you need anything, hit the red button on the mic."

"Where are we heading?" asked Buck.

"Oklahoma. Agent Clancy will fill you in once we arrive. Please sit back and enjoy the flight."

Buck grabbed a bottle of water and what looked like a roast beef and cheddar sandwich out of the cooler and sat back as the pilot lifted off. He had never been a big fan of flying, especially in helicopters. He didn't like the noise and the vibration, except this helicopter was much quieter than the ones he'd flown in during his time in the army. Surprisingly, he dozed off about halfway through the flight and only snapped awake when the pilot touched down on a road in the middle of nowhere. The last vestiges of daylight were fading over the horizon as he stepped out of the helicopter and looked around. All Buck could see for miles in any direction were yellow fields.

A black FBI SUV was parked along the paved road about a hundred feet from the helicopter, so Buck headed in that direction. A tall, fair-skinned FBI agent with short blond hair stepped out of the car and opened the rear door. He extended his hand.

"Agent Taylor, Agent Tom Corwin. Please climb in, and we can be on our way."

"Nice to meet you, Tom. Please call me Buck." He looked around. "Where in the hell are we?" he asked.

"We're about twenty minutes from the location. Agent Clancy will explain everything when we get there."

Buck slid his backpack across the back seat, shut the door and climbed into the front seat. Agent Corwin pulled off the shoulder and headed west until he reached a dirt road in a wooded area that seemed to appear out of nowhere. After fifteen minutes of driving on the bumpy road, Buck saw, in the distance, the flashing lights of emergency vehicles. He could make out the outline of a decent-sized lake in the distance.

The SUV pulled behind several other black SUVs, and Buck opened the door, grabbed his backpack and slid out. He was standing in front of a log cabin, colored gray from prolonged exposure to the hot sun. The cabin was lit up like an amusement park, but he sensed that nothing about this scene was going to be amusing.

Agent Corwin directed him towards the front entrance, so Buck slung his backpack over his left shoulder and headed for the door. Hank Clancy stepped out of the front door as Buck approached. The two men shook hands. Buck noticed how tired Hank looked. It had been a while since they had seen each other in person, and Hank looked thin and drawn.

"Sorry about all the cloak-and-dagger stuff, Buck. We're trying to keep this low profile."

"What's going on, Hank? From the number of cars in the lot and the number of suits I see, I'm betting this has something to do with Alicia Hawkins."

Hank led Buck into the cabin. At first glance, it was a warm, cozy cabin with rustic wood furnishings and several good-sized fish mounted on planks of old barn wood and hung on the walls. This was obviously a well-cared-for property.

Hank spoke as they started down a hallway towards, what Buck assumed, were a couple bedrooms.

"The cabin belongs to Jack Pendleton. Been in his family for years. He rents it out on one of those vacation rentals by owner websites. Sight unseen, I might add. He never sees the tenant or has any personal contact with them. Everything is done online. Two weeks ago, he rented it to a woman named Susan Carson. She gave him a credit card number in that name, and the deposit went through with no issues. A week later, he collected the rest of the fee for the one-week rental. Susan Carson requested no cleaning service for the week she was here, which was fine with the owner since it saved him a lot of money. This morning the cleaners showed up and discovered a mess."

Hank stepped aside and let Buck walk into the bedroom. The first thing Buck noticed was the smell. Had it not been cold the last couple days, Buck imagined the smell would be a lot worse. The body was lying naked and exposed on the blood-soaked bed. There was blood on the walls, and the carpet was soaked with blood. There were bloody footprints heading into the bathroom connected to the bedroom. Buck looked inside the bathroom as they passed, and there was blood everywhere.

Buck stepped up to the bed as one of the FBI evidence techs stepped aside. His expression said it all.

"This is a male," he said. "If Alicia Hawkins did this, she's stepped up her game. I'm gonna assume the cause of death is exsanguination. It looks like she drained every ounce of blood this poor kid had. There are also a lot more cuts than the last case." He looked at Hank. "She's getting better at this. She's keeping them alive longer while she slices. How long?"

"Medical examiner figures three, four days max," said Hank.

"One more thing you need to see before we leave this body. Go ahead and turn him over, Doc."

The medical examiner and his assistant reached across the body and turned it on its side. Buck had no problem seeing through all the blood. Carved into the young man's back was Buck's name.

"There doesn't seem to be any doubt who did this, Buck. She left you a message," said Hank.

Buck stared at his name carved in the young man's back. He had no idea why she would single him out, but there was no doubt she had.

Buck nodded. "You said 'before we leave this body. Is there another?"

Hank led Buck out of the bedroom and down a flight of stairs at the end of the hall that led to a finished basement. The scene here was almost as bad. The walls and floors were covered in blood, with the same bare footsteps leading into another bathroom, this one also covered in blood. The young woman hanging from two chains screwed into the wall, with her feet shackled, dangled like a butchered piece of meat in a slaughterhouse. The look in her clouded-over eyes told of a horrible death.

"Fuck, Hank. Two in one week. How many does this make?"

"Thirteen and fourteen, if everything we found so far is hers." Hank turned and headed up the stairs.

Hank and Buck stepped out onto the front porch and

watched as the ME's gurney was lifted into the back of a hearse.

"Any identity so far on either body?" asked Buck.

"Not so far. We've only been here for seven hours. What do you make of her carving your name into the male victim?"

Buck thought for a minute. "I think she is sending me a message that this is not over yet. Maybe she's blaming me for sending her down this road. Who the hell knows with crazies like her?"

"You don't think it's a warning that she's coming after you? Maybe I need to get you protection," said Hank.

Buck looked at him with an intensity Hank hadn't seen before. "Don't even think about sending your agents to watch over me. I've got too much going on right now, and I don't need your people in my way."

"What about your family? You should, at the very least, tell them to watch their backs."

"My kids can all take care of themselves, but if it keeps you off my back, I will send them her picture and let them know to be careful with strangers."

Hank held up his hand in surrender. "Okay, Buck, but watch your ass, and if you see her, you make sure you call me. We're going to be here for another day or two before we regroup in Denver and see if we can figure out her next move. You get any thoughts, give me a call. Corwin will drive you back to the chopper."

Buck shook hands with Hank and headed back to the SUV. He slid onto the seat and didn't look back as they headed back to where the helicopter was parked. Buck thanked Corwin and climbed aboard the helicopter. He put on his headset and was asleep before they were airborne. Buck had been threatened before and would handle this threat the same way he'd handled all the others. He would do his job, and when the time and the opportunity presented itself, he would arrest Alicia Hawkins.

CHAPTER TEN

A shley Baxter walked up to the front desk at St. Mary's Hospital, and the same thing happened that always happened when Bax walked into a room. Men noticed her, at least until they saw the badge and gun that were clipped to her belt. Bax wasn't supermodel gorgeous, but she would be considered pretty by most people's standards. She had long blond hair that she wore in a ponytail that hung through the back of her CBI cap and amazing jade-green eyes.

She had a nice figure—not thin, but not heavy either. What used to be called a "mountain girl" figure. A little stocky, but with curves in all the right places. She carried herself with the grace of an athlete, and she moved with a certain fluidness that came from being a track star in college and years of running marathons with her dad. She stepped up to the desk, flashed her badge and asked where she could find the Claremonts. She was directed down the hall to the surgical waiting area. She was told that Henry Claremont was still in surgery. She thanked the volunteer at the desk and headed down the hallway.

She found Theresa Claremont sitting all alone in the empty waiting room, staring into space, the tear stains on her cheeks marking the passage of time. She looked up as Bax entered the room, surely wishing instead that it was the doctor coming to tell her that Henry was going to be all right. She gave Bax a half-hearted smile and went back to staring at the wall. Bax sat down next to her and opened her cred pack, so Theresa could see her CBI identification card. She slid the wallet back into her back pocket.

"Mrs. Claremont, I'm Ashley Baxter with the Colorado Bureau of Investigation. First, I want to tell you how sorry I am about what you are going through. A situation like this is never easy. We are investigating the home invasion at your place, and I'd like to ask you a few questions while things are still fresh in your mind. Would that be okay?"

Theresa Claremont gave her a tiny nod.

"If at any time this becomes too much for you, let me know, and we can stop and sit for a while. Can you tell me what you remember about last night?"

Bax sat back in the chair and let Theresa Claremont tell her story in her own way. Sometimes she would go on for a while talking with clarity, and then she would stop, the tears would flow and the conversation would lag. Bax didn't mind. One of the things she'd learned from working with Buck all these years was patience. On several occasions, she'd watched Buck sit in an interrogation room for hours with a suspect and never say a word. Just sit there and stare off into space. Never ask a question or even talk to the suspect, just sit there. She was amazed at how often the suspect would blurt out a confession just to break up the silence. Buck was the best interrogator she had ever seen, and patience was a huge part of his success.

Theresa Claremont was able to confirm the information Buck had gotten from the children. She did remember the southern accent, and she agreed with her daughter's assessment that it wasn't harsh like her brother-in-law's accent but was smooth and soft. She agreed that the woman seemed to be in charge, and she didn't understand why the woman had given her husband such a beating. She confirmed that her husband did mouth off to the woman and called her a bitch at one point. The tears began to flow.

Bax held off on asking about the audiotape Buck had sent her. Instead, she asked Theresa a series of conversational questions. Nothing about the case, but about her family and her life in Telluride. After a while, the conversation seemed to get more relaxed, and Theresa started to get comfortable talking to her. She was trying to figure out how to broach the subject of the tape when Judge Morgan walked into the room.

Bax stood up and met Jane at the door, and they shook hands.

"Hey, Bax, how are you doing?"

"Good, Jane. Nice to see you. I've been sitting here with Theresa, having a nice conversation about her family. Maybe you could sit with her for a while, so I can make some phone calls and see how her children are doing?"

Jane smiled. She was wearing jeans, a flannel shirt and boots, and she looked nothing like a judge, which was what she'd hoped for. Right now, she was just Jane and was here to help. Her petite figure and amazing smile helped her look younger than she should after almost thirty years on the bench.

Jane had listened to the tape a second and third time on the way over from the courthouse, and she knew what information Buck needed for his case. Her priority, however, was to help the victim, and even though she wasn't acting in her capacity as a municipal judge or as an attorney, she still held herself to a higher standard, and that included confidentiality. Buck knew, when he involved her in his cases, that she would invoke attorney-client privilege to protect the victim. She would do her best to get the victim to a point where she would feel comfortable telling Buck her story, but she would never tell Buck anything confidential without the victim's consent. Buck accepted that, and in all these years, he had never crossed that line.

Jane watched Bax walk down the hall and then sat down next to Theresa Claremont and introduced herself. At first, their conversation was very casual and was designed to help Theresa relax. At one point, the surgeon came out, dressed in his light blue scrubs, and sat down next to Theresa. Jane offered to leave, but Theresa grabbed her hand.

The surgeon told her that they had repaired as much of the damage to Henry's brain as they could. He would know more once the swelling went down, which could take a few hours or a few days. He told her that if her husband survived the next forty-eight hours, his chances of surviving would improve dramatically, but there was still a chance that he would suffer some brain damage. How much, there was no way of knowing, until he came out of the coma. He said that her husband would be in recovery for a couple of hours, and then they would take him to intensive care. She would be able to see him there.

The doctor put his hand on her shoulder and told her that he was available if she needed him. He bid them both a good night and walked back towards the surgical area.

Jane sat with Theresa and held her for a while until she sensed that Theresa might be ready to talk. She started the conversation slowly and ran into the same resistance she usually got from abuse victims. Nothing had happened. Her husband would never. People didn't know. Their marriage was a happy one. Lots of love. Jane had heard it all before over the twenty years that she and her husband had run the shelter. She listened and let Theresa talk and argue and cry, and then she played the tape for her. Theresa sat there, stunned, and all of a sudden, she started to tell Jane a story, and it all came out, every lurid detail. When she was finished, she sat back, exhausted, and closed her eyes. She had never told anyone the story before.

Jane pulled out her phone, called Bax and asked her to

come back to the waiting room. And to bring some coffee.

CHAPTER ELEVEN

P IS pushed through the back door of the Celtic Club, one of his favorite bars, and stepped into the alley between East Hopkins Avenue and East Hyman Avenue. As he let the door close behind him, he looked up and down the alley. It was late, and the alley was deserted. There was a fall chill in the air, and he felt warmed by the nightly glass of brandy he had just finished in the bar. He buttoned his linen coat, snugged down his black beret and turned up his collar against the chilly breeze. It was a beautiful night, and the sky was full of stars.

PIS had lived in Aspen for the past twenty-some years and was considered one of its most colorful characters, in a city filled with colorful characters. Everyone in Aspen either had heard of or knew PIS, except that no one really knew much about him. PIS was tall, about six feet two and gangly, as folks used to say. He probably weighed one hundred fifty pounds soaking wet. He had long gray hair pulled back in a ponytail, piercing gray eyes and a three-day growth of stubble on his face. The odd thing was, no matter what day or time you encountered PIS, his stubble was always the same. It never seemed to grow out or look untidy.

Unlike most of the homeless characters in town, PIS never smelled like a homeless person. He wore the same clothes every day but never looked dirty or unkempt. His outfit hadn't changed in over twenty years. He wore calf-height brown leather lace-up moccasin-style boots, light gray tuxedo pants with a dark gray stripe down each leg and a worn white dress shirt, frayed and yellow with age. Around his waist, he wore a bright red cummerbund, and around his neck, he wore a bright red ascot.

No matter what time of year or what the temperature was, PIS always wore the same tattered brown linen coat and a black beret. He looked rather elegant for a homeless person. His only other possession was a well-worn leather backpack that looked like it had traveled the world. The initials p.i.s. were stamped on the flap, and since no one knew his name, everyone called him PIS, which he never seemed to mind. His demeanor was always jovial and friendly, and no one ever complained about feeling threatened by his presence. Most striking was his British accent. Not the harsh Cockney accent you associate with street people, but a silky smooth accent that exuded sophistication.

No one ever saw him panhandling for money, yet he always seemed to have enough to visit one of the local pubs for his nightly glass of brandy. As it turned out, PIS also had an incredible talent, which helped him generate some income on a regular basis. PIS was an amazing tracker. There wasn't anything he couldn't find, whether it be an animal or a missing child, and his abilities had come to the attention of many of the local hunting guides, who paid him a daily fee to help them find game for their out-of-town clients. PIS's tracking skills had also come to the attention of the local police and sheriff, and over the years, he had been involved in finding many lost hikers or missing persons in the rugged mountains surrounding Aspen.

Early on, when he'd first arrived in Aspen, many people tried to engage him in conversation to try to determine his real name or his background. It was rumored that several times, people had tried to follow him as he left the downtown area and headed for the forest at the end of the day. No one was ever successful. Within minutes of entering the forest, PIS would completely disappear, leaving his followers bewildered. No one had any idea where he went at night or where he slept, but every morning he was right back downtown walking the alleys between East Hopkins Avenue and East Hyman Avenue, rummaging through trash dumpsters. If you asked people to guess PIS's age, you would get answers from forty to eighty. He truly was a mystery.

The sheriff had run his fingerprints once when an overzealous deputy tried to arrest PIS for vagrancy, and his prints came back as flagged, meaning some agency had restricted access to his information. PIS had become furious at the intrusion into his privacy, and ever since, there had been a truce between local law enforcement and PIS. He would provide his tracking services for free to any agency that needed such services; in exchange, local law enforcement would no longer try to determine his true identity. That truce had lasted almost twenty years.

PIS turned towards South Galena Street and started walking. Even though you couldn't see it, PIS was always aware of his surroundings. Passing the midpoint of the alley, PIS heard what sounded like someone whimpering. Never one to pass up someone in need, especially one of his homeless brethren, he started checking behind and alongside the bearproof dumpsters he passed. The crying grew louder.

Almost at the end of the alley, PIS spotted a brown lump lying next to the back door to the bookstore. His senses on full alert, he looked up and down the alley to see if there might be some help available if needed, and slowly he approached the lump.

"Hey, fella, are you okay?" he said softly.

The lump moved and made a moaning noise. PIS, sensing that this person was in serious trouble, stepped forward and knelt next to the lump. He was worried that this might be a drug overdose, which had become a serious problem amongst the homeless population.

With the opioid crisis in full swing, PIS had helped countless people in the shadows, and the Pitkin County sheriff had supplied him with several doses of Narcan, since he was the first responder for a lot of these folks. Knowing that fast action was essential in a drug overdose case, PIS had already pulled a Narcan dose out of his coat pocket as he approached the lump.

He reached out and touched the shoulder of the lump and pulled the person flat so he could evaluate them. The first thing he noticed was the purple-striped blond hair and the smell of vomit.

"Hey, young lady, can you hear me?" The only response was a long moan, and the young girl pulled her legs up tighter into her abdomen and rolled onto her side.

"Sweetie, what did you take?" PIS asked, his concern for her well-being growing.

The young girl started to moan louder, and PIS dropped his guard, grabbed her by her shoulder and pulled her, so he could lay her flat on her back. He barely felt the thin blade of the knife as it penetrated his coat, sliced through his faded white shirt and slid deep into his chest cavity. Momentarily stunned, he just stared as the young girl looked into his face with those piercing jade-green eyes.

She started to pull out the knife and then drove it into his heart even deeper, and then she smiled.

"When you see Buck Taylor in hell, tell him Alicia says hello."

She pushed PIS away, and the knife slid out of his chest. He was leaning back on his arms and was losing blood fast. Alicia Hawkins stood up and looked down at him, deciding whether it was worth it to slit his throat. No, she decided. It was better if he died slowly.

Suddenly, a voice came from down the alley.

"Hey, what's going on down there?"

Alicia Hawkins spotted a short man running down the alley towards them and decided it was time to go. She wiped the knife on PIS's coat, walked around the corner and disappeared down Galena Street.

Hector Martinez reached PIS just as he fell onto his back. He pulled back his coat and saw the blood seeping through the white shirt.

"Oh, my god," he said with a thick Mexican accent. He made the sign of the cross and pulled out his phone.

"Nine-one-one, what is your emergency?"

"This is Hector Martinez. Someone stabbed Mr. PIS. He is bleeding very badly. Please hurry!"

"Hector, where are you?" asked the 911 operator.

"The alley off Galena by the bookstore. Hurry!"

He dropped the phone on the pavement, pulled off his jacket and pressed down hard on the bloody wound in PIS's chest. He heard sirens in the distance and said a silent prayer that they would get there in time.

CHAPTER TWELVE

The home invasion team sat around the table, playing cards and drinking beer. The downtime felt good, as they had pulled off six major jobs in the last seven weeks. The time off was good for morale, and it was good to keep them off the radar for a while.

Their dad grabbed another beer from the fridge and sat down. "Good job on the watches and jewelry, guys. Our take was almost half a million dollars after service fees."

Everyone at the table high-fived, and they toasted their success. They knew from listening to the police networks across the state of Colorado that they had gotten away clean. They also knew that their last male victim was in the hospital in critical condition.

Jessie didn't feel bad about beating him to a pulp. He was a pig and had abused his wife on more than one occasion, and they had only been monitoring the family for a week. Who knew how many times in the past he had done the same thing?

Jessie was a tough woman. She had been a star softball player in high school and college, back when she and her family had lived an almost normal life. They knew about hardship growing up poor in North Carolina, but that all changed when Victoria Larsen entered their lives. The kids didn't know a lot about her past before she married their father, but they knew a lot of her life was still classified. They knew she had retired early from the Central Intelligence Agency, and they knew she was a master hacker of the highest order. The rest they didn't care about because they had more money now than they had ever seen before and were having a wonderful time with their new careers as home invaders and car thieves.

Jessie's brother Earl was dealing the next hand when their stepmom walked out of her office and sat down at the table with a new manila folder in her hand. She had a big smile on her face.

"First off, I got a call from our friend in Europe. They deposited six hundred thousand into our account for the McLaren. It's safely on the boat and will be in Germany by the end of next week. Great job all around."

She opened the manila folder and handed everyone at the table a copy of the dossier for their next victim. They each took a minute to look over the information.

"We may have hit the jackpot with this one. Our friend in the Middle East has a buyer already standing by if we can deliver." She slid a printed page over to Jessie. She read the paper and said, "Wow."

Victoria continued. "If we can pull this off, our split for the car alone will be two point five million dollars, and the money is already in the bank waiting. We will also be famous for stealing one of the most expensive cars in the world."

They all laughed and high-fived again.

"This will not be easy," she said. "I found one available here in Colorado. If we can take this one, we can pull out of here and head towards Montana for a couple weeks of rest before we head out to California. I already have several clients lined up in California who have what we need to keep our customers abroad happy for a long time to come."

Jessie's youngest brother, Toby, asked Victoria about security. He had heard about this next victim and knew this man could pay for some of the best protection available.

"You're right, Toby," she said. "This one is not going to be a walk in the park. Everything will need to go like clockwork. I have already started monitoring his location, and I am running software to try to crack his internet encryption. Besides the car, this guy has some incredible jewelry pieces in his collection. This could be a huge payday if we don't get sloppy. Now let's get some rest. We still have one more order to fill in Colorado before we try for the big prize, and you guys need to be on-site within the next two days. We promised the buyer that this would be in his collection by the end of the month, so we don't have a lot of time. While you are sitting on this next project, your dad and I will be heading to Aspen to start our surveillance."

They were too wired to rest, so Jessie and her brothers decided to hit the Rodeo Bar and Grill and listen to some of Telluride's best country rock.

CHAPTER THIRTEEN

Buck was sitting at a booth by the window in the Elkhorn Diner on Main Street in Telluride. Because of the lateness of the helicopter flight, he'd decided to stay and rent a room for the night at the Elkhorn Lodge, a quaint twelve-unit B&B a block off Main Street. He'd stayed here once before when Lucy was still healthy. That seemed like a long time ago, even though she'd passed away a little over two years ago.

He thought about his life with Lucinda Torres, Lucy to everyone who knew her, and how she'd decided, during senior year in high school, to take a chance and date a jock. She'd always assumed he was conceited and would spend their entire date talking about his prowess on the football field. What she found was a soft-spoken, sensitive gentleman who was interested in her. After that first date they were inseparable.

Buck cut into the French toast he had ordered for breakfast, took a bite and washed it down with a swallow of Coke, his first one of the day. There would be several more before the day was over. His Coke drinking was legendary around the CBI office in Grand Junction. He was about to take another bite when his phone rang. He looked at the number, frowned and slid the red button to the left, sending the call to voice mail.

Buck finished his breakfast, left a nice tip for the waitress and headed for his state-issued Jeep Grand Cherokee. His plan for the day was to head to the office in Grand Junction and meet up with Bax. He wanted to see how her interview with Theresa Claremont went and to see if the judge had had any luck getting her to talk about the possible assault. He was sliding into the car when his phone rang. It was CBI Director Kevin Jackson. This time he answered.

"Yes, sir," said Buck.

"How did your trip to Oklahoma go? Is this Hawkins woman gonna be our problem again?"

"It might be, Director. It was definitely her kill, and it appears she's heading in our direction."

The director was silent for a minute. Jackson had become the youngest person ever appointed to head up the Colorado Bureau of Investigation when he was tapped by Governor Richard J. Kennedy to run the agency. He spent the early part of his career on the administrative side of the Colorado Springs Police Department and was highly regarded by the law enforcement community. He was not only an effective manager, but a seasoned investigator in his own right. Buck held the man in high regard.

"I understand she left a personal message for you, Buck. You okay with that, or do we need to send you on a long vacation?"

Buck knew the director wasn't serious about the vacation, but he wondered if maybe there wasn't a little bit more to his offer. The director held Buck in high regard as well. He'd almost lost Buck a few years back, during a drug investigation Buck was running in Durango against the Sonoma Cartel out of Mexico. In the end, it wasn't the cartel that tried to kill him, but two suspects in a triple homicide that Buck was also working at the time. The director didn't want to face the prospect of losing him again.

"No, sir. Won't need a vacation. I doubt she would try to

come after me, and there is little information about my family available in the public record. Besides, they can all take care of themselves, and I'm going to give them a heads-up that she's on the loose."

"Okay, Buck. You need anything, you let me know. How are you coming with the car theft cases?"

Buck filled him in on the limited information they had so far, and he told him that he would get back to him once he had a chance to talk to Bax. The director thanked him, told him to yell if he needed anything and hung up. Buck went to put his phone away when it rang again.

"Hey, Bax. I was just leaving Telluride for Grand Junction. What's up?"

"Wanted to fill you in on the time we spent with Theresa Claremont. We wrapped up the conversation about an hour ago. Jane headed home to get ready for court, and I got Mrs. Claremont situated in a hotel near the hospital. By the way, Jane was awesome. Once she got her talking about her life with Henry Claremont, we couldn't stop her. She did confirm that the audio file is her and her husband, and it was not the first time it happened. It seems her husband has a short fuse and doesn't accept no for an answer."

Bax took a breath, and Buck asked, "Does she have any idea how the recording was made?"

"No. She was as shocked as we were when she heard it. She can't imagine how it happened, but I had an idea, and I wanted to catch you before you left Telluride. Can you run back to their house and see if they have a digital assistant?"

"Sure thing. Are you thinking someone hacked into their internet feed?"

"Possibly, or there could be electronic bugs in the house. It's the only two things that make sense."

"If I have the digital scanner in my backpack, I'll run a

quick sweep of the house while I'm there and see what turns up. Why don't you go home and crash for a while and let's meet this afternoon in the office and compare notes? How is her husband doing?"

"Not good," said Bax. "According to the surgeon, if he survives the next forty-eight hours, he will be out of the woods, but he could still be a vegetable. The damage to his brain is extensive. Oh, how was your helicopter ride last night? Do we have anything to worry about?"

"Maybe. I'll fill you in later. Go rest."

Buck hung up, called the sheriff and asked him to meet him at the Claremont house. Then he started his car and followed the route he had taken last night.

The sheriff was standing by the front door when Buck pulled his Jeep into the driveway and parked next to the sheriff's SUV. He opened the hatch, grabbed his backpack and headed towards the front door.

"Hey, Buck. How's Henry Claremont doing?"

"Not good, Matt. The next forty-eight hours will tell the tale." Matt Anderson nodded.

Buck explained to the sheriff what he was looking for, the sheriff unlocked the door and they entered the front foyer. Since the house was huge, they decided to separate to cover more ground. As the sheriff headed upstairs to the private space, Buck pulled out a portable scanner from his backpack and started scanning the ground floor for electronic bugs.

After two hours, they met back in the kitchen. The sheriff hadn't found any recording devices in the private spaces on the second floor, and Buck's scan of the ground floor came up empty. It was possible that the home invasion crew had removed any bugs that were in the house, but Buck thought that was unlikely. He was putting the scanner back in his backpack when he spotted the white tower sitting on the counter next to the coffee maker.

Buck walked over to the counter, picked up the device and faced the sheriff.

"Is this what they call a digital assistant?"

The sheriff walked over and looked at the device in Buck's hand. "I believe that is. My son has something like this in his house. Gives him the weather and traffic in the morning. I think it does other stuff too, but technology is not my thing."

"Do you think this could have picked up sound from the bedroom, sitting here on the counter?" asked Buck.

"I'll bet not, especially in a house this size. I know my son has a few—I think he calls them pucks—spread out around his house, so he can talk to this thing from anywhere. Let's take a quick look and see if we can find something like that."

By the time they got back to the kitchen, they each carried a half dozen pucks they'd found in various rooms. They laid them on the kitchen counter and looked at the small pile. Buck took a picture of the tower, the information tag on the bottom and the information that was printed on the pucks. Once he got back to Grand Junction, he would have Bax contact the manufacturer to see how vulnerable these things were.

Buck thanked the sheriff, stowed his backpack in the back of his Jeep and headed for Grand Junction.

CHAPTER FOURTEEN

J essie and Toby drove by the target house and slowed down as they approached the driveway. The gate was imposing: at least ten feet tall, solid wood, with two massive brick columns on either side. They couldn't see the house from the road, but Victoria had included a Google Earth picture in the dossier. The property wasn't as big as the place outside Telluride, but the house was huge. This was some serious money.

As they passed the driveway, the two sections of the gate started to swing open. Jessie pulled to the side of the road and looked in the rearview mirror. She hoped that once whoever was pulling out of the driveway went by, they would have time enough to turn around and get a view of the house before the gates closed.

The sound of the car was the first thing they heard. The throaty roar of pure power immediately kicked their adrenaline into high gear. They watched in awe as the lime-green car pulled through the gate, stopped momentarily at the edge of the road and then blasted out onto Highway 34, flying past them. All they could see of the driver was long blond hair blowing in the wind and mirrored aviator sunglasses, and in a flash, she was gone, leaving a cloud of dust behind her.

Jessie pulled off the shoulder and swung the car around. The gates were still standing open as she drove by. Toby took pictures of the inside of the property as they went, concentrating on the area around the gate, where they could see a security camera mounted to a pole. There were no signs of any guards or a keypad. It looked like the only way to open the gate was to be seen approaching the gate by the camera. It must be monitored from somewhere in the house. This was going to complicate things.

She turned the car around and risked one more pass in front of the gate. She was looking for something she didn't see. There were no cameras on the street side of the gate. She wondered how someone driving up to the gate could notify whoever was watching from inside that they needed entry. It was possible there were cameras mounted in the trees surrounding the gate, or it could be a sensor in the ground in front of the gate. Whatever it was, they were going to have to do a lot more research.

Pulling away from the gate before she attracted any unnecessary attention, she headed down 34. The plan was to meet Earl at a small restaurant in Estes Park and start to put together a game plan. Victoria, as always, provided them with all the access codes and passwords they would need to access the house. They had a complete dossier on everyone in the house, as well as the domestic staff. They would watch the house, both electronically and visually, for a couple days until they could get a feel for how the family went about their daily business, and they would focus on the perfect opportunity to strike.

Jessie cruised down Highway 34 and turned right onto West Elkhorn Avenue. She slowed down as they approached the center of town and looked for a parking space. She was stunned when she spotted the Lamborghini parked in front of the same restaurant where they were meeting Earl. What were the odds? They had never been to Estes Park, yet of all the places to eat, they'd chosen the same place as the driver.

Jessie found a parking space half a block down from the

restaurant, and she pulled in. There was a crowd of what she assumed were mostly tourists standing on the sidewalk, gawking at the car. Even standing still, it looked like it was traveling at two hundred miles an hour.

Jessie and Toby strolled by, looking like locals with their dark brown Stetsons, jeans and cowboy boots. Toby even wore a large Western-style belt buckle. They stepped into the restaurant and removed their sunglasses to let their eyes adjust to the light. Earl was sitting at a table for four in the back corner with a view of the dining room, and he waved as they walked in. He was dressed like his brother and sister. Since there were several other people having lunch who were dressed just like them, they felt comfortable.

Earl casually nodded and shifted his chin slightly to the left. Jessie followed his movement and spotted an attractive blond woman sitting at a table for four with three other women. They were drinking wine, laughing and giggling like schoolgirls. Jessie and Toby sat down at the table, with Jessie taking the chair that gave her the best view of the woman.

They made small talk while the server took their orders, and then they got down to business. They discussed the wooden gates and the fact that they could not see any active surveillance equipment anywhere near the property. They decided to give Victoria a call after dinner and ask her to look into possible security systems that matched what they had been able to see. It was agreed that Earl would take the first surveillance shift, and he told them he'd found a spot down the street where he could watch the gate. As for inside the house, the information would have to come strictly from what they could pull off the internet, but they were lucky there. Victoria had spotted a vast number of cameras showing almost every area of the interior.

The woman and her friends laughed out loud at something one of them said and ordered another bottle of wine.

They didn't seem to care that they were attracting attention, which Jessie thought was typical of people like that. She pulled out her phone and opened the dossier from Victoria and perused the pictures. She looked from her phone to the woman.

Based on the pictures, the woman was Constance Fontaine. She was the wife of almost-billionaire Jerry Fontaine, industrialist, philanthropist and recently announced owner of the Las Vegas Knights, NFL team and current Super Bowl champs. The car, according to Victoria, had been a gift for his wife to celebrate their fifteenth wedding anniversary. According to the dossier, they did not have children, which led Jessie to wonder what they did with all that space in the house.

The women were still laughing when Jessie paid the bill for dinner, and they headed for their cars. They would head out in different directions and make their way back to the RV parked in the Mary's Lake campground. As they walked past the car, Earl stopped to look in the dark-tinted windows. It was hard to make out anything with all that shading. He stepped up on the sidewalk and whispered in Jessie's ear.

"Why don't we stop her on the road when she heads home? The way she's been drinking, her reaction time would be way out of whack. We could take the car and leave her on the side of the road. That would save us a lot of work trying to figure out how to get through the gate."

Jessie looked at him. "We've never taken a car without doing a lot of research before we struck. You know Victoria doesn't like spontaneity. Every contingency must be accounted for. You think we could put this together before she leaves the restaurant?"

Earl nodded. "All we need to know is how close Dad is. If he's within a half hour or an hour of here, we could meet on a dark road and make the transfer."

"That would get us to Aspen four days before we were planning to be there," said Toby.

Jessie thought about it, stepped away from the car and pulled out her phone. Victoria picked up on the second ring, and Jessie told her what they had seen so far, and then she told her about the start of a plan she had formed in her head. Victoria listened without comment until Jessie was finished.

"It makes sense, especially based on what you saw at the gate. I would hate to miss out on an opportunity that's right in front of our faces, but I'm worried about the logistics."

"Logistics is my job, yours is information. I think we can set it up and execute it, as long as Dad is close by."

"Okay," said Victoria. "Let me call your dad and see where he is and discuss it with him. I need to make sure he's ready to make the long drive on such short notice. Give me a few minutes, and I'll call you back."

Victoria hung up, and Jessie walked back to her brothers. "Victoria is calling Dad. Earl, why don't you head back along the highway and see if you can find a good spot to make the stop? Start working out how we're going to do it. Toby and I will wait for Victoria to call back."

Earl nodded and headed towards his SUV, while Jessie and Toby sat on a wooden bench a block from the car. They were discussing the approach when Jessie's phone rang.

"Your dad is on the Peak to Peak Highway. He said he will meet you a mile north of Allenspark; it should take you about twenty-five minutes to get there. He said there's a wide spot in the road near a picnic area. He'll be ready for you. One last thing. Don't force it. If it doesn't look good, abort, and we will try to figure out the gate issue. I'll monitor the police bands and the house and keep you apprised."

Jessie hung up the call from Victoria, smiled at Toby and called Earl.

"It's a go. Toby will stay here and watch the car until she leaves. I will head your way so we can set up the approach."

Jessie hugged Toby and headed for her car.

CHAPTER FIFTEEN

Buck was sitting at a table near the back wall of Santini's Italian Restaurant on Main Street in Grand Junction when Bax walked in and grabbed the chair opposite him.

"Hey, Bax."

He slid the menu across the table. Bax picked it up and, before looking at it, ordered a glass of pinot noir from the waiter, who had appeared, almost ghostlike, at the table. This was one of Buck's favorite spots to eat when he needed to be at the CBI office in Grand Junction.

While Bax looked at the menu, several people stopped by to say hi and chat for a minute with Buck. Bax looked over the top of the menu.

"Is there anyone you don't know?" she asked.

Buck smiled and picked up his glass of Coke. His phone rang before he had a chance to take a sip, and he looked at it and frowned. He slid the red button to the left and put the phone back in his pocket.

"Do you need to get that?" she asked.

"Nah, I'll deal with it later."

The waiter appeared, and Bax ordered the cheese ravioli with vodka sauce. She handed the menu to the waiter and picked up a piece of Italian bread off the plate on the table and dipped it in the seasoned olive oil.

"So, tell me about Oklahoma. It's not every day you get to ride in an FBI helicopter. Was it Alicia Hawkins?"

Buck looked around the restaurant to make sure no one was listening.

"Yeah. This time she left the FBI two bodies, and one was a male."

Bax stopped chewing and looked at him. "Is she stepping outside her comfort zone? So far, she's only done women. This is a new wrinkle."

"And not a good wrinkle. She appears to have honed her craft to a new level of sick. It also appears she was able to keep the male alive a lot longer than any of her previous victims. The number of cuts was astounding."

Buck lowered his voice and looked around the restaurant. He didn't want to be overheard, giving gory details in an Italian restaurant.

"Do they have an ID on either victim?"

"Yeah, the male was a young cowboy. No family they could find. He worked on a cattle ranch about a half hour from the cabin he was found in. I talked with Hank on the way here. The FBI spoke to the other cowboys from the ranch. They were all together in a bar and that's where she picked him up. The other cowboys were shaken up, since most of them had tried, at some point during the evening, to pick up the pretty girl with the purple-striped blond hair."

"Are they certain it was her and not a copycat? I heard she has quite an internet following."

"Yeah, Hank wouldn't have dragged me out to Oklahoma if he wasn't sure this was her. Her DNA was everywhere. She doesn't try to hide her identity anymore. I think she believes she is smarter than all of us, and so far, she might be right. The FBI is chasing their tails."

"Do you think she's coming here? Back to Colorado?" asked Bax.

Buck finished his mouthful of food. "I don't doubt it for a minute, but I can't figure out why she would risk it. In almost a year, the FBI hasn't even gotten close to her. Why now?"

Bax thought about it while she ate some of her ravioli. She held off answering until the waiter walked away from the table. The second glass of wine went down too easy.

"Maybe the FBI got it wrong. You said yourself that her DNA was everywhere, but if the FBI hasn't processed it yet, assuming it's her, then maybe they're wrong."

"They didn't get it wrong."

"Then maybe this is a fake-out, like Georgia. Fuck, Buck. From Oklahoma, she could be heading anywhere."

Buck set down his fork and looked at Bax. "It's not a fake-out." He hesitated a second. "She left a message."

Bax looked surprised. "What kind of message?"

"She carved my name in the kid's back."

Bax almost dropped her glass of wine. "Seriously? But why your name? You're not even involved in the investigation and haven't been since the Feds took over. She must know that?"

Buck's frown said it all. "Yeah, that's the problem that has the FBI confused. The profilers have no idea what it means."

"Well, it sounds to me like she's calling you out. Do you really think she would come after you?"

"Hank's worried she might try to go after my family. None of it makes sense."

"Have you called your kids to fill them in? They need to be on alert."

"I was going to make those calls tonight to give them a

heads-up."

"Buck, are you all right with this?"

Buck smiled. "She comes after me, and her life as a serial killer will end abruptly."

"Okay, tough guy." Bax smiled. "What do you need me to do?"

Buck thought for a minute. The FBI was running a nation-wide manhunt, but Colorado was Buck's world, and he had no intention of sitting back and waiting for the FBI to do their job. This was where knowing a lot of people might come in handy.

"Can you pull her college photo from the file and some-how add purple streaks to her hair?"

"If I can't, we have an entire building of talented people. I'm sure someone can. What do you want to do?"

"Let's put out an APB to all of Colorado, and let's cover Wyoming, Utah, Kansas, Nebraska and New Mexico, just in case she did decide not to come here. Let's also get the CBI Public Information Office to circulate her picture to all the TV, radio and newspaper outlets, here and in those states as well."

"How about hotels, motels, VRBOs and social media?"

Since the internet was not Buck's friend, he didn't even know how that stuff worked, but if Bax could do it, then why not? He nodded in agreement.

"On the VRBO sites, let's mention single woman looking for an isolated location," he added.

"What are you going to do?" she asked.

"Tomorrow, I'm heading to Aspen to talk to her family, to see if any of them have heard from her."

Buck finished his dinner. While they waited for dessert, he

switched gears.

"Were you able to get ahold of the company that manufactured the digital assistant to see if they think someone could hack their machine?"

"I did one better. I subpoenaed their records. The judge mentioned that she read a trial transcript from another state, and these machines can record the conversations that take place around them. The companies keep those recordings. She signed the subpoena and suggested we get all the records for that individual unit and see what it has to say. The hard part will still be trying to see if someone was able to hack the unit and listen to the recording, but one step at a time."

"Great idea. It's good to have a judge on our side. Once the records come in, get them over to the techs and see what they can find. In the meantime, let's proceed with the plan as we discussed."

They paid their bill, and they each left a hefty tip since they had occupied the table a lot longer than most of the surrounding diners. They grabbed their backpacks and headed out into the night. Bax zipped up her vest against the chill. They turned down Main Street, and Buck walked Bax to her car, which was parked on the next street over. Buck was a dinosaur in many respects, and even though he knew Bax was as tough as they come, he still felt it was his duty to escort her safely to her car. Chivalry was still alive in Buck's world.

They said goodnight, and Bax slid into her Jeep and headed for home. Buck walked two blocks over and stepped into the lobby of his hotel. He had some calls to make before he crashed for the night. It had been a hell of a couple of days.

CHAPTER SIXTEEN

Buck got back to his hotel room, clicked on his laptop and grabbed a Coke from the refrigerator. He sat down at his desk and signed into the case file for the home invasion–car theft case. Carefully and with precise detail, he entered a synopsis of everything that had transpired during the past couple days, read the entries and saved the file. He then went into the folder labeled Lab Results and reviewed the latest information from the crime lab. There wasn't much.

Other than prints and DNA from the family and the staff, there was no other DNA to be found. He closed the file and opened the files for the other home invasions. He read through Bax's case notes and looked over the lab reports. It was like he was reading the same report each time, except for the violence. With the information he'd gotten from Bax about the conversation with Theresa Claremont, he felt he understood where the violence stemmed from, but he wasn't sure what had set it off.

He clicked out of the file, sat back in the chair and put his palms against his temples.

"These folks are stealing high-end cars that should stand out like a sore thumb, yet no one sees or hears a thing. How is that possible? How are they moving the cars without being noticed?"

He looked around the room and said out loud, "This is great. Now I'm talking to myself. Sometimes I think I'm getting too old for this shit!"

He took another sip of Coke, grabbed his phone and dialed his oldest son. David was a police officer with the Gunnison Police Department. He looked a lot like his dad when his dad was his age. Slightly taller than Buck and slightly heavier, but the resemblance was striking. Unlike his father, David still moved with the ease of a young man.

David was a sergeant and was now the night shift supervisor. He liked working the night shift and had been a patrolman on that shift for many years. He enjoyed the calm and quiet of a small mountain town in the early morning hours.

David answered on the second ring. "Hey, Dad, what's up?"

"Hey, yourself. Do you have a minute to talk?"

"Yeah, it's a good time. I'm covering the desk for a while, and so far, it's been quiet. What's going on?"

Buck filled him in on the home invasion case, and they bounced around a couple ideas, but nothing that made a lot of sense. He then got to the point and told David about the new information they had on Alicia Hawkins and the message she'd left for Buck.

David listened carefully. "Hold on a minute, Dad." He could hear the printer running in the background.

David picked up the phone. "Just got an APB from your office. Pretty girl. Doesn't look like a serial killer."

Buck looked at his watch. Bax hadn't gone home after they left the restaurant. She must have gone back to the office and spent the last hour putting together a current picture of Alicia Hawkins. Buck's email alert chimed, and he opened his laptop. There she was in all her glory, purple streaks included. Buck left the email open and went back to his call.

"Yeah," he said. "Pretty girl who has already killed fourteen people in less than a year. Do me a favor. Give Judy and the kids copies of her picture, without the description of her crimes, so they can have it with them for the next couple weeks. Let the kids know that if they see this girl, they need to get to the nearest adult and call 911."

"No worries, Dad. Do you think she would really come after you or us?"

"I don't know, David, but I don't want to take any chances. This girl is extremely dangerous, and I don't have a clue what her next move is going to be."

They talked for a few more minutes about the kids, and then Buck hung up. He reopened the email from Bax, read the information and was pleased. He couldn't have done a better job. He forwarded the email to Jason and Cassie and closed his laptop.

He dialed his youngest son and Jason answered the phone. Jason was an architect, and he lived in Boulder with his wife, Kate, and their three children. He listened in silence as Buck told him about Alicia Hawkins. Buck knew Jason would take it differently than David had. Jason was more sensitive, and he tended to take things to heart and worry a lot more than his brother or sister. Of all of Buck's kids, Jason was the one who had continued to follow Catholicism, just like his mom, and he'd seemed to get more involved in his church after Lucy died. They had the same conversation, including talking about the kids, but it took a little longer to convince him that the email was just a precaution. Buck hung up and took another sip of Coke. He wasn't worried about the kids being able to take care of themselves. He'd made sure when they were growing up that they knew how to handle a weapon, and they each had concealed carry permits. He'd also spent a lot of time on the range with his older grandchildren, and he was confident in everyone's abilities.

His last call was to his daughter. Cassandra, or Cassie to

everyone she knew, was the middle child, and she was every bit a middle child. In high school, she'd played soccer, ran track and played volleyball. She lettered in all three sports. She was also the one who got in trouble for violating curfew, drinking and getting into whatever other mischief she could find. Buck was surprised when she was accepted to the University of Arizona with a full scholarship for volleyball. He was even more surprised when she was accepted into law school. Cassie had never been one for regimented education.

Three years ago, she suddenly dropped out of law school, and her career path took a different track. She joined the Forest Service and was now working as a wildland firefighter with the Helena Hotshots, one of the country's elite firefighting teams based out of Helena, Montana.

Buck had not been surprised by any of this. He never saw her sitting behind a desk as a lawyer. She loved the outdoors, and she was as tough as they come. Lucy wasn't pleased that she quit school without any discussion, and she always worried whenever Cassie was called out on a fire, but she also knew her daughter, and if this was where she was happy, then so was her mom.

Cassie's phone went straight to voice mail, so Buck assumed she was out on a fire line somewhere. He left her a message about the email he'd forwarded to her and told her to call when she had a minute. He hung up and decided to call it a night. He closed his laptop, set his alarm for six and climbed into bed. He knew tomorrow was going to be a busy day, but he had no idea how soon tomorrow was going to start.

CHAPTER SEVENTEEN

Toby sat on a wooden bench across the street from the bar and licked his chocolate ice cream cone. Most of the shops on the street had closed, and the street was almost vacant of tourists. The sounds coming from the bar meant that there was quite a party going on, and he wished he could be inside having a drink with a pretty girl instead of sitting outside in the cold watching a car, but this was his job, and he would do as he was told.

He pulled up the collar of his jacket and settled into the bench when the door to the bar flew open, and the four laughing women stumbled out the door. Toby didn't need to use the microphone app on his phone to hear what they were saying. Anyone within half a block could have heard. They all promised to get together again, and then they hugged and each headed for their cars.

Toby figured that women who looked like that never worried about getting a DUI. All they would need to do was slide up their miniskirts a little, and most cops would turn a blind eye. He figured it must be nice to be rich and gorgeous, and these four women had the whole package.

He watched Constance Fontaine fumble with her key fob, and then she threw her purse onto the passenger seat, climbed in and fired up the turbocharged engine. He was certain the noise must have woken up half the people in town. She put the car into reverse and pulled away from the curb, never looking to make sure she wasn't going to hit anyone.

She threw the car into drive and stomped down on the gas. The car took off like a shot, her blond hair flying wildly in the wind.

Toby speed-dialed Jessie and looked around to make sure no one was watching. "She just left the bar and is heading your way." He hung up, sat back on the bench and settled in. Once Jessie and Earl were done, one of them would be back to collect him.

Jessie hung up her phone and called to Earl, "She's on her way, get ready."

Jessie had changed into a miniskirt that showed a lot of leg, high heels and a sequined blouse. They'd decided that a woman would be more inclined to stop to help another woman, especially a woman who was dressed similarly to herself. Jessie also had on a long brown wig to cover her blond hair and dark sunglasses to hide her eyes.

Earl, in the meantime, had positioned Jessie's car in a conspicuous spot and opened the hood. He was walking back into the woods along the road when he heard the throaty roar of the approaching car. He could tell from the sound that she was really moving, and he yelled to Jessie to get ready.

Jessie leaned into the engine compartment as Constance Fontaine blew through the stop sign and blasted onto Highway 34. From down the road, all you could see were these beautiful long legs leaning into the car. It was a sight that would have made any guy stop, but would it be enough to stop Constance Fontaine?

That question was about to be answered. Constance blew past them. They thought they had miscalculated, then the red brake lights came on and the car stopped. The white back-up lights popped on, and the car flew backward, making them worry if she was going to stop, but she did, right in front of Jessie's car.

The door flew open, and Constance bounced out of the car, long blond hair flying in the air. She stumbled, stopped, reached down and slipped off her high heels and walked barefoot back to Jessie.

"Hey, girlfriend, what's going on?" she slurred. She stumbled again and almost went down but caught herself and walked up next to Jessie.

Jessie told her she had no idea what was wrong with the car and would she be kind enough to call a tow company? Constance never even questioned why Jessie didn't have a phone of her own, but she nodded and then leaned into the engine compartment like she had some idea how to fix the imaginary problem.

Earl walked up behind her and jammed the needle into her exposed thigh. Between the sedative and the excessive alcohol, she barely flinched. She fell over the side panel and didn't move.

Jessie pulled two pairs of flex-cuffs off the front seat and looked up and down the highway.

"Okay," she said. "Like we planned. Carry her back into the woods, tie her hands and feet and then follow me to Dad, then we can run back and get Toby. She should be out for at least an hour, if not longer."

Earl lifted Constance over his shoulder and headed back into the woods. He had picked out a good spot where she would be comfortable and couldn't be seen from the road. Victoria would alert the authorities once the car was secure and they were on their way.

Earl carried her to the spot he found and laid her on the ground. As he did, her skirt slid up, and Earl couldn't help but notice that she wasn't wearing anything under the skirt. He found himself getting aroused, and he knew he had a minute or two before Jessie was changed into her jeans and ready to leave, so he pulled down his pants and slid into Constance.

He was almost finished when he heard a car pull to a stop on the road, so he pulled up his pants, secured her hands and feet and silently approached the road. The car was an older Ford Explorer, and a guy in a dark suit was standing next to it.

"Excuse me, miss, where is Mrs. Fontaine, and who are you?" he asked.

Jessie froze. She had already gotten dressed in her jeans and a T-shirt and was leaning into the car, pulling her shoes out when the car stopped.

Thinking fast, she said, "I'm Ashley Rivers, we were together at the bar tonight. Constance is on the other side of the car, throwing up. I stopped to give her a hand."

The guy in the suit reached into his jacket and pulled out a phone, keeping a close eye on Jessie. As he dialed, he heard someone step onto the gravel behind his car, and he did the most foolish thing he could have done: he momentarily glanced behind him. He didn't see Earl, but when he turned back, he dropped his phone on the ground and pushed back his jacket, revealing a holstered pistol. He pulled his gun, but that momentary glance was all Jessie needed. She had reached into the car, pulled her silenced pistol and fired as he turned. In the quiet of the highway, the silenced shot still sounded loud, but her aim was true. The bullet struck the guy in the forehead, and he fell back and slammed into the ground.

Earl came around the corner of his car, looked at the body on the ground, picked him up and headed into the woods. He placed the body next to the now-immobile Constance Fontaine and headed back for the car.

Jessie grabbed the phone and pistol off the ground with gloved hands and threw them into the woods. She looked at

Earl. It had been almost five minutes since they had drugged Constance, and they were behind schedule. They needed to move.

Earl mentioned that he'd spotted a dirt road about a half mile down the road, and he would take the guy's car down there and hide it and then come back and retrieve Jessie's car. He told Jessie to take off in Constance's car, and he would catch up with her. She nodded, headed for the car, jumped in and put the car in gear.

Earl was worried. He had taken longer with Constance than he should have, and it had almost cost his sister her life. He wouldn't let that happen again. He pulled the guy's car back into the woods on the narrow dirt road, ran back to Jessie's car, slid in and headed towards Allenspark.

CHAPTER EIGHTEEN

Buck wasn't sure if it was the ringing in his ears or the nightmare that had woken him, but whichever it was, he was not happy. The nightmare was the same one he had been having over the past couple weeks, and it always ended the same, with his late wife, Lucy, being sliced up by Alicia Hawkins. He didn't understand why he was having this nightmare. He couldn't remember ever having them before, about any of the cases he had worked, and he had worked some pretty gruesome cases. There was something about Alicia Hawkins that he seemed to be having trouble dealing with, but he couldn't put his finger on it. He knew one thing for sure when he woke up. The bug that ran around in his brain when he got involved in a case was bouncing around wearing combat boots, and that got his attention.

The other thing that got his attention was the phone ringing next to the bed. He turned on the bedside lamp, checked the number and answered.

"Hey, Bob. What's up?" Buck wiped the sleep from his eyes and took a long drink from the warm Coke bottle sitting on the nightstand.

Robert Brady was the Aspen, Colorado, police chief, a position he had held for nearly fifteen years. He and Buck had worked together on several cases over the years, but the most noteworthy was a case involving a missing thirteen-year-old heiress that had happened twelve years ago. Every investigator had that one case that got away or that kept them up at night, and that case was the one that Buck carried with him everywhere he went. The old dog-eared file had a special place in Buck's backpack, and he reviewed it weekly.

The young girl had disappeared from what, for all intents and purposes, was a safe, happy home. Her wealthy parents —her father being an heir to an international shipping company—were vacationing in Aspen at the time with the young girl and her brother and sister. The family had several security guards they traveled with, and the house had the latest in security technology, yet no one saw anything, and the security system didn't catch anything unusual.

Buck was called in when the locals ran into a brick wall, and he wasn't able to make any headway. He followed up on a couple potential suspects, but nothing panned out, and a nationwide Amber Alert led nowhere. It was as if the girl had vanished into thin air. Buck and his friend PIS, a member of the Aspen homeless community and one of the best trackers Buck had ever met, spent countless hours in the woods around the house, trying to find any sign of the girl, but to no avail.

Buck still spoke with the girl's mother periodically. Her father had passed away a couple years back, never knowing what happened to his little girl.

Buck hadn't spoken with Bob Brady in several months, so when he saw the name on his phone, he wondered if something in the case had broken open. He couldn't have been more wrong.

"Sorry to call so early, Buck, but I thought you'd want to know." He hesitated for a second. "PIS was stabbed tonight. He's in critical condition at Aspen Valley Hospital. They are getting ready to take him into surgery. He lost a lot of blood."

Buck had to clear his mind to make sense of what Bob Brady said. "Is he going to be all right?"

"Too early to tell. Doc says the blade went in deep, and whoever stabbed him knew what they were doing."

"Bob, any idea who did it? Was it another homeless person?"

"We just started investigating, so we have no idea. We know he was at the Celtic Club, and that he left a little after midnight, and we know Hector Martinez called nine-one-one at twelve twelve a.m., so it happened right after he left the bar and started walking down the alley."

"Do you have Hector in an interview room?"

"Right now, he's here in the hospital with the rest of us. He went in the ambulance with PIS. Doc says he probably saved PIS's life. You can talk to him when you get here. I've got to run. Get here as soon as you can, before it's too late."

Buck hung up his phone, grabbed a quick shower, got dressed and clipped his badge and gun to his belt. He threw some clean clothes in his go bag, grabbed his coat and then stopped to pull out his phone and send a text to Bax.

PIS STABBED. HEADING TO ASPEN. I'LL CALL WHEN I KNOW SOMETHING

He ran out of the hotel, jumped into his Jeep and hit the gas. As soon as he pulled onto I-70 Eastbound, he called the state police dispatcher and told the woman who answered that he was en route to a crime, where he was heading and that he had his emergency flashers on. He didn't want to blow by a state trooper and end up in a chase, especially this early in the morning. He flipped the switch on his dash that activated the red, white and blue flashers that were buried in his grill and rear window and punched it.

It was typically a two hour and fifteen minute drive from Grand Junction to Aspen, but Buck made it in a little over an hour and twenty minutes. He pulled into the parking lot and sat for a minute to calm down.

The last time he had been at this hospital was when PIS was brought in to remove a five-inch chunk of wood from his shoulder. A year ago, PIS had helped Buck and the Pitkin County sheriff search for a missing Parks and Wildlife ranger after her dog was found shot in a parking lot near the Maroon Bells trailhead.

The female ranger, Susan Corey, was found murdered, her body concealed in a ravine several miles from the trailhead. PIS had used his tracking skills to find the body, which was no easy task. After finding the body, he led Buck and two Pitkin County sheriff's deputies on a search for the killers. They found an old cabin and were ambushed by the killers, who turned out to be two young boys. They were living in the woods with an old Vietnam vet and several younger kids, all of whom had been kidnapped by the one young killer's mother. The cabin had been rigged to explode, and PIS was able to push Buck out of the way, just in time, but he ended up getting a chunk of wood driven into his shoulder. Both young boys were killed during the gun battle that took place around the cabin, as was the older vet.

It was while PIS was being worked on by a Gunnison County deputy who had EMT training that they noticed that his back was covered with deep scars. It was another interesting piece of information to add to the mystery they all called PIS.

PIS had survived that encounter, but Buck was concerned about his chances of surviving this encounter. He would hate it if PIS died without anyone knowing his real story. He was also worried about who would want to hurt him. He didn't know any of the details, but he did know that everyone who knew him thought the world of him. He was soft-spoken and easygoing and didn't act like any homeless person anyone had ever met.

Buck slid out of the Jeep, grabbed his backpack and headed

into the hospital. The sun was coming up over the mountains, and he knew this was going to be a long day.

CHAPTER NINETEEN

J essie pulled the Lamborghini to a stop at the end of the ramp. Her dad stood to the side and watched as she slowly drove up the ramp into the back of the semi, pulled to the front end of the trailer and shut off the car. She climbed out, walked back towards the ramp and closed the intermediary doors behind the car. Her dad was in the process of sliding the cargo racks back into place.

The cargo racks could be slid out of the back of the trailer and swung aside. This had been an expensive addition to the trailer, but well worth it. Before they had the racks installed, they had to unload the boxes by hand and then put them all back, in the correct position, to hide the hidden compartment. This took a lot of valuable time that they could ill afford.

Now, all they had to do was push a button on the controller to slide them out of the way, fully loaded, and when they were ready, push another button to slide them back. The entire process took less than five minutes, and any inspector or cop on the road would only see full boxes of clothing as far into the trailer as they could see.

The company that had built the system was one of Victoria's contacts from her CIA days and had performed the same kind of work for several government agencies and private contractors. The system was designed initially to hide human beings that needed to be moved from one location to another without being seen. According to Victoria, many of the world's dictators had escaped their countries using the very same system. She also said the system was used by Tier 1 operators, SEALs and Delta Force, to get into locations too hot to use conventional insertion techniques.

They were putting the last rack in place when Earl pulled into the picnic area parking lot.

Jessie was not happy. "What the fuck were you doing when that security guy showed up?"

Earl looked surprised. "What? You told me to make sure she was tied up, so I was working on that when I heard the car pull up."

Their dad walked up after closing the trailer doors. "What's going on?"

"Nothing," said Earl.

"Nothing, my ass." Jessie turned to face her dad. "I had to kill a guy who stopped on the road. He showed up as we were getting ready to pull out. I had to wait for Earl while he dumped the woman in the woods. The guy heard Earl coming out of the woods and went for his gun. I had no choice."

"What did you do with the guy?" asked their dad.

Earl turned. "I put him next to the woman; she was still out cold. When she wakes up, she's going to be freaked out." He laughed.

The scowl on their dad's face said it all. "Did you put your sister in a compromising position while you fucked around? She asked you a question."

"And I answered her. I was securing the woman. I took her back a ways from the road so no one would see her. I was finishing up when I heard the car pull up."

Jessie looked at him with laser-focused eyes and started to say something. Their dad put up his hand for silence. "We're losing time. Go get your brother and head for Aspen.

Victoria will text you the location of the RV."

He turned and walked towards the cab, climbed up inside and put the transmission in gear. He pulled out of the picnic area and headed south. In less than an hour, he would be turning onto I-70, and in two days, he would be at the warehouse in Long Beach, California. Three days total and the car would be on its way to Asia, to some wealthy media mogul, and their bank account would be a lot fuller.

Jessie punched Earl in the arm. She could tell by looking at him that he was not telling the truth. She had been able to read him like a book since they were little kids. She wanted to say something, but they were wasting time. In a couple hours, the sun would be up, and she wanted to be out of Estes Park and on the way to Aspen. Just another group of tourists enjoying Colorado.

They pulled into Estes Park and found an empty parking space on Main Street. They spotted Toby sitting in a small restaurant having breakfast, walked in and sat down. The waitress came over with a coffee pot in one hand and two menus in the other. She poured the coffee while they read the menus, and they ordered.

Toby leaned in closer. "Three cop cars went by about ten minutes ago. I called in, and Victoria said she made the call a few minutes before that. She said Dad called and told her you guys had a problem."

Jessie looked across the table at Earl, who diverted his eyes to his cell phone. "Nothing we couldn't handle. It's all good," she said.

She glared at Earl, and Toby could sense the tension, but he let it go. The restaurant was no place to discuss this issue. They were almost finished with breakfast when two sheriff's department cars blew by with lights and sirens, followed by an ambulance. They paid their bill, left a decent tip and stepped out into the morning air.

They made their way down Main Street, looking in some of the shop windows as they went. They looked like all the other tourists that were starting to congregate on the sidewalk. Once they reached their SUV, they climbed in, pulled out of the space and headed back the way they'd come. In a couple hours, they would be in Aspen, ready to start their next project.

CHAPTER TWENTY

B uck walked into the surgical waiting room, looked around and spotted Bob Brady, the Aspen police chief, sitting against the back wall next to a short, older Hispanic man with black wavy hair. Hector Martinez was still wearing his blood-covered janitorial company shirt and pants. Bob Brady looked up from his phone, spotted Buck and met him at the door; they shook hands.

"Thanks for coming, Buck."

"Any word?" asked Buck.

"No. Still in surgery." He looked at his watch. "Been about four hours."

"Bob, what happened?"

"Not sure. I've got everyone I can spare working on this." He waved over Hector, who walked up and shook Buck's hand.

"Hector, this is Buck Taylor, from the Colorado Bureau of Investigation. He is a friend of Mr. PIS, and he could use your help."

Buck smiled at him. "Hector, first, thanks for helping PIS. They tell me you saved his life." Hector shuffled his feet and looked embarrassed.

"I hope I did enough. Mr. PIS is always good to me." A tear formed in his eye.

"Hector, would you mind answering a few questions for

me? I know you've already told the chief everything, but I'd like to hear it for myself if that's okay?"

Hector nodded, and Buck pointed towards a couple chairs. They sat down, and Hector wiped his eyes.

Buck put his hand on Hector's shoulder. "It's okay. Can you tell me exactly what you saw and did last night? Don't leave out any details, no matter how small."

Buck clicked on the voice recorder on his phone and set it on the arm of the chair.

"I had just finished cleaning the bank building, like I do every night. I stepped out back into the alley to have a cigarette. I cannot smoke at home. Maria, my wife, does not allow it." He smiled. "I had just lit up when I looked down the alley and spotted someone leaning over a pile on the ground. Something did not seem right, so I started walking down the alley. That was when I saw it was two people. I yelled to see what they were doing, and the person kneeling next to the person on the ground looked up, saw me, said something to the person on the ground and stood up and walked around the corner."

"I ran the rest of the way down the alley and spotted Mr. PIS on the ground. I reached down to see if he was okay, and my hand came away covered in blood. I used my phone to call the police. There was so much blood."

Hector's hands started to shake, and he looked at the bloodstains on his pants. Tears filled his eyes, and he looked up at Buck. "Who would do such a thing? Mr. PIS, he never hurt anyone."

Bob Brady handed Hector a bottle of water, and he took a long drink.

"Hector, did you recognize the person who was kneeling next to Mr. PIS?"

"It was dark, and I did not get a good look at the face. The person was wearing one of those sweatshirts with the hood on it like all the kids wear."

"Could you tell if it was a man or a woman?"

"It could be a man, but he would be very short, I think shorter than me, so maybe it was a woman. I wish I could help."

Buck told him he was doing fine and gave him a minute to take another drink and compose himself.

"You said the person said something to Mr. PIS. Could you hear what was said?"

"No, I was too far away. I saw the person lean down to his ear, and I saw his mouth move, but I could not hear the words."

"Hector, did you notice any kind of weapon in the person's hand?"

Hector squinted his eyes and thought back on the events of the night. He nodded. "I think I saw a knife."

He looked surprised as he squinted a little harder. "Yes, something flashed in the light from the street when the person stood up." He looked at Bob Brady. "I do not know why I did not remember this when I spoke to your detective."

Bob Brady told him it was okay and explained that he was probably in shock and that he might have new memories pop up over the next couple of days, and it was important that he contact the police if that happened.

Buck continued. "Hector, you said the person stood up and walked around the corner. He didn't run, he just walked away? Are you sure?"

Hector thought for a minute. "No, I am sure. He walked away like he was not in a hurry." He looked puzzled.

Buck nodded his head to Bob Brady and stepped out into the hallway. The chief followed.

"Anything about his story seem odd to you?" asked Buck.

"Yeah, probably the same thing that's bothering you. The guy was spotted by someone running down the alley, and he took the time to say something to PIS and then walk away like he had nowhere to be."

Buck thought about this for a minute. In his career, he had seen criminals do a lot of weird things, but this seemed odd.

"Anything at the scene that might cast doubt on Hector's story?"

"Can't say for sure. I'll check in with my detectives and see what they've found. What are you going to do?"

Buck looked at Hector, who was sitting alone in the waiting room. "I'm going to stick around a while and wait for the doctor. Can you get Hector home and have someone collect the clothes he's wearing? I want to get them down to the State Crime Lab as soon as possible."

Bob Brady nodded and walked back into the waiting room. He spoke with Hector for a minute, and then they both stood up and walked out the door. Hector stopped and reached out his hand to Buck.

"I will stop by the church and pray for Mr. PIS. I hope you will find the person who did this."

Buck shook Hector's hand and watched as Hector and Bob Brady walked down the hall towards the front entrance. Buck grabbed a seat along the back wall, sat back and closed his eyes.

CHAPTER TWENTY-ONE

Bax pulled her Jeep in behind a Larimer County Sheriff's Department SUV, grabbed her backpack and headed for the group of cops standing along the road. She presented her ID to the officer at the crime scene tape and asked for the officer in charge.

Detective Lawrence Boyd was an average-height black man with a bald head and a thin mustache. He had been with the Larimer County Sheriff's Department for fifteen years and was a seasoned investigator. Detective Boyd was talking with two crime scene techs when Bax walked up and introduced herself. The detective dismissed the techs and turned to face Bax.

"Detective Boyd, Ashley Baxter, CBI, nice to meet you."

"You as well, Agent Baxter. The sheriff said you'd be arriving. So what can I do for you?"

"The first thing you can do is call me Bax; everyone does." He nodded. "Secondly, can you run me through the scene?"

Detective Boyd nodded, stepped off the shoulder of the road and headed into the woods. They ducked under the crime scene tape and walked back about fifty yards until they came to a group of technicians working in various locations around the body, which was lying near a tree. Boyd asked one of the techs if it was okay for them to approach, and he said it was.

Bax pulled a pair of black nitrile gloves out of her backpack and pulled out her cell phone. She approached the body, and about five feet out, she started to circle it, using her phone to record her progress. The body was a middle-aged man of average height with brown hair and a good build. She figured he was about forty years old. He also had a bullet hole above the bridge of his nose.

She knelt next to the body and took a couple still photos of the wound.

"Caliber?" she asked.

"Nine mil," said Boyd.

She asked the tech to roll the body and noticed minimal damage to the back of the head. She'd expected more.

She looked up at Boyd. "No exit wound. Any idea how far away the shooter was?"

"We found blood on the gravel on the shoulder, next to tire marks. We found another set of footprints about twenty-five feet in front of those. The techs think the gun might have had a silencer, which slowed the bullet down. That's why it didn't blow out the back of his head. We'll know more once the pathologist can dig it out."

Colorado was one of about a dozen states that still used the coroner system, instead of the medical examiner system. The coroner for each jurisdiction was an elected official, and that person did not have to have any experience or even be a medical professional. Anyone could run for coroner. The system was gradually evolving so that the coroner was required to complete a formal training program in death investigations, but it was a slow process. Unlike in the medical examiner system, and since the coroner did not have to be a doctor, coroners would contract with a licensed forensic pathologist to handle any investigations that required an autopsy. These forensic pathologists were highly trained doctors who split their time among several jurisdictions to keep costs down. Many of the forensic pathologists were current or former medical examiners, and several were retired, working part-time to keep their hands in the game.

Bax stood up, turned off her phone and stepped back from the body.

"Tell me about the other victim," she said.

Boyd pulled up his notes on his iPad. "The victim is Constance Fontaine." Bax let out a low whistle, and Boyd nodded.

"From what we were able to get out of her before we got her to the hospital, she was out drinking with some friends in Estes. She was still pretty wasted when we found her, and we think she might have been drugged as well. Anyway, she said something about pulling over to help a girlfriend and not remembering a thing after that until she woke up in the woods with her hands and feet bound, lying next to a dead body."

Boyd looked a little uneasy. "Something else, detective?" Bax asked.

He looked down at his tablet. "The first officer on the scene thinks she might have been raped. She is missing her underwear, and the female officer who checked her over said it looked like she had dried semen on her thigh. The officer accompanied her to the hospital, and I called the hospital and asked them to do a rape kit."

Bax looked down at the body. "Who's this guy, and how does he fit in? Good Samaritan in the right place at the wrong time?" she asked.

"His name is James Woodbridge. He works on the security detail for her husband, Jerry Fontaine. He was on his way to work. All we can figure is he saw her car on the side of the road and stopped. We don't know what happened after that, except that he was shot on the road, carried in here and his car was driven about a half mile down and pulled into a dirt road. Techs are going over it now for prints."

"How did you find her?"

"Nine-one-one got a call at two twenty-five a.m. about a possible kidnapping attempt. It was odd. The caller's voice sounded disguised, and the operator was given coordinates, instead of street information, like it came from someone unfamiliar with the area. The first officer on the scene followed the coordinates with a handheld GPS and found the body. Mrs. Fontaine was starting to come around, and she started screaming when she saw the body next to her. According to the officer, her miniskirt was pushed up to her hips, and she was without any underwear. That's when she saw the dried semen."

Bax and Detective Boyd walked back to the shoulder on the road, and she used her phone again to take pictures of the bloodstains, the tire tracks and the footprints. She got down on her knees and took a closer look at the prints.

"These are high heel marks, and if I'm not mistaken, there are two different sizes here." She moved a few feet back. "These look like a man's shoe," she said, pointing her camera at the print. Boyd knelt next to her and looked at the footprints she indicated. He called over a tech and told him to photograph all three prints. They stood up.

"Good catch, Bax. Looks like we have a male-female team. How did you see those?"

"I got lucky with the light. Where is her car?"

"We think the car was the target, that's why we called you guys. The sheriff read about your home invasions, and even though this didn't fit, it was the car that attracted our attention."

He looked down at his notes. "Car was a 2019 Lamborghini Aventador SVJ. I was told that there were only eight hundred made, and the base cost is about six hundred thousand."

"The car cost a little over a million dollars."

Bax and Boyd turned around. The man approaching them was six feet tall and had a little paunch, but otherwise looked in good shape. He had a full head of blond hair and a dark tan. He walked up to the officers and reached out his hand.

"Jerry Fontaine," he said.

Bax and Boyd shook hands and introduced themselves.

"Is this where it happened?" he asked.

Bax nodded and pointed out the approximate location of the car.

"I bought that car for my wife as an anniversary present. I've been so busy lately with the team that I think she felt a little neglected. We only took possession a month ago, but she loved to show it off. Do you think whoever did this was after my wife or the car? She is a beautiful woman, and I always worry about kidnappers."

"We don't know for sure, but we think they were after the car. Does your wife travel with a bodyguard? Is that what James Woodbridge was doing here?"

"No. We live here because it's a small town and everyone knows her. We felt it was safe, so when she was going into town to meet her girlfriends, she didn't take security. James was a member of my detail and was on his way in late because we were leaving for Vegas first thing this morning. I need to call his wife." He wiped the tears from his eyes.

"Mr. Fontaine, this may seem like an odd question, but do you guys have digital assistance devices in your house?" asked Bax.

Jerry Fontaine looked at her with a suspicious look. "No.

I won't allow them in the house. We have enough security issues to deal with. May I ask why you want to know?"

"It's possible your wife was the victim of a group of very sophisticated car thieves, but we won't know for sure until we finish our investigation. I would like to speak to your security chief. Can you arrange that?"

"Whatever you need, Agent Baxter." He pulled out his phone and called the house.

CHAPTER TWENTY-TWO

Buck woke up with a start and looked around the surgical waiting room. Several people now occupied seats, waiting on word about their loved ones. The surgical waiting room was not a place of good memories for Buck. He had been dreaming about the long wait he'd experienced while his wife, Lucy, had her double mastectomy. It was one of the longest days of his life, waiting for word from the doctor that they had gotten all the cancer. And when the doctor finally walked into the waiting room, Buck almost broke down.

The good news that day was that Lucy had survived the surgery. The bad news came from the lab a couple days later, when they discovered additional cancer in her spine and lung. Devastating was the only word Buck could think of to describe that day.

Buck stood up, stretched and checked his watch. PIS had been under the knife for almost seven hours. He knew PIS was one tough son of a bitch, but seven hours is a long time, and he started to worry. He checked his messages and saw that Bax had called and was about to call her back when the doctor, dressed in blue scrubs, walked in and signaled for him to follow.

Buck walked into the hallway and shook the doctor's hand.

"Good to see you again, Buck."

"Good to see you too, Doc. How is he?"

"He survived the operation, but he lost a lot of blood. If he survives the next twenty-four hours, he should be okay. Whoever did this was very skilled and knew exactly where to put the knife for maximum effect."

"Bob Brady said he was stabbed in the heart. How did he manage to survive the initial attack?"

"The blade penetrated the chest wall, exactly where his heart should be."

Buck looked up with surprise. "If he was stabbed in the heart, why isn't he dead?"

"You didn't hear what I said, Buck. He was stabbed where his heart should have been if he was a normal person, but he's not normal."

"What are you talking about?" asked Buck.

"I thought you knew from the last time he was here, when we pulled out that chunk of wood. PIS's heart is on the right side, not the left. As a matter of fact, all his organs are on the opposite side."

Buck was astonished and speechless, something he had never been accused of. He looked at the doctor, trying to comprehend what he was saying. He finally gathered his wits about him and asked, "How is that even possible?"

The doctor explained that it was not a common condition, but that it was also not uncommon. PIS had survived because his heart was not where the knife-wielder expected it to be. He'd lost so much blood because the blade nicked an artery, and they had trouble getting the bleeding to stop.

"Truth is, Buck, if PIS were normal, we would be having a very different conversation. He has a condition called situs inversus totalis. In simple terms, all the organs in his body are reversed. He is a mirror image of most of the rest of the population. The doctor explained that situs inversus totalis affects about one in ten thousand people and is a genetic condition, so although rare, it is not uncommon. It could happen to anyone but is most common in mirror-image identical twins.

Buck was having a hard time grasping what the doc was saying. He had never heard of this condition and was finding it hard to believe that someone could live with all their organs on the opposite side.

"I studied this condition in medical school, but until we operated on PIS last year, I'd never seen an actual case. Since then, I have been doing a lot of research, trying to figure out why he has the condition. The only conclusion I can come to is that ..."

"He had a twin sister, an identical twin sister, and she did not have the same condition."

Buck and the doctor turned to see who was talking, the heavy Scottish accent surprising them both. Walking down the hall was a mountain of a man with a balding head of red hair and a neatly trimmed red beard. He looked to be several inches over six feet and close to three hundred pounds, and he walked with a limp, using a wooden cane for support.

Buck looked him up and down. "I'm sorry. Did you say something?"

"Aye. I said he had a twin sister. We weren't sure when we saw his picture that he was our comrade, but hearing that he survived another attack because of his heart thing means he probably is."

Buck looked at the doctor, who shrugged his shoulders. "Who would you be, sir?" he asked.

He stepped up to Buck and reached out a huge right hand. "My apologies for eavesdropping. I'm Sergeant Major Michael MacDonald, SBS retired. Please call me Mac."

Buck introduced himself and the doctor. "You say you saw a picture of the person who was attacked, and you think he might be a friend of yours?"

"Correct, but we didn't know he had been attacked. We were on a military tour in Washington, DC, when Devlin spotted an internet story about you, and in the picture was a gentleman with long gray hair wearing a costume. Could have knocked us over with a feather when he showed us the picture. It's been over thirty years since the last time we saw him."

The doctor asked, "How do you know PIS?"

Mac laughed a hearty laugh. "That's what he calls himself now? PIS. What kind of name is that? The man I knew would have killed anyone that called him something like that."

Buck interrupted. "PIS is the only name we know him by. He's never told anyone his real name, and the only thing the people in town had to go on were the letters p.i.s. stamped on an old leather backpack."

Mac scratched his chin, his mind deep in thought. "His father gave him that backpack when he entered the Royal Marines. That was a long time ago."

Buck could have sworn he saw a tear form in the corner of Mac's eye. He asked Mac how he had tracked them to the hospital.

"We weren't sure where to start, so I stopped by the local constabulary to inquire about you. We figured if we found you, we might find him, since the article said you worked together on cases."

He told them that when he and his two comrades saw the picture online, they were stunned. They had no idea he was in the United States. They weren't even sure if he was alive, but they figured, since they were here, they should try to find him, so they ditched the tour group, took a cab to the Greyhound station and bought three tickets to Aspen, Colorado. They'd spent four days on the bus and arrived in town about an hour ago.

"My traveling companions needed to take a rest, so I dropped them off at the motel and walked around a little. I asked a gentleman sweeping the sidewalk in front of his shop if he knew where I might find the man who dressed funny and worked with the police. He gave me directions to the police station. Based on the description I gave them, they said I should come here, and here I am."

Buck suggested they sit down in the waiting room, but the doctor offered up his office, and they followed him down the hall and into a small but comfortable office. The doctor sat behind his desk, and Buck and Mac took the visitor's chairs. Buck felt uneasy, remembering the day he'd sat in an office very similar to this one with Lucy, listening as the doctor said those three horrible words: metastatic breast cancer. Buck shook off the memory.

The doctor asked, "Can you tell us your friend's real name?"

"That's easy. His name is Pheasant Iverson-Smythe. He was a captain in the Special Boat Service during our last posting. It's very much like your Navy SEALs. We've been friends since we were kids." This was a name Buck had heard before.

Mac asked if it would be possible to see his friend, to make sure it was the same person he knew as Pheasant, but the doctor said that wasn't possible since he was in recovery in the intensive care unit. Mac looked disheartened until the doctor clicked a couple keys and brought up a picture of PIS that had been taken by the ER nurse. He turned his computer to face Mac, who took a pair of glasses out of his pocket, put them on and looked carefully at the picture. Buck could see a light shine in his eyes as he removed his glasses, sat back and shook his head.

"That's him, all right. I'd recognize him anywhere."

He smiled, but Buck could see that there was a pain behind the smile. Mac pulled out his phone. "I need to call my friends, if you'll excuse me."

He stood up, opened the door and stepped out of the office into the hallway. Buck and the doctor looked at each other, not saying a word.

CHAPTER TWENTY-THREE

B uck and the doctor caught up to Mac in the waiting
room as he hung up his phone.

"My companions will come by tomorrow since we
can't see him anyway. Would it be possible to see where he
was attacked?"

Buck had made plans to head over to the alley, so he
nodded, but before he could answer, the doctor asked. "Mac,
what can you tell us about PIS . . . sorry, Pheasant's medical
condition? Any information might be helpful as to how we
treat his wound."

Buck smiled. He knew the doctor was sincere in his quest
for information, but there was also a little bit of bullshit in
that statement. The doctor was as curious as Buck was about
PIS's past, but he used medicine as a pretext for asking the
question Buck was trying to figure out how to ask.

Mac stepped to the back of the waiting room and sat
down, and Buck and the doctor did the same. Mac got a serious look on his face. It was obvious he was struggling with
how much he was willing to tell these folks about Pheasant's
life, especially since he had lived amongst them for over
twenty years and they knew almost nothing about him. He
sat deep in thought for a minute before finally answering.

"Pheasant's mom died during childbirth. His dad never
gave us much detail, but I guess the strain of delivering twins
was too much on her heart. Pheasant is younger than his sister by a minute or two, and she used to love to tease him

about being his older sister. According to things we learned over the years, no one knew Pheasant was different until he broke his arm when he was three or four, falling out of a tree. They knew he wasn't like the other babies, right from birth, but it wasn't until they took a bunch of X-rays that they discovered that all his organs were reversed. The doctors did some tests on his sister, and Sparrow was perfectly normal. According to family lore, the doctors told Pheasant's dad that he probably wouldn't live more than a year or two. I guess he surprised them all."

"Did his condition affect him while he was growing up?" asked the doctor.

"Not a bit. I've known him since he was four, and he did everything the other kids did and usually better than any of us. He was as tough as they come, and he had no fear."

"Is his sister still alive?" asked the doctor.

"No. She died about ten years back. They said it was a brain tumor. It was the first time anyone could remember her being sick. She was as tough as Pheasant and just as fearless. Spent her entire adult life at Scotland Yard. She was so proud of Pheasant when he graduated from SBS training. It was a huge achievement for someone who wasn't supposed to live a year or two at most."

"What can you tell me about his wounds? We couldn't help but notice that his back is covered with scars, as if someone whipped him. There's also an X carved in his chest where his heart should be, with a scar from a bullet right in the middle."

"Doctor, I think I've said enough right now. Agent Taylor, I'm getting tired, so if we can head for the alley, I would appreciate it."

Buck could see the disappointment in the doctor's face. He was hoping for more insight into PIS than he got from

Mac. Buck understood where Mac was coming from. He was not about to reveal any of PIS's secrets and violate his friend's trust, even a friend he hadn't seen in over thirty years.

Buck left his business card with the doctor and led Mac down the hall to the hospital entrance and out into the parking lot. They reached Buck's Jeep and slid onto the seats. Buck pulled out his phone and called Bob Brady to let him know he was heading to the alley to look around, and he would report back later. He pulled out of the parking lot and headed downtown.

Buck was always amazed at how much the little mining town had grown over the years. The first time he'd visited Aspen as a kid was with his dad. They had driven up in his dad's tow truck to pick up a car for one of his dad's customers. Buck's dad owned the only gas station in Gunnison back in the day, and everyone came to his dad's station when they needed gas, an engine repaired or a tire fixed. It was also the neighborhood gathering place, where the town's old-timers could hang out, drink a couple beers from the old cooler and shoot the shit about politics and the troubles of the day. It was nothing like the new travel centers that now dotted the landscape. This was a down and dirty mechanics garage. A place for working men to get together, out of earshot of the womenfolk. There was no convenience store attached to it, only two old greasy repair bays and two restrooms located out back, which would have been condemned by the Board of Health today but were perfectly fine back in the day.

Buck's thoughts turned back to Aspen and how, even since his last major crime in the city ten years before, the little town had grown up even more. More mansions were being built than middle-class homes, and he wondered how the average Aspenite was able to survive in the place now. It was also apparent, he noticed as he turned down the alley, that the homeless population had grown. Several small groups and individuals were scrounging through the dumpsters that lined the alley, looking for tonight's dinner, or possibly scouting out a better place to live once winter arrived, which wouldn't be too much longer.

Buck's phone rang, and he looked at the number and frowned. He pushed the red button to the left and put the phone back in his pocket.

The drive over from the hospital was quiet, and Mac sat and looked out the window. Buck could tell that Mac was trying to work something out in his mind, so he decided not to press him. He imagined that the sudden reappearance of Pheasant in his life was a hard thing to deal with. Buck didn't know the particulars, but it was evident that something had happened a long time ago that led PIS to leave the life he knew as a soldier, disappear into the world outside Britain and lose contact with those who had been his friends. He wondered if, now that they had located him, Mac thought it might have been a mistake to make the journey to Aspen. After all, it had been over thirty years, and PIS had had no contact with his friends and comrades in arms. What if this visit was not something that PIS wanted?

Buck pulled up behind the bookstore and stopped the Jeep. They climbed out, and Buck asked Mac to hang back for a minute. The smell from something rotting in the dumpsters in the unusually warm weather was unpleasant, but Buck put it out of his head and walked to the back of the Jeep. Since Buck hadn't been here before, to him, this was a new crime scene, and he needed to handle it like he dealt with any crime scene, even though he knew the local forensic team had already scoured the area. He pulled a pair of black nitrile gloves out of his backpack, put them on and stepped up to the yellow crime scene tape that still hung between the power pole and the dumpster.

He walked along the perimeter of the yellow tape, looking at the overall scene. He noticed Mac out of the corner of his eye, looking at the homeless as they wandered about. He wondered what was going through his mind.

Buck focused on the job at hand and slipped under the tape. He knelt next to the bloodstain that had dried on the pavement and scanned the surrounding area. As far as crime scenes went, this one was pristine, except for the blood. He stood up, looked around and spotted cameras on several of the buildings. He made a mental note to call Bob Brady and see if his detectives had pulled the tapes from the cameras. He realized as he thought it that most of these cameras didn't use tape anymore, that everything was stored in a cloud somewhere in digital space. He didn't have a clue how to find this cloud, but he knew a lot of people who did, including his grandkids. Maybe he really was a technological dinosaur. He cleared away that thought. He looked over towards the edge of the dumpster and spotted a dried pile of something on the ground next to one wheel. He stepped over and pushed the dumpster out of the way enough to see that the pile was vomit. He had no way of knowing if it was connected to PIS's attack, but for the moment, it was evidence.

He pulled his phone out and dialed Bob Brady. "Bob, did your detectives take a sample of some vomit that is next to the dumpster?"

"Yeah," said Bob. "They sent it to the State Crime Lab for analysis. Why?"

"I wanted to make sure before I grabbed another sample. I'll call the lab and see if they can rush the sample. Oh, before I forget. Was there anything on any of the cameras in the alley? I noticed several behind the buildings."

"Not really. One showed something, but it was fuzzy. We sent it to your tech guys to see if they could clean it up. The others were either not working or had a bad view. I will email you a copy of what we have, and you can look for yourself."

"Thanks, Bob."

Buck hit one of his speed dial numbers. Maxine Clinton answered right away.

"Buck Taylor. How's my favorite cop?"

"Hey, Max. Doing good. How're things at the crime lab?"

Dr. Maxine Clinton, Max to her friends, was the director of the State Crime Lab in Pueblo. She was a matronly woman in her early sixties, about five feet five with short gray hair. She probably thought she carried around an extra fifteen pounds she didn't need, but she was still a handsome woman.

Married for forty years, Max had four children, eleven grandchildren and six great-grandchildren. She lived in a 150-year-old farmhouse in Pueblo, where she liked to tend her garden and sit on her porch and drink iced tea. She was also a bourbon girl and could easily drink most people under the table. She was loud and outspoken, but she knew her job.

Max had received her PhD in Biology from the University of Colorado and worked as a biology professor for twenty years before joining CBI and accepting the challenge of running the lab, which under her leadership had become one of the top crime labs in the country. She was a hard taskmaster, but she had a belief system that didn't allow for defeat. Her goal was to give the crime investigator, no matter which department or municipality they worked for, all the information they would need to solve any crime. She held that as a sacred obligation to the victims. She was incredibly dedicated, and her team at the lab practically worshipped her.

Buck would be included in that group. Many times, during a complicated investigation, it had been Max and her team that lit the spark that led to a breakthrough. Max was one of Buck's favorite people, and she felt the same way about him.

"Couldn't be better," she said. They spent a few minutes catching up before Max asked how she could help him today.

"Aspen PD sent you a sample of some vomit they found at a crime scene. I wanted to see if you had any results yet."

Buck heard Max clicking away on her computer. "Here it is. We received the sample earlier today, and it is being processed. You're not on the notification list. What's your interest?"

"The victim is a good friend of mine. I'm in town to help if I can. Can you put a rush on this, Max? It's important."

Max didn't even hesitate. "I'll put this in for an overnight DNA test. I'll call you tomorrow when I have the results. Is your friend okay?"

"Right now, he's in critical condition after a knifing. The vomit could be from the perp."

"No worries, Buck. We won't let you down."

She ended the call the way she always did. "You're a good man, Buck Taylor. God will watch over you. Stay safe."

Buck hadn't been to church since he received his confirmation, but he always appreciated Max's little blessing. It wasn't that he didn't believe in God. He wasn't sure what he really believed in. He didn't like organized religion, but he never held that against anyone. A lot of people had prayed for his wife during the five years she fought metastatic breast cancer, but in the end, Lucy still died. Although he had been mad at first, he soon realized that to be angry at God, he first had to believe in God, and he could never get there. He always felt there were forces in the world that he couldn't explain, and he always thanked the river spirits whenever he had a chance to do some fly-fishing. He didn't have a place for one God in his life. He never held Max's beliefs against her. He always figured that it couldn't hurt if she believed he was worthy.

He called Mac back to the Jeep, and they slid in and headed for Mac's hotel. Mac was once again quiet on the drive over.

CHAPTER TWENTY-FOUR

Alicia Hawkins was parked outside the bus station in Glenwood Springs. She wore a black wig and dark sunglasses and hid her face anytime someone drew near. She had been parked for a couple hours looking for that perfect person, her next victim, and she was running out of time. Three days in Aspen had not rewarded her with one opportunity, and she was getting concerned. She needed her fifteenth victim before she went after the bar owner. It was a promise to her grandfather that she meant to keep. Besides, she still hadn't put together a solid plan of how to take the bar owner. She was fit for her age, and the bouncer always seemed to be somewhere close by. She was working on a plan, but that would depend on how she felt about the two fanboys she had been communicating with since Key West.

Alicia was stunned by the number of fans she had on the internet. She assumed most people would be turned off by her activities, but there was a large group that seemed to worship her, and she was amazed to find that there was even a private Facebook page dedicated to her. What a crazy world. She was already more famous than her grandfather, and that both excited and repulsed her. She figured it was like those women who married convicted killers in prison, knowing they would never have a normal life.

Anyway, two of her fanboys, Josh and Louis, had taken a real interest in her work and had been reaching out lately. They wanted to get together with her and become her students. She had no idea if they were serious, but they were persistent, and the more she thought about it, the more it sounded like fun. Think of how famous she would be if she had an army of killers working with her—well, maybe not an army, but a couple enthusiastic followers trained in her methods could be a good thing.

She decided to reach out to them through the dark web and ask them to meet her in Aspen. They were due to arrive in a day or two, and she would see how they fit in. She was worried that they might be part of the FBI, but she had to take a chance. She would need help getting to the bar owner, and these two guys might be just what she needed. And if things didn't work out, well, maybe they could be victims seventeen and eighteen.

She checked the schedule she had picked up on her first visit to the bus station. The last bus from Denver had arrived, and she watched patiently as the passengers exited the bus. She wondered if any of the travelers would ever realize how close they had come to being the victim of a serial killer. The thought made her smile, and she visualized what she would do to each one of them as they walked away from the bus,

She was about to call it quits and head back to the cabin she was renting when she spotted a petite young girl standing at the curb, looking lost. She hiked up her coat against the chilly breeze and looked around like she was waiting for someone to come pick her up.

The bus pulled away from the station heading for the parking lot, and within minutes she was all alone on the sidewalk. Darkness had long ago settled over the Roaring Fork Valley, and with it came the possibility of snow and colder temperatures. It was early fall, but winter could occur at any time.

Alicia watched her for a few minutes to make sure she was alone, and then she slid out of her car, grabbed a rolling suitcase out of the trunk and skirted around the girl towards the entrance to the station. Once inside the revolving door, she turned around and headed back out the door, looking like any of the other passengers exiting the station. She walked past the young girl and stopped.

"Hi. You look lost. Can I help you?" she asked.

"That's okay," she said. "I just need to find a place to eat."

"Where are you heading? Perhaps I can give you a ride?" asked Alicia.

The girl nodded and shrugged her shoulders.

Alicia smiled at her. "Look. It's too late to find an open restaurant, and hotels here are expensive. I am heading home, and I've got lots of food and a warm place to stay. Why don't you join me? It's better than sleeping outside in the cold."

The girl looked at her suspiciously and pulled back. Alicia reached out her hand. "There's nothing to be afraid of. I'm the Reverend Monica Chase. My church is the First Presbyterian Congregation in Aspen, and I have a cozy cabin in the woods outside of town. Please. Let me help you."

The religious introduction must have struck a chord, and the young girl smiled and reached out her hand and shook Alicia's hand. "Karen," she said. "Karen Holcomb from Portland, Maine."

Alicia's smile was warm and comforting. "Well, Karen. It's a pleasure to meet you. We can talk more once you are fed and warm. My car is over there." She pointed towards the small green car, one of the few left in the lot. They headed for the car, Alicia pulling her roller suitcase and Karen swinging her backpack over her shoulders.

Alicia stowed the bags in the trunk and climbed in next to Karen, who was unzipping her coat now that she was inside a warm car. Alicia was worried that the warm car might make Karen question her decision. It didn't seem to occur to her that if Alicia was coming back from a bus trip, her car shouldn't be warm, but the question never came up. She just snuggled into the warmth and closed her eyes. Before they left the lot, Karen was asleep.

Alicia headed down Highway 82 towards Aspen. About a mile south of town, she turned down County Road 21, drove about a mile and turned down an unmarked dirt road and headed back into the trees. The house was a cozy little hunting cabin she'd found on one of the vacation rentals by owner sites on the internet. The owner was out of the country and was happy to rent it to a member of the clergy for a couple weeks of solitude and reflection.

She pulled into a small circular parking area and stopped the car. She softly tapped Karen on the arm, and the girl slowly opened her eyes. She saw Alicia's smiling face and smiled back.

"Come on. We need to walk back about a half mile to the house. Grab your backpack out of the trunk, and don't be afraid of the dark. I walk this trail every night after work, and I know it like the back of my hand."

Karen slid out of the car and pulled her backpack out of the trunk. She didn't question why Alicia didn't take her own rolling suitcase. She closed the trunk and followed the glow of Alicia's flashlight. The path wasn't difficult, and they soon crested a small rise and saw the lights of the cabin burning brightly in the distance.

Alicia unlocked the front door to the cabin and stepped out of the way so Karen could step in first. She closed the door and turned off the outside light. The cabin was large and open, and the lights gave the honey-colored wood a soft, warm glow. Alicia lit a fire in the gas fireplace and told Karen to make herself at home while she threw some dinner together. She walked into the kitchen, thinking that this was way too easy.

She cooked up some pasta and sauce and called Karen to dinner. She put candles on the table and took two bottles of wine from the closet down the hall. Everything was perfect, and Karen dug in like she hadn't eaten in days. They talked about life and food, and then the conversation turned to Karen.

Karen had walked out on an abusive boyfriend and hopped on the first bus out of town. Her parents had moved to Oregon a couple years back, and she figured she might head that way and surprise them. She had no intention of telling her ex-boyfriend where she was heading, and for now, she was going to play it by ear.

Alicia offered her another glass of wine and then excused herself and took the glasses over to the counter to fill them. They finished dinner, walked into the family room and sat on the carpet in front of the fireplace. The warmth was comforting, and it didn't take long before Karen got a glazed look in her eyes and started yawning. She leaned back against the couch and finished the last of her wine. The glass slipped from her hand, and Alicia caught it, and then the lights went out, and Karen fell into a deep sleep. The sleeping pills in the wine had done the job.

Alicia felt her excitement start to build as she half dragged, half carried Karen to the ground-floor bedroom. She hadn't bolted the shackles to the wall but had decided to strap Karen to the bed. That method had worked well with the cowboy in Oklahoma, and she hoped it would work as well this time. She stripped off Karen's clothes and looked over her petite body. Her skin was fair, her short brown hair shined in the candlelight and her breasts were small but perfect. Alicia strapped her hands and feet to the bed frame and walked out to the family room to turn off the rest of the lights and blow out the candles. She walked back into the bedroom, stripped off her own clothes and spent a few minutes getting herself aroused. Feeling good, she unrolled her bundle of knives and pulled out a thin four-inch scalpel. It was time to begin.

CHAPTER TWENTY-FIVE

Bax pulled her Jeep up to the gate, followed by Detective Boyd in his unmarked LCSD SUV. She glanced around and noticed there was no call box or gatehouse, and she wondered how she was supposed to let the people inside the gate know she was waiting. That question answered itself as the gate swung inwards. They pulled both vehicles through the gate and followed the dirt road for about a quarter mile before arriving at an enormous modern mountain home. It appeared to be one story, with lots of wood, stone and glass, and it covered a huge swath of ground. They parked in front of the massive entry doors and slid out of their vehicles. Bax grabbed her backpack off the seat, and Detective Boyd did the same.

The entry doors opened before they reached the top step, and a short, bald man wearing dark-rimmed glasses stepped through the door. She wondered if he was the butler or house boy until he reached out his hand.

"Officers, Martin Campbell. Mr. Fontaine's head of security."

Bax and Detective Boyd both shook hands with him and introduced themselves, although Bax had no doubt that he probably had their pictures in his phone along with their profiles. He waved his hand towards the entry and stepped slightly aside so they could enter.

Bax stepped into the foyer and stopped and stared. The hall and attached great room were huge, with a massive brass-and-stone circular fireplace in the middle of the great room. Everywhere she looked, the views out the huge walls of windows were impressive. Martin Campbell asked them to follow him, and they walked through a chef's dream kitchen and down a flight of stairs to the security office. Bax stepped into the room and thought she had stepped into NASA or a television studio. One entire wall was covered with monitors, each showing an almost continuous path around the property. There were four technicians seated at separate consoles, and each person was busy working their keyboard or moving around a joystick.

"Mr. Fontaine asked us to review the past two days of tape and report on any unusual vehicles that passed our gates. We've found one vehicle yesterday that fits that profile. Marcus, please pull up the tape we reviewed earlier."

Bax and Detective Boyd stepped over to Marcus's console, and he clicked a few keys and directed them to look at the screens to the right. He pushed a button, and what had been twelve separate camera views turned into one large picture. He rolled the camera forward as they all looked on.

At first, it was just traffic on the highway, but then a slow-moving vehicle came into view and appeared to almost stop as it drew even with the gate. The SUV's windows were tinted dark, and it was impossible to see who was in the car, except for the shadows of what appeared to be three people.

"The vehicle is a 2016 Ford Explorer. It appears to be either dark blue or black," said Martin Campbell.

Bax asked Marcus to freeze the picture, and she looked closer at the car. "How can you tell the make and model? There are no markings on the side of the vehicle," asked Bax.

Marcus clicked a couple more keys, and the side view of the vehicle was replaced with a head-on view. Bax was impressed.

Because the front windshield can't be tinted in Colorado, they had a perfect view of the driver and passenger. As Marcus pulled the camera view back, they also got a view of the license plate. The plates were from North Carolina, and Detective Boyd pulled out his iPad and started to type in the information.

"There is no need for that, Detective. We ran the vehicle through our vast database to get the make and model. We will forward the videos to you. We have also taken the liberty of running the plates through the North Carolina Department of Motor Vehicles, and we have included that information in the email to you and Agent Baxter as well."

Bax stepped back from the console. "Mr. Campbell, this is an amazing system you have here. May I ask? Does it cover the entire property, as well as the highway?"

"I'm sorry, Agent Baxter, that is proprietary information that I cannot divulge, but suffice it to say, there is very little that can happen on this property that we are not aware of. Mr. Fontaine is a very private person, and he can afford the very best."

"One last question. Do you have a digital assistant in the house?"

"No, Agent Baxter, Mr. Fontaine does not allow anyone in the household to have a digital assistant. He is concerned about privacy."

Detective Boyd looked up from his iPad. "Would it be possible for us to interview Mrs. Fontaine?"

"Mrs. Fontaine is waiting for you in her sitting room. I will take you there now, if you will follow me."

The sitting room was as big as Bax's apartment in Grand Junction and was as impressive as the rest of the house, with a large fireplace flanked by a wall of windows. Mrs. Fontaine sat on a leather couch that Bax figured probably cost more than she made in a year. They introduced themselves to Mrs. Fontaine, and Martin Campbell stepped out of the room and closed the door. Mrs. Fontaine pointed to the two chairs opposite the couch, and Bax and Detective Boyd sat down and sank into the softest leather chairs either one of them had ever sat in. The leather was like butter.

Constance Fontaine was sitting cross-legged on the couch with her bare feet tucked under her legs. She wore jeans and a flannel shirt, and she was stunning. The only thing amiss was that she looked terribly hungover. She took a sip of water from the bottle on the table next to her and looked at her visitors.

"My husband asked me to speak with you, but please be aware that I can't seem to remember anything that happened after I left the bar. It's like the whole evening disappeared. The doctor at the hospital said I was drugged with a fast-acting sedative."

"Mrs. Fontaine," said Detective Boyd. "We believe that shortly after you left the bar, you stopped along the side of the highway. There are indications that there might have been a car parked on the side of the road and possibly another woman. We found a second print from a high heel shoe that is smaller than yours. Do you recall stopping to meet someone?"

Mrs. Fontaine looked deep in thought and, after a minute, rubbed her forehead with her fingers.

"I seem to still be hungover. Now that you mention it, I think I did stop to help someone. There was another woman. She was all alone, and the hood of her car was up. I remember walking back to her car, and then the lights went out until I woke up and found that poor security guard lying next to me. It was horrible." She started to cry and took another sip of water.

Bax handed her a tissue from the box on the desk. "Mrs.

Fontaine, do you remember anything about the woman or the car? Anything that might help us?"

Constance Fontaine shook her head. "I'm so sorry. I wish I could remember more, but my head is empty. It's a terrible feeling."

Bax and Detective Boyd stood up to leave. It was obvious that they were not going to get anything more out of Constance Fontaine. They turned and headed towards the door.

"My husband didn't say much at the hospital, but I could tell from the tests the nurse ran. Was I raped while I was unconscious?"

Bax stepped back to the couch and looked into Constance Fontaine's eyes. "We believe you were, but we will know more once the tests come back. I'm so sorry."

Constance Fontaine nodded, and Bax turned, and they left the room. They could hear her crying behind the closed door.

Bax and Detective Boyd thanked Martin Campbell for his help and walked to their cars.

Bax said, "I will call the crime lab and put a rush on the samples. Can you make sure they get to the lab right away?"

"No problem, Bax. I will also run the video of the car through facial recognition and call a friend of mine in North Carolina to see if they can get a line on the owner of the SUV."

They shook hands, and each slid into their respective vehicles with a promise to call as soon as something popped. Bax pulled out her phone and called Max Clinton.

"Hey, Max," she said. "I need a favor."

"Hiya, Bax. How can I help?"

Bax told her about the possible rape and that this case might be tied to the other home invasion that she and Buck were working on, and could she rush the results? Max, as usual, was willing to do whatever she needed to do once the samples arrived. They talked for a minute about the cases and bounced some ideas around, and then Max told her that God would watch over her, and they hung up.

Her next call was to Buck to fill him in. Buck answered right away.

"Hey, Bax. How'd things go in Estes Park?"

"It's crazy, Buck. From what we can tell this same crew has committed five break-ins and stolen five expensive cars. In each case the MO was exactly the same, and then all of a sudden we have two cases, in less than a week, and neither one fits the MO. I feel it in my bones that this is the same crew. I can't figure out what changed."

Buck thought for a minute. "Tell me what's different about these last two cases."

"Well, the first thing that stands out is the increase in violence. In the case in Telluride, they beat the husband almost to death, and in this case in Estes, they killed a security guard and possibly raped the victim."

Buck wasn't aware of the rape and expressed his surprise. "Walk me through the Estes case step by step."

Bax spent the next fifteen minutes giving Buck a quick synopsis of the events surrounding the stolen car. When she was finished, Buck was quiet for a minute.

"It sounds to me like this was a crime of opportunity. From what you described, it is possible they were staking the place out and couldn't figure out how to get through the security system. You said it was seriously sophisticated."

"That's what I was thinking too. They must have been looking for a way in when they encountered the car on the road, or someplace outside the compound. We know she was drinking in town with some friends. It's possible the crew spotted her in town and decided to take the chance and hit her after she left the bar."

"Was the deceased security guard on her security detail?"

"No. I think this was wrong place, wrong time. The security guard was driving into work and must have seen the car on the side of the road. Buck, whoever shot him was good. Real good. It was one shot, and he was down for the count. He was a good-sized guy, so I doubt the woman who belonged to the heel marks was the one who carried him into the woods."

"Okay. Until we get the DNA results back on the semen and we can track down the ownership of the SUV, let's work this with the theory that it is the same crew, and that something caused them to escalate their level of violence. Let's do this. See if someone in the office can run a motor vehicle computer check on the most expensive cars in Colorado. We are talking megabucks cars, so there can't be that many, and let's see if we can't anticipate their next move. The prices of the cars seem to be going up in value, so we might get lucky."

"You got it, Buck. By the way, how's PIS?"

"He's out of surgery, but he's not out of the woods yet. I'm going to spend a couple days here and see if I can help. Call me if you find out anything new."

Bax hung up and called the office to get one of the techs working on the computer search. She pulled out of the driveway and passed through the gate. She'd decided while she was talking to Buck that she would check out the bar and the surrounding shops and see if anyone remembered anything that might help. She headed into town.

CHAPTER TWENTY-SIX

The RV was parked in a small campground, a couple miles outside the Aspen city limits. Jessie, Earl and Toby were lounging on the couches listening to music or reading their posts online while Victoria Larsen worked the keys on her laptop, like a maestro playing a fine instrument. She was hard at work, trying to crack through the firewalls of their next victim's digital presence.

Victoria wasn't concerned that it was taking a little longer than she had planned. She was highly trained, and there were very few systems she couldn't crack. She didn't have any qualms about using the talents the government had taught her for evil instead of good. During her time with the CIA, she'd seen and done a lot of things she would consider as not necessarily good, and if the government could use her to do evil things, why not do them on her own and get paid a lot of money? Besides, it wasn't like she was stealing government secrets or passing false information to a political campaign. They were stealing cars from wealthy people who could well afford the loss.

Jessie stood up to stretch and walked over to the table Victoria was working at. They had been sitting around for two days, and they were getting bored. As far as she was concerned, the digital crap was a small part of what they did. She believed that most of their information came from watching the house and the people in it. Of course, the digital information did give them a foot in the door, and she knew it was a big help. She just hated to admit it.

Victoria leaned back in her chair and stretched, a big smile on her face. "Got it," she said. She leaned into her laptop and started clicking keys with lightning speed.

Jessie kicked Earl in the foot, and he took off his headphones and moved from the couch to the table. Toby still sat in the corner, playing a video game on his phone. They sat opposite Victoria and waited patiently while she ran through the digital systems she now had access to.

She pushed back from the laptop. "Okay, I have access to the security system and the digital assistant. I also have Bluetooth access to his entertainment system, which is extensive."

She clicked a couple more keys. "I transferred all the access to your laptops and phones. Go ahead and log into the system so I can authenticate you, then you can begin surveillance."

"Who's our victim?" asked Earl.

Victoria Larsen looked up. "James Murphy."

Earl looked at Jessie and then back to Victoria. "James Murphy, the actor? The guy who was in all those fast car movies?"

"One and the same," she said. "Murphy owns one of only three hundred Bugatti Chiron Sports in the world. The car is worth three point six million dollars, and from what I can tell, it is sitting in the garage of his house, which is about three miles from where we are sitting. What we need to determine is whether anyone is actually in the house. His security system is low-end compared to his entertainment system. I guess when you are the highest-paid actor in the world and you are only twenty-eight years old, your priorities are a little skewed."

Earl looked at Jessie. "Sounds like it's time to get our gear and find a place to set up on the house." He held up his phone for her to see. "I pulled up Google Earth, and his house is surrounded by forest on three sides, and the closest neighbor is across the street, a quarter mile away, front door to front door. Should be a piece of cake."

Jessie looked at the picture. "Looks right. Why don't you and Toby go scout a spot and take shifts, while I start to search for security codes and passwords."

Earl grabbed Toby as he passed by, and they headed for the rear of the RV to gear up. Jessie set her laptop up on the table opposite Victoria and logged into the system.

"Did you have to kill the security guard?" Victoria asked without looking up from her laptop. "I've been monitoring the local emergency service channel, and there is a lot of chatter. You stirred up a hornet's nest."

"We had no choice. He came out of nowhere. If Earl hadn't been gone so long, we might have been able to subdue him, but since I was alone with the victim's car, what was I supposed to do?"

"I can't answer that. I wasn't there, but . . ."

"No, you weren't there. I did what I needed to do to survive, so what gives you the right to question my response? I don't see you risking your ass to steal these cars. All you do is sit back in your little digital world and listen to people's lives. We take all the risk."

Jessie stood up and walked back to the small side bedroom and slid the door closed. Victoria was concerned. They had pulled off some serious heists in the past couple weeks, and she'd known eventually it would take its toll on the team. She was glad this would be the last project for a while, and in less than a week, they would all be home in Montana for a much-deserved rest. She hoped Jessie could keep it together for a few more days. This heist was going to need their full attention.

She turned back around to her laptop and sent an email to their broker in California, letting him know that they should have information on the car in the next couple days and to make sure the buyer was ready to take delivery. The idea of a big payday helped clear a little of the concern she had for Jessie.

Earl and Toby, dressed in camo, walked out of the back of the RV. They looked like typical elk hunters except that neither one carried a weapon. The last thing they needed was to get caught in the woods with a firearm. Instead, they carried field glasses and cameras, and if anyone asked, they were taking photos for a wildlife magazine. They each gave Victoria a hug and headed for the SUV. They still had a little light left to find a place to camp so they could start their surveillance tonight. They couldn't wait for this last heist to be over. The previous two had taken a toll on them as well.

Victoria watched them leave and called up the tracker she had placed in Toby's backpack. She hadn't told their father about the tracker, but she felt more comfortable knowing where they were. She hadn't said anything to any of them, but she wondered why Earl had been gone so long in Estes Park. She knew Earl had a past, but she'd never gotten into the specifics with his father. Now she wondered if that was a mistake.

She set up the laptop to record everything that came through the various systems she'd discovered in the house, and now all she needed to do was wait until someone logged into the system from inside so she would have the passcodes she needed. She also logged back into the Larimer County Sheriff's Department server to see if there was any new information about the shooting of the security guard. She needed to keep apprised of what was going on with the investigation. The last thing any of them needed was a midnight raid on their RV by law enforcement.

She pushed the laptop aside and stepped over to the window. She hoped Earl and Toby had dressed warmly enough. The nights were getting colder, and soon it would snow. Hopefully, they would be back in Montana before that happened, for a much-needed rest.

CHAPTER TWENTY-SEVEN

Buck pulled up in front of the motel where Mac and his traveling companions were staying. He asked Mac if they would like to join him for dinner, and Mac said he would check with his buddies and be right back. He slid out of the car and limped to unit seven and used his key. A few minutes went by, and the door opened and out walked Mac, followed by two other elderly men.

Buck thought they were a sad sight. Mac with his cane, followed by a shorter, heavyset fireplug of a man with a full head of white hair who was using a walker. The third man appeared much younger than Mac or the other man, and he was shorter than Mac but taller than the fella with the walker, and he still had a military air about him. They slid into the Jeep, and Mac made the introductions.

"Agent Taylor," Mac said, pointing to the man with the walker. "This is Sergeant Devlin Kyle, and this taller fellow is Sergeant Willie Carlisle, both former SBS, now retired. Gentlemen, this is Agent Buck Taylor."

They shook hands, and Buck asked them if steak was a good choice for dinner, and they all nodded. Buck pulled out of the space in front of unit seven, pulled onto Main Street and headed for The Ranch.

The Ranch was an excellent steakhouse in town, mostly a local joint, and didn't have the same kind of prices as some of the other restaurants in town. It had a Western feel with lots of wood and leather, and the owner was fond of showing off his hunting abilities by hanging a bunch of animal heads on the walls. It was a fun environment, and Buck hoped the travelers from Britain might enjoy a little mountain hospitality.

Buck let the travelers out at the front door and pulled through the parking lot to find a space in the back. By the time he got back to the entrance, his guests were being seated by the hostess. She smiled as Buck stepped up to the table, handed them all menus and then left them to their own devices. The waiter brought glasses of water and took their drink orders. Three beers and a glass of Coke.

Buck offered them some words of wisdom about the menu, and after receiving their drinks, they each ordered. Buck didn't let the conversation lag, and he used his interrogation skills to find out everything he could about PIS and his life before Aspen.

"So, you were in the SBS together? If I remember correctly, that's the Special Boat Service, correct?" asked Buck.

Willie was the first to respond. Buck noticed a bit of harshness in his accent, unlike the silky smoothness of PIS's accent. "That's correct. It's much like your Navy SEALs. We were trained to go anywhere, anytime, to handle whatever needed to be done."

"Was Pheasant your squad leader, since you mentioned you were all sergeants?"

Devlin took over. "He was a fresh-faced lieutenant when we were first assigned to his unit. Mac and Pheasant had been friends since grade school, and he was already assigned to Pheasant's squad when we came along."

"How is it that Pheasant and Mac ended up together?" Buck asked. "I would assume since they were friends, they wouldn't have been assigned to the same unit."

They all laughed, then Mac responded. "Pheasant got anything he asked for. With status comes perks."

They ordered another round of beers and dug into their meals. "What kind of status did Pheasant have?"

Devlin replied, "Not did have. I guess technically he still does have."

Buck looked confused until Devlin clarified his statement. "Pheasant is royalty." Buck watched as Mac signaled to cut him off, but he continued. "At the time we served together, Pheasant was tenth or eleventh in line for the throne."

Mac said, "I don't think we need to bore Agent Taylor with all this old history."

"That's okay, Mac. We know so little about him that it's fascinating to find out about some of his life before he got here."

"I don't think we should be speaking out of school. He must have had his reasons to keep people in the dark, and it's not our place to expose his past."

Devlin apologized for speaking out of turn and took another sip of his beer.

"I didn't mean to pry, Mac. I consider Pheasant to be a good friend, and we have been through a lot together. His life before Aspen is a mystery, and whatever you tell me here tonight will remain here."

Mac looked at Buck with serious eyes and held his gaze. Buck sensed that Mac was trying to get a feel for the kind of man he was. He must have believed Buck had only the best intentions, because he started to loosen up a little.

"Pheasant's father was the Royal Gamekeeper. He oversaw all the forests in Great Britain. He was also a duke, which put him fourth in line to the crown. That was where Pheasant developed his tracking skills. He and his sister spent hour upon hour in the woods with their dad, hunting and tracking. It became a family game, trying to hide from each other. I was a good tracker in the early days, but I couldn't hold a candle to Pheasant, or his sister for that matter. Those two would rather be in the woods than in school, and by the time we were ten, Pheasant was one of the best trackers in England, and not just for someone his age. He was one of the best at any age."

Mac took a big gulp of his beer and continued. "Pheasant decided early on that he wanted to be in the boat service, so against his father's wishes, we both joined up together. His dad, even though he disapproved, pulled some strings and got us into SBS training. Pheasant excelled and dragged me along with him. We graduated first and second in our class. Was about the hardest thing I ever did, but Pheasant breezed through it. He was able to pull some strings of his own and got us assigned together. We chose Devlin and Willie to fill out our squad."

"We served in a lot of places together before we were chosen as one of the first anti-terrorist groups, but we spent most of our time rescuing British citizens and diplomats from hot spots around the world. We were in some hairy places."

Devlin and Willie both nodded in agreement.

Buck hated to interrupt, but he wondered about something PIS had said when they were lying on the ground behind the blown-up cabin. "Did you guys ever serve in Vietnam? Pheasant made a comment when we were in the middle of an ambush, about methods the U.S. Marine mortar crews used on the enemy, and I was curious about the comment."

Willie continued. "Most of the files are still kept under lock and key, and we could be imprisoned for even talking about it, but the answer would be yes. We had several missions in both North and South Vietnam, along with our counterparts in the SAS. That was where we almost lost Pheasant."

CHAPTER TWENTY-EIGHT

Vietnam, 1969.

T he war had already started to go badly for the Americans, and the British government chose not to publicly support their American friends with British military personnel. The British had already fought one war in Vietnam back in the forties, and they didn't want to get mired down in another one. When we arrived in the country, our mission was to cause confusion in the enemy ranks, and that included killing as many of their officers as we could find. We were also supposed to make our way to every little hamlet we could find and escort out any British citizens we found there, of which there were many.

We made a lot of trips from Vietnam to Cambodia to bring out British doctors, priests and journalists, and we also put a dent in the officer ranks of several of North Vietnam's army units. One general took a particular dislike towards us, and he made it his personal goal to track us down and destroy us. He almost succeeded.

We were in a nothing little village in the north, not far from the Laotian border, interrogating the village elders about an NVA unit we were tracking, when we got word about a British emissary who had gotten stranded behind enemy lines when his chopper was shot down.

Pheasant told us to finish up with the elders, and he would head for the area of the downed chopper. It wasn't unusual for him to head out on his own and break trail, so he grabbed his gear and headed into the forest. We knew Mac would be able to track him, so we weren't concerned. Pheasant managed to get to the chopper a few hours ahead of the NVA. The pilots were both dead, and the emissary and his assistant were in bad shape. He was trying to render aid when an NVA unit showed up. He knew if he started a firefight that it would end badly for the civilians, so he tried to hide them in the woods. He walked right into an ambush. Now, Pheasant was a big prize, but the emissary and his assistant held no value to the general, so he had them both shot where they lay. Pheasant was taken captive.

It took us four days to track him down from where we found the bodies. It's still hard to talk about the things they did to Pheasant during the time he was held captive. When we got to the camp, it was abandoned. We found Pheasant tied to two crossed logs, and we thought he was dead. As we approached, he tried to raise his head, but he had lost a lot of blood.

His NVA interrogators had taken pleasure in beating him across his back with wet pieces of bamboo, and his back was torn to shreds. Then, the bastards decided to use him for target practice. We found out later that the general had had his men turn him around on the crossed logs and use a knife to cut an X where his heart should have been. The general stepped up, pulled his pistol and shot him right through the middle of the X. If Pheasant had been any other person, and not a person with a unique condition, he would have been dead. The general's shot was perfect, and he must have figured he would die soon, since he'd shot him in the heart, so they left him for dead and moved on.

By the time we got to him, he was all but gone. We cut him down and hightailed it for the border. Once across into Laos, we headed for a small hospital we knew about. It took us three days of tough travel to get there, but we were able to keep him alive.

The hospital was able to get him stable, we were able to get word to our command and they arranged for a chopper to evac us out. Our journey finally ended in a British hospital in India. Pheasant spent four months in rehab, and we were temporarily reassigned to another squad. By the time we got back to India, Pheasant was healed up, and he had fallen head over heels in love with a young British doctor. Her name was Charlene Quinn, and she had been at his side the entire time he was there. They were inseparable, and we figured that sooner or later, they would get married, and he would probably leave the service.

We were so very wrong.

CHAPTER TWENTY-NINE

Bax parked her state-issued Jeep Grand Cherokee on West Elkhorn Avenue, down the street from the bar Constance Fontaine and her girlfriends had patronized the night before. It was a chilly afternoon, and there wasn't a cloud visible in the Colorado bluebird sky. Bax stepped out of her Jeep and looked up and down the street.

"This is going to be hard without a description," she thought to herself as she grabbed her backpack and locked the Jeep. She wasn't expecting anything to come of this little excursion, but she knew that sometimes the answers came from the strangest places when investigating a crime. So, no matter what, she knew she had to try.

She started at the bar; she walked in and presented her credentials to the bartender. He introduced himself as Barry as he dried his hands on the bar towel. She pulled up the picture of Constance Fontaine on her phone and showed it to him. He looked at the picture.

"Sure. Mrs. F was in here last night. She's in here a lot with her girlfriends, and they are quite a group. Good looking, loud and really good for business."

"Did you notice anyone paying attention to the group of women?"

"It would be easier to tell you who wasn't paying attention to the group. They always attract attention."

"Anyone watching them but trying to do it without being

noticed?"

Barry thought for a minute as he loaded the washed beer mugs into the chest freezer next to the tap. He waved over one of the waitresses. Vicky was tall, thin and attractive. Her dark hair was done up in a quick bun, and she was setting the condiments out on the tables. She walked over to the bar, and Bax introduced herself.

"I heard Mrs. F ran into some trouble last night. Is she okay?" asked Vicky.

"Do you all call her Mrs. F?"

"She prefers it," said Vicky. "She told us that 'Mrs. Fontaine' makes her feel like her mother-in-law. She's pretty hip for an older lady, and she's a great tipper."

"Vicky, was anyone paying any special attention to Mrs. F and her friends, maybe trying not to look obvious?"

Vicky looked serious for a moment. "There was this one table. When Mrs. F is here, she attracts a lot of attention, but the three people at the table near the back tried to make like they weren't even interested, but I got the feeling they were watching her anyway."

"Tell me why you got that feeling?"

"Nothing specific. It was like they kept glancing over towards her table, but like they didn't want anyone to notice. Kind of sideways glances. They were also here for quite a while after they finished their dinner."

"Can you describe these three?"

"Sure. The woman was a honey blonde. She was tall and pretty. Blue eyes and a small birthmark on her cheek. She had a real sweet Southern accent. She also seemed to be doing most of the talking. The one guy was a good size. Around six foot but built like a football player. He had dark curly hair, and you could tell he was interested in the women. I spotted him a couple times, checking them out. The other one was shorter and younger. He also had curly dark hair, and he had some acne on his cheeks. He was quiet the entire time they were here. I need to get ready for the rush. I hope that helps."

Bax thanked her and made some notes on her tablet. She would transfer all this information to the investigation file once she got back to her hotel. The descriptions weren't great, and the description of the woman differed from the picture they'd gotten from the surveillance camera at the Fontaine place, but it was a good start. She thanked Barry and headed out into the fading afternoon light. A light rain shower had passed through while she was in the bar, and the air felt a bit cooler, but the smell of wet pine trees always made her smile.

Bax stopped at all the stores and restaurants on either side of the bar but didn't get any additional information. The night before had been busy, and all the shops were filled with tourists. She was glad to see that the small city had been able to recover from the flood. Estes Park had been one of her favorite places to visit with her family when she was growing up. Her dad wrote a lot of magazine articles about the recreational activities in the area, and it was one of the first places he took her rock climbing. It also brought back memories of the flood.

The flood had started at six a.m. on July 15, 1982, during the height of the summer tourist season. Lawn Lake was a natural lake that sat at 11,000 feet in Rocky Mountain National Park. In the early 1900s, it had been dammed to increase its capacity and used for irrigation. The morning the dam failed, the wall of water rushed down the side of the mountain, scouring out a massive amount of dirt and debris as it went. The water roared down the Roaring River valley, flowed into the Fall River—overwhelming the lower Cascade dam and rushed through the town of Estes Park. The flood ended when the water settled into Lake Estes at the eastern edge of town. The aftermath of the flood was devastating. Several lives were lost, and seventy-five percent of the commercial operations in town were destroyed.

The town had made an incredible recovery and continued to make improvements to attract more and more tourists. Bax remembered reading about the flood in *Life Magazine*. Her dad had come back a couple months after the flood so he could do an article for *Life* about the flood and the recovery efforts. She remembered looking at his photos many years later, and all she could see were piles of mud and debris. Now the street was wall-to-wall tourists.

Bax dodged a couple cars and decided to hit a few more shops along the opposite side of the street. For the next hour, she chatted with several shopkeepers. They all remembered seeing Mrs. Fontaine's car parked near the bar, and some of them remembered Mrs. Fontaine roaring down the street as she left the bar, but no one remembered seeing anyone watching the bar. She was about to call it a night when she reached the small ice cream parlor almost directly opposite the bar. She needed a break, so she walked in and ordered a chocolate ice cream cone. While she waited for the cone, she started a conversation with the woman behind the counter, who happened to be the owner. When Bax mentioned a curly-haired young man with acne on his face, the woman stopped and looked at her.

"I remember him, sweetie," she said. "He seemed a little odd to me, and for quite a while, he sat outside on the bench and watched the street. Even after he finished his ice cream, he sat there and watched. He was there a good couple of hours."

"Do you know when he left?" asked Bax.

"Not really. We got busy, and I almost forgot about him. When the rush was over, I looked to see if he was still there, but he was gone."

"Did he pay cash or use a card?"

The woman thought a minute. "I think he used a card. Let me get my box of receipts."

She walked into the back of the shop and disappeared. Bax couldn't believe she could get this lucky, and she hoped it was true, so she sat at one of the small round metal tables and finished her cone.

The owner walked back into the shop about five minutes later and handed Bax a small receipt. Bax noted the time on the receipt, which matched the period of time the woman had observed the young man.

"I think this is the one," she said. "I hope it helps."

She stepped away to help a family of four, and Bax took a picture of the receipt. She felt excited, but she needed to keep it in reserve. She still had a job to do. She called fellow CBI agent Paul Webber.

"Hey, Bax. What's up?"

"Hey, Paul. Do you have time to do me a favor?"

"Sure thing. Whatcha got?"

"I'm gonna send you a picture of a receipt. Can you see if you can get Visa to tell you the address and full name of the owner of the credit card?"

"Is this about the murder in Estes Park?"

"It could be. These guys may have finally made a mistake. I could have the break we need, right here in my hot little hand."

"No worries, Bax. Send it my way, and I will do what I can to track it down."

Bax thanked Paul, hung up and sat for a minute. She sent the picture of the receipt to Paul Webber, and then she dialed Buck. The call went to voice mail, so she left him a message and hung up. She suddenly realized how tired she was, and she decided to head for her hotel and call it a night.

CHAPTER THIRTY

Alicia Hawkins sat down on the edge of the bed, exhausted and satisfied. She looked at Karen's body lying there and was pleased with how well she'd done. She hadn't lost count this time, like usual, and she was able to keep Karen alive through seven hundred fifty-seven cuts. Looking at the body, she felt it was a new personal best. Her grandfather would be proud of her.

She lay down on the bloody sheets, smeared blood on her breasts and stomach and relived the experience until the thrill of the kill finally faded. She already had a good bit of blood on her, but the blood she smeared on herself now was still warm, and she wanted more. She wanted to remember this day for a long time.

Karen had woken up about halfway through the cutting, and the look in her eyes showed the utter fear she was feeling. Alicia couldn't believe how excited she got, but she kept to the pace she wanted to set, and it paid off in the end. This time, she made sure all the cuts were shallow, so as not to nick an artery.

She stood up and stepped away from the bed, turned and looked at Karen. This was a true masterpiece, and she couldn't wait until the FBI saw this victim. She smiled at the thought. She felt she had turned a corner and was well on her way to reaching the one thousand cuts her grandfather had tried to achieve.

She walked into the bathroom and ran a hot shower,

which felt good on her sore muscles. It always amazed her how tired and sore she was after killing someone. It hardly seemed like work at all. She let the hot water wash over her body and tried to relax.

When she climbed out of the shower, she was clean and felt refreshed. She got dressed, grabbed her coat and her keys and headed for one of the fast-food restaurants in Glenwood Springs. She felt safer using the drive-through, and she put on her black wig and sunglasses.

She had a couple hours to kill before she met Josh and Louis. She wanted to meet them the first time in a public spot, so she'd chosen the Lowe's parking lot. She figured with all the men coming and going, if something went wrong, she could always scream and figured someone would come to her rescue.

She sat in the parking lot, eating her burger and fries and watching the people coming and going. She could just as easily pick one of these poor saps for her sixteenth victim and not have to worry about the bar owner. It would be so much easier. She'd already seen several young women who would fit the bill nicely. She spotted a couple young men that might be an interesting challenge, especially since she was feeling more confident since the kill in Oklahoma. She was looking forward to trying again.

The problem was, she'd made that promise to her grandfather that she would complete his legacy by killing his sixteenth victim, the one that got away. She intended to live up to that promise, but she was going to have to move quickly. The anniversary of her grandfather's death was rapidly approaching.

She was sitting there daydreaming when an old Chevy van pulled up alongside her. She almost couldn't believe her eyes. The van was white, which wasn't too bad since most workers used white vans. The problem was all the demon art that was painted on the side facing her, and the words born to kill in huge letters. She looked around to see if anyone was watching them. She felt more conspicuous than she had in months, and she cringed, hoping she hadn't made a colossal mistake inviting these two neophytes into her world.

Josh and Louis climbed out of the van, approached the driver's side and introduced themselves. Josh was white, stood about five feet five, was overweight with shoulder-length hair and dressed like he had fallen into a used clothes bin. Louis was a fair-skinned black kid with spiky hair and a feeble attempt at growing a beard. He too was dressed in clothes that most poor people would throw away. They stood smiling at her like two goofs, and she signaled for them to get into the car.

Josh gushed all over her as she shook his clammy hand. She looked at his lily-white hands and wondered if this kid had ever done a hard day's work in his short life.

"God, Alicia. What a thrill to finally meet you in the flesh." Josh giggled like a schoolgirl. "We have been dreaming of this day for weeks. We're so glad to be here."

Josh almost couldn't contain himself in the back seat. "When do we start? I can't wait to claim my first victim."

Alicia looked startled. "Look, fellas. If we are going to do this together, we need to set a couple ground rules. First, never ever mention a victim in public. If you want to survive more than one victim, you need to be invisible. And speaking of invisible. What the fuck is the deal with the van? You look like a traveling billboard for a creep mobile."

They both looked ashamed, and they got quiet. "Sorry, Miss Alicia," said Louis. "We were so excited to come here, we never thought about the van. Our friends think it's cool. We didn't mean anything by it."

Alicia felt like she had kicked a puppy. "Okay, guys. Let's

forget about the van for now. Tell me about yourselves. Where you're from and why you think you are cut out to do this kind of work. Pardon the pun."

They both laughed, and that eased the tension. Louis told her he was from West Virginia, and that his father was a drunk. His mom had died in childbirth, and he had been raised by his grandmother in Florida. He'd learned early on how to hunt, and he always got a thrill cutting out the guts of the small animals he killed.

Josh had had an equally sad life, and he was also from Florida. They had been friends since kindergarten. He told her they'd started to follow her career, and her kills, and they knew they had to meet her. He told her they would work harder than anyone she ever knew, and all they wanted was a chance to prove themselves.

Alicia asked them some questions about their families and their habits, and after they were done talking, she told them to meet her later that night on the street in front of the Jackpot Bar in Aspen. She told them to park the van on the next block and walk back to her car. She shook their hands, and they slid out of her car. She had a lot to think about now that she had met them. She felt good about their enthusiasm, but she didn't have a sense of how they would act when the time came to kill a human being.

Alicia headed back to Aspen. She needed some sleep, and to do some internet research on her two new friends. She wasn't convinced that they weren't FBI, but they were so odd that she had trouble seeing them as anything but a couple young weirdos. She was about to enter a critical period in her serial killer career, and she hoped these two wouldn't be her downfall.

CHAPTER THIRTY-ONE

Buck picked up the check, and they stepped out into the cool night air. Mac invited Buck to join them for a drink, but Buck refused. He wanted to get back to the hospital in case PIS woke up, so he bid his new friends good night and walked to his car. The night had been filled with new and interesting revelations, and Buck needed some time to process the things Mac and his crew had told him.

PIS was royalty. Buck would have never guessed that. He knew PIS must have had a good upbringing, and from the way he carried himself, he obviously went to some excellent schools, but royalty? That was hard for Buck to fathom. He had never met royalty before, but the more he thought about it, the more he felt he could see PIS in that role. The other thing that was hard to believe was that someone who looked like PIS—tall, thin and wiry—could have been an elite soldier, what today is called a Tier 1 operator. Buck had met SEALs and Delta Force guys while he had been stationed at various bases during his time in the army. Most of them looked like Mac and his friends—stout, solid, muscular men, hardened by their experiences and training. PIS was none of those things. Buck knew he had some mad skills. He had seen them in action, but he didn't look like a special operator.

PIS was quiet, respectful and looked more like an accountant. Yet PIS had proven his value on more occasions than Buck could count. He also thought back to the conversation he'd had with PIS about someone setting up a scholarship fund for ranger Susan Corey's son and how PIS had blown off the fact that someone had done that. Now, he wondered once again if PIS was the one who set it up. The problem now was that none of this made any sense. If he was wealthy, why did he live in the woods?

At that point, the investigator in Buck kicked in, and he wondered if maybe PIS did have a place he went home to every night, which was why no one was ever able to track him. After all, he always had clean clothes on, and he never smelled like most of the homeless Buck had encountered. He might even have someone taking care of him. Buck thought if he was royalty, maybe he had an entire team of servants.

Buck pulled into the parking lot of the hospital, stopped the Jeep and slid out. He shook off the ideas about PIS that had been rolling around in his head and walked through the front doors.

One nurse was working at the counter at the entrance to the ICU, and she nodded as Buck walked in.

"Evening, Agent Taylor. Did you have a nice dinner?"

"Hi, Ramona, how's our patient tonight?"

"No real change, sir. The doctor came by about half an hour ago, and PIS is still sleeping."

"Thanks, Ramona, I'm going to head in there and stick around for a little while."

Ramona nodded, and Buck walked down the hall. He opened the door to PIS's room and stood in the doorway. PIS was sleeping soundly, but it was all the medical machinery that mesmerized Buck. One time, when Lucy had had a reaction to a new chemo drug, Buck had taken her to the hospital. She'd spent a couple days in intensive care, and Buck remembered the sounds of all the machinery and the blinking lights that never stopped. He shook off that memory and walked into the room. The sights, sounds and smells were all too familiar, and he almost turned around and walked out, but he knew he needed to support his friend.

Buck sat in the chair next to the bed, pulled out his phone and checked his messages. He checked the voice mail from Bax and smiled. Bax was making progress on the car theft case, and for a moment, he felt bad. He should be helping her, but he knew she understood that he needed to be right where he was. The message indicating that she had tracked down a receipt from one of the possible car thieves was great news. He checked his watch and decided it was too late to call her now, even though he knew she was probably wide awake and still working.

The second voice mail was from Hank Clancy. He wanted him to know that the task force had lost track of Alicia Hawkins. They still believed she was heading to Colorado, so they were now working out of an office in the Denver Field Office. He also found out that Buck and Bax had sent out a warning to all the papers and news outlets in the state, and he was hoping they hadn't scared her off. They were still trying to figure out if there was something significant about her coming to Colorado and why she would take the risk.

Buck deleted the message and was about to put his phone away when it buzzed with an incoming call. He checked the number and smiled.

"Hey, kiddo. How ya doing?" he said.

"Doing all right, Dad. I got your message when we came in from the fire line, and I wanted to call you right away. I saw the picture of the serial killer girl. You really think she'd come after us?"

"Not sure, Cassie, but I wanted to make sure you had the information and were on alert. I didn't want to scare you, but we all thought it was the best thing we could do."

"Do you have any idea where she is?"

"We think she's heading for Colorado, but we can't figure

out why. She has to know we would be all over her if she showed up here, so we're trying to work through it."

"Okay, Dad. I showed the rest of the team her picture, and my guys will watch out for me, so don't worry about me. Listen, Dad, I had a message from Aunt Beth. She said she left you several messages, but you won't call her back. She thinks you're avoiding her, and she said it was important. What's going on?"

"I've been busy lately. I'll get around to calling her soon, but not right now."

Cassie interrupted. "She said Grandpa's sick, and he wants to see you."

"Yeah, he's sick, all right. Look, Cass, they chose to go live in Arizona with Beth because she can take care of them. She's the doctor in the family, and she knew I wanted nothing to do with either of them, so I really couldn't care less that he's sick."

"Dad, I don't know what happened between you and Grandma and Grandpa, but whatever happened, it was a long time ago, and since you refuse to talk about, we can't help you. I know Grandma would like to see you."

"Beth can deal with them, that's the way she wanted it."

"You're punishing Grandma for something that Grandpa did, and it's not fair. Mom changed. I don't know why you won't."

Buck stared at the phone. He had no idea what she was talking about. He hadn't seen either of his parents since Lucy had gotten sick.

"What do you mean, your mom changed? Since when?"

"Dad, we're not stupid. We know when Grandpa was sitting around the gas station with all his old cronies, he used to call us kids his 'little beaner babies,' and then laugh about it. Yes, he was a racist. He never liked the fact you married a Latina, and we know he said he was too busy to go to your wedding, but we are proud of our Hispanic heritage, and he is still our grandfather, so we accepted him as he was."

Buck was speechless. He didn't realize the kids knew about his history with his father. The man was a racist, and he was also a drunk, and when he got drunk, he said a lot of stupid shit, most of which Buck could live with by avoiding him. What bothered him was that his mother never did or said anything about it. Lucy always tried to smooth things over when his father got out of hand, but Buck would never forgive the old man for what he'd said when he found out Lucy was dying. He could look past the "beaner baby" stuff, but when his father told Lucy that her cancer was God punishing her for marrying outside her race, Buck had had enough, and he and his father almost came to blows before Buck threw both his parents out of his house. Neither of them bothered to show up for Lucy's funeral, and he would never forget that.

His father was always putting down Lucy's father in front of his friends even though he was one of the hardest-working people Buck had ever met. What was so crazy was that Fernando Torres's ancestors had been in this country a hell of a lot longer than Buck's family. Fernando's ancestors had settled in the country as part of a land grant issued by the Spanish king in the late 1600s. Lucy's family had a rich and proud history, and he was glad that his children were a part of that heritage.

"Grandma flew in a few weeks before Mom died, and they had a long talk. We didn't tell you because Mom thought you'd put a stop to it. David arranged it, and she stayed at his house. Grandma apologized to Mom for everything bad Grandpa had said about her, and they buried the hatchet. She came in again after Mom died, and she and Grandma Rose spent hours down at the dock where we spread Mom's ashes, and they just talked. According to David, they walked back to his house arm in arm. You were out of town on a case and we thought it was the perfect time. I know this may be hard to believe, and we didn't mean to do it behind your back, but we all thought it was important. You never told us what Grandpa said to Mom, and we know it was pretty bad, but if Mom could make it all okay, maybe you can too."

Buck sat and stared at the phone. He didn't know whether to be aggravated or be relieved that it was all out in the open. He found it hard to believe that Lucy would keep that kind of secret from him. He'd had no idea they had spoken. He didn't know what to say, so he told Cassie he would call her back, and he disconnected the call. He put his phone away and stared out the window. He looked at PIS and all those tubes and wires he was connected to, and he wondered if a man avoided his family for all those years, what the toll on that person would be. He closed his eyes and leaned his head against the back of the chair. With everything he had learned about PIS and now everything he had learned about his own family, he was going to need some time to make sense of it all.

CHAPTER THIRTY-TWO

Alicia Hawkins was sitting in her car across the street from the Jackpot Bar, running the plan through her mind one more time. She knew what she needed Josh and Louis to do; she hoped they could pull it off. Her internet search had found little information about the two. They had a Facebook page and a Twitter account, but other than that, there was almost nothing of value on the web. She was going to have to go with her instincts alone. She needed them to pull this off, and she only had a few days to make it happen.

She spotted them coming around the corner, and she waited as they slid into the car, one in front and one in back. Once settled, they looked out the windows.

"What are we looking at?" Josh asked.

"You see the Jackpot Bar across the street? That is where my next victim is coming from, and I need you to help me abduct her. She may be an older woman, but I am worried she is going to be formidable."

"Who is she?" asked Louis, now staring out the back window.

"She owns the bar, and every time I've seen her, she is with this huge bouncer."

"Why did you choose her?" asked Josh.

"I didn't choose her, my grandfather did."

They looked at her like she had lost her mind. They had

read all the stories in the newspaper and online about her grandfather's exploits as a serial killer, and they knew he was dead, so they were unsure how her grandfather could have chosen this woman.

"My grandfather chose her when she was a young woman and was on the way to his tunnel when he ran off the road and almost died in the crash. The woman in the car with him, who no one knew existed until I discovered her, was supposed to be his sixteenth victim." She wrapped her hand around the jade horse hanging around her neck.

"Two days from now is the first anniversary of my grand-father's death, and as a tribute to him, I am going to kill his sixteenth victim, who will also be my sixteenth victim."

The two young men almost couldn't contain themselves; they were so excited. They were thrilled to be part of such a moving tribute, and they were excited to be a part of history. This was so great that people would be talking about it for years to come. They could almost see their names in the history books, next to Alicia Hawkins's name as well as all the now-famous serial killers in history. This was a stroke of genius, and they pledged then and there not to let her down.

Alicia slowly walked them through the plan, as she saw it, and asked them for their input. She was putting a lot of faith in these two unknown characters, but she wanted to see what they thought of the possibility of the plan's success.

After listening to her plan, they agreed that it was possible. The variable would be the bouncer. If they could get past the bouncer, then getting the bar owner shouldn't be a problem. They walked through the details once more, and then Josh and Louis slid out of Alicia's car and headed for the bar. They wanted to get a good look at the bouncer and the owner.

The bar was packed and noisy as usual with young people, and the band on the small stage in the corner was playing covers of current hits by various artists. It was so loud that they could barely hear themselves talk. They paid their ten dollars each at the door and noted the muscles on the bouncer. He was one big dude. They smiled as they walked past him and found two seats that had just been vacated at the bar.

Due to the busyness, there were three bartenders behind the bar tonight, but it was easy to pick out the owner. Alicia had been right on point with her description, and they had a hard time believing this woman was somewhere in her late sixties, early seventies. She was drop-dead gorgeous, and the sleeveless top she was wearing showed a lot of cleavage and a well-toned, muscular body. They sat for a minute staring at her, until they realized the male bartender was standing in front of them, waiting for their order.

They each ordered a bottle of Coors and looked around the bar. They had never drank Coors, but they'd heard it was made in Colorado, and they wanted to look like they fit in with the rest of the crowd. For the next thirty minutes, they sat, listened to the music and worked out the details of the abduction. Their conclusion was that if they had to, they would kill the bouncer. After all, they were going to be serial killers; what did it matter if their first victim was the bouncer or some old lady?

They finished their beers and headed for the door, once again noting how big the bouncer was as they walked past him and out the door. Alicia was still parked across the street, and they slid into the car and gave a nod.

"Piece of cake," said Josh.

Louis didn't look as sure as Josh did, but they were buddies, so he went along. Alicia told them to plan it all out like they had discussed and get ready. They needed to deliver the woman to Alicia's cabin in the woods in two days.

Alicia pulled away from the curb, and they followed her

in their van to the cabin. They clocked the drive from the bar to the cabin parking area at ten minutes. They climbed out of their vehicles, and Alicia led them down the darkened path to the cabin, which shone like a beacon in the night. Josh and Louis noted the steepness of the trail in one spot because they wanted to make sure they didn't slip carrying the woman. They didn't care about hurting her; she was going to die anyway. They were more concerned about hurting themselves and not being able to help Alicia with the kill.

Alicia led them into the cabin and led them downstairs to the bedroom. She wanted to gauge their reactions when they saw Karen, dead and still tied to the bed. They both stopped in the doorway and stared. Josh walked towards the end of the bed and got closer for a good look. He looked up at Alicia with admiration in his eyes.

"Incredible, look at all those cuts," he said. He circled the bed and looked at the body from several angles. He asked Alicia if he could touch the body, and Alicia handed him a pair of blue nitrile gloves. Her DNA was already on record, but she wanted to make sure their DNA wasn't found on the body. This was her kill, and she wanted all the credit. She glanced over at Louis, who was still standing in the doorway. She thought he was paler than when she'd first met them.

"Come closer, Louis. If you are going to be a part of this, you need to find out if you have the stomach for it."

Louis took a few hesitant steps into the room and looked at the bloodstained sheets. Other than in books, he had never seen a dead body before. Josh laughed and told him to stop being a pussy and come closer. This was going to be their legacy someday. Louis took another tentative step, swallowed hard to keep the bile from getting into his throat and ran from the room and out the front door, where he proceeded to vomit in the shrubs next to the door. When Josh reached him, he was on his knees, wiping his mouth.

"Sorry, man. I've never seen a dead body. God, there's so much blood. Sorry, man."

Josh patted him on his back and grabbed his arm to help him up. "Hey, don't worry about it. You'll get used to it, but in the meantime, you can help with grabbing the victims. I'll do all the cutting."

Louis smiled. He knew Josh would have his back, and that made him feel better. He turned around to walk back into the house and saw Alicia looking at him from the front door. He thought he should apologize, but Alicia turned and walked back into the cabin. A cold chill ran up his spine, and it made him uneasy. He shook it off and walked into the warm cabin and closed the door.

Josh came in a few minutes later, carrying two sleeping bags and two AR-15 rifles. He had a pistol clipped to his belt. Alicia looked at the weapons, said nothing and headed for the bedroom, carrying a large black plastic trash bag. While Louis set up their gear in the living room, Alicia asked Josh to help her move the body from the bed. She needed to sleep, and she wanted to put some clean sheets on the bed.

Josh helped her pick up Karen and carry her to the walk-in closet next to the bathroom. They dumped her in the middle of the floor, stripped the stiff sheets off the bed and placed them in the bag. They flipped over the mattress, and Alicia put the new sheets on the bed while Josh carried the trash bag to the mudroom off the kitchen. Once done, Alicia said good night and closed the door. Josh grabbed Louis's car keys, and they headed back to their van. They planned to sit on the bar for a while and hopefully follow the bar owner back to her house. They were now in the research portion of the abduction, so they sat outside the bar and waited.

Alicia stood by the bedroom window and watched Josh and Louis head into the woods. She was feeling okay about Josh, but she was having serious doubts about Louis, and she started to formulate a plan. A plan that would make Louis her seventeenth victim.

CHAPTER THIRTY-THREE

Bax had just sat down to breakfast when her phone rang. She looked at the number and answered. "Hey, Paul. What's up?"

Paul Webber had been doing research on expensive cars registered in Colorado. "Hey, Bax. I sent you a couple cars that might be candidates, but after speaking with some of the owners, I think I've narrowed it down to one that makes sense. Most of the owners I spoke with have either moved their cars out of state for the winter or have them locked away in a secure automotive storage facility. I spoke with one of those facilities in Denver, and if the owner is even half truthful, these places are like Fort Knox. I doubt our thieves would try to hit one of those facilities, but I have passed on the information, and the guy I spoke with is going to add more security, both physical and technological."

"Great, Paul. So, what does that leave us?"

"Out of twenty-seven mega-dollar cars we were able to find, we have spoken to all but one owner. The owner is that actor from all those fast car movies, and according to his agent, he is working on a film in Italy, and the car is locked in his garage in Aspen, along with a half dozen other cars."

"What makes you think this might be the car?"

"The car is a red Bugatti Chiron Sport. It is one of only three hundred made in 2019, and according to the registration, it was purchased four months ago for three point six million dollars."

Bax let out a long whistle. "You have to be kidding. Someone paid *that* much money for a car? People must be nuts."

"I guess if you can afford it, and this guy certainly can. He made fifty million dollars for his last movie, he likes fast cars and this is one of the fastest, most expensive cars in the world. That's like the perfect storm for a car guy. You wouldn't spend that much on a car if you had it?"

Bax laughed. "I'd need to talk to my accountant first. Paul, can you text me his address? Is there a security person or anyone I need to talk with?"

"Yes, and get this. The only security on the car is the locked garage and a video camera, which is there only because the insurance company required it. Right now, the only people on the property are the handyman, who's in his sixties, and a housekeeper, who is not much younger. You want some help?"

"Yeah. Why don't you meet me in Aspen? Buck is in Aspen already, but he is tied up between PIS and the Alicia Hawkins case. I'll give him a call and fill him in. Great information, Paul. Thanks."

Bax hung up, took a sip of her coffee and was about to put a fork full of scrambled eggs in her mouth when her phone rang again. She checked the number and hit the answer button.

"Hi, Max. You're up early. What's up?"

"Hi, Bax. I wanted to catch you before you started your day. We got the DNA results from the Fontaine woman's rape kit, and the perp is in the system."

Bax set her fork back down on the plate. "Local?"

"No. The information was put in the system in Mount Airy, North Carolina. I requested a copy of the arrest report, and it's rather unimpressive. It appears that a high-school prank got a little out of hand, and an underage girl was groped. Her father pressed charges. The problem was, the kid who was arrested was eighteen, so they charged him as an adult and made him register as a sex offender. The sex offender designation required him to have a DNA sample on file. Bad for him, lucky for us."

"That's a pretty harsh sentence for a prank, Max. I wonder if there was more to it than that?"

"I can't tell without requesting a copy of the court ruling, but my guess would be that you're right. But anyway. His name is Earl Richard Jefferson, twenty-six, six feet four and two hundred forty pounds. I knew you were on the road, so I sent everything we have over to Paul Webber, so he can do a deep dive into Mr. Jefferson."

"Max, you're awesome. I'll touch base with Paul on my way to Aspen. Thanks, Max."

Bax hung up and asked the waitress if she could pop her eggs and bacon in the microwave for a few seconds to warm them up, and the waitress said she'd take care of it. When she returned a few minutes later, she had a plate full of fresh scrambled eggs and crispy bacon, and she refilled Bax's coffee cup. She smiled at Bax and left the check on the table. Bax finished her meal, put a twenty-dollar bill on the table and headed for her car.

She threw her backpack on the front seat, pulled out her phone and dialed Buck. Even though it was early, she knew Buck would be awake. Buck answered and, with a whisper, said, "Hey, Bax. What's up?"

Bax filled him in on the DNA match and the information she had gotten from Max Clinton. She also told him about the information Paul had been able to gather on the expensive cars. Buck was silent for a minute, and she heard a door quietly close behind him.

"Sorry, Bax. I didn't want to disturb PIS."

Before he could continue, Bax asked him how PIS was doing. Buck took a few minutes to fill her in on PIS's condition and gave her some of the highlights from his conversation at dinner with Max, Devlin and Willie.

"Royalty, huh? I always wondered if he was more than he appeared." She hesitated for a minute. "Knowing how private PIS is, do you think he'll want to see his former teammates?"

"I have been wondering about that myself. As far as I know, PIS has never told anyone about his past life, and I still don't know what made him disappear all those years ago, but I'm wondering if them coming here to find him might have been a bad idea. I sat here all night, hoping he might wake up so I could tell him before they show up for another visit. The doctor is due in about an hour, and I might know more then. So, fill me in."

"I'm leaving Estes Park. I should be in Aspen in a couple hours."

She told him about the call from Paul and the car he'd located in Aspen, and she gave him a quick rundown on the DNA results.

"The information on Earl Jefferson works with the North Carolina license plate we are running down, from the video at the Fontaine house." She also told him about the young guy who had been on what appeared to be a stakeout across from the bar in Estes Park. She planned to have one of the techs from Denver travel to Estes and create a composite sketch of the kid on the bench.

"Great work, Bax. As soon as you can get an address for this guy Earl or a hit on the plate, call the state police in North Carolina and see if they have an investigator who can check out the house. We need to know if Jefferson is in town and who might be with him. Give me a call when you get to Aspen, and we can swing by and look at this Bugatti together."

"Buck, anything new on Alicia Hawkins?"

"No. I was going to call Hank Clancy in a little while and see if they were making any progress. Any luck with the information you put online?"

"I haven't had a chance to check. I'll call Paul and see if someone in the office can run a check on the social media and VRBO sites. I'll see you in a couple hours."

Bax pulled out of the parking lot and headed towards Aspen. As she left town, she dialed Detective Boyd and filled him in on everything that had happened since she'd left him the night before. He thanked her for the information and said he would run an internet search for Earl Jefferson. She told him to call when he had anything, and she would do the same.

Bax called Paul Webber and asked him to also do a background search on Earl Jefferson. It wasn't that she didn't trust Detective Boyd, but CBI had access to a lot of resources that the detective didn't, and she wanted to cover all the bases. She hung up after talking with Paul and concentrated on the road. Hopefully, by the time she reached Aspen, she would have more to report to Buck.

CHAPTER THIRTY-FOUR

Buck stepped back into PIS's room, grabbed his backpack and was about to run out for some breakfast when his phone rang. He looked at the number and answered.

"Hey, Bob. What's up?"

Bob Brady sounded distraught. "Hey, Buck, sorry to call so early, but we've had a little disturbance in Wagner Park this morning, and I could use your help."

"What kind of disturbance, Bob?"

"My officers are holding your three friends. Get here as soon as you can."

Buck looked confused, then it hit him, and he wondered what kind of trouble Mac and his team had gotten themselves into. He left the hospital, climbed into his Jeep and headed for the park.

He turned onto South Monarch Street, parked behind an Aspen Police Department SUV and an Aspen Fire Department ambulance and walked towards the crowd gathered near one of the wooden picnic tables.

Mac, Devlin and Willie, with the cane and walker sitting next to them, were handcuffed and sitting on the bench next to the table. Willie was being treated for a cut on his forehead, and Mac was holding a towel against his bloody nose. They looked up as Buck approached. An EMT was also working on some cuts and scrapes on a homeless man sitting on the ground.

Bob Brady turned and walked towards Buck, who raised his hands in a "What the hell happened?" gesture.

Bob Brady started laughing. "Your three new friends are some characters. They attacked a homeless vet in the park. That's him sitting on the ground, and they refuse to speak to anyone but you."

Buck looked at the table and was confused. "How is that possible? Two of them can barely walk."

Bob laughed again and walked towards the bench. His officers stepped away as they approached and were trying, with great difficulty, to not laugh themselves.

Buck stepped up to the trio. "Mac, what's going on? The chief says you attacked a homeless vet."

Mac looked up at Buck and nodded. "He's the fella who stabbed Pheasant."

"I did not," yelled the vet sitting on the ground.

"Mac, why don't you start at the top," said Buck.

"We stopped in that Irish pub for a drink after we left you. You know, the one Pheasant was drinking at the night he was stabbed. We were talking to people in the bar, and someone mentioned that they had seen that fella there"—he pointed to the vet— "get into a fight earlier in the day with Pheasant, and Pheasant had him pinned to the ground. When several other people mentioned it, we decided we should have a little talk with the fella, so we went looking for him. We talked with some homeless folks, and they told us where to find him and to be careful because he was crazy. We found him sleeping under this table, and we politely asked him to come out and talk to us."

"I assume, since we're all sitting here and you're in handcuffs, that he refused to speak with you?"

"Aye. He spoke with us in a foul manner, so we decided to teach him a lesson. The rest is why we are here in handcuffs."

"Mac, you guys aren't that young anymore. You could have been hurt."

"Nonsense," said Willie. "A few more minutes and we'd have had him."

Buck was not amused. "Why do you think he hurt Pheasant?"

"We don't know why, but they were seen rolling around in the grass, and Pheasant had to restrain him. Heard there was a lot of foul language."

"He also had a knife," said Devlin.

Buck looked surprised, and he looked, questioning, towards Bob Brady. Bob handed him a sealed evidence bag containing a military-issued Ka-Bar knife. Buck examined it through the plastic.

"Might be some blood on it," said Bob Brady.

Buck looked over to the vet. "Mind if I talk to him?"

Bob Brady nodded, and Buck stepped over to the vet. The EMT wrapped up what he was doing, and the officer guarding him stepped aside. Buck knelt next to him.

"What's your name, soldier?"

The vet looked Buck up and down. "I didn't hurt PIS, he's my friend."

"That's fine, but what's your name?"

"People call me Stick. Real name's Paul Stickley."

"Where'd you serve, Stick?"

"All over. Afghanistan, Iraq. Was with the 101st Airborne. Captain." He asked Buck to reach into his upper jacket pocket. Buck did and pulled out a silver star medal. Buck asked him if the medal was his, and he nodded. Buck put it back in his pocket.

"Okay, Stick. You want to tell me what happened?"

"Those crazy old coots attacked me. I was sleepin' under the bench when they grabbed me and started pounding on me. Big guy hit me with his cane, and the guy with the walker set it on my chest and held me down. I didn't do nothin'."

"They say you stabbed PIS. Is that true?"

"PIS is my friend. He helps me when I need help. I wouldn't hurt him."

"They found a knife in your things. Looks like it has some blood on it."

"I use that for cutting up meat. Had a rabbit two nights ago and skinned it with the knife. Never stabbed PIS with it."

"Stick, tell me what happened the other day when you got in a fight with PIS?"

Stick looked around like he was unsure what to say. Buck leaned in closer and looked at him. Buck had learned over the years that silence makes people uncomfortable, and he'd turned it into an interrogation technique that had worked well for him. His patience was legendary.

Stick watched Buck for a few minutes without saying a word. He finally gave up.

"PIS saved my life. We weren't fighting. I got some bad dope and was ODing. PIS was trying to give me the Narcan, but I couldn't stop thrashing. He finally laid down on top of me. The Narcan brought me around. There was no fight."

"Thanks, Stick." Buck stood up, and a young homeless woman standing off to the side said, "It's true, Officer. I was there. We had been partying all night and got some bad junk. Stick would be dead if PIS hadn't come along."

Buck thanked her and walked back to Bob Brady, who had

overheard the whole thing. "I think this was a misunderstanding. My suggestion would be to let them all go. Let's give him back his knife. I doubt he wants to file charges against PIS's friends."

Bob Brady agreed and had his officers remove the handcuffs from everyone. Buck walked back over to Stick. He spoke quietly with him for a minute, so no one could hear, then he reached into his pocket, pulled out a twenty-dollar bill and handed it to Stick. They shook hands, and Stick and the homeless woman walked away.

Buck walked back to the trio of Brits as the EMTs and police officers cleared the crowd that had gathered. He asked Mac if they had eaten breakfast yet and told them to head for his Jeep and that he would be along in a second. He walked back to Bob Brady.

"They are lucky Stick didn't kick their asses. He's got a pretty good build under that coat. You want to grab some breakfast with us? Might be interesting."

Bob Brady headed back to his SUV, and Buck walked back to his Jeep. He wondered how much more trouble these three were going to be before PIS woke up.

CHAPTER THIRTY-FIVE

The restaurant was crowded, but the hostess was able to find them a table in the back corner. They all sat down and ordered drinks. Coffee all around and a Coke for Buck. The waitress took their breakfast orders and walked away.

"What the hell were you guys thinking?" asked Buck.

Willie was the first to respond. "We thought we had him dead to rights. Several people in the bar said they saw the incident and described it as a fight. How were we to know?"

Bob Brady looked up from his coffee. "You should have come to either Buck or me. That's our job. You can't take the law into your own hands, even if PIS is your friend."

They all looked contrite, and the conversation turned to PIS's condition and progress on the case. Of which there hadn't been much. Buck decided to take the conversation in a different direction.

"You guys told me about how Pheasant got the scars on his back, and about the doctor he fell in love with. He carries around an old cigar tin with a small china teacup, a plate and a tea ball in it. At the bottom is a black-and-white picture of a pretty young woman. Is that a picture of the doctor who treated him after he was injured in Nam? When I asked him about it one night, he told me that some things were better left unsaid."

A sad silence seemed to come over the trio, and they

looked at one another. It was as if no one wanted to tell the story of the tea set. It was apparent to Buck and Bob Brady that there was something important about that picture. Devlin took a sip of his coffee and set the cup down. He looked at the others, who nodded, and he looked at Buck.

"That tea set brings up some bad memories. We got called up to evacuate some British citizens from a small hospital in Uganda. We had been stationed in Africa for a couple months, and this had become part of our routine. Sometimes we did three or four evacuations in a week. The fighting in Uganda at the time was brutal, and we went wherever we were needed. We choppered into an area near the hospital and made our way through the jungle. Before we got to the hospital, we knew something was wrong. It was eerily quiet. Even the birds and animals were silent."

"We moved silently into the hospital grounds, and the scene was something none of us will ever forget. There were bodies scattered everywhere. Many were missing limbs or heads, and many of the women and girls had been raped before being butchered."

He stopped for a minute and took a sip of coffee. The eggs that had arrived a few minutes before were getting cold, but Buck and Bob Brady were focused on Devlin.

"Pheasant had no idea until we walked into the hospital that Dr. Quinn was even in the country. The last they'd spoken, she was working in a hospital in London. Somehow, her letter to Pheasant arrived after we left the base. The hospital's doctor had taken ill, and she had been asked by the hospital in London if she would be willing to fill in for a couple weeks. She had only arrived at the hospital two days before we got there."

"We found the ill doctor on the floor as we entered the hospital. He had been disemboweled and shot repeatedly. There were two patients in the two operating rooms that had been hacked to death, and then we found Dr. Quinn. She had been tied down to a hospital bed, stripped and raped by god knows how many men and boys. When they finished with her, they slit her throat. It was horrible."

There was silence at the table as everyone listened to the story. Willie wiped the tears from his eyes and continued. "Pheasant walked in before we could stop him, and he stood there and didn't say a word. He seemed numb. While we took care of burying the bodies, Pheasant was in her room, which had been ransacked like everything else. Among the debris, he found one cup and one saucer from a tea set he had bought her while we were on leave in London. The rest of the set was destroyed. Hidden in a niche in the wall, he found the small teapot and the tea ball."

"When we got back to him, he was sitting amongst the ruins with the cup and saucer and odd things he had found, including the picture. We found an old tin box, put the items in it for him and led him outside."

"Mac had been speaking with a couple young women who had managed to escape into the forest. The carnage had been caused by a local warlord who called himself General Mutombo. He wasn't any kind of recognized general, just a thug who had a few dozen men and boys he had recruited to help him. According to the women, it was the general himself who had killed the two doctors."

"We radioed in our situation, and since it was dark, we were told to wait until morning for evac. Sometime during the night, Pheasant disappeared into the jungle. By the time we noticed he was gone, he had about a five-hour head start. Mac was able to track him, and half a day later, we caught up with him, or I guess I should say, we found the destruction he had left in his wake."

"We reached the rebel camp late in the afternoon, and what we found was unimaginable. There were bodies everywhere, and like at the hospital, many were hacked to death, many were shot, and there wasn't a soul left alive. We found the general tied to a tree. He had been castrated, and his throat had been slit, almost taking his head off. In the middle of the camp, we found Pheasant's uniform and his weapons. We never saw him again after that. Mac tried to find his trail, but Pheasant was too good, and we never found a trail to follow. We didn't know if he was dead or alive. All we knew was that he had killed a lot of people that day."

"We left the camp as we found it, took Pheasant's uniform and weapons and made it back to the hospital, where we were evac'd back to base. The SBS sent several teams back to the area to search for Pheasant, but after a week, they called off the search. The SBS interrogated us about Pheasant's disappearance and about what we had found at the hospital. I don't know if they ever found the general's encampment, but no one ever mentioned it to us. He was officially listed as missing in action, and we moved on with our careers."

They ate their breakfasts in silence, and Buck could see that even to this day, it was hard for these men to talk about what had happened that day. If he were to try to understand, he would have a hard time picturing PIS as a stone-cold killer. Buck, more than anyone, had come to respect PIS over the years, and he tried to imagine PIS living with the nightmare of finding his girlfriend brutalized and the aftermath of what he did out of revenge. Buck wasn't sure, under those circumstances, if he would have reacted any differently. His family was his whole world, yet he figured he'd spent too many years as a cop and would have a hard time setting that aside to seek revenge. But then who knows how anyone would react in that situation?

He did know one thing. He now had a better understanding of why PIS had chosen to stay out of society and avoid living a normal life. He was even more worried that the presence of Mac and his buddies, after all these years and with all the emotions associated with that tragic day, might not be a good thing for PIS. He had no idea how PIS would react to them being in Aspen, but he wondered if he should suggest that they leave now and not wait around until PIS woke up.

Finished with breakfast and emotionally drained, Mac asked Buck if he would drive them back to their hotel. Buck picked up the check off the table, paid the bill and left a nice tip for the waitress. He said goodbye to Bob Brady and headed for his Jeep. They drove back to the hotel in silence. Buck told the trio that he would call them when Pheasant woke up, and he would pick them up if PIS wanted to see them. He let them out in front of the hotel, pulled onto Main Street and headed back towards the hospital. He was almost to the parking lot when his phone rang.

Buck answered the phone, and Max Clinton greeted him the way she always did. She then told him that the DNA results from the vomit in the alley where PIS had been stabbed were back from the lab. Buck listened, thanked her, hit his flashers and spun the car around in the street. He speed-dialed Bob Brady, told him to meet him back at Wagner Park and hit the gas.

CHAPTER THIRTY-SIX

Earl and Toby dropped their backpacks next to the RV and stepped through the door. They looked tired and cold. Victoria Larsen and Jessie were sitting at the table looking at pictures on Victoria's laptop. They both looked up as Earl and Toby walked in.

"We have everything we need from watching the house. There is no one home but a housekeeper and a maintenance guy. This should be a piece of cake."

Jessie nodded and asked them to look at the screen. "We got the same impression. Haven't seen anyone who looks like a movie star or anyone other than the folks you saw." Victoria had been monitoring the security cameras and digital assistants for the past couple days.

Victoria continued. "Your dad will be here tomorrow night. We've spent enough time in this town, so let's plan on going for the car as soon as he arrives. We've set up a rendezvous point at a turnout heading up Independence Pass."

She pulled up a local map on her laptop and pointed to a turnout near an old abandoned mining camp. During the day, it was a local tourist trap, but at night no one went there. She highlighted the route they would follow once they had secured the car, and Jessie studied the map and memorized every street, including a couple backup routes, just in case something went wrong.

Earl and Toby slipped off their camo gear and crashed on their beds. They needed a couple hours of sleep, and then they would start making their final plans. The hardest part would be getting into the gated property, but they had no doubt that Victoria had already devised a plan to circumvent the security systems at the front gate. They were looking forward to a couple months off at the ranch in Montana.

In the meantime, Jessie and Victoria were going back through the camera feeds from the house to make sure they hadn't missed anything. They were all tired, and with this being their last job for a while, they didn't want any loose ends or mistakes.

After reviewing three days' worth of videos taken off the digital assistants and the security cameras, Jessie was feeling more and more confident that they were ready to make the grab. The older couple taking care of the house had developed a standard routine they followed to the letter every day, and it concluded with a couple hours of television-watching in the evening, checking all the doors and setting the perimeter alarms and retiring to their room in time for the nightly news.

Jessie had narrowed down the timeline before they went off to bed. Victoria had all the alarm codes, so gaining access to the house after the alarms were set would not be a problem. The only unknown was a ten-minute window when the maintenance guy was out of the picture. Since it happened every night, Victoria was convinced it was a dead spot in the alarm coverage. She had backtracked the entire system several times, but she couldn't say where the guy was going or what he was doing. She had located all the alarm zones, and she knew it had nothing to do with the system, but she was at a loss as to what he was doing during the ten minutes he was missing from view.

She chalked her concern up to a little paranoia and made sure that when she and Jessie set the schedule, they avoided that ten-minute window. By the end of the night, they had a plan that got them in and out in less than three minutes, and they were pleased. Victoria ran the plan through the simulator program she had on her laptop, and each time the results were the same. The successful removal of the car from the premises. She also had finished capturing all the police and sheriff's department frequencies, and they were now plugged into her laptop, so she could monitor everything that was happening with local law enforcement. By the time they slipped into bed, everything was running on autopilot. They each fell asleep dreaming about what they were going to do with all the money that was sitting in their online bank account.

The last thing Victoria did before calling it a night was check in with her broker. The deal was already set, and the money had been transferred to his bank. Once the broker received word that the car was en route, he would transfer the money to Victoria's account. This would be their biggest payday yet, and she was very proud of her adopted family.

CHAPTER THIRTY-SEVEN

J osh and Louis thought they were ready. They had spent the last two days watching the bar owner, and they were confident that they knew the best time to grab her. Luckily for them, the bouncer did not go home with her after they closed the bar. Like a good soldier, he made sure she was safely in her car before he headed to his own house. They followed the same routine every night.

Once she got home, the bar owner would park her car in the garage that was separated from the house by about fifteen feet. She would open the back door to her house, walk in, shut off her alarm system and then come back and close the back door. This was the only mistake they saw her make, and this was where they would grab her. They would need to be close to the door when she got home, so they decided to split up. Josh would stake out the backyard of her house, while Louis would keep watch at the bar. Once she was in her car, assuming there was no sudden change of plans, Louis would race the half mile to her house and be ready for Josh's call. There was a blind spot on the side of her garage between the garage and some trees where they could hide without being seen from the street. From that spot next to the garage, they were also hidden from her neighbors. They felt good about their plan.

The sun was clearing the mountains by the time they headed back to Alicia's place in the woods. They were passing by a park when they noticed a lot of police activity. They pulled to the curb and watched for a minute, hoping this didn't have anything to do with them. The police had a couple old geezers handcuffed and sitting at a wooden picnic table. They also had some homeless guy sitting on the ground a few feet away. He was also handcuffed.

They watched as an older fellow walked up and talked to one of the cops, who they figured was the chief of police, from all the stars on his collar. The older guy then walked over and spoke to the homeless guy on the ground. Josh recognized the older guy right away. That was that state cop, Buck Taylor. Alicia had told them to be on the lookout for him and let her know if they spotted him. They didn't know that much about his role in all of Alicia's plans, but she seemed spooked whenever she mentioned this guy. She also seemed pissed.

Having seen enough, they decided that whatever was going on in the park had nothing to do with them, so they pulled back onto the street and headed for Alicia's. They wanted to run their snatch-and-grab plan by Alicia to make sure they hadn't missed anything. They also wanted to get some sleep so they would be ready when it was time to grab the bar owner.

Alicia wasn't pleased when they told her that they had seen Buck Taylor in the park with a bunch of cops. She had them describe everything they saw, then she sat back quietly and contemplated her next move. It would be so incredible to hit Buck Taylor. Revenge would be so sweet, but she couldn't jeopardize her commitment to her grandfather. This was her tribute to him, and nothing would stand in her way. She also wondered why Buck Taylor was still in town. It had been several days since she had killed his homeless friend, and she'd figured he would probably help with the investigation, but by now they should have had their suspect in custody, and he should be moving on. She wondered if that was what all the police activity was in the park. Maybe they'd gotten the DNA results back and were attempting to arrest the homeless vet. She wished she could get in her car and drive over to the park to watch, but she was too close to take that chance.

If the opportunity presented itself after she was done fulfilling her tribute, maybe she would take on Buck Taylor.

Alicia walked through the plan for the abduction with Josh and Louis one more time as they fine-tuned it. Feeling good about what was to come, she changed the subject. She was still concerned that the FBI was already in Aspen looking for her, and she had a plan to cover her ass.

"I want you two to find a couple good spots along the trail to the cabin, and I want you to set up an ambush. Once we have the bar owner, I am going to need time, and I am worried that the police and FBI response might be faster than I expected."

Josh looked disappointed. He had hoped they could be there while Alicia did her work, and they could learn more about her techniques. He had studied everything written online about her, but getting the chance to see it all up close and personal, well, that was what he had been hoping for.

"Do you really think that could happen? How would they even find you?" asked Josh.

"Look, Josh. I know you want to see how this is done, but this kill is important to me. I promise you that once we are out of here and headed for California, there will be plenty of opportunities to teach you the proper way to use a scalpel and keep your victim alive. You will have my undivided attention, okay?"

Louis tapped Josh on the arm. He was relieved that they were not going to be in the room while Alicia sliced up her next victim, but he tried not to show his relief.

"We promised to help Alicia with whatever she needed. Besides, it might be fun to kill a couple FBI agents, and who knows, maybe that Buck Taylor guy will be with them and we can kill him too."

Josh smiled, and he and Louis high-fived.

"Don't you worry, Alicia," said Josh. "We will make sure no one gets anywhere near this cabin."

They grabbed their coats and headed for the front door. Once they were gone, Alicia sat down at the kitchen table and sipped her cup of tea. She hated the waiting, especially after she'd already picked out her next victim, and more than anything, she hated to have to rely on people she didn't know she could trust. Everything depended on these two guys. She hoped they could deliver. The plan was sound, and she felt reasonably confident that it would work, but there was always that element that couldn't be accounted for. She finished her tea and cleaned the cup.

Alicia Hawkins sat by the fireplace and cried. It was the first time she had cried in a long time, and she wasn't sure what had brought this on. She had been thinking about her grandfather and how much she missed him. In a short time, she had been able to achieve everything he had achieved, and because of the internet, she was world-famous, which he had never achieved. Maybe it was all finally catching up to her. She was tired of hiding and never being able to sleep more than a couple nights in any one location. She also missed her family more than she realized. She knew her grandmother and her parents were concerned about her, but she couldn't stop now. This kill was important on so many levels.

She got hold of her emotions and started to move into killing mode. It wouldn't be long before she would have her next kill. She walked to the other bedroom, opened the closet door and looked at the plastic tarp that contained the bloated body of her last kill. She smiled a wicked smile and closed the door. She would be ready when the boys came back with the bar owner, and if the FBI or Buck Taylor tried to stop her, there would be hell to pay.

CHAPTER THIRTY-EIGHT

B uck pulled to the curb, slid out of his Jeep and headed to the small congregation of homeless people milling around the picnic table in the corner of the park. He spotted Bob Brady and two of his officers coming from the other side of the park. They reached the table at about the same time, and the conversation among the homeless stopped as they moved into the crowd. Stick was sitting at one corner of the table, sipping a beer.

"Stick," said Buck. "We need to talk to you."

Stick put his beer down on the table and looked around like he was trying to find a way out. One of the police officers reached him, grabbed his arms and pushed him down on the table. The crowd around them started to get noisy, especially when they handcuffed him.

"What the fuck is going on?" yelled Stick. "I answered all your questions. What more do you want?"

Bob Brady pushed through the crowd. "Stick, you're under arrest for stabbing PIS." While Stick stood there looking bewildered, Bob read him his Miranda rights, and the two police officers escorted him towards the waiting patrol car. Buck and Bob Brady headed for their own vehicles.

Back at the police station, Stick was put in a holding cell while Buck and Bob Brady reviewed the DNA report that was now on the screen of Buck's laptop.

"DNA came back as a perfect match," said Buck. "The lab

was able to get access to his military file, which contained a copy of his DNA."

"Yeah, I get that," said Bob Brady. "But how do you explain it? His alibi was confirmed by the girl in the park, and no one there raised any doubt about his story."

"I can't explain it, so let's go talk to him and see if we can figure this out."

The officer who had put the cuffs on Stick walked back to the holding cell and led Stick to a small interview room. Buck and Bob Brady deposited their guns in a wall safe outside the room, and the officer buzzed them in.

Stick was sweating and looked more afraid than anyone Buck could remember. He looked at Buck with pleading eyes.

"I didn't hurt no one. You got to let me out of here, I can't stand small spaces." His entire body shook.

"Okay, Stick. But we have a problem. You see, we gathered some evidence in the alley where PIS was stabbed, and your DNA was a perfect match. Can you help us understand how that's possible?"

Stick stopped shaking. "I told you about PIS saving me."

"That's right, you did, but that was in the park earlier. We think you caught up with PIS in the alley later and stabbed him. Maybe it was dark, and you didn't realize it was PIS, or maybe you had a beef with him from earlier."

"I didn't hurt PIS. He's my friend, and he saved my life."

"Why don't you tell us what really happened in the alley?"

"I never go into the alley. Ask anyone. I stay in the park."

"Stick, where do you get food, if you don't go into the alley?"

Stick turned pale, knowing that he was caught in a lie. All

the homeless frequented the alleys, since there were no restaurants or trash dumpsters near the park. The closest place to find food was in the alley.

Stick put his head in his hands and closed his eyes. "Talk to anyone. PIS was my friend. I wouldn't hurt him." He lifted his head and looked at Buck with tear-filled eyes.

Buck looked at the DNA report on his laptop. "Stick, you said that PIS gave you Narcan that night when those British fellows said you and PIS had a fight. Do you remember that night?"

Stick nodded his head. "I got some bad dope, like the girl in the park said. PIS gave me the Narcan, or I would have died."

"Did you get sick from the dope? Maybe vomit?"

"No. I hadn't eaten anything since the day before. Nothing in my stomach to throw up. Why?"

"When was the last time you were in the alley? And remember, we can check the security cameras and see when you were there."

Stick thought for a minute, not sure what was going on. "I hadn't been down that end of the alley in a couple days. The restaurants are all at the other end, not by the bookstore. So most of us never go down that end. There's never anything good to eat."

"Stick, we found your vomit in the area where PIS was stabbed. Can you explain that?"

Stick's expression said it all: confusion, bewilderment and something else that Buck noticed. For the first time since they'd brought him in, Buck could see a question looming in Stick's mind. Was it possible he'd stabbed PIS and didn't remember doing it?

Stick buried his face in his hands and cried. Buck and Bob

Brady decided to give him a minute to think about it, so Buck picked up his laptop and they stood up. The officer on duty outside the interrogation room buzzed the door, and Bob Brady pulled open the door. Buck was about to close the door behind him when he heard Stick say something that stopped him in his tracks.

"The girl with the purple stripe in her hair can tell you when I got sick."

Buck stepped back into the room and stood by the table. "Stick, what did you say?"

Stick looked up and wiped his runny nose on his sleeve. "I just remembered. I got sick from some bad food a couple days ago, and a girl with a purple stripe in her hair helped me out, so I wouldn't drown in my own puke. If you can find her, she will tell you I didn't get sick in the alley."

"What else do you remember about this girl you say helped you?"

By this time, Bob Brady had stepped back into the room and was looking at Buck.

"Not much," said Stick. "She rolled me over so I could puke easier, and she found me a blanket and covered me up. That's all I remember."

"Buck," said Bob Brady. "What are you thinking?"

Buck led Bob Brady out of the interrogation room and sat on the edge of a desk, his mind racing as he considered the possibilities.

"This is going to sound far-fetched, but try this. Stick gets sick, and this girl helps him, then scoops up his vomit and leaves it in the alley after she stabs PIS."

"Okay, that's a little bizarre, but why?"

"To throw us off the track. I think Alicia Hawkins is in Aspen."

"Buck, that's a hell of a jump. We're gonna need a lot more than the drug-induced memories of a homeless guy. Besides, why hurt PIS? If I remember right, he didn't have anything to do with the serial killer case."

"That I can't answer, but I know someone who might. I'm heading back to the hospital to see if PIS is awake. Let's keep Stick on ice for a while till I can figure this out."

Buck grabbed his backpack off the desk, slid his gun back into his holster and headed for the door. He needed answers, and he needed them fast.

CHAPTER THIRTY-NINE

Buck pulled into the hospital parking lot, grabbed his backpack and raced for the front door. He took the elevator up to the ICU and stopped short when he got to PIS's room. The room was empty. He walked back to the nurse's station, where he found out that PIS was awake and had been moved to a regular room. He took the elevator up to the third floor and found PIS's room.

PIS was indeed wide awake and talking with the male nurse assigned to his room. He stepped into the room.

"Ah, Agent Taylor, a pleasure to see you, sir."

"PIS, are you okay? You had us all pretty worried."

"A minor inconvenience. I shall be up and about in no time."

The nurse left the room, and PIS's jovial expression turned serious. "I believe you have an enemy about, Agent Taylor."

Buck had tried for years to get PIS to call him Buck but to no avail. No matter the circumstances, PIS continued to call him Agent Taylor, even in private.

"What are you talking about, and how much do you remember about the attack?"

"I remember it all very clearly. My attacker was a young woman, that was what caught me off guard. I thought she was having a drug reaction, so my focus was on helping her. I never saw the knife until it was too late. I must be getting old. That would have never happened in my youth."

"What does that have to do with me having an enemy?"

"After she stabbed me, she whispered in my ear, 'When you see Buck Taylor in hell, tell him Alicia says hello.'"

"Are you sure she said, 'Alicia says hello'?"

"No doubt. If it helps any, I did notice that she had a purple stripe in her hair. If I remember correctly, that sounds like your serial killer to me. What I don't understand is how she connected me to you."

Buck sat back in the chair and thought for a minute. PIS may have been homeless, but he had a good grasp of things going on in the world around him, so it didn't surprise him at all that PIS knew about Alicia Hawkins. A lot had gone on in Aspen during that week a year ago, but what confused him was that PIS hadn't had anything to do with Alicia Hawkins, so why target him?

A crazy thought occurred to him. They had all been concerned about the possibility of Alicia Hawkins targeting one of Buck's children. It never occurred to him that she might target his friends. PIS was old and homeless and looked weak and frail; he would be an excellent target if she felt she couldn't get to Buck. But how had she connected them?

"Agent Taylor. From what I understand about this young woman, she is evil. She is back in Aspen for a reason, and you are a part of it. If you find her, you need to finish this. She does not deserve the benefit of the doubt. You must take her out."

Buck stared at PIS, and he could see the intensity in his gray eyes. What made PIS's words even darker was knowing what he knew now about PIS's past. He had no doubt that PIS would have no qualms about taking Alicia's life, but Buck was a cop. He had a different moral code that had served him well. Deep down inside, he knew PIS was probably right, but Buck was still about justice and not revenge.

"PIS, I'm a cop. When the time comes, I will arrest Alicia

Hawkins, and she will be tried and convicted. If the state or the federal government wants to execute her for her crimes, that's up to a judge and jury to decide. I will not play judge, jury and executioner."

PIS looked at Buck and smiled. "I understand how you feel, Agent Taylor. I once had those kinds of values, but that was long ago. I know, in the end, you will do the right thing."

"PIS, talking about long ago. Some friends of yours from the past are in Aspen and would like to see you."

PIS cut him off. "I know they are here, Agent Taylor. I will deal with them in my own way, but I have left orders with the nurses that they are not to be allowed in my room."

Buck wasn't surprised by PIS's comment. He had wondered how their arrival would sit with the secretive Brit. Buck dropped the subject and pulled out his phone. He hit a speed dial button and waited.

Hank Clancy answered. "Hey, Buck. What's up?"

"Hey, Hank. I have good reason to believe that Alicia Hawkins is in Aspen."

"What makes you think that? It's like she's fallen off the radar. Why Aspen?"

"I don't know the why, but a friend of mine was stabbed a couple days ago, and he just woke up. He said the person who stabbed him was a young woman with a purple streak in her hair, and she left him a message for me."

"Is this friend someone she would have known about or been able to find out about?"

"I'm still working on that, Hank, but it would not have been easy to connect us. I'm not sure how she found him, but I believe she did."

"Okay, Buck. You keep your guard up. I'm gonna roll the task force, and we will get there as soon as we can. Stay safe."

Hank hung up, and Buck looked at PIS. He was about to say something when Bax walked into his room.

"Agent Baxter, how wonderful to see you again."

Bax nodded at Buck and walked over to the bed and gave PIS a slight hug. She didn't know PIS as well as Buck did, but they had worked together on a couple cases with Buck, and like everyone else, she had a deep fondness for the strange man.

"PIS, you don't look too worse for wear. How are you feeling?"

"Not bad. Nothing a few days in this luxury resort won't cure. I'll be back on my feet in no time at all."

Bax now turned her attention towards Buck. "Paul Webber is on his way and should be here in a couple hours. We are going to contact the owner of that expensive car that lives here in Aspen, or at least his caretakers, and see if they have noticed anything out of the ordinary."

She noticed the dark expression on Buck's face. "Did I interrupt something?"

Buck told her about the call he'd made to Hank Clancy and about their belief that PIS had been attacked by Alicia Hawkins. She looked stunned.

"Why would she come back to Aspen, Buck, and how would she even know about PIS?"

"That I can't answer, but maybe we can do a little research and see if there is anything important happening here in Aspen that might have brought her home. As far as how she found out about PIS, I have no idea."

Bax pulled her laptop out of her backpack and fired it up. "I have some time until Paul arrives. Let me do a little data mining and see what I can find."

Buck looked over and saw that PIS had his eyes closed and

was breathing softly. He wasn't sure what to think anymore. Sleeping like he was, PIS looked almost angelic, but Buck knew there was a side to PIS that no one else knew about. He hoped that knowledge wouldn't impact their relationship going forward.

Buck picked up his phone from the table and called Bob Brady. "Bob, PIS is awake, and he confirmed Stick's story. He was stabbed by a woman with purple hair. I just got off the phone with Hank Clancy, and he is mobilizing his task force. You need to be prepared for a sudden influx of federal agents in your town. Go ahead and release Stick. Also, can you have your guys check and see if there are any missing person reports in the area?"

"No worries. What are you going to be doing?"

"I'm going to talk to her family and see if any of them have heard from her."

CHAPTER FORTY

M ac, Devlin and Willie climbed out of the Lyft car they had ordered and headed towards the hospital entrance. They were hoping PIS was finally awake, and they would be able to visit with him for a while. Mac had mentioned at breakfast this morning that they should probably think about heading back to Washington, DC, to rejoin their travel group. No doubt, the tour guides must be wondering what happened to them, since they disappeared without telling anyone where they were going. He was surprised that no one had alerted the authorities to their disappearance.

They were crossing the hospital driveway when a Cadillac SUV pulled to the curb in front of them, and the driver stepped out of the car and held open the back door.

"Gentlemen. Someone wishes to have a word."

Mac looked at the others, and they all nodded. The driver's accent was British, but it was somewhat Americanized, possibly a Midwestern twang. They stepped over to the door and slid inside, taking their cane and walker with them. They were not sure who they were about to meet, and they were all on high alert. The driver closed the door, slid into his seat and drove away from the hospital.

Mac tried to ask the driver a couple questions, but the only response he received was silence. They also noticed that the windows were so darkly tinted that they could barely see out of them. They drove a few miles outside of town and turned down a dirt road, which eventually opened into a large field with an incredible view of the mountains. The driver pulled to a stop next to another SUV, and the driver of that vehicle slid out, walked over and slid into the front passenger seat of the SUV they were in.

"Good afternoon, gentlemen. It is nice to see you again."

The man doing the speaking seemed familiar in some way, but they couldn't be sure. He was tall, with short gray hair and a gray Van Dyke beard. He was impeccably dressed, and his accent was as smooth as silk.

It was Willie who made the connection and spoke up. "Stanford, is that you?"

"Yes, Mr. Willie. It is."

They stared at one another in disbelief. A member of the Stanford family had been employed by the Iverson-Smythe family at all times since the 1300s. The Stanford family had always served as majordomos to the duke and ran the family estates. Their histories were so intertwined, it was hard to tell where one started and the other left off. To say the trio was stunned would have been an understatement. The idea that a Stanford was in the United States and still working for Pheasant's family boggled the mind, especially since they assumed Pheasant had ceased all contact with his family when he disappeared. That was obviously not the case.

"I can see you are a bit confused by all this, but trust me when I tell you that I am not here today to clear up any of your questions. I come with a request from Pheasant. He appreciates the fact that you were able to locate him, even if by accident, and that you felt compelled to come all this way to track him down. However, he would prefer that things remain as they are. He does not wish to see you at this time. Towards that end, we feel it is best if you either return to your tour group or return to England without further attempts to visit him in the hospital."

Mac was the first to speak up. "I don't understand. We've come all this way to visit a friend we thought was dead, and all you can say is go home? I'll be damned if I'll do that without at least an explanation."

Devlin and Willie started to agree, and Stanford held up his hand. "Gentlemen, I know how you must feel, but it is for your own good that we make this request. There will be no further discussion of the matter. I'm sorry. Tomorrow afternoon, a jet will arrive at the Aspen airport. The pilot is prepared to take you wherever you would like to go. If you want to rejoin your tour in Washington or if you would like to fly directly back to England, just let the pilot know." He pointed to the driver. "Gerald will pick you up once the plane arrives and take you to the airport. You will not need any flight documents, just yourselves and your bags. Please enjoy your last night in Aspen. Gerald will make arrangements for you to have dinner in one of Aspen's finest restaurants. I know this is very difficult to understand, but please know that we appreciate your discretion. Safe travels."

With that, Stanford slid out of the car, closed the door, climbed into the other SUV and drove away. The trio were too stunned to speak. They had no idea what they had gotten themselves into or what Pheasant was involved in, but whatever it was, they had been clearly told that their being in Aspen was bringing undue attention to Pheasant, and that attention was not appreciated. Was it possible that after all these years, Pheasant was still involved with the government? He was definitely not a soldier anymore, at least not in the classic sense, but what the hell had happened during the last thirty years, and why was he in Aspen?

Gerald dropped them off outside their hotel and told them he would pick them up at seven for dinner. He pulled away from the curb, and they just stood there and looked at one another. Over the years, they had found themselves in some unusual situations, but this was strange.

Devlin and Willie headed to their rooms, but Mac stayed outside to have a smoke. He finished his cigarette, pulled out his phone and clicked on the Lyft app. He entered the hospital as his destination and waited for the driver. He had been friends with Pheasant for too long to just walk away.

CHAPTER FORTY-ONE

Buck pulled up to the little Victorian house on West Hallam Street, turned off the engine and sat for a minute looking at the house. The last time he had been here, the Hawkins family's lives were turned upside down. Not only had they found out that their father and grandfather, Thomas, had been a serial killer starting back in the fifties and sixties, and that his wife had been having an affair with the local sheriff following the accident that left her husband a quadriplegic. The worst of all was finding out that Alicia—daughter, granddaughter and college student —was following in her grandfather's footsteps. Buck was amazed that after all they had been through, the family had been able to stay together.

He was about to step out of the car when the front door opened, and Judith Hawkins stepped out onto the front porch and stood against the rail looking at him. Judith was the matriarch of the family. She looked older now than she'd looked on the day she found out her husband had murdered fifteen women, but she still stood tall. Buck could only imagine how the last year of her life must have gone, with the whole town talking about her husband and now her granddaughter. She lived in a world of monsters, but she still held her head up high.

Buck walked up the steps to the porch and shook her frail, translucent hand. She shivered at the touch.

"Mrs. Hawkins, it's nice to see you again."

"Agent Taylor, it's nice to see you as well. Is there some news of my granddaughter?"

"We're not sure, ma'am. We've heard rumors that she may be back in the area, and we were wondering if she had tried to contact you or anyone in the family?"

Mrs. Hawkins sat down on the swing, and Buck sat down next to her. She pulled her shawl tighter around her shoulders. Buck could see the sadness that still filled her eyes. The last time they'd sat on this very swing and spoken, Mrs. Hawkins had asked Buck to please find her granddaughter.

"I doubt she would try to contact us, Agent Taylor, and it's odd that she would come back here, where she is so widely known. Are you certain of your information?"

"No, ma'am, this is all just speculation at this point. The FBI has been tracking her, and they lost her somewhere in Oklahoma. We were hoping she had tried to contact you folks."

"Do you really think we would tell you if she had?"

The voice coming from behind the screen door belonged to Thomas Jr. Buck looked up as he pushed open the screen door and stood next to his mother.

"Haven't you people caused us enough grief for one life-time? My mother barely leaves the house anymore. She can't go to church or the supermarket without someone calling her names and spewing vile filth in her direction. We are prisoners in our own house. The whole town hates us, and you have the nerve to show up on our doorstep to see if we have heard from that monster. I want you off my porch and out of our lives."

"Thomas, enough." Mrs. Hawkins still wielded power over her son, and he shut up and stepped closer to the screen door. If looks could kill, Buck would be fighting for his life right now.

Mrs. Hawkins said, "Agent Taylor did not create this problem. This is your father's doing, and he didn't force your daughter to become a monster, just like him, that was her choice. Agent Taylor has treated us with nothing but respect, and no matter what our circumstances, we will not treat him with anything less. I am sorry, Agent Taylor. With the first anniversary of Thomas's death fast approaching, we are all a little emotional."

"Ma'am, if I may ask, when did your husband pass away?"

"It will be one year tomorrow. We had him cremated, and we scattered his ashes at a location that was special to him. We were afraid that if vandals found out we had buried him, they might destroy his grave either out of spite or looking for ghoulish souvenirs. Tomorrow will be the first time we have been back to that location since then."

Buck hadn't noticed it before, but the little bug that ran around in his brain when something started to make sense about a case felt like it was doing an Irish jig on his skull. Could it be that simple? Could she be coming back to visit the site where they'd scattered her grandfather's ashes?

"Ma'am, does Alicia know where you scattered your husband's ashes? Does she know about this special location?"

Mrs. Hawkins sat silently and thought for a minute. If she made any connection, it did not show on her face.

"I don't believe she did know about that place. Even my children didn't know it until I told them about it. It was a place only Thomas and I knew about, and I don't believe it was ever discussed. Why do you ask?"

"I'm just trying to figure out if there is a special reason she might come back to Aspen now. Why she would take the risk?"

"You're barking up the wrong tree, Agent Taylor," said Thomas Jr. "My daughter is far away from here, and if she ever did show up, we might find out that I have the same tendencies my father had, and I might save you the trouble of arresting her."

"Thomas, enough of that talk. She is still your daughter and my granddaughter, and she may have done some terrible things, but I will not have you talking that way in my house."

Thomas Jr. pushed through the screen door and let it slam behind him. Mrs. Hawkins shivered and pulled her shawl up around her neck.

"I hope you find my granddaughter, Agent Taylor, before someone who doesn't care about her finds her first. It was nice to see you again."

Mrs. Hawkins stood up from the porch swing, shook Buck's hand and stepped into her house. Buck stood for a minute playing the conversation back in his head. The presence of the little bug in his brain told him that what they had discussed was important. He just needed to figure out why.

Buck walked back to his car, pulled out his phone and dialed Bax, who answered on the first ring.

"Hey, Buck, I just left you a text. Paul and I are heading to speak to the folks about the car, but I found something interesting. I couldn't find any newsworthy event happening this week in Aspen that might attract Alicia Hawkins, but I think I figured out how she found out about PIS. Look at the text, and I'll call you when we finish here."

"Okay, Bax. Stay safe."

Buck hung up, slid into his Jeep and headed back to the hospital. He wanted to talk with PIS a little more about the attack. He had a muddy picture in his brain, and he needed to clear up a few things to bring it into focus.

CHAPTER FORTY-TWO

Bax pulled up to the massive weathered steel gate and pushed the button on the communication tower. She held up her CBI ID card so the camera could see it and waited.

"May I help you, Officer?" The female voice was clear and distinctive, without the hint of an accent.

"CBI Agents Baxter and Webber. We would like to speak with Mr. James Murphy, please."

There was silence for a minute, and then the gate started to swing open. Bax was amazed. The gate looked old and covered with rust, yet it swung open with hardly a sound. She pulled through the gate and followed the long driveway past several fenced fields containing a variety of horses. Bax had grown up around horses, and she could see that these weren't thoroughbreds but working horses, and they looked well cared for.

She parked her Jeep in front of a log-and-stone house that looked more like a Western apartment building than a private residence and seemed ideally suited for its location against the backdrop of Aspen Mountain in the distance. They grabbed their backpacks and walked towards the two massive wooden front doors.

The door on the right opened silently as they approached, and an older gentleman wearing a beat-up cowboy hat, jeans and a flannel shirt stepped out onto the porch.

"If I could see your IDs again, folks. Can't ever be too careful," he said. Bax noticed that he had a touch of an accent, but it sounded more East Coast than Western. He put on a pair of reading glasses and carefully compared the photos to their faces. He handed them back their IDs.

"Thanks, folks. Sheriff said you two were okay, but I like to be sure. Come on in."

He stepped to the side and let Bax and Paul pass through the door into a room that Bax could only describe as huge and warm. There was wood everywhere, except for the massive stone fireplace that sat in the middle of one wall. All the furniture was rustic wood and leather, and the fire burning in the grate gave the room a soft glow.

"Sir, you checked us out from the time we pulled up to your gate until we walked up to the door?"

The older man turned and faced Bax. "Yes, ma'am. We have an arrangement with the sheriff's office. We had a bit of a stalker problem a while back, and, well, we support the sheriff's office in their volunteer programs, and they, in turn, help us keep track of who's coming and going. It's a good relationship."

"Did the sheriff tell you why we are here?" asked Paul.

An elderly woman stepped out of a doorway next to the fireplace. "He just told me it was important," she said. She walked over and held out her hand for a handshake, which Paul noticed was strong and firm. "I'm Mary Winslow, and that good-lookin' cowboy is my husband, Roy. It's nice to meet you both."

They shook hands all around, and then Mary invited them into the kitchen, where she had a fresh pot of coffee brewing and an apple pie cooling. Bax stopped them before they entered the kitchen and leaned in close.

"Is there a spot in the house not covered by the security

cameras or the digital assistants?" she asked softly.

Roy looked at his wife and nodded, and she headed down the hall past the kitchen to a single door in the back of the house. They stepped through the door and found themselves in a small office space. Mary closed the door.

Roy said, "This is our space. I hate all that electronic gadgetry, so I had them leave a space for just us, to get away from it all."

The room was comfortable, and it contained a small desk, a couch and a large TV mounted to the wall.

"If I may ask, Agent Baxter. This seems a little mysterious. What's going on?"

"We believe a team of car thieves might be targeting Mr. Murphy's Bugatti. They have stolen several very expensive cars in several states, and they have been working in Colorado for the past couple weeks. Mr. Murphy's car is one of the most expensive cars registered in the state, so we are trying to be proactive."

Roy looked disgusted. "I told Jimmy not to buy that damn car. Told him it would be nothing but trouble. But why the secrecy?"

Paul took over. "We think the team is hacking into home security systems and digital assistance devices and using them to study the houses and the residents' movements. That's why we wanted to speak out of earshot of anything internet-connected. Have you noticed anyone around or noticed anything odd concerning your internet or your security system?"

"I can't say I have, but then I try to avoid the internet thing as much as possible," said Mary.

"Are you folks here alone, right now? I read that James Murphy is in Europe, filming a movie."

"Yeah," said Roy. "We take care of the place while our grandson makes movie magic."

Bax and Paul looked at each other. "You're his grandparents?" Bax asked.

"Yes," said Mary. "I'm sorry. I thought you knew. We've been taking care of him for years, since his mom, our daughter, died. Breast cancer. When he hit it big, he bought this place and moved us out here from Indiana. We love the solitude and the beauty, and Roy loves the horses. We also have a couple day workers who help around the ranch. It's a good life." She hesitated. "Are these car thieves dangerous?"

"I don't want to scare you," said Bax. "They have injured several people and possibly killed one man."

Mary and Roy looked at each other nervously.

"What do you need from us?" asked Roy.

Paul pulled out his laptop and sat down at the desk. "I'd like to have you call your security company and ask them to give me access to your account. I want to see if anyone has tried to get access without your knowledge. While I'm doing that, I want to put your security cameras into a loop so Agent Baxter can go to the garage and put a tracker on the car."

"We would also like to put you folks up in a hotel for a couple days. Will the horses be okay without you for a bit?" asked Bax.

"Yeah. That's not a problem," said Roy. "I'll let the boys know. They come by in the morning to feed and water them, but they're usually gone by noon."

Bax handed Roy her phone. She didn't want him calling from his cell or the house landline, just in case they had been compromised. He dialed the security company, spoke to someone for a few minutes and then handed the phone to Paul. Paul talked to the person on the other end and started clicking keys. After a few minutes, he looked up at Bax.

"We put the camera system into a loop. Go ahead and put the tracker on the car," he said.

Bax and Roy left the office, and Paul continued working on his laptop while talking to the technician on the other end. By the time Bax and Roy got back, he was finishing up with the tech. He hung up and sat back in the chair.

"The system was definitely hacked. The tech I was working with can see the intrusion, but they can't figure out how their system was breached. To say they were stunned would be an understatement. Bax, this was some world-class hacking. Whoever broke in has some mad skills. I will remove the loop once we leave, then Mary and Roy can go on with their lives until they are ready to leave."

"Awesome," said Bax. "I called the director from the garage, and he is making arrangements to put the Winslows up in a hotel in town. Can you monitor the cameras and the system remotely?"

Paul nodded. He had access to the entire system, and they would know as soon as someone entered the house.

Bax called Pitkin County Sheriff Earl Winters and arranged to meet with him and his SWAT team at their office. Since they had a tracker on the car, her plan was pretty simple. Let the bad guys grab the car and then have several SWAT units spread out around town and see where it went.

She was helping Mary pack a couple bags when her phone rang. She didn't recognize the number.

"Baxter."

"Hi, Agent Baxter. This is Detective Sergeant Leroy Johnson with the North Carolina State Police. My commander asked me to call you about that individual you wanted us to check out. Do you have a minute?"

"Good afternoon, Sergeant. Please, go ahead."

The sergeant explained that he'd stopped by the last known address of Earl Richard Jefferson, and he found the house empty. The neighbors said the family had loaded up their RV and moved out about two months ago. He also said he did a search for other family members. He found a Jessie and a Toby Jefferson listed at the same address, as well as Frank Jefferson and a Victoria Larsen. He also found a civil marriage certificate showing that Frank and Victoria had been married about three years ago.

"One other thing of note. Frank Jefferson was investigated several years ago for auto theft. The case was dismissed for lack of evidence. That was in 2008, and he's been clean ever since. He has a commercial driver's license, and I was able to find a semi registered in his name. I'm emailing you everything I've got. Hope this helps."

Bax thanked the sergeant for his help and hung up. She was excited. The semi was a huge lead. She needed to call Buck and the CBI director, but first, she needed to set up a surveillance net with the sheriff. She called the CBI office in Grand Junction, reached the cyber unit and asked them to start doing a deep dive into the Jeffersons and Victoria Larsen. She asked them if it was possible to check the most recent travels of the semi registered to Frank Jefferson. The cyber tech told her that it might be possible to follow them by checking state weigh stations and ports of entry, starting in Colorado, and then checking the neighboring states to see if they could get a travel direction. He told Bax he would get the team right on it and would call her back if they found anything.

CHAPTER FORTY-THREE

Buck found PIS sitting up talking with one of the nurses. The nurse left the room when Buck walked in. PIS looked much better than he had the day before. This Brit constantly amazed Buck with his stamina and ability to heal. A year ago, PIS had checked himself out of the hospital just a couple days after having surgery to remove a five-inch-long chunk of wood from his right shoulder.

"Good morning, Agent Taylor. Any luck with locating your young serial killer?"

Buck filled him in on his conversation with Alicia Hawkins's grandmother. He also asked him to walk through the night in the alley when he'd gotten stabbed.

PIS, slowly and deliberately, retold the events of that evening. He knew Buck was keying in on everything he said, looking for even the smallest detail. He had worked with Buck enough to know that nothing was to be left out of the narrative, no matter how minor.

PIS stopped his narration and looked up at Buck. "I suppose the doctor filled you in on my unique condition, which is the very reason I am not now lying on a slab, instead of resting comfortably in this bed?"

"He told me. Said you most likely have a twin somewhere who is perfectly normal. He also told me it looked like someone had marked your heart a long time ago and shot you. I'll bet that's an interesting story."

Buck didn't want PIS to know that his friends had spilled the beans on some of PIS's adventures. He hated lying to him, but he figured it was more of an omission than a lie. PIS was a very private person, and Buck figured that if he wanted to tell him about his past life, he would.

PIS just brushed the comment off with a wave of his hand. "Possibly a tale for another day. Right now, we need to concentrate on your serial killer."

Buck pulled out his phone and opened the text that Bax had sent him. He read her summary and then looked at the photo she'd attached. Buck hadn't seen this picture before, but he assumed this must be the same picture that Mac had referenced. It was a picture of Buck and Sheriff Winters standing near the search and rescue truck, and standing just off to one side was PIS. The note under the photo indicated that the homeless man in the background had aided the search teams looking for the missing ranger. Buck showed PIS the picture.

"Well, Agent Taylor, I believe that is one mystery solved. Your young serial killer was born and raised around here. She would have known who I was. She probably did her research and figured out that you and I had worked together on several cases. She probably assumed we were friends."

"I still don't get what she hoped to achieve by attacking you instead of coming after me."

Buck was about to say something else when the little bug in his brain smacked the side of his skull. It was something her grandmother had said. Buck hadn't kept track of when Alicia's grandfather died, but Mrs. Hawkins said that he would be dead one year tomorrow. Buck sat back in his chair. PIS looked at him.

"I've seen that look before, Agent Taylor. I believe you are on to something important."

"I think I am, PIS. According to her grandmother, her grandfather died one year ago tomorrow. Now think about this. Her grandfather killed fifteen women before his accident. He was planning to kill his sixteenth victim the night of the crash. When Alicia left Oklahoma a couple weeks back, the FBI listed that kill as her fourteenth. A lot of death in just a year. Suppose she wanted to make a big statement to mark her grandfather's passing. Suppose she wanted to mark the first anniversary of her grandfather's death by killing her sixteenth victim. The victim he never got to kill."

PIS looked serious. "That would be quite a tribute to her grandfather, but that would also mean that somewhere out there is another body. By your reasoning, number fifteen is probably already dead. If you are correct, you need to stop her today."

"Fuck, Buck. That's a hell of a theory."

Hank Clancy stood in the doorway with two of his task force agents. He looked exhausted. He also was not wearing his typical government-issue uniform, as Buck liked to call it. Instead, he had on jeans, Western boots and a leather jacket. He ran his hands through his hair.

"Your friend is right. If this is some grand scheme to honor her grandfather, then we are already too late to save some poor soul from her wrath, but that still doesn't answer why she tried to kill your friend here. It's almost like she was inviting you to be a witness to her depravity."

Buck introduced Hank to PIS, and they shook hands. They exchanged some pleasantries, and then Buck cut them off.

"How could she know I would show up? Nothing in the article indicated that PIS and I had anything more than a working relationship. There was no guarantee that I would get here, and she did her damnedest to cover her tracks. I don't think she was focused on me being here. I think she found a way she thought might hurt me. No offense, but if you had seen PIS around town, he looks thin and frail. I think he was an easier target in her mind than me."

"Okay. For now, let's put that aside," said Hank. "The question is, how do we find her before someone else dies?"

Buck pulled out his phone and speed-dialed a number. Bax answered. "Hey, Buck. What's up?"

"Hey, Bax. Did you ever get any responses to the information you posted on the vacation rentals by owner sites?"

"As a matter of fact, we didn't. I didn't check today, because of the car theft thing, but let me pull up my email and see if anyone responded."

Bax came back a minute later. "Nothing, Buck. Sorry."

"That's okay, Bax. Any idea of how many VRBOs are in the Aspen Valley?"

"Couple hundred, I would guess. Why?"

"I've got an idea. Let me talk to Hank and get back to you. How'd it go with the car owner?"

"I've got a tracker on the car, and we have access to their security cameras. We are putting the two people who live there up in a hotel, and I'm just walking into a meeting with Sheriff Winters to set up a surveillance net."

"Nice work. Keep me posted."

Buck hung up his phone, and it rang again. Buck recognized the number and answered. "Yes, sir."

"Buck sounds like we've got a lot of activity going on in Aspen. Can you give me a quick rundown?" asked Director Jackson.

Buck filled him in on the car theft ring, and then they spent a few minutes discussing Alicia Hawkins and Buck's latest theory. The director listened without comment until Buck was finished.

"Do you think your friend PIS was a substitute for you, and this was a revenge thing? That seems like a stretch, since you had nothing to do with her grandfather dying. If I remember right, he was already dying when you finally found the connection."

"Correct, sir. I think it was a spur-of-the-moment response when she saw the picture on the internet. I think in her twisted mind, at that moment, she blamed me for her not being able to go to his funeral or say goodbye. I think PIS was an easy target, but right now, none of that matters. We need to figure out how to find her."

"Buck, based on your report from Oklahoma, she rented an out-of-the-way cabin. Do you think she did the same thing in Aspen?"

"We were just discussing that. Bax has not had any response from any rental owners about renting to a single woman, which didn't surprise me."

"Buck, can the FBI help with this?"

"Yes, sir. Hank is here with me now. We just spoke with Bax and were moving on to the next step. I will call you back as soon as we have an idea."

Hank was just finishing up a call when Buck disconnected his phone. "Hank, can your computer folks pull up a list of all VRBOs available in this market?"

"Great minds, Buck. That's what I was doing while you were on the phone with your director. I asked them to pull up every rental and start calling the owners. The SWAT team will land at the airport in about two hours. If we have any sort of list, we can have them start physically checking rentals."

"That's going to take a lot of time. I wish there was something we could do in the meantime to narrow down the list."

PIS had nodded off again, so Buck and Hank stepped out

into the hallway. Buck's phone rang, and he looked at the number and answered.

"Hey, Bob. What's up?"

Buck listened for a minute, asked a couple questions and hung up.

"That was Bob Brady. His dispatch just got a call about a possible missing person. He doesn't think it's related to Alicia Hawkins because she doesn't match the profile. This woman owns a bar in town, and she is in her seventies. He is on his way to check it out, and I told him I would meet him there. You coming?"

Hank nodded, and they headed for the door.

CHAPTER FORTY-FOUR

Josh and Louis couldn't have hoped for a better situation. Maggie Stevens, the bar owner, lived in a small house that sat back off the road and was partially hidden from the street and her neighbors' houses. Her driveway was hidden by trees on one side, and Josh was able to unscrew the lone driveway light hanging off the front of the garage, placing the garage and the back door into total darkness. The sky was cloudy, and the moon was hidden, making the night feel darker. All things considered; Josh felt good about the set up.

He set his backpack down in the spot he'd picked out behind her trash cans along the side of the garage. He pulled out the taser, checked to make sure it was fully charged and laid it on the ground. He had asked a friend of his, back in Florida, to purchase the taser so there was no record of it in his name. He then checked to make sure his semiautomatic pistol was loaded. He had a round in the chamber, and the safety was on. He stuck the gun into his belt. Next, he pulled out a length of rope and a couple large wire ties that he had picked up at a local hardware store. He snugged his coat up against the mountain breeze and sat down next to the cans to wait.

He was concerned that Louis was getting cold feet and that he might not be able to pull off the initial attack to subdue Maggie Stevens, so he'd changed the plan at the last minute, and he sent Louis in the van to keep an eye on the bar and alert him when she was leaving. He wasn't sure if Alicia Hawkins had noticed Louis's hesitation about this whole serial killer thing.

He had decided the night before that if Louis screwed up any part of the abduction, he might have to make Louis his first victim. He didn't want to think that way. He liked Louis, but he was concerned that Alicia Hawkins might feel the same way and decide to do away with them both. He liked Alicia, but he sensed she could be unpredictable, so he would now have to keep an eye on them both.

Louis had parked the van a block from the bar and had a perfect view of the front door. He wasn't sure what he was supposed to do next. He had seen plenty of stakeouts on television cop shows, but those shows never really dealt with the boredom that comes with just sitting in the same place for an extended period of time. He noticed that the bar was busier than the first night he and Josh had staked it out. He realized he needed to pee, and he was getting colder. He knew Josh would not like it if he ran the van so he could use the heater. Josh had told him the fastest way to get spotted was smoke from the tailpipe.

He finally gave in to his baser urges and decided he would go into the bar and use the restroom. As crowded as it was, he figured no one would notice him, so he slid out of the van and headed for the front entrance.

The noise, when he opened the door, was deafening. The local band was playing a mix of heavy metal and country, and it hurt his ears. He nodded to the bouncer and stepped towards the crowd.

"Hey, you," said the bouncer.

Louis froze. He wasn't sure what he had done wrong. After all, he had just walked in. What could he have possibly done to attract the bouncer's attention? He turned slowly and faced the bouncer. He could feel his stomach gurgle, and he was afraid he was going to vomit right there in front of the bouncer. He swallowed hard.

"Yes, sir?"

The bouncer pointed towards the sign on the wall. Louis looked at the sign and realized his mistake. There was a twenty-dollar cover charge, and he needed to show his ID. He breathed a sigh of relief as he pulled out his driver's license and a twenty-dollar bill from his wallet. The bouncer put the twenty in a drawer, compared his face to the picture on the license and handed him back his ID. Louis nodded and headed for the restroom and then to the bar, where a tall cowboy-looking dude was just getting up. He slid onto the stool and waited for the bartender.

Louis turned around on the stool and got lost watching the people until someone tapped him on his shoulder, and he almost jumped out of the seat. He spun back around as if he had been caught doing something wrong and stared right into the face of Maggie Stevens. His heart almost jumped out of his chest. She was speaking to him, but he could barely hear her over the band.

"What'll it be?" she asked a second time.

Louis leaned into the bar. "Coors, please," he said, louder than he'd expected it to come out. She nodded and walked away, grabbing a mug from behind the bar. Louis watched her walk away, and he caught himself staring. This woman was beautiful. Alicia said she was in her seventies, but she looked like she was in her forties. He watched her tight ass as she walked down the bar, and she had nice firm breasts. He suddenly had serious doubts about killing this woman. She turned and headed back in his direction, and he diverted his eyes. He was afraid his thoughts would give him away. She set the beer on the bar, and he pulled a ten out of his wallet and handed it to her.

He took a long drink from his glass and closed his eyes for a second. What was he doing here? Not just here in the bar, but here in Aspen? Josh was his best friend, but maybe he shouldn't have let him talk him into this. He knew deep down inside that he was no serial killer. He'd never hurt anything in his life, especially people. What would his grandmother say if she found out about this?

The problem now was he was in too deep. He should have called the cops when Alicia showed them her most recent kill. "She's nuts," he thought to himself. He'd found no joy in seeing that dead body, only sadness, but he was doing this for Josh. His hands started to shake, and he tried to control his thoughts. He watched the bartender, and several times she looked back, and he diverted his eyes. His mind was racing. This was a bad idea, coming in here like this, so he finished his drink and headed for the door. He hoped his quick departure didn't raise any suspicions.

Outside the bar, he stopped on the sidewalk and tried to calm down. He took a deep breath and leaned over with his hands on his knees. After what seemed like an eternity, he stood up and walked back to the van. He thought about maybe just driving away and leaving Josh here. He was scared, but he'd made a promise to Josh, and he would never go back on a promise. But this was it. Once they were done with this job, he was going to head off on his own. He had no idea where, but it didn't matter. He was just going to get out of town.

Sitting in the cold van gave him time to calm his nerves and thoughts. He almost fell asleep but woke suddenly when he heard a noise outside the bar. He looked over and spotted the bouncer and the bar owner locking the front door. They said good night, and he watched the owner walk into the small lot next to the bar and slide into her car. He pulled out his phone and sent Josh a text.

SHE'S LEAVING NOW.

Louis started the van and pulled away from the curb. He didn't need to follow her because he knew where she was heading. He drove the three blocks and pulled to the curb a couple houses down from hers. He watched her car turn into her driveway and disappear behind the row of trees. He slid out of the van, looked around the empty street and walked towards her driveway. He stopped at the end of the driveway and waited.

Maggie Stevens pulled into her garage, slid out of the car and closed the garage door. She stopped for a minute and looked at the burned-out bulb over the garage door. She looked around slowly and then headed for the back door. Using her key, she unlocked the back door and stepped into the kitchen, leaving the back door open behind her. Josh had positioned himself just outside the back door, and he watched as she hit the buttons on the alarm panel. She turned, and Josh was in her face. He fired the taser, and the two leads shot out and stuck in her chest. Josh was stunned to see confetti fly out along with the two electric barbs. He had no idea where the confetti had come from. The owner never made a sound, and she hit the floor hard. Josh jumped on top of her, pulled the syringe out of his pocket, stuck the needle into her shoulder and pushed the plunger. Maggie Stevens lay quietly on the floor, and Josh sat on the floor next to her body and tried to calm down. He set the syringe down on the floor next to the body. Everything had gone like clockwork.

Louis had stood at the back door in the shadows and watched as Josh stabbed her with the syringe Alicia had given them. Without a word, and just like they'd planned, he raced back to the van, started it and, with the lights off, backed down the street and pulled into her driveway. He jumped out, ran around the van and slid open the side door, then ran inside and helped Josh carry Maggie Stevens out to the van. Once Maggie was in the back of the van, Louis ran back into the house and started picking up the tiny pieces of confetti. He didn't know what they were for, or why they'd shot out of the taser, but he didn't think it was a good idea to leave them lying around. He gathered up every piece he could find in the dark and ran back to the van, stuffing the papers in his pocket.

While Louis was picking up the confetti, Josh jumped into the back seat with the body, grabbed the large wire ties and bound her hands and feet. Louis slid the side door closed, jumped into the driver's seat and pulled out of the driveway. Halfway down the block, he turned on the headlights, and walking across the street, directly in front of him, was a man in a green army jacket. Louis jammed on the brakes and turned the wheel hard to the left, just missing the guy. He almost had a heart attack, and Josh, who was tying up Maggie Stevens, flew forward and slammed into the back of the front seat.

"What the fuck, Louis," yelled Josh as he picked himself off the floor, rubbing the side of his head.

Louis's hands were shaking as he stepped on the gas and careened around the corner. "Fuckin' guy came out of nowhere."

Louis stomped down hard on the accelerator. The last thing he saw, through the side mirror, was the guy in the green coat yelling and waving his arms and then giving him the middle finger.

Louis headed for the cabin, keeping one eye on the speedometer and one eye on his side mirrors, hoping the guy didn't call the cops. The last thing he needed was to get stopped by a cop for speeding, or for almost running over that guy. His adrenaline was pumping, and his entire body tingled. He felt like he wanted to throw up. His mind cleared, and the reality and the gravity of what they had just done burned deep into his brain. He shuddered as he thought that he had just helped sign this woman's death warrant. He wondered again what his grandmother would think.

CHAPTER FORTY-FIVE

Bax and Paul Webber walked through the front door of the Pitkin County Sheriff's Office, checked in with the desk officer and were buzzed through the security door. They walked back to the conference room and shook hands with Sheriff Winters and Sergeant Jamie Winters, the sheriff's daughter and lead SWAT officer. Sergeant Winters had six SWAT officers with her, and they all grabbed chairs around the table.

"Bax, Paul. It's good to see you again. How can we help?"

"Thanks, Sheriff. Here's what we know so far. This team has stolen at least five extremely expensive cars in Colorado that we are aware of. They have also beaten a man almost to death, raped a woman during one of the thefts and killed a security guard. They only target the highest-valued cars, and you have one of those cars here in Aspen."

"Murphy's car?" asked one of the SWAT officers. "Always thought that car would end up being trouble."

"Correct," said Bax. "We know that the security cameras at the Murphy property have been hacked. We assume the hackers have also been monitoring the location through the family's digital assistants. We are confident that they are going to go after the car, but we have no idea when."

Paul took over. "We have placed a tracker on the car, we are monitoring the cameras and we have made arrangements for Mr. and Mrs. Winslow to spend a few nights in a hotel in town."

Bax pulled up a street map of Aspen on her laptop, connected to the projector on the table and put the map on the wall behind the table. "Here's our thoughts." Using a laser pointer, she started pointing to spots on the map. "We would like to position several teams at these locations. Once we know the car is moving, we can move in and make the arrest."

Sergeant Winters said, "The reports we read seemed to leave out how they are moving the car. Do we know if these cars are still in the state, or are they someplace else?"

"Excellent question," said Bax. "We spoke with the state police in North Carolina, where our DNA suspect is from, and we might have a better idea of how they are moving the cars. The father of our suspects is an over-the-road truck driver. We think they meet up, soon after the grab, put the car in a trailer and the dad drives it someplace. We have been told that California is the most likely shipping port for these high-end cars."

Paul passed out photos and information sheets on the five suspects, and everyone was reading intently. One of the SWAT officers—Kramer, according to the name tag on his uniform—spoke up.

"If I could make a suggestion? There are not many places in the valley where a tractor-trailer could sit and not arouse suspicion. We are also looking for an RV. What if we have our patrol units start driving through all the RV parks between here and Carbondale? We're between seasons, so their occupancy should be low. If the RV is here, we should know in a couple hours. Then we can sit on the RV, and that cuts our surveillance needs down by half. Then we could position ourselves on both sides of the highway leaving Woody Creek and wait for the car to move."

Woody Creek, Colorado, population 263 as of the 2010 census, is a small town located along Highway 82, north of

Aspen. It makes up for its small size by being home to many celebrities, authors, musicians, politicians and actors. This was the location that James Murphy, actor, entrepreneur and philanthropist, had chosen to build his magnificent ranch house.

"I agree," said Jamie Winters. "There are only two ways out of Woody Creek. If they head south, they are going right through the middle of Aspen. That car is going to stick out like a sore thumb. Either way, they have to get on Highway 82 before they can do anything. I would like to put one of my units at the entrance to Aspen, and then we can put our three other units and you guys north of town, and we wait."

"In the meantime," said Sheriff Winters. "I'll have my patrol units start looking for a parked semi and the RV. I'll call Bob Brady and see if he can have a couple of his officers check the RV sites in town."

They spent the next few minutes going over the plan and the placement of the units. Bax reminded everyone how dangerous these people were and to be careful.

Sheriff Winters stepped back into the room. "We may not get much help from the Aspen PD. Seems they have a missing woman, and they are trying to figure out if it's related to Alicia Hawkins. Bax, Buck is on his way to the missing woman's house and asked if you and Paul could meet him there." He handed her a slip of paper with an address on it.

Bax and Paul thanked the team for their help and agreed to meet back in the office at eight p.m. to strategize one more time and set up their teams. They shook hands all around and headed for the door.

Bax pulled out of the parking lot and headed down Main Street. The address the sheriff had provided was only a couple blocks from the Sheriff's Office, and Bax pulled to the curb in front of a small wood-framed house tucked back a little off the street. She spotted Buck's car as well as several black government SUVs. She slid out of the car, grabbed her backpack and waited for Paul, who pulled in behind her. They headed for the congregation of law enforcement officers standing in the driveway.

Buck made the introductions for those who did not know Bax or Paul Webber, and he filled them in on what they knew.

"First, we're not sure this is connected to Alicia Hawkins. According to the woman next door, she spotted the back door open when she let her dog out. She has a limited view of the house from her yard, barely enough to see the door. She thought it was odd that the door was open. She knows the owner of the house gets home late. She owns a bar in town. The first thing Aspen PD did was check with the bar as soon as they got the call, but she has not shown up at the bar yet today."

Bob Brady continued. "The thing that makes us believe it is not connected is that the missing woman is seventy-two years old and is not homeless. According to the bouncer at the bar, she is also one tough lady and can handle herself in most situations. She definitely does not fit the pattern."

"What's the woman's name?" asked Paul.

"Her name is Maggie Stevens, she owns the . . ."

"Jackpot Bar," said Paul.

Everyone looked at Paul, and Bax broke the silence. "Paul?"

"Buck, this is definitely related to Alicia Hawkins."

Paul started to explain when Buck got a strange look on his face. "Shit. I completely forgot."

Now everyone turned and looked at Buck.

Paul spoke up. "Maggie Stevens was supposed to be Thomas Hawkins's sixteenth victim. She was in the car with him the night he crashed. She spent months in the hospital and had almost no recollection of that night. I spoke to her during the investigation because the most recent victim had been seen in her bar the night she disappeared. A subsequent interview, and information we gathered on the accident, led us to believe she was on her way to being the sixteenth victim. She also identified a small jade necklace that Alicia Hawkins wore that looked like something she remembered having before the accident."

Paul pulled out his laptop, opened it and started clicking keys. He was in the process of pulling up the investigation file—the murder book, as it used to be called. With CBI going totally digital, he had immediate access to all the files for every investigation CBI had been involved in for the past ten years, with more files being added every day.

"This all makes sense," said Buck. "We were wondering why she would come back to Aspen, and now it all works. She wants to honor her grandfather on the anniversary of his death, and what better way to do it than to kill the woman who was supposed to be his sixteenth victim, and will now be hers. That also means we have a fifteenth victim out there somewhere. We need to find Alicia Hawkins and fast. The clock is ticking."

A sense of urgency flooded the group standing in the drive-way. Hank pulled out his phone and started calling the task force, and Bax was on the phone calling the forensics team in Grand Junction. She told them she needed them there as soon as possible. Paul was pulling up more notes from the interviews with Maggie Stevens to see if he could find any-thing that could help.

Buck walked away from the group and stood looking out into the street. Bob Brady walked up and stood alongside him. "We all miss shit, Buck. We've all had a lot on our plates."

"It's not that, Bob. I should have remembered Paul interviewed her, and that's got me pissed off. We could have put her under surveillance. That's important, but the reality is we didn't lose any time today. What's bugging me is the way it was done. Alicia Hawkins is not a strong woman. Her victims have always been young, petite women, except for the young man in Oklahoma, and even he wasn't a big guy. These were people she could control. This looks like a blitz attack. This woman owned a bar and has for years. From everything you know about her, and what her employees told us, she is no-nonsense and hard as nails. Definitely not the type Alicia Hawkins would go after. What I can't figure out is how Alicia Hawkins pulled this off."

Buck caught Bax's attention and waved her over. "How'd things go with the sheriff?"

"Good. Jamie Winters has her team spreading out looking for the RV and possibly a semi. Tonight, we will position ourselves around the area and wait for the car to move. We will have to play it a little loose until we see where the car is heading. In the meantime, it's a waiting game. What do you need?"

"Hank has the FBI folks checking VRBO rentals in the area. I know his computer people are good, but I trust you guys. I know you said you didn't hear back from any of the owners for the ads you placed, but do you think you and Paul can dig into the internet world and figure out a way to speed up the process? We need to find her lair."

"We'll give it our best shot."

Buck nodded, and Bax headed over to Paul, pulling out her laptop as she went. Buck knew he could count on his people, above all else. If anyone could find Alicia Hawkins, it would be Bax and Paul Webber.

CHAPTER FORTY-SIX

Buck walked into PIS's hospital room and found the Brit sleeping. He sat down in the visitor's chair and watched him for a moment. PIS stirred and opened his eyes. He looked at Buck.

"Good afternoon, Agent Taylor. It's nice to see you."

He looked at Buck and saw something in his eyes that he rarely saw.

"Something is troubling you, my friend."

Buck filled PIS in on the events of the day. He told him about the missing bar owner, and how he had missed the signs of what Alicia intended, and it was probably going to cost this woman her life. Buck didn't usually deal in self-pity, but he was feeling bad. His job had almost cost PIS his life, and now it was going to cost this woman her life. He felt helpless, which was also an affliction that rarely hit him.

PIS raised the head end of the hospital bed and got a serious look in his eyes. "That is ridiculous, Agent Taylor. I was stabbed because I let my guard down. She may have been trying in some strange way to hurt you, but I am the only person who could have prevented the stabbing, and I failed. As far as the bartender is concerned, fate gave her many years of good life that could have ended the day of the accident. Once again, you had nothing to do with that. There is no way you could have known that that evil bitch would decide to celebrate a perverted life by finishing its final act. No one could have known that."

Buck had never heard PIS talk like this, and it hit a nerve. He was being foolish, and he needed to get his head on straight.

"You must change your focus," said PIS. "You need to focus on finding and ending this evil creature before she can hurt anyone else."

Buck looked at PIS and could see something in PIS's eyes he'd never seen before. PIS looked malevolent, and it took Buck a second to gather himself. He wondered if what he was seeing was really there, or a reaction to the story Mac and his friends had told him. He shook off the thought.

"I will find her and arrest her, PIS. That's what I do. She is entitled to her day in court. I can't just execute her. I couldn't live with myself. I would be no better than she is if I did that." Buck caught himself, but it was too late.

PIS looked at him and smiled. "They told you, didn't they?"

"I'm sorry, PIS. They were regaling me with tales of your time together, and it came out."

"That was a long time ago, Agent Taylor. That person died in the jungle. What I say to you now is logical. She has killed fourteen or fifteen people. She is evil and needs to be stopped. Prison is too good for someone like her, but I also know you, Agent Taylor, and I know you will do the right thing. You are a man of conscience, which is why I value your friendship. Please disregard the ramblings of an old man."

Buck smiled. This was the PIS he knew. He stood looking out the hospital window. "Where are you, Alicia Hawkins?"

PIS had fallen back to sleep, so Buck pulled out his phone and called Hank Clancy. Hank answered right away.

"Hey, Buck."

"Hank, any luck with the VRBO search?"

"Nothing yet. There are over a thousand VRBOs in this area. We've eliminated a bunch, but we have a ways to go. In the meantime, I have every member of the task force out, looking for anything that might help."

"Thanks, Hank. Call me if you get anything."

Buck hung up and dialed another number.

"Hey, Buck. I was about to call you," said Bax.

"You had some luck with the VRBO search?" said Buck.

"Not yet. Paul's still working that angle, but here is something new to think about. The forensic team from Grand Junction is at Maggie Stevens's house. Someone discharged a taser. The team found several taser ID tags in the kitchen. Not as many as there should be, which means someone tried to clean them up but missed a few."

Buck stopped abruptly, his mind running in a bunch of different directions. "Alicia Hawkins never used a taser before, at least there's no evidence on any of the bodies to indicate that."

"Maybe she used it this time because she knew Maggie Stevens was going to be a challenge to take down," said Bax.

Buck thought for a minute. "There's another explanation. Alicia Hawkins had help."

"Fuck, Buck. Up until now, everything we know about Alicia Hawkins tells us she works alone. That's a seriously scary thought that she could have someone working with her. Shit. That would change everything."

"Keep working with Paul on the VRBO stuff. I am going to run back to Maggie's house and see if they found anything else. Let me know if you find anything, or when you head out to meet the sheriff's team."

Buck hung up his phone and sat down in the visitor's chair. The idea of Alicia Hawkins having a helper was something that had never crossed his or anyone else's mind. His mind was filled with questions. Most importantly: How would she have met or recruited this person? Buck picked up his backpack and left the room. The little bug in his head had gone into overdrive.

CHAPTER FORTY-SEVEN

Victoria Larsen went through the camera feeds from the Murphy house. She spotted the two people who drove up in the Jeep and followed them as they entered the house. She didn't know who they were, but she was running the license plate through the Colorado motor vehicle registry. She grew concerned when she lost them for a few minutes after they met with the two residents of the property.

She knew what James Murphy looked like. She had seen all his movies, so she knew he wasn't in the house. It's possible these were friends of the two older people; she had been watching for days now.

She ran through all the cameras and was surprised to see a suitcase by the front door. She hadn't seen it there earlier. The old couple opened the door, and the man picked up the suitcase and carried it out to a waiting SUV. He put the suitcase in the back while the woman set the alarm, locked the door and slid into the passenger seat. The man climbed in the driver's side, started the car and pulled out. Victoria followed them with the exterior cameras until they drove through the gate and left the property. Victoria's radar was on high alert.

Jessie slid into the chair across from her and saw the concern in her face. "What's going on, Victoria?"

"I'm not sure," answered Victoria. "The old couple in the Murphy house just drove away, and they had a suitcase with them."

"Well, that's great news," said Jessie. "If they're gone, they won't get in the way when we go for the car."

"Maybe. Or maybe not. They had a couple visitors earlier, and I lost them for a little bit. There must be a spot in the house that doesn't have security coverage."

"Are you getting anything from the sheriff or the Aspen police?"

"Nothing about us. I picked up a lot of activity this morning from the police. Something about a missing woman."

"Look," said Jessie. "Maybe it's our lucky day. Let's take the car tonight, as planned, and get the hell out of here. I feel like we've been here too long already."

"You might be right, but I have this feeling that . . ."

"Look, Victoria. Your feelings aside, sometimes we need to move when the timing is right. This is going to be our biggest score, and it will set us up for a long time. Let's move on it and go. Dad will be in the area in a couple hours, and by midnight we could be cleared out of here and on the road. You keep monitoring the police and sheriff and watching the cameras. If nothing happens by nine p.m., then Toby can drop us off, as planned. It will take us an hour to get from the drop point to the house, through the woods. That will give you another hour to abort if something doesn't look or feel right. If all looks good, we move. Okay?"

Victoria looked at her. "Okay. Go tell your brothers to get ready. Ten p.m. will be our drop-dead time. I'll let your father know."

Jessie hurried off to tell her brothers and to start to get their gear together. The hike from the drop point to the house was not rugged or steep, just long. They had walked it twice before and knew that an hour was a good estimate. They'd found a great spot to the west of the house that gave them a view of the entire property and the surrounding area. They would have no trouble seeing anyone who might be watching the house. With the old folks gone for the night, this was the perfect opportunity. They'd made a lot of money over the past couple weeks, but this would be the capper. This would set them up for years, and she couldn't wait to be off the road.

She found Earl and Toby sitting outside the RV at a picnic table playing video games. She laughed when she saw the game. They loved those car theft games, which she found weird, mostly because she knew how utterly unrealistic they were, but they enjoyed blowing stuff up, so she never stopped them from playing. It helped them relax, and it also kept them from being underfoot.

CHAPTER FORTY-EIGHT

S tick walked through the front entrance of the hospital and, after stopping at the front desk, was directed to PIS's room. He noticed how the volunteer at the front desk pulled back when he stepped up to the counter, and he noticed the security guard move a little closer. As he stepped into the elevator, he saw the security guard key the microphone he had attached to his pocket. He understood that his appearance made people uncomfortable, but maybe if he wore his silver star on his jacket, they might treat him with a little respect. After all, he was a war hero who'd gotten addicted to painkillers because of the injuries he'd suffered in battle. No matter how he looked, people should respect that.

He stepped off the elevator, and a second security guard walked up.

"Can I help you, sir?"

Stick stopped and looked at the security guard. He could feel his agitation building as he balled his fists. Sometimes he did that as a defense mechanism, and sometimes he did it to keep the pressure, building inside, under control. He wasn't sure which it was today.

"I'm here to visit a friend, sir."

"What friend?" asked the security guard.

He was about to respond when he heard a familiar voice. "Hey, Stick. What brings you to the hospital? You okay?"

Stick looked past the security guard and tried to remember the man's name. Then it clicked. He was the cop from the park. The one who'd given him twenty dollars so he could get some food.

"Here to visit PIS, sir."

Buck stepped up to the security guard. "Is there a problem here, Officer?"

The guard looked at Buck and noticed the badge clipped to his belt and the intensity in his eyes.

"Just trying to help this fella find his friend, sir."

The guard smiled through crooked teeth, and Buck thought to himself that if he wasn't in the hospital, he would have broken this guy's nose.

Buck turned to Stick and pointed down the hall. "Fourth door on the left. PIS will be glad to see you."

Stick stepped away from Buck and the security guard and headed for PIS's room. Buck pushed the down button for the elevator and leaned in a little closer to the guard.

"That man won a silver star for saving his entire unit from being killed. He is a war hero, and if you can't respect him, then at least stay away from him."

The elevator door opened, and Buck turned to leave, then turned back suddenly. "If I ever hear that you disrespected him again, I will come back and find you, and you won't like it." The security guard's smile disappeared.

Buck stepped into the elevator and headed for the parking lot. He was running out of time, and he hoped the forensic team at Maggie Stevens's house had found something helpful.

Stick walked into PIS's room and stood in the doorway. It looked like PIS was sound asleep, and he didn't want to disturb him, but he also didn't want to leave and face the security guard again. He had just decided to leave when PIS rolled over in the bed and smiled.

"Stick, how wonderful to see you, my friend. Come in, come in." PIS raised the head end of the bed as Stick walked over to the side of the bed. Stick reached out his hand, and PIS took it in his.

"I wanted to come by to thank you for getting me out of jail. The cops didn't want to believe I didn't stab you. You know I would never do anything like that." A tear ran down his cheek.

"I know you wouldn't, Stick. I'm glad I was able to help. Are you doing okay?"

"Yeah. That cop who just left gave me money for some food. I had a good meal, and I bought some food for some of the others too."

"That cop is a good man. If you ever need help, you let me know, and I will make sure Buck is there for you. Okay?"

Stick smiled and nodded. "Okay, PIS."

"So, what's going on in the alley, Stick? I heard Maggie from the Jackpot Bar is missing. What's the word on the street? You hear anything?"

Stick thought for a minute. "I heard some talk that she might have been grabbed by the girl who stabbed you. I don't think so. Maggie is a hard woman."

"Have you seen anyone hanging out around the bar that you didn't know?"

Stick looked deep in thought. "Just the death van that almost ran me over last night."

PIS looked at Stick and leaned forward in the bed. "What death van?"

"One of those vans like we had when I was younger. Has some weird pictures of demons and shit painted on the side.

Saw it a couple times parked on the street down from the bar. Never saw who was in it."

"Good, Stick, very good. You said it almost ran you over last night. Tell me about it."

"I walked to the alley after dark to see who was around and find something to eat. Passed the van parked a block or so away from the bar. I fell asleep in the alley by the Chinese restaurant, got cold and woke up really late. I was heading back to the park when this van came down the street with its lights off. They turned the lights on just as I was crossing the street. Like to scare the shit out of me. Guy turned the wheel hard and blew around the corner."

"Okay, Stick. I need you to think really hard. What street did this happen on?"

"I don't remember. It was late, all the bars were closed, but it might have been three or four streets from the park, near the small church on the corner."

PIS pictured the street map of downtown Aspen in his mind. Three or four streets from the park, near a small church. He was having trouble picturing a church on any of the corners, then it hit him. It wasn't a church any longer. It was a private home, but it still had the sign out front because it was a historic building. That church was on the corner of Maggie Stevens's street.

"Stick, did you see the driver?"

"Caught a glimpse. Black kid, short hair."

PIS thought back to when he'd first been moved from the ICU to his room. He reached for the nurse's button and pushed it. He was trying to remember the conversation the two nurses were having when he first woke up in the room.

Jennifer, the friendly day nurse, walked in and asked him what he needed. She looked at Stick but changed her focus back to PIS.

"Good afternoon, Nurse Jenny. I was wondering if Mark or Nathan are on duty today?"

"Mark is working on two. Why?"

"Would you be a dear and give him a call? I need to ask him something unrelated to the hospital, but it is vitally important."

"Sure. I'll give him a call. Don't go anywhere." She laughed as she stepped out of the room.

PIS and Stick talked about the gang from the park for a few minutes, and then Mark McCloud stepped into the room.

"Hey, PIS. You doing okay?"

"Yes, thank you. Doing fine, Mark. I was wondering if you could help me out? When they brought me up to the room the other day, you and Nurse Nathan were discussing tattoos." Mark's left arm was covered in tattoos, and his right was partially covered.

Mark stood next to the bed and thought for a minute. "Oh, yeah. I remember. I saw some awesome art on an old van, and I was showing Nathan a couple pictures to see if he thought they might make good tattoos. Why?"

"Do you still have the pictures?"

"Yeah, they're on my phone." Mark pulled his phone out of his pocket and opened his gallery. He flipped through some pictures and handed his phone to PIS, who flipped through a couple pictures and then asked Stick to take a look.

Stick looked carefully at the pictures and nodded. "That looks like the same van."

PIS handed the phone back to PIS. "Mark, where did you see this van?"

"It was in the parking area at the end of East Lupine Drive. There's a hiking trail there we like to take sometimes." He looked at PIS.

"Isn't there a private home back in there too?"

"Yeah, about a half mile back. The parking area is like two small circles. One side is for the trail, and the other side is private. The van was on the private side. What's going on, PIS?"

"My friend Stick here said a van with lots of pictures on it almost hit him, and I was curious, since I did not remember seeing a van like you both described around town. Thank you, Mark. You have been most helpful."

Mark left the room, and PIS told Stick that he was getting tired and wanted to take a nap. They shook hands, and Stick left the room.

Stick spotted the same security guard standing by the nurse's desk, talking to a couple nurses. He had been hoping to get out of the hospital without another confrontation. The security guard stood up tall as he approached. He stepped over to the elevator and pushed the down button. Stick moved, hesitantly, into the elevator.

"You have a nice day, sir, and thank you for your service," said the security guard. The elevator door closed, and Stick smiled. It had been a long time since anyone thanked him for his service.

CHAPTER FORTY-NINE

Buck pulled to the curb outside Maggie Stevens's house. The CBI forensic van sat in the driveway, and several Tyvek-clad techs moved back and forth from the van to the house. Hank Clancy stood to one side of the back door, watching the techs working inside the kitchen.

Buck walked up to the back door. "Hank, anything new?"

"Hey, Buck. We found more taser ID tags under the kitchen table. Alicia must not have turned on the lights when she was cleaning up. I have one of my agents running down the ID number. With any luck, we will ID the person who purchased it for her."

"Any luck with the VRBO search?"

"We came up pretty much empty. Way too many variables, plus we can't get hold of a lot of the owners. Finding their contact information isn't easy since most of their reservations are handled electronically. I still have people working on it, but I am not holding out much hope. I think the ID tags might get us closer."

Buck thought about the approach they had been taking. The little bug in his brain was nagging at him, and he wasn't sure why. All he knew was that they were running out of time.

"Agent Taylor," one of the forensic techs called.

Buck and Hank Clancy walked to the door. The tech was holding an evidence bag containing a syringe they'd found in the kitchen. "We found this syringe alongside the toe kick of the kitchen cabinet. We pulled off some partial prints that we know belong to Alicia Hawkins. She doesn't even try to hide them anymore, but we found a second partial print that is not hers. We are running it through AFIS now."

The tech walked away, and Buck looked at Hank. The bug in his brain stopped jumping up and down.

"I think she had help."

"Seriously?"

"Yeah. Think about it. We agree that it would be hard for her to take down Maggie Stevens alone. Yet there's no sign of a struggle in the house. She would have struggled to get Maggie's limp body into a car, and now we have a fingerprint from an unknown person."

Hank's mind was trying to wrap itself around the possibility of Alicia having help. "Do you think it could be another family member?"

"It's certainly possible, but I doubt it. I think she found an acolyte. Maybe someone who wants to be like her. Do you have a couple analysts we can pull off the VRBO search?"

"What'd ya have in mind?"

"I know there are websites devoted to Alicia Hawkins. Bax told me she has quite a following, which personally I find sick, but how about we have a couple analysts go through every site that mentions her name, including on the dark web, and see if anyone jumps out at us?"

Hank pulled out his phone, dialed a number and explained to the person on the other end what they were looking for. He hung up.

"I pulled everyone off the VRBO search and put them on this. Fuck, Buck. This will add a whole new wrinkle to finding her."

Buck's phone rang, and he looked at the number and slid the red button to the left. He knew he was going to have to deal with this sooner rather than later, but right now, he had a more pressing issue.

Buck called the director and filled him in on the possibility that Alicia Hawkins had an accomplice. He explained what the FBI analysts were working on and told him about the second fingerprint on the syringe.

"Okay, Buck. You need anything, call me."

He hung up and put his phone away. He was thinking about their next move when his phone rang again. He looked at the number and answered.

"Hey, Max."

"Hi, Buck. How's my favorite cop?" Buck never got tired of that greeting from Max Clinton, and he knew she only called if she had something that would help.

"Doing okay, Max. What's up?"

"We have an eighty percent match on the partial print the team found on the syringe."

Hank's phone rang, and he stepped away to answer it.

"You got a name?" said Buck.

"You bet. Print belongs to Joshua Kirby. He is listed as a juvenile offender. We are trying to get his file unsealed. Our estimate would be that he is in his mid-twenties right now. We also launched a search for his contact info. I will call you back as soon as we have it."

"Max, that's awesome."

Max ended the call the way she always did. "You're a good man, Buck Taylor. God will watch over you."

Buck turned just as Hank Clancy hung up his phone. Hank looked excited. "We've got a possible match on the partial from the syringe."

"Joshua Kirby," said Buck.

Hank's smile disappeared. "How the hell?" he said.

"Max Clinton called. They are trying to track down his juvy record."

Hank looked pleased. "Hah. I already have it, and I have agents en route to his last known address in Florida. I also asked the analysts to focus on his name for the internet search."

Buck smiled. He didn't mind if Hank and the FBI won one once in a while, so he'd let him have this little victory.

Hank's phone rang again, and he answered. He pulled a small pad from his pocket and wrote something down. He hung up the phone.

"Kirby was arrested when he was sixteen for assault. He was sentenced to two years in juvy. He's been clean ever since. Now, this might be interesting. He was arrested with another kid, one Louis Thompson. There was a phone number for Louis in his file, and the number still worked. My agents spoke with his grandmother. She says Louis and Kirby left a week or so ago to meet a friend. She couldn't remember where they said they were going, or even if they did. She said Louis has been following Kirby around since kindergarten. She never liked that kid. Thought he was a bad influence on Louis. She said they were driving in Louis's van. It's old and has lots of demonic paintings on the sides. We're going through Florida Motor Vehicles to get his plates."

Buck knew they were on the right track. The little bug in his brain was silent. Now, all they needed to do was find the van. The problem was it was late, and in a couple hours, it would be the anniversary of Alicia Hawkins's grandfather's death. He had no idea if Maggie Stevens was still alive, but if she was, she wouldn't be for long.

CHAPTER FIFTY

Alicia Hawkins stood at the end of the bed and looked at Maggie Stevens. She admired the shape the woman was in. Too bad she was going to have to mess that up, but that was life . . . or death.

She injected Maggie again to keep her unconscious. The last thing she needed was Maggie waking up before she had a chance to strip her clothes off and get started. She didn't care if Maggie woke up after she started. She enjoyed watching the faces as they realized she was slicing them up. The fear in their eyes made her heart beat faster.

Josh and Louis were standing in the living room and had kept watch over Maggie while Alicia slept. Tonight was going to be a long night, and she needed to be well rested. She made sure to let them know before she sacked out that Maggie was off-limits. They were not to touch her. Alicia could see the lust in Josh's eyes. She knew if she left him to his own devices, he would have his way with the unconscious woman. This woman was special. She was a sacrifice in her grandfather's honor.

She had been watching Louis most of the day, and she was not sure what she was reading in his eyes. Ever since they'd carried her body up the trail from the van, Louis had been unusually quiet, yet she thought she could see his mind working, and she didn't like what she saw. She made sure both guys stayed in the cabin while they waited. She wasn't sure if she could trust Louis.

They ate dinner in silence, but she could see they were both getting restless. After dinner, she asked them to inspect the perimeter of the property and make sure they didn't have any unwanted guests. They still seemed disappointed that they would not be able to watch her slice up Maggie Stevens. Josh had been hoping that since they'd done such a good job kidnapping her, Alicia would have a change of heart and let them observe, or maybe even help a little, but that was not to be. He finally resolved himself to the fact that Alicia was not going to change her mind.

At the appointed hour, Alicia asked them to take up their positions along the trail so they could ambush anyone coming up to the cabin. Once she started, she didn't want to be disturbed. Reluctantly, they grabbed their assault rifles, checked to make sure they each had three additional magazines, grabbed their camouflage coats and hats and headed out the front door.

Alicia looked at her watch. She knew it was too early to start slicing on Maggie, but she wanted the time alone to reflect on her grandfather's legacy and how far she had come in such a short period of time. When her grandfather had first suggested that she would be the one to follow in his footsteps, she was appalled by the idea. She had never killed anything in her young life, and she didn't believe that she could actually do it. Boy, had she proven herself—and everyone else—wrong. Not only had she done it, but she did it in front of the entire world, and she managed to stay two steps ahead of the FBI while she was doing it.

She spent the next couple hours listening to music on her phone. She used the smooth jazz to calm her soul and her mind. She needed to be completely in the moment. This one was too important. She opened her eyes and looked at her watch. The time was fast approaching, so she got up from the couch, turned off the music and headed into the bedroom.

Maggie Stevens was still unconscious, and Alicia walked over next to the bed, leaned down and checked her pulse, which was strong, and her breathing, which was smooth and regular. She undid the buttons on her blouse and slipped it off her shoulders. She had to use a pair of scissors to cut the sleeves, so she could get it over the ropes binding her to the bed. She cut off her bra and admired the woman.

Her pants were next, and Alicia had to cut those and her panties off due to the bindings. Lying naked on the bed, she was quite a specimen. Alicia had no idea what Maggie had looked like on the day her grandfather was supposed to kill her, but she felt sad that he'd missed out on such a beautiful creature.

Alicia stepped into the bathroom and removed her own clothes. She walked back out to the bedroom and sat on the edge of the bed, next to Maggie. She ran her left hand over Maggie's body, stopping periodically while she pleasured herself, to the point of being in a frenzy. Having finally exploded, she lay down for a minute next to the body and rested. She was spent but exhilarated.

She kept her eye on the clock on her phone as she lay there and watched the numbers slowly clicking towards midnight. The time had come.

Alicia sat up, walked over to the dresser and opened her leather sheath, which contained her collection of knives and scalpels. She ran her hands over the instruments of destruction, looking for the perfect blade. She wished the FBI hadn't confiscated her grandfather's knives. If she could have used one of his knives, that would have been perfect. Her hand slowed and stopped over a small scalpel with a three-inch blade. She held the blade up to the light and admired the way it sparkled. This was the one.

She turned and walked back to the bed and stood watching Maggie Stevens breathe. She knew in a matter of hours that that would end, and it made her smile. She said a silent prayer to her grandfather and stepped to the side of the bed. Alicia Hawkins was about to begin.

CHAPTER FIFTY-ONE

Victoria Larsen ran one more check on the cameras and security system at the house. There was no indication that anything was amiss. She sat back and looked at Jessie.

"It's all clear. You should probably get going. I will do one more check once you are at the edge of the property, and if it's all good, you can go. There is nothing on any of the local police frequencies."

She handed Jessie a slip of paper with the coordinates for the location where her dad would be. Jessie plugged them into her handheld GPS and set the paper back on the table.

"See you soon," said Jessie, and she turned and walked out the front door of the RV. She slid into the front seat of her SUV and told Toby, who was driving, to head out. They pulled out of the RV park and headed north on Highway 82. After about a ten-minute drive, they turned onto an unnamed county road, drove a half mile and Toby pulled to a stop. Jessie programmed the coordinates for their dad's truck into the car's navigation system, pocketed the GPS and she and Earl slid out of the car, grabbing their backpacks. No additional words were needed, since they had followed this same procedure for several months, in several states, and it always worked flawlessly.

Toby pulled forward as Jessie and Earl ran into the woods, the darkness so complete that within seconds they were invisible. Toby headed for a little restaurant near the RV park, stopped the car and stepped inside. He would wait in the restaurant until he got the call from Victoria that everything was a go, and then he would head for the rendezvous point.

Jessie and Earl made good time, and they arrived at their hiding spot at the edge of the property with ten minutes to spare. Slightly out of breath, they sat down and waited for Victoria to run her last security sweep.

The call came fifteen minutes after their arrival. Victoria gave them the all clear, and they grabbed their gear and raced towards the back of the house. They ran up onto a large deck and waited at the back door to the kitchen. The house had electronic security locks on all the doors, and within seconds of their arrival, they heard the latch retract, and they opened the door and went inside.

The house was as quiet as a church, and they waited a minute in the kitchen to make sure no one was hiding in the house.

Satisfied that they were alone, they headed for the master bedroom. On one of her sweeps, Victoria had spotted a code for a possible wall safe connected to the system. Jessie and Earl entered the room and started looking everywhere for a safe. They finally found it behind a bookcase. Jessie pulled out an electronic meter, connected two leads to the safe and texted Victoria that they were ready. Several lights on the front of the meter started flashing, and then all the lights turned green. Jessie pulled the leads and put the meter away, turned the handle and opened the safe. She was shocked at what she found.

Inside the safe were several bundles of hundred-dollar bills and a dozen Rolex watches. She had no idea how much money they were looking at, but it would make a nice little addition to their bank account. She slid everything into a black bag, and they headed for the garage. Earl found the keys to all the cars hanging on a hook in the kitchen closet.

He grabbed the Bugatti key, and they headed for the door to the garage. The Bugatti was parked in the center bay of a five-bay garage. Jessie stood for a second and admired the car, then signaled Earl to open the door, which he did with a push of the button on the master garage door panel. The door slid up, and he stepped to the side and waited.

Jessie fired up the engine and was mesmerized at the sound of power and the luxury of her surroundings. The car was a lot quieter than they had been expecting. She put the car in gear and pulled out of the garage. Earl hit the button to close the door and raced towards the car, being careful not to trigger the reversing mechanism on the door. They watched until the door closed, then they each stripped off their camo gear and put it into their backpack, replacing it with dark nylon windbreakers.

Feeling confident, they jumped into the car, and Jessie headed down the driveway to the main gate. They watched as the camera on the back of the gate tracked their approach, and then silently, the gate swung open. Jessie pulled forward, checked to make sure there were no other cars on the road and then headed for Highway 82.

CHAPTER FIFTY-TWO

For a man who had made patience an art form, Buck hated to wait, especially when he knew he was running out of time. He was trying to figure out what his next step should be when Hank's phone rang. He answered, made some notes in his little notebook and hung up. They were sitting in Bob Brady's office, so the next step was easy.

"I've got the plate number from Florida," he said. He handed Bob the slip of paper with the number on it. "My guys in Florida have the name of the guy who bought the taser, and they are on their way to his address right now." Bob Brady picked up his desk phone and called dispatch.

"Connie, it's Bob. I have the plate number for that van you put out over the airwaves earlier." He read her the number, and Buck copied it down into his own notebook. "Go ahead and update the BOLO and send it statewide."

Buck grabbed his backpack off an unused desk and headed for the front door, followed by Hank Clancy and Bob Brady. While they'd waited for the call from Hank's analyst, they had broken the town up into sections and assigned every available patrol unit and reserve officer they could gather up, along with all the FBI agents they had available, to specific patrol areas. They blanketed the town, hoping to find the van. Buck and the others headed to their assigned areas. He didn't think it would be that hard to spot a van that looked like this one, but he was wrong.

After a couple hours, frustration was building as time ran

short. They needed a break. He pulled over to the curb and sat for a minute. They had to be missing something. Truth was, they weren't missing anything except, perhaps, more bodies. There were too many side roads and forest service roads that led to cabins. This was like looking for a needle in a haystack, only the haystack was a huge valley. Buck rubbed his eyes. If only they had more time.

He was about to pull away from the side of the road when his phone rang. He answered right away.

"Bob, anything?"

"We're not sure. We received an anonymous call on the nine-one-one line. The caller refused to identify himself and didn't stay on long enough for us to get a trace; he gave the dispatcher an address and hung up."

"Doesn't tell us much, other than an address. We don't even know if it pertains to Alicia Hawkins or not. It could also be a diversion," said Buck.

He looked at his watch. It was almost midnight, and they were out of time. He didn't want to get overly excited, but they needed to do something.

"Bob, I think we need to check it out. Give me the address and call everyone in. I am going to check it out and see if the van is at the address. If it is, we're going to have to devise a plan on the fly."

"Okay, Buck, but wait for backup." He gave Buck the address and called Hank and had dispatch recall all the patrols.

Buck plugged the address into his nav system and headed out. If he didn't miss any turns in the pitch-black night, he should be to the address in five minutes. Luck was on his side. He pulled to the end of the street, and there were directions to two parking areas: one public, one private. He parked his car in the public lot, grabbed his night-vision goggles out of his backpack and headed towards the private parking area, and there, sitting in the middle of the drive-way, was the van, next to an old green sedan.

Buck approached the van from the passenger side with his pistol drawn and shined his flashlight into the passenger window. There was nothing visible except for some soda bottles and fast-food wrappers.

He walked back to his car, pulled out his phone and called Bob Brady.

"Is it there?" said Bob.

"Yeah. Let's get the FBI SWAT team here, ASAP, and tell them no lights. There is a trail leading to the cabin, but I can't see the cabin, so I have no idea how close we are. We need total silence. Keep everyone else away. We'll bring them in when we need them."

Buck hung up and opened the Jeep's back hatch. He slipped on his ballistic vest, clipped a backup pistol in a thigh holster to his leg and unlocked the gun case that was welded to the floor of the cargo area.

He pulled out his AR-15 and put four spare clips in the holders attached to his vest. He slipped on his navy-blue CBI jacket and put on his CBI cap. He closed the hatch, locked it and walked towards the road.

It didn't take but a minute for the first government-issued black SUV to arrive, followed by several more. Bob Brady and Hank Clancy slid out of the first SUV and walked up to Buck. Next to arrive was the FBI SWAT commander, who pulled out a topographic map and placed it on the hood of the car.

"We may have a bigger problem," said Hank Clancy. "We got word that Joshua Kirby's father owned several guns registered in his name, including two AR-15s. We could be walking into a trap."

"This is the path to the cabin. It looks to be about a quarter to a half mile," whispered the SWAT commander. "I think our best bet is to avoid the path and proceed through the woods. I would like you, Agent Clancy and Chief Brady, to remain behind us until we can secure the location. We are going in blind, and I am a little uncomfortable with that, but we have no choice."

The SWAT team agents were checking their weapons and communications gear, while Buck and the others reviewed what little bit of plan they had.

"I wish we knew more about the two guys and what their motivation is. Do they want to be like her, or are they here for protection and to help her abduct her victims? I would hate to think these guys want to go out in a blaze of glory and take a bunch of law enforcement people with them."

"I'm with you, Agent Taylor. We need to proceed with caution, but we need to go if we're going," said the SWAT commander.

Everyone looked at Hank Clancy, and Hank nodded. "Let's go."

The SWAT agents fanned out and entered the woods about ten feet apart. The plan was as simple as it gets. Move forward until you run into opposition or until you get to the cabin.

Buck, Hank and Bob Brady entered the woods about fifty feet behind the SWAT team. They moved cautiously from tree to tree and stayed as quiet as possible. Buck estimated that they were roughly halfway to the cabin when he heard one of the SWAT agents call the commander.

"SWAT seven to one. We have a body."

Everyone stopped moving.

"Six and four. Move up on seven and secure the area. Is it another female victim?" asked the commander. Everyone was aware that somewhere out there was Alicia Hawkins's fifteenth victim.

"No, sir. This is a male. He's dressed in camo and was holding an AR-15. His throat was slit."

Buck looked at Hank. "What the fuck?"

"Got me, Buck. Looks like someone saved us from getting into a shoot-out."

"Yeah," said Bob Brady. "But that still leaves at least one other armed person out there, that we know of."

Hank keyed his mic. "We may still have another armed person in the woods. Stay alert. Commander, head to the cabin. We will head for seven's location."

"Roger."

Hank, Buck and Bob Brady headed for the body while the rest of the SWAT team headed for the cabin. Their sense of urgency grew by the minute.

Buck walked through the trees to where SWAT seven was standing next to the body. He pulled a pair of nitrile gloves out of his pocket and put them on. The other two SWAT agents were on high alert, keeping lookout around them. He knelt next to the body. From the limited description they had of both Josh and Louis, Buck could tell that this was not Louis. This person was a white male. Buck looked at the wound in the neck.

"Whoever killed this kid knew what they were doing. The knife slid in here." He pointed to the start of the slice under the right ear. "Then sliced from right to left, through the windpipe. The kid would have never had a chance to scream. The slice is clean. Knife was incredibly sharp."

He stood up and removed his gloves. "Hank, let's keep these guys here, and as soon as we get to the cabin, I'll call the forensic team I had at Maggie Stevens's house."

Hank nodded, as did the three SWAT agents.

"Agent Clancy, SWAT one. We are at the cabin. Definitely someone home, but all the curtains are drawn, so we have no visual. We are preparing to breach."

Hank looked at Buck and Bob Brady, and they both nodded. He hated sending the team in blind, especially in a hostage situation, but they needed to move.

"Breach," said Hank.

Up ahead, they heard wood splintering and then several flashbangs go off. They heard muffled shouts, and then silence. Hank's radio crackled.

"Agent Clancy, SWAT one. Cabin secure. You are going to want to see this."

CHAPTER FIFTY-THREE

Bax was starting to nod off. It felt like they had been sitting in her Jeep for hours waiting for something to happen. Maybe they were wrong. Maybe, at this very moment, the car thieves were zeroing in on another car, someplace else. Maybe her gut was wrong.

She was starting to feel sorry for herself when Paul Webber looked up from his laptop screen.

"The security system just shut off."

Bax stopped feeling sorry for herself, started the Jeep and sent out a mass text to the sheriff's SWAT team.

ALARMS OFF. WE ARE IN PLAY.

Paul pulled up the interior security camera feeds and spotted two shadows entering the kitchen through the back door. He watched them as they paused for a minute and then followed them into the master bedroom, where he saw them deactivate the electronic locks on a wall safe behind a bookcase and remove what looked like cash and several watches.

Since their faces were covered, Paul couldn't get a good picture of them, but he was recording the entire event anyway. He now switched cameras and spotted them in the garage as they pulled the car out and then removed their camo outerwear and put on windbreakers. He got two excellent face shots as they were turning to make sure the garage door closed behind them.

Paul then switched to the app for the tracker Bax had

placed on the car, and they started following the blip. The car passed through the main gate and turned left, exactly as they had expected. The car followed the street in a circular path and turned left onto Highway 82. Bax was surprised. They were heading towards Aspen.

Bax kept her lights off as she sent another text.

TURNED TOWARDS ASPEN.

She stayed in the parking lot of the convenience store with her lights off until she spotted the headlights for the Bugatti. As it passed by the store, she slowly pulled onto the highway behind them. Thanks to the tracker, she didn't have to keep them in sight. The tracker seemed to be working perfectly.

Paul followed the car with the tracking app as it drove through Aspen and continued down the highway towards Independence Pass, the back way out of Aspen before the road was closed for the winter. The highway was a little more open here, so Bax backed off even more. She watched as the car pulled off the side of the road into a chain-up area.

Up ahead, they spotted a large semi sitting in the chain-up area at the bottom of the pass. She crept slowly forward and stopped. Paul, using a night-vision scope attached to a video camera, filmed the whole thing.

The trailer was open, with what looked like boxes suspended in the air around the opening. There was a long ramp connected to the trailer, and they watched as the car pulled into the parking area and drove straight up the ramp and into the truck. There didn't appear to be a moment's hesitation by the driver. The two car thieves jumped down off the back of the trailer, and the old guy pushed what looked like some kind of controller, and the suspended boxes started sliding back into the trailer.

"Are you getting this?" asked Bax.

Paul nodded. "Amazing. No wonder no one has been able to catch these guys. They have this down to a science."

They watched, and within ten minutes, the truck was reloaded, and they were shutting the doors. The driver gave them each a hug, climbed in and fired up the big diesel. As they watched, another car that had passed them earlier came back down the pass and pulled into the chain-up area. The two thieves from the house climbed into the car, with the woman moving into the driver's seat, and they headed back towards town. The tractor-trailer pulled out of the area and slowly started up Independence Pass.

Bax sent another text as she swung the car around to follow the SUV.

EXCHANGE COMPLETE. STOP TRUCK AT TOP OF PASS.

Bax closed the distance to the SUV as they drove through Aspen. Paul sent a text to the team with the license plate number and called the sheriff to let him know what was happening. They were hoping the SUV would lead them back to the RV, so they could wrap up everyone at the same time.

Two members of the sheriff's SWAT team blew past Bax, coming from the other direction, as they headed for the top of the pass. The pass was steep on the Aspen side of the mountain, and they knew it would take the truck a while to get there. As a precaution, they had a couple state troopers and a couple Lake County deputies stationed in a parking area at the top of the pass.

Bax followed the SUV as close as she could, and as they passed through an area between Woody Creek and Basalt known as Wingo, the SUV pulled into the Wingo Junction RV Park, drove around the loop and parked in front of an old RV with Colorado plates.

Bax pulled to a stop out of sight and sent a text to the teams following them. WINGO JUNCTION RV PARK.

Paul ran the tags, and within a minute, he received the notice that the plates were stolen. "No wonder we couldn't find the RV. We were looking for North Carolina plates."

Bax watched as the group from the SUV ran into the RV. Sergeant Winters pulled in behind her, followed by two other SWAT team members. She walked up to Bax's Jeep.

"Sergeant. What do you think?"

Sergeant Winters looked at the RV and called over a member of her team. "Brian. Go back around the loop and pull in quietly and cut off their back retreat. Amy, take Gus and work your way to the back of the RV." Gus the dog wagged his tail. This was what he lived for. "I don't want them running. Bax and I will pull our cars up to the RV from this side and box them in. Wait till they step out of the RV and hit them with your lights. Be ready for anything."

Bax and Paul were wearing body armor, and Paul pulled an assault rifle from the back seat and started moving, in the shadows, towards the RV. Bax and Sergeant Winters slowly rolled their cars along the loop road and parked in front of the RV, blocking any possible escape path.

Bax spotted Paul off to the side of the RV and watched as Brian pulled his car across the road, blocking the back of the RV. They all got out of their cars and positioned themselves behind the cars and waited.

They didn't have to wait long until the door to the RV flew open, and the three people bolted for the SUV, carrying backpacks. The lights from the patrol cars came on and blinded them, forcing them to stop and try to see what was going on. Bax was on her radio.

"Police. Freeze. We have you surrounded," she said as the radio blared her message.

There was stunned silence as the three thieves stopped and banged into one another, not sure which way to move.

Jessie dropped her backpack and reached towards her hip. Paul was the first to respond as she raised her pistol, and the sound was deafening in the still night air. The bullet hit Jessie in the shoulder, and she went down hard. Before anyone else tried something dumb, the SWAT team, along with Bax and Paul, were all over them.

Two of the SWAT officers threw a flashbang into the open RV door and then charged inside. They came out a minute later with a stunned Victoria Larsen in handcuffs. Within seconds everyone was on the ground in cuffs, and Sergeant Winters was reading them their rights off the Miranda warning card. By this time, several more Pitkin county deputies had arrived, along with Sheriff Winters, who reported that the truck was stopped at the top of the pass without incident. He shook Bax's and Paul's hands and then made the rounds, checking on his deputies.

Bax sent a quick text to Buck. She wasn't sure where he was at that moment, but she didn't want to call him.

CAR THEFT RING BUSTED. CAR AND TEAM SAFE.

She and Paul leaned back against Bax's Jeep and watched as the sheriff took over and loaded his prisoners into several patrol cars for the quick ride back to the county lockup. She patted Paul on the shoulder and smiled.

CHAPTER FIFTY-FOUR

J osh and Louis had found a couple hiding spots on either side of the trail. They had a good view of the trail and of the woods next to it. No one was getting through. The more they talked about the plan, the more Louis was growing concerned. He wasn't keen on what Alicia was doing, but he was having a harder time dealing with the idea of getting into a firefight with police. This was not what he had signed up to do. He wasn't sure he wanted to follow Josh down this road any longer. His hands were shaking as he took up his position behind the rock outcropping and waited. He started to think that maybe when the shooting started, if there was any, he would surrender when the time came. At least that way he wouldn't get killed.

He was still thinking of a way out when he heard a twig snap behind him. Fear filled his eyes as he started to turn his head. Out of nowhere, a hand grabbed the side of his head, and a knife sliced into his neck, below his right ear, and swept across the front of his throat. Louis tried to scream, but nothing came out, and the last thing he saw in this life were the stars above, as his attacker laid him down next to the rocks.

Josh thought he heard something, but Louis was too far away, and he didn't want to yell for him, so he settled in with his AR-15 at the ready and waited behind the downed tree. He was prepared to kill as many cops as necessary to protect Alicia Hawkins. His adrenaline was through the roof, and he wondered if this was how soldiers felt right before the big battle. He smiled and subconsciously ran his hand over the barrel of the rifle. He never heard death as it arrived at his doorstep.

A hand came out of nowhere and grabbed the side of his head. He startled and tried to find the trigger of his rifle as the knife plunged into his neck and swept across his throat. The last thing he felt was the warm blood running down his neck, and he died probably still wondering if this was how soldiers felt.

Alicia Hawkins leaned over the bed and was about to make her first slice when a cool breeze ran up her spine from behind her. She paused with the scalpel, barely touching Maggie Stevens's right breast, and she got angry.

"I told those guys to stay outside and not come near me. What the hell are they doing now?" she said to no one. She set the scalpel down on the edge of the bed, stood up and turned, and was stunned as she looked straight into the gray eyes of a man she had already killed. She stood mesmerized. "How is this possible?" she thought to herself. She had stabbed him in the heart. There was no way he could have survived.

Alicia Hawkins was so fixated on the gray eyes that she never felt the knife slide in under her left breast. She winced when she finally felt the pain, and then the man spoke, with a soft British accent.

"I've stopped the blade before it enters your heart because I want you to be fully aware of what death feels like. Your period of evil is over, and you can now join your grandfather in hell."

PIS slid the knife in another half inch and swept the tip from side to side, slicing Alicia Hawkins's heart in half. He held her close as he watched her life slip away. He slowly laid her on the floor, checked her pulse and stood up. He walked over to make sure Maggie Stevens was still alive and was pleased to see her breathing softly. There was no evidence that Alicia had started her terrible ritual. He left her hands and feet tied to the bed and covered her with a blanket he found balled up in the corner.

He quickly checked the rest of the cabin and found the other victim in the downstairs closet, wrapped in plastic. Even through all the wrapping, the smell was turning the air foul, and he walked back upstairs, shaking his head.

He pulled out the cell phone he had taken from Louis, dialed 911 and gave them the address and hung up. He removed the battery and put the phone back in his pocket. He would dispose of it on his way.

He left the knife with Louis's fingerprints on it stuck in Alicia, stepped out the front door of the cabin, removed his vinyl gloves and headed into the woods. Within minutes he was no longer visible.

CHAPTER FIFTY-FIVE

Buck, Hank and Bob Brady walked through the cabin door and followed the SWAT commander into the bedroom. The first thing they noticed was the smell of death, and the SWAT commander pointed down the stairs.

"We found a body, female, wrapped in plastic. Probably been dead a couple days."

Hank looked at Buck. "I guess we found victim number fifteen." There was no expression on his face as he said it. They stepped farther into the bedroom, and Buck took in the scene.

A SWAT agent who was trained as a medic was sitting on the bed next to Maggie Stevens, who was covered with a blanket, and he was checking her vitals. She was unconscious. He was talking on the phone to someone, and from the sound of the conversation, that someone was most likely a doctor at the hospital.

Buck looked over to where Bob Brady was standing and looked down at the floor. Alicia Hawkins looked almost angelic lying there, except, of course, for the knife sticking out of her chest. The first thing Buck noticed was that there was not a lot of blood. The autopsy would later reveal that most of her blood had flowed into her chest cavity. Whoever had made the cut was exceptionally well trained.

Hank Clancy walked up and stood next to Buck. "Looks like someone stopped her from realizing the tribute to her grandfather. We couldn't save victim number fifteen, but whoever did this saved Maggie Stevens. What do you make of this?"

Buck didn't answer at first. He was staring at the red piece of fabric that was tied around Alicia's neck. It looked like a man's tie or ... an ascot. He looked at Hank.

"I think someone did us a favor," said Hank. "At first light, we will start searching for Louis. From the looks of things, I'd say if we don't find him dead in the woods, then he is most likely the one who took out Alicia and the guy in the woods. We'll need to dive deeper into his background and see if someone trained him. This was done by a pro."

Buck didn't say anything, but he thought to himself, "I don't think we'll ever find Louis."

"I bet the profilers will have a field day with the red scarf," said Hank. "Must be a subliminal serial killer thing. Part of her ritual, I guess." Hank stepped away, and Bob Brady looked sideways at Buck and nodded. He never said a word.

Buck called the director and filled him in on the situation at the cabin. To say the director was ecstatic would be an understatement. He asked Buck several questions about the scene and listened as Buck described what they'd found. He was silent for a long minute.

"Well, Buck. We'll just have to wait for the forensics and see what the science tells us. Great job on saving the sixteenth victim."

He told Buck about the arrest of the car thieves and that Bax and Paul had done a great job. It had been a busy night in Aspen, with two major crimes brought to a safe conclusion. He was proud of his team. The director hung up, and Buck walked through the cabin and stepped out onto the front porch. He pulled a warm Coke out of his backpack and took a long drink.

He dreaded the next part of the approaching morning.

Once the site was wrapped up, he would have to go visit Mrs. Hawkins and tell her that her granddaughter was dead. This was one part of the job he didn't like, but he knew it needed to come from him. He finished his Coke and sat against the rail.

Within minutes a long line of lights appeared down the path as the paramedics and the forensic team entered the cabin site. Everyone was asked to leave the building as the forensic team suited up. The paramedics worked quickly to remove Maggie Stevens from the house, and they headed off to the hospital with a police escort.

Hank stepped out onto the porch. "I've sent out a nation-wide BOLO for Louis Thompson. He couldn't have gotten far since we have his van. We'll find him in no time. Buck, you did excellent work on this thing right from the start."

Buck nodded. He didn't do what he did for the credit. It had always been about seeking justice for the victims. He wished he could take credit this time, but he didn't think that was possible.

He pulled out his phone and checked his messages. He had a text from Bax, which he replied to, and a voice mail from his sister. He listened to the message, hung up and wiped a tear out of his eye. He knew he needed to call her back, but once again, that would have to wait. He leaned against the porch rail and, one by one, texted his kids to let them know that he was okay and the danger from Alicia Hawkins had passed. He didn't usually text his kids, but tonight he didn't want to talk to anyone.

By the time Buck left the cabin, the forensic team was well underway with their evidence-gathering routines. The bodies of Josh, Alicia and the unknown fifteenth victim had been removed and taken to the morgue, and Hank scheduled a press conference for ten a.m. Buck saw the sun starting to crest over the mountains, and he knew it was time to handle the last detail of this case. He headed for his car and drove the quick drive to see Mrs. Hawkins.

Buck pulled to the curb in front of the Hawkins home and saw Mrs. Hawkins standing at the front window. She stepped out onto the porch as he walked up the path.

"She's gone, isn't she," she said as Buck stepped up onto the porch. She snugged her shawl around her shoulder and sat down on the porch swing.

Buck nodded. "I'm afraid so. I wanted you to hear it from me before the reporters showed up. Alicia was a big story, and you need to prepare for what's coming."

Tears formed in her eyes as she looked at Buck. "Did she hurt anyone else?"

Buck didn't want to answer, but he had never lied to this woman. He told her the truth, and she took it stoically and without comment.

"I will tell the others. Thank you, Agent Taylor."

She stood up and walked into the house, closing the front door behind her. Buck sat for a minute and then walked to his car. He needed a shower, something to eat and a little sleep.

CHAPTER FIFTY-SIX

Buck, feeling refreshed after a little sleep and a shower, walked through the front entrance of the Aspen Police Department and was buzzed into the back. The reporters had all left, and Buck found Bax and Paul talking with Hank Clancy in the back office area. They shook hands all around, and Buck told Bax and Paul how proud he was of them and what a great job they had done on the car thieves case.

Bax explained that Hank's FBI task force would be taking over the case and trying to figure out how the cars had been moved out of the country. Hank was confident that the arrest of the family was only the tip of the iceberg and that this case would go international in a hurry.

Hank handed Buck a file. He opened it, read it and gave it back to Hank. The initial fingerprint report on the knife that had killed both Josh Kirby and Alicia Hawkins led back to Louis Thompson. Hank had no idea what caused the kid to have a change of heart, but he was confident he would find out. The file also had some background the analysts had pulled off the dark web.

There was a lot of chatter praising Alicia Hawkins tracked back to Josh Kirby, expressing his desire to be like her to the point of almost worship. Some of what they found was downright scary. Here had been another serial killer in the making. Buck wondered how many more of these people were out there in the real world, plotting their first kills.

Buck walked over and grabbed a Coke out of the refrigerator. He shook hands with Hank, and they promised to get together the next time Buck was in Denver for a nice dinner. Hank was on his way to Washington, DC, to close out the Alicia Hawkins case.

Bax and Paul had finished their paperwork and were heading back to Grand Junction. Buck thanked them for all their help on both cases and told them to take a couple days off. They deserved it. He said if they needed him, he would be home, fishing, but he had something to do first. He also wanted to swing by the hospital and see PIS before he left.

Bax asked how things had gone with PIS and his friends from England, and Buck gave them the highlights. He told them he had gotten a voice message from Mac, thanking him for his hospitality and letting him know that they had run out of time and that a plane was waiting for them at the Aspen airport to take them back to England. They were disappointed that they hadn't gotten to see Pheasant before they left, but perhaps another time. Buck thought that would be unlikely, and he deleted the voice mail.

The hospital was quiet as Buck walked through the front door and took the elevator to PIS's floor. He walked down the hall and turned into the room and stopped short. The hospital bed was empty, and the room was clean and waiting for its next inhabitant. Buck stood for a minute, staring into space.

A shadow appeared next to him, and he looked over to see the doctor standing there.

"He checked himself out a few hours ago. I tried to talk him out of it, but you know PIS. Can't stay in one place too long."

He handed Buck a small envelope. "He asked me to give you this the next time I saw you. Have a good day, Buck."

The doctor walked away, and Buck stood for a minute and looked at the envelope. He was no expert on stationery, but he could tell this was a high-quality product. He opened the flap and slid out the note. At the top of the page was a family coat of arms, which confirmed for him that the story Mac and his friends had told was true. He looked at the beautiful script written on the page. Buck admired anyone who could write with a flair, since his script, and even his printing, was hard to decipher. The words reminded Buck of a conversation he and PIS had had one night in the woods, sitting around the campfire, while looking for the missing thirteen-year-old heiress. Buck had seen the picture of the pretty woman in the metal tin that held PIS's tea set and had asked about the picture. The same words PIS had spoken that night appeared on the note in his hand.

MY DEAR AGENT TAYLOR,

SOME THINGS ARE BETTER LEFT UNSAID.

YOUR FRIEND, ALWAYS,

PIS.

P.S. DO NOT WORRY ABOUT ME.

I WILL SEE YOU SOON.

Buck slid the envelope into his pocket and left the hospital. He had one thing left to do.

EPILOGUE

Buck sat in the rental car and watched the people gather at the top of the hill. The morning had dawned beautifully, and the hot desert breeze had held off, making the morning pleasant. From his vantage point, he had a great view of the place, the marble headstones all lined up in perfect rows no matter what direction you looked at them from. Here were thousands of men and women who had made the ultimate sacrifice to fight evil, no matter where it occurred. He looked out over acres and acres of headstones and smiled.

He watched as his son David, his wife, Judy, and their children slid out of the first black SUV. They were dressed in their Sunday best, and he was pleased to see that none of his grandchildren were playing games on their phones. They all looked so grown up in their suits and dresses.

Cassie, his daughter, greeted them all with hugs as they stood next to the cars. It had been so long since Buck had seen her without her green-and-yellow hotshot uniform on that he almost didn't recognize her. He thought she had gained a little weight, but she looked fit and tanned in her black pantsuit and white blouse. With her long black hair hanging down her back, she looked like Lucy standing there.

Buck was surprised to see Lucy's mom, Rosalie, standing next to Cassie. He hadn't expected her to make the trip. Grandma Rose, as the kids called her, stood tall, at a shade over five feet, and hugged everyone as they exited the car, showing them where they needed to stand. Buck wasn't surprised. Rosalie was never shy about taking control of any situation.

Jason, Buck's youngest son, and his wife and kids were the last to arrive, and more hugs were exchanged.

A thunderous sound grew in the distance as a contingent of volunteer honor guards arrived on their Harleys, followed by the hearse and two black limos. The motorcade pulled to a stop at the curb, and the family lined the sidewalk. The volunteer honor guard, in their leather vests full of military patches, formed a line starting at the back of the hearse and waited.

Buck's sister, Beth, her husband, Roger, their three grown children and their families climbed out of the limos and stood with the family. Roger helped Buck's mom get out of the limo. It had been years since Buck had seen his mom, and he was surprised how frail she looked. She stood proudly as she hugged each member of the family and spent a lot of time holding Rosalie.

While the family was meeting on the sidewalk, the Marine honor guard arrived. They unfurled the flags they'd come with and stood at attention, waiting to lead the procession. A gunnery sergeant, in full dress uniform, removed the urn from the back of the hearse, and the family followed the honor guard up the path to the top of the hill. Buck watched as the American flag was marched up the path, followed by the Marine Corps flag, but it was the third flag that caught his attention.

He had grown up seeing that flag all the time, displayed in its place of honor in the Gunnison VFW hall. This morning, the light blue flag with the thirteen white stars in the center glowed in the morning sun. The Medal of Honor flag was something Buck's dad had always cherished but never spoken about. Tears formed in Buck's eyes.

Buck knew he couldn't put it off any longer, so he turned off the car and slid out into the warm desert air. He walked up the hill alone, wishing that Lucy was here with him. She was so much better at family gatherings than he was. By the time he reached the top of the hill, everyone was gathered around the grave, and a military chaplain had begun the service.

Buck looked at all the family and friends gathered around his mom: the honor guard, friends from the retirement village and from the local VFW. They all listened as the chaplain spoke. He glanced over his shoulder and saw something that made him pause.

Standing on a small hill a hundred feet or so away was a tall, thin man in a dark suit, his long gray hair tied back in a ponytail. What caught Buck's attention was the bright red cummerbund the man wore around his waist. Buck removed his sunglasses, wiped the tears from his eyes and, once the service concluded, looked back towards the hill, but the man was no longer there. He wasn't sure if the vision had been real or not, but it made him smile.

Buck stood next to David and Cassie. He caught his mother's eye, and she smiled. He smiled back and nodded his head. Cassie reached over and took his hand.

"I know Mom is proud of you," she whispered.

ACKNOWLEDGMENTS

A special thank-you to my daughter Christina J. Morgan, my unofficial editor-in-chief. She devoted a significant amount of time making sure the book was presented as perfectly as possible.

Thanks to my editor, Laura Dragonette whose efforts helped turn my manuscript into a polished novel. Her help is greatly appreciated. Any mistakes the reader may find are solely the responsibility of the author.

Also, I would like to thank my family for all of their encouragement. I have been telling them stories since they were little, and I always told them that someone should be writing this stuff down. I decided to write it down myself.

I want to thank my closest friend, Trish Moakler-Herud. She has been encouraging me for years to write my stories down. I hope this will make her proud.

A special thanks to my late wife, Jane. She pushed me for years to become a writer, and my biggest regret is that she didn't live long enough to see it happen. I love her with all my heart and miss her every day. I think she would be pleased.

Finally, thanks to the readers. Without you, none of this would be important.

ABOUT THE AUTHOR

Chuck Morgan attended Seton Hall University and Regis College and spent thirty-five years as a construction project manager. He is an avid outdoorsman, an Eagle Scout and a licensed private pilot. He enjoys camping, hiking, mountain biking and fly-fishing.

He is the author of the Crime series, featuring Colorado Bureau of Investigation agent Buck Taylor. The series includes *Crime Interrupted, Crime Delayed, Crime Unsolved* and *Crime Exposed,* and *Crime Denied.*

He is also the author of *Her Name Was Jane,* a memoir about his late wife's nine-year battle with breast cancer. He has three children, three grandchildren and one dog. He resides in Lone Tree, Colorado.

OTHER BOOKS BY THE AUTHOR

"*Crime Interrupted: A Buck Taylor Novel* by Chuck Morgan is a gripping, edge-of-the-seat novel. Right from page one, the action kicks off and never stops, gaining pace as each chapter passes." Reviewed by Anne-Marie Reynolds for Readers' Favorite.

"This crime novel reads like a great thriller. The writing is atmospheric, laced with vivid descriptions that capture the setting in great detail while allowing readers to follow the intensity of the action and the emotional and psychological depth of the story." Reviewed by Divine Zape for Readers' Favorite.

"Professionally written in the style of a best-selling crime novelist, such as Tom Clancy, *Crime Unsolved: A Buck Taylor Novel* by Chuck Morgan is a spellbinding suspense novel with an environmental flair. Intriguing subplots of fraud, survivalist paranoia, and murder weave their way through the fabric of the plot, creating a dynamic story. This is an action-filled, stimulating tale which contains fascinating details that are relevant in our present climate." Reviewed by Susan Sewell for Readers' Favorite.

"Chuck Morgan has a unique gift for plot, one that makes *Crime Exposed: A Buck Taylor Novel* a hard-to-put-down book. From the start, readers know what happens to Barb, but they become curious as they follow the investigation, wondering if the characters will find out what happened to her. The descriptions are filled with clarity, and they offer readers great images. The prose is elegant, and it captures both the emotional and psychological elements of the novel clearly while offering vivid descriptions of scenes and characters. This is a fast-paced thriller with memorable characters and a criminal investigation that is so real readers will believe it could happen." Reviewed by Romuald Dzemo for Readers' Favorite.

"Crime Denied is the fifth book in the Buck Taylor series by Chuck Morgan, a compelling thriller that follows a dangerous serial killer. A cunningly plotted and gorgeously written entry in a compelling series, Crime Denied explores the psyche of a serial killer and the perversity of human nature while taking readers on an exhilarating investigation. Chuck Morgan has the knack for creating characters that are realistic and genuinely flawed, scenes that are focused, and a conflict that builds up quickly and that escalates into a crisis point. Crime Denied is a page-turner for fans of sleuth and murder fiction." Reviewed by Romuald Dzemo for Readers' Favorite

www.ingramcontent.com/pod-product-compliance
Lightning Source LLC
Chambersburg PA
CBHW072007020726
47501CB00006B/1723